Praise f[...]

"A gripping contemporary story that g[...]
to reveal the diversity in individual p[...]
and love, in family, friendship, and pub[...]
club selection."
—*Booklist*

"The intersecting destinies of the three heroes present a portrait of Turkey at
once tender and compassionate. I am sure they will have a deep influence
upon French readers just as they have conquered the hearts of more than a
hundred thousand of your compatriots."
—President Jacques Chirac of France in a letter to the author

"A fascinating look at the diversity of Turkey today." —*Library Journal*

"Draws one into the disparate worlds of traditional and modern Turkey. This
exciting, sensitively written novel educates and illuminates not only the
plight of women but also a society in conflict."
—Bestselling author, historian, and activist Barbara Goldsmith

"A compelling premise, set in a part of the world that many American readers
are curious about...hard to put down." —*The Plain Dealer* (Cleveland)

"Livaneli's novel paints a picture of contemporary Turkey and its archaic culture and shows how torn this country and its people are...Livaneli reveals the
beauty and violence of this country, as well as how much collective obedience,
respect, and honor mold people and keep them from their happiness. This
novel is smart, honest, and a singular occurrence in Turkish literature. It
allows us to understand Turkey and its people a little better and sympathize
with them." —Necla Kelek, German-Turkish sociologist and author of
the bestsellers *The Foreign Brides* and *The Lost Sons*

"A lyrical novel." —*The Wall Street Journal*

"Lyrical, poetic, and magical!.... Livaneli is an extraordinary writer and a master of language, who describes in this book an incredibly violent but at the
same time magical, almost surreal world. I like the way he depicts the real
and the unknown life of the simple people who live deep within the East with
their own age-old codes of life...they show their own 'truth' about life and
death, their own views about right and wrong.... You will read this book in
one breath, without a pause."
—Mikis Theodorakis, composer of the score for *Zorba the Greek*

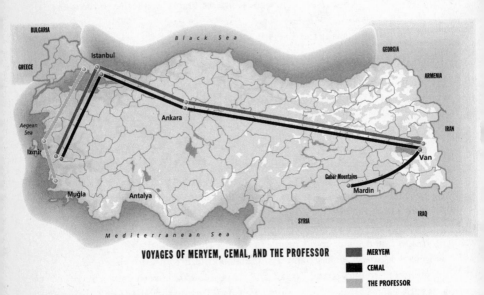

VOYAGES OF MERYEM, CEMAL, AND THE PROFESSOR

MERYEM
CEMAL
THE PROFESSOR

BLISS

O. Z. LIVANELI

 St. Martin's Griffin ☙ New York

BLISS. Copyright © 2002 by O. Z. Livaneli. Translation copyright © 2006 by O. Z. Livaneli. Translation by Çiğdem Aksoy Fromm. All rights reserved. Printed in the United States of America. No part of this book may be used or reproduced in any manner whatsoever without written permission except in the case of brief quotations embodied in critical articles or reviews. For information, address St. Martin's Press, 175 Fifth Avenue, New York, N.Y. 10010.

www.stmartins.com

Excerpt from "Away" from *The Poetry of Robert Frost,* edited by Edward Connery Lathem. Copyright © 1969 by Henry Holt and Company. Copyright © 1958, 1962 by Robert Frost, copyright © 1986 by Leslie Frost Ballantine. Reprinted by permission of Henry Holt and Company, LLC.

Library of Congress Cataloging-in-Publication Data

Livaneli, Zülfü, 1946–
    Bliss / O. Z. Livaneli.
        p. cm.
    In English, translated from Turkish.
    ISBN-13: 978-0-312-36054-2
    ISBN-10: 0-312-36054-1
    I. Title.

PL248.L58 B53 2006
894'.353—dc22

2006045828

First published as *Mutluluk* by Remzi Publishing in Turkey

First St. Martin's Griffin Edition: September 2007

10 9 8 7 6 5 4 3 2 1

CONTENTS

ACKNOWLEDGMENTS

When this novel was published in various languages, I received many questions from readers around the world. I was not surprised when I received similar questions from Turkish readers, too. The diverse styles of culture in Turkey—a country that shelters acute conflicts to the point that it might seem there are, in fact, two or three different countries within the same country—evoked such questions. Even some Turkish readers were unaware of the details of these varied cultures and lifestyles.

My valuable editor, Diane Reverand, who interpreted the novel like a virtuoso, provided superb guidance during the preparation of the American edition, enabling me to make necessary changes and incorporate answers to many possible questions. I am indebted to St. Martin's Press and Diane Reverand for this special English edition.

Words are insufficient to express my gratitude to my dear friends Leyla Topal and Jim Ottaway, who helped bring the novel to New York and to St. Martin's Press all the way from the shores of the Aegean Sea, ensuring that it landed at its destination safely. My thanks also go to Robert and Peter Bernstein, who represented the book excellently.

In addition, I extend my thanks to Çiğdem Aksoy Fromm, who

translated the novel from Turkish to English; to Brian Johnson, who proofread and edited it; and to Angela Roome, who re-edited it. Finally, I must express my deep gratitude to my dear wife, Ülker, and my daughter, Aylin, who were by my side during the process of writing the novel and supported me with their ideas and valuable criticism.

In Turkish, there is a saying that "one hand has nothing, two hands have sound," meaning that two hands are better than one and that many hands make the work lighter. This novel was brought to you through the hands of many people. The art of literature in the world continues to stand erect thanks to numerous honorable hands.

BLISS

MERYEM'S FLIGHT

In a dream as deep as the waters of Lake Van, fifteen-year-old Meryem was flying through the air, her pale naked body pressed against the neck of the phoenix. The phoenix was as white in color as Meryem's own slender form, and it flew as lightly as a feather, carrying her smoothly and safely through the clouds.

Clasping the bird's neck, Meryem felt full of bliss. The cool breeze gently caressing her bare neck, shoulders, and legs made her shiver with happiness.

"O bird!" she whispered to herself. "O holy bird! O blessed bird!"

This was the bird of her grandmother's stories; the bird praised nightly by that tall, thin woman, whose looks terrified everyone. The bird had come at last, gliding through the vast infinity of the sky, to land right in front of their house. Picking out Meryem from among everyone else there, the phoenix had risen into the sky, carrying her on its back.

Meryem knew from her grandmother's tales that the phoenix must be given milk when it squawked and meat when it sang. If these conditions were fulfilled, it would carry you from one land to another without stopping, but if it did not get what it wanted, the sacred bird would become enraged and fling you from its back. Meryem had often heard this and knew it must be true.

Far below glittered the blue waters of Lake Van. On its shores there rose a great city, resembling, by all accounts, the city of Istanbul, about which Meryem had heard so much. She could hardly take her eyes off it.

Suddenly, the phoenix squawked, a sound that reverberated stridently in her ears.

"Where can I find milk for you, blessed bird?" Meryem wondered. "What can I find to milk in the sky, supported by a thousand pillars?"

The bird squawked again.

"Where in heaven's name am I going to find milk?" she asked again. "The sorrel cow whose full udders I milk each morning isn't here."

The giant bird squawked even louder, frightening Meryem, for the bird shook itself angrily, as if it wanted to hurl her from its neck.

"Please!" she begged. "Can't I give you milk when we get back to earth? I'll milk the sorrel cow and give you as much of its sweet milk as you wish."

At that moment, it occurred to Meryem that if the cow had huge udders, she had her own small breasts. Squeezing one of them, she saw that drops of milk trickled from the rosebud nipple. She bent forward, wetting the bird's head with her warm milk. Suddenly the flow increased; the first few drops became a stream, then poured out in a copious fountain.

The sacred bird drank the warm milk that dripped down its neck and was appeased.

As the cool breeze caressed her body, Meryem floated on without a care. She felt weightless, as if she were one of the pure, white clouds drifting along beside her.

After a time, she heard the voice of the phoenix again. It was now singing sweetly.

"Ah, my dear bird, where in the seven circles of the universe am I going to find meat for you?"

The bird repeated its song, and once more she began to plead with it—this time she really had nothing to turn to. The phoenix then screeched so hideously that Meryem felt the end of the world had come.

"O glorious bird! Holy, blessed bird!" she cried. "I beg you, please don't throw me down!"

Her fears were not realized. The phoenix did not fling her from its neck.

Meryem saw that they were approaching a mountain piercing the sky with its towering summit. The mountain was so high that the clouds hung below the serrated cone cutting through the white mist. The bird placed Meryem on the sharpest rock of this lofty peak, which seemed to stab into her back. Her slim, naked body shook violently, shuddering with cold and fear.

Without warning, the phoenix began to change. Sprouting coal-black feathers, its white head turned to darkest ebony, and its beak lengthened into a pair of bloody pincers. The phoenix screeched, jarring heaven and earth, and all the other birds fled away in fear.

Meryem was terrified. "I know it wants meat," she thought. "It must have meat, so it must want to eat my flesh. First it drank my milk, now it's my flesh it wants to devour."

The giant bird plunged its bloody beak between her thighs—into that disgusting and accursed place of sin. "I'm just imagining it," Meryem reassured herself. "It's just a nightmare, that's all. It can't be real." But this thought brought her no comfort.

Meryem struggled to push the bird's coal black head away from her thighs, but the phoenix was too strong for her. It took no notice of her tiny hands, but kept digging into her, ripping out pieces of her flesh.

Suddenly, in a flash, the bird's head became human, and she saw a man's face covered with a dark growth. Meryem recognized her uncle with his black beard.

"Uncle, please give me back what you've torn out," she begged.

The bird with the human head and bearded face gave her the mangled pieces of flesh and flew off into the heavens.

Meryem was left alone on top of the mountain. She gathered the pieces one by one and put them back where they belonged. Each piece adhered to its place and healed immediately.

With a start, Meryem suddenly awoke.

"I don't want to wake up," she thought. "I don't ever want to wake up!" Her dream had frightened her, but the reality was more horrifying.

She opened her eyes—the eyes that everybody in the village talked about. Large, unusual eyes, where a thousand and one different shades of green and hazel blended, those unseeing eyes, which had inspired admiration in some and in others enmity. Her grandmother, before she died, had often embraced her, saying, "This girl's eyes outshine the sun."

Meryem realized she had been clasping the place between her thighs so tightly with both hands that it hurt.

In one respect, at least, it was good to be awake. At least she no longer felt so afraid. She had wiped the thought of her uncle from her mind; now it was the phoenix that replaced him in her memory.

She no longer remembered the hut by the vineyard at the edge of the village where she had gone to take her uncle his food. She no longer recollected how the man had thrown himself on her and violated her; nor how she had fainted; nor even later, when she had come to her senses, how she had rushed out of the hut and ran madly down the road. It was all buried deep in the shadows of her mind.

Two young men had found her near the graveyard, her skin scratched by thornbushes, dried blood on her legs. Delirious with fright, she had fluttered like a wounded bird. They carried her through the village marketplace and brought her home—where everyone was stunned into silence. Too afraid to discuss the incident, Meryem's family had locked her in the damp and dingy outhouse they called the barn.

Meryem spoke to no one about the rape in the vineyard hut, nor did she reveal the identity of her attacker. In fact, she began to doubt it had ever happened. Perhaps it had just been a dream. Her memory was blurred, and she could not remember what she had done after regaining her senses. It was all so confused, so impossible to think of, though she could not imagine ever saying "uncle" to him again. She thrust the event to the farthest corner of her mind. Yet, even there, out of conscious reach, it still lay lurking—ready to surface again in her dreams.

The barn, where her thin mattress lay on the ground, was dark. Feeble beams of light from the courtyard flickered through the cracks in the aged wooden door and the tiny hole in the ceiling. In the dimness, the shapes of discarded saddles, saddlebags, halters, harnesses, a pitchfork abandoned in a corner, bundles arranged in rows on the wooden shelves, a bag used to store dried phyllo dough, thin sheets of sun-dried grape pulp, and grain sacks were all indistinguishable, but Meryem knew by heart the place of each and every one of them.

She had spent her entire life in this place on the shores of Lake Van, this place half town, half village. She knew each house, each tree, each bird there. Every detail of the abandoned Armenian house, two stories high, in which they lived was stamped on her mind: the granary, the simple bathroom, the earthen oven, the stable, the chicken coop, the garden, the poplars, and the courtyard. Even with her eyes closed, she could easily find the smallest thing, as if she had put it there herself. On the wooden door of their house were two knockers—one big, one small. The larger knocker was used by the men and the smaller one by the women who visited the house. The women of the household understood from the sound who was at the door, and when they heard the banging of the bigger knocker they had just enough time to cover themselves for the male visitor.

Since Meryem had never left the village or even seen the other side of the hill that was always there in front of her, she sometimes thought she knew nothing of the world. But this did not bother her. After all, she could go to the city of Istanbul anytime she liked; whenever people talked about some acquaintance or other, they always seemed to remark, "She went to Istanbul" or "He came from Istanbul." Meryem was certain that it lay just beyond the distant hill. She had always believed if she climbed to the top, she would see the golden city about whose glories the villagers never tired of telling.

To go to a city so near might not have been difficult, but now it was quite impossible. Quite apart from going to Istanbul just over the hill, now she could not go even to the fountain, the bakery from which she used to fetch bread, the store full of sweet-smelling, colorful cloth she had been taken to by her elders, or the public bath where once a week they used to spend the whole day. She was now imprisoned in the barn into which her family had thrust her, then locked the door. An outcast, she was in solitary confinement.

Meryem could not even go to make water with her aunts and female cousins anymore. On summer evenings, after the evening meal, the women used to gather in the far corner of the backyard, squat down, and urinate—gossiping together all the while. She remembered the evening when everyone else had finished but her gentle splashes continued without stopping. "Listen to that." Her aunt had laughed. "Meryem's so young, yet she has so much pee!"

"Oh, Mother!" her daughter Fatma objected. "What's the connection between being young and peeing?"

Meryem had no mother. The poor woman had died a few days after giving birth to her. Despite the protests of Gülizar, the village's elderly midwife, who knew how little strength her mother had left, various treatments had been inflicted on her. She was hung upside down by her ankles, breathed on by the village imam, and subjected to the many folk remedies prescribed by all and sundry. After a few days, she had expired and was laid to rest in the old, overgrown graveyard outside the village, the haunt of snakes and centipedes.

In the afternoons, Meryem's aunts and stepmother would lie on their beds in the two-story stone house. Resting their heads on soft cushions, they chatted for hours. With the exception of her mother's twin sister, all of Meryem's aunts were fat, their buxom bodies bulging in every direction without any definite shape.

No longer could Meryem listen to their gossip, join them in the garden, or share their meals in the kitchen. She had no right even to eat the fish from the lake. In fact, the waters of Lake Van were so alkaline no fish could live there, but the mullet caught near Erciş, where the river flows into the lake, were delicious. Canned fish were eaten throughout the year. Meryem was now cut off from everything that might be termed enjoyment.

Her father's third wife, Döne, brought her food occasionally, and she was permitted to relieve herself in a secluded corner of the garden. But that was all. She had no other link with the outside world, and no idea what was to become of her. Once or twice, Meryem had plucked up the courage to ask Döne, who was near to her in age, about this matter, but always received the same malevolent reply, "You know the punishment for what you did." This only served to frighten her more; the next time Döne came, she mentioned Istanbul.

Meryem had not seen her father since the incident when the sinful part of her body had been violated. Her father was quiet and withdrawn, and her uncle dominated the family. No one, not even Meryem's father, dared to speak freely in front of him. He was highly regarded, not only in their village but throughout the neighborhood, and visitors, bearing gifts, would often come to kiss his hand and pay their respects. Strict, quick-tempered, and intimidating, he recited verses from the Quran, invoked the *hadiths* of the Prophet Muhammad, and acted as a guide in all matters of daily life. As he was the head of the religious sect of that area, he had many followers, even in Istanbul on the other side of the hill.

It was Meryem's uncle who had confined her to the barn. She

could still hear his furious shout, "Lock up that accursed, immoral whore!" and the memory of his cruel words made her tremble even more.

As Döne was quick to tell her, Meryem had thrown the family honor into the dust. No longer could they walk through the village with their heads held high.

"What happens to girls who get into trouble like this?" Meryem had asked her stepmother.

"They get sent to Istanbul. Two or three have already gone there."

Meryem's fear lessened. Her punishment would only be to go over the hill there behind them. But then she noticed Döne's expression—as if she were saying, "You'll get what you deserve, my girl!"

Döne had always despised Meryem as much as the sin she had committed, and the sneer on her face sent a chill through Meryem. As she walked out of the barn, Döne added, "Of course, the ones who hang themselves aren't sent away. Some have solved their problems by finding a rope."

After her stepmother had gone, Meryem gazed at the braided halters and coiled ropes lying in heaps on the floor around her. Had they shut her in the barn so she could hang herself? The beams on the ceiling, the cross timbers, the ropes, all were ready there at hand. If someone wanted to hang herself, the barn was just the place to do it.

Meryem began to understand the implication behind Döne's cruel words and sneering face. She must have discussed the matter with Meryem's father. As his youngest and newest wife, who had given him two children, she had influence, while the second wife remained barren.

So this is what her family had decided her punishment should be. Meryem was to hang herself in the barn quietly, without fuss, and soon all would be forgotten. Who in this place would think of inquiring into a young girl's death or suicide? When, previously, two young girls had hanged themselves, everyone, assuming the false mask of grief, had gossiped about it endlessly in every detail.

Meryem picked up a coil of rope that lay in one corner. The plaited cord, old and worn, unraveled in her hand. She looked at the sooty, cracked beams above, black as the deed itself. She had heard talk of how it should be done: Throw the rope over the beam and fasten one end of it with a knot, climb up on a log, make a noose in the other end, and slip it over the head. All that remained to do then was to kick the log away. Her neck might hurt a little at first, but in a couple of minutes everything would be over. Death must be like the sleep she had awoken from a little while before, but a sleep in which she would never see that terrifying phoenix.

"Do the dead dream?" Meryem wondered. No one had ever returned from the dead, so no one could know the answer to this question. Perhaps her mother was dreaming of her now, watching reproachfully as she prepared to kill herself. Of course, what mother could bear to watch her daughter commit suicide?

Meryem fingered the rope for a while before flinging it to the ground as if it were a poisonous snake.

"Go away!" she shouted.

At once she felt relieved. Something soothed her fears, and her reaction was to giggle at herself for talking to the rope.

"Don't cry, Mother," she said softly. "See, I didn't kill myself."

Then Meryem realized what it was that had changed her mind—Istanbul. According to Döne, the girls who did not hang themselves were sent to Istanbul. In that case, Meryem, like those others, would simply go over the hill to that magnificent city. "If they'd let me, I'd walk there now, all by myself," she thought. She could probably reach the city by the end of the day, but she could not go at all unless her uncle commanded it. She would not think of running away, because he was all-knowing and had demons that told him everything, down to the smallest detail.

According to Meryem's uncle, all human beings were sinners but women were especially accursed. To be born a woman was punishment enough in itself. Women were devils, dirty and dangerous. Like their forerunner, Eve, all of them got men into trouble. Get them constantly with child and regularly give them a good hiding, for they are a disgrace to mankind. Meryem had heard this continually as she was growing up, and so she hated being a woman. She would cry out bitterly, "Dear God, why did you make me a woman?" and constantly question it—until she was up to her neck in sin.

Life used to be easier when she was a little girl, thin as a beanpole with scrawny arms and legs. She played with the other children from dawn to dusk, running through the streets of the dusty township of stone and mud-brick houses, through the middle of which ran a polluted stream, and where broken wagons with wheels leaned against garden walls. With her cousin Cemal, who was four years older, his best friend Memo, and the other girls and boys, they even went to the lake, where they ran along the shore and splashed each other as they stood knee-deep in the water. She splattered the sides of buildings with handfuls of mud, squabbled over the skeleton cars they made from old pieces of wire, or climbed up precipitous walls to demolish bird's nests.

When her chest sprouted twin buds and her body found its curves, when the bleeding started between her legs, she knew she was different from Cemal and Memo. They were human, and she was a transgressor. It was considered proper for her to cover herself and hide away, to serve others, and to be punished. This was the way things were. She was now one of those creatures called women, for whose transgression the world was doomed.

So Meryem's head was covered. With a scarf on her head and every inch of her body enveloped in thick clothes, none of which she was allowed to remove, she sweated out her punishment in the heat of the sun, which in summer sometimes reached a temperature of 120. On the day she stepped into womanhood, she also understood why she had no mother. Her mother must have received her punishment by dying in childbirth. God would not have punished her if he had created her a man, because then she could not have given birth and died.

Now Meryem herself was enduring the punishment of being a woman. It must be that place of sin that was responsible for all the trouble women had to go through and all that happened to them. Meryem knew this must be true. It was that which caused sin. It was for this that punishment was given. She had prayed to God so many times to take that aperture away, hoping to find on waking up one morning that it was closed shut and gone forever. Yet, every morning, her hopes were dashed when she realized that the ugly hole was still there.

When Meryem was little and wet her bed, her aunt would always threaten to burn that part of her. Once she even lit a match and brought it close to Meryem's legs but changed her mind at the last moment. Later, Meryem regretted that her aunt had pulled the flame away.

Meryem's problems had all started after the visit to the tomb of

Şeker Baba's, a holy figure to whom the villagers prayed for their wishes to come true. They visited his tomb to pray and pour out their troubles, beg for cures, and leave votive offerings. When Meryem was a little girl, her aunts had taken her to visit the shrine. They even let her ride on a donkey so that she would not get tired. She must have been four or five years old at the time. The journey up the crooked path to the top of the arid hill where the tomb was located seemed to last forever as she swayed backward and forward in the saddle. When they finally reached the shrine, they found people sitting on the ground all around it, eyes closed and palms stretched upward. Bewildered, Meryem asked her aunt what they were doing but was hushed with the reply, "Ssshh, we're going to sleep now." Pointing to the women sitting with their eyes shut, her aunt had added, "Look, everyone's sleeping. Go on, close your eyes and take a little nap."

Meryem sat down, held out her hands, palm upward like the others, and closed her eyes, but it was impossible to fall asleep like the others because she needed to pee. She wriggled around in a desperate effort to keep from wetting herself and tried hard to keep the pee from coming.

Meryem opened one eye and glanced around. Everyone had her eyes shut and appeared to be in a deep trance. She could control herself no longer, and she felt the warm fluid pour out, soaking her legs. She again opened one eye and looked around to see if anyone had noticed. Thank God, they were all still sleeping and had noticed nothing. Now she could go to sleep comfortably, too. Hands opened to the sky, she closed her eyes and fell into a daydream.

A short while later, Meryem's aunt roused her from her reverie. "Come on," she said, "we're leaving." Meryem was not sure whether she had really fallen asleep or not. But then, as Meryem was mounting the donkey, her aunt noticed what had happened. "What's this?" she hissed. "Couldn't you have found another place to pee?" She went on to tell Meryem at great length how those who urinated at Şeker Baba's tomb were punished horribly, how the place between her legs would break out into sores. On the way back, her legs became chafed from riding on the donkey. Her aunt's words had frightened her so much that, for a long time, she could not rid herself of the idea that evil spirits would curse her, or the red devil would come to snatch her away, or festering sores would open in the sinful place. Her eyes became swollen and bloodshot from constant weeping.

From that day on, Meryem had no doubt that Şeker Baba would punish her on account of that shameless, unwished-for place of sin, and something terrible would happen to her. And, in the end, it had. The bird had ripped into her sinful body, and now she sat in the barn awaiting a more severe punishment. Where would it end? Would she be sent to Istanbul like other girls whose sinful parts had been pecked at, or was something worse in store for her? It all depended on the head of the family, her uncle.

Even Meryem's father, Tahsin Agha, gentle and good-tempered, always busying himself with duties on the farm, went in fear of his elder brother, who had the advantage over him in age and also in religious standing and therefore was to be respected. Tahsin Agha, a grown man, never smoked in front of his brother. If he were accidentally caught smoking a cigarette, he would quickly stick it in his trouser pocket or extinguish it in his palm.

Meryem's uncle devoted most of his time to religious matters and to the followers who visited him. Thus, the burden of running the family farm fell on Meryem's father. He had to supervise the collection of the crops gathered from the land rented out to sharecroppers and to see these got stored in the granaries, as well as manage the livestock and take care of the shepherds and day laborers.

The old farmhouse, which was large enough to accommodate all the members of the family, had originally belonged to an Armenian named Johannes, who was remembered affectionately by the villagers for his willingness to lend a helping hand. One day soldiers had come and ordered all the Armenians to collect whatever belongings they could carry and assemble on the outskirts of the village. Frightened and weeping, the Armenians obeyed and were led off, casting backward glances as they trudged away from the village. Not one of them returned. According to rumor, the soldiers had taken them to a distant land, yet nobody dared to say this aloud. Some of the Armenians had entrusted their valuables to their Muslim neighbors, hoping to come back to retrieve them. Decades had passed, and no one had ever returned.

There was another strange rumor connected with this. It was whispered that some of the older village women were, in fact, Armenian. During those languid, soporific afternoons when Meryem's aunts would chat together, this was a frequent topic of discussion. They would tell how, on that ominous day so many years ago, having no idea of what fate held in store for them, some Armenian families had left their daughters in the care of their Muslim neighbors. Such names as Ani or Anush were changed to Turkish names like Saliha or Fatma, and their adoptive families raised these girls as their own, eventually marrying them off. The gossip in the village was that, as they had never converted to Islam, it was questionable whether it was right for them to be married according to Islamic practice. Even more disputed was their right to a funeral and a final resting place alongside Muslims.

At a funeral, the imam asks those who gather to pay their last respects, "How did you regard the deceased?" The mourners reply in unison, "We considered her a good person," invoking God's favor upon her. The imam then pronounces, "In favor of the deceased woman," and starts the *namaz*. Perhaps the Muslim men of the village who followed their imam in the ritual prayers for one of these dead women were performing it for a Christian—that would, indeed, be going too far!

After the Armenians had been taken away, Muslims took over their houses, fields, and workplaces. The house now belonging to Meryem's family was one of the largest of these properties in the village. Meryem had for a long time believed that her great-grandfather, Ahmet the Wrestler, had won it for himself through the strength of his arms. In that area his splendid physique was still talked about and had become the subject of legendary stories. These were still some of Meryem's favorites, especially the one about the cream.

According to the tale, when her great-grandfather was small, his mother would always give his brother the cream off the milk. Although he resented this, Ahmet never uttered a word. One day when his mother was out, he led their donkey out of the barn, lifted it, and put it on the flat roof of their two-story house. His parents returned home from the fields to find the donkey on the roof. They could not find a way of getting it down from there. Knowing her son's strength, Ahmet's mother begged him to take the animal off the roof. Grinning, he responded that whoever ate the cream should bring it down.

The story would stop there and up until a few years ago, Meryem would recall great-grandfather's exploit whenever she gazed up at the roof of the family home, wondering if the donkey was still up there. But when she grew older, she realized that their house could not be the one in the story—there was no donkey on top of it.

When Meryem asked if any of the villagers' tales were true, her aunt assured her that those about the forced departure of the Armenians were certainly false. Instead, she declared, a miracle had caused them all to disappear in a single stroke. The wind had blown so fiercely one stormy February day that the minaret of the mosque toppled down, trees were uprooted, and roofs flew off houses. At the same time, the storm must have swept up all the Armenians in the village and blown them away into the sky. One could not question God's mercies. The divine wind had not touched a single Muslim, but every Armenian man, woman, and child had been taken up into the heavens. Maybe the Armenians were actually God's favorites and had ascended to heaven like Jesus, may his name be praised.

Meryem preferred to think that they were up in the sky. She would close her eyes and try to imagine the Armenian girls flying across the sky. Their parents would call out to their children flying joyfully here and there, "It's getting late, children. Come back to your clouds!"

Although most of the family members lived in Johannes's former house, Meryem was glad her uncle was hardly ever at home during the day. He usually went to the hut in the distant vineyard, where he would welcome visitors with their offerings or pray by himself in deep solitude. The children of the family would take him baskets of food. Even Meryem's father saw his brother only in the mosque at the hour of prayer.

After the prayers at sunset, the women of the house would spread a cloth on the floor and serve dinner to the men and wait on them. Only when they had been fed and the table cleared away could the women gather in the kitchen to eat the leftovers. If any of them talked or lingered too long over their food, Meryem's uncle would become angry. According to his understanding of religion, eating could be an act of sensuality. One ate in order to live. It was a duty to be carried out in the least possible time. So the women rapidly spooned down hot soup, stuffed their mouths with meat and pilaf, and caused the baklava to vanish in the twinkling of an eye. After the meal, it was time for the bedtime prayers. Meryem's uncle, as imam, would lead them and

Meryem's father, and her uncle's son, Cemal, would stand in line behind him. During the holy month of Ramadan, after breaking their fast, the men would go to the mosque for special prayers.

Tahsin Agha's first wife had died while giving birth to Meryem, his first child. His second wife was barren, so for many years he had had no further children until he took Döne as his wife. She had given him two children, one after the other, but both of these were still very young. Meryem's uncle and his wife had three daughters and two sons. The older boy, Yakup, had gone to Istanbul two years before with his wife Nazik and their two children. According to Yakup's infrequent messages, they were prospering and doing well in the "golden" city. When the younger son, Cemal, went to do his military service and was posted to the southeast, and the two daughters, Ayşe and Hatice, married, the large house became quite empty. Cemal's mother, who was a miserable, lusterless woman oppressed by her tyrannical husband, was barely perceptible in the house. Whether she existed or not did not make much difference.

Cemal was with his commando unit in the Gabar Mountains, where he was known to be fighting against the Kurds. His father made constant invocations asking that "the power of God, the Almighty, protect his son from all evil." Since he had forbidden all "non-Muslim inventions," including radio and television, to enter the house, the family could not learn the names of the soldiers killed daily in action, and they had little news of Cemal other than his letters, which came at rare intervals.

THE PROFESSOR IN CRISIS

Wᴡʜɪʟᴇ Mᴇʀʏᴇᴍ ᴡᴀꜱ ʟᴏꜱᴛ ɪɴ ɢʟᴏᴏᴍʏ ᴛʜᴏᴜɢʜᴛꜱ in that dusty village on the edge of Lake Van, more than seven hundred miles to the west, in Istanbul, where Asia and Europe meet, a man with the impressive title of Professor İrfan Kurudal cried out in his sleep and woke himself up. The forty-four-year-old professor knew he had been asleep less than half an hour; recently it had become a habit with him to wake up shortly after going to sleep.

He had never before suffered from insomnia, nor had he changed his normal routine—going to bed as usual right after midnight and dozing off effortlessly. Yet, each night for the past two months, he had woken up in a panic, with the same horrible feeling that a black bird was flapping its wings in the middle of his chest. The ominous vision chilled his heart. He had tried various remedies, even turning to alcohol, but there was no improvement.

He used to sleep soundly until eight in the morning and start the new day fresh, but now he was weary and overwrought. No matter how hard he tried, he could not fall asleep once he had been jolted awake.

From all appearances, the professor seemed to have no problems: He had a beautiful wife, was respected at his university, appeared fre-

quently on television as a commentator, and the moderators listened
reverently to his words. He had been on television before, but now
that he was appearing on a weekly talk program, everyone from the
owner of the grocery store to the stranger on the street began to recognize him. No one who saw this tall, well-built man could fail to recognize his face again, so striking was the contrast between his jet-black
hair and his gray beard. The professor was not a man one could over-
look.

İrfan lay still in the somber bedroom dimly lit by the lights of the
garden, trying to contain his fear and not awaken his wife. He knew he
could not overcome the terror without pills.

He rose, walked softly to his private bathroom, and flicked on the
lights, illuminating the expensive fixtures and the bright porphyry
marble floor. Sitting on the edge of the tub, he began the accustomed
swaying backward and forward.

"You're healthy . . . everything's going well," he said to himself.
"Don't be afraid. This is your home. Your name is İrfan Kurudal. The
woman in your bed is your wife, Aysel. There's nothing to fear. You
had a great time this evening at the Four Seasons Hotel with your
brother-in-law, Sedat, and his wife, İclal. The sushi was excellent, don't
worry. You drank two cool bottles of beer. After dinner, Sedat brought
you home in his Range Rover. You took a look at the gossip shows on
television and, as always, enjoyed looking at those young models with
their long legs and large breasts. You know Aysel doesn't mind. She's
not bothered by such things. There's no reason to be afraid."

But dread still clutched at his heart. It was as though he was not
Professor İrfan Kurudal; it was as though someone else was living in
his body. For the past few months, he had been observing himself
from without.

He had once dreamed that he was going to visit a patient in the
hospital. In his dream, he had entered a sick man's room, put the flowers in a vase, and sat down at the foot of the bed. The patient, dressed
in pajamas, was sitting up in bed facing him. İrfan stared at him, and
saw it was himself. He, İrfan Kurudal was visiting himself. The man sitting opposite him and having the dream was not İrfan, the patient, but
İrfan, the visitor. Neither of them said a word. He stared at his pale,
sick face for a long time.

Slowly, another figure began to materialize next to the patient, and İrfan began to tremble and sweat in his dream. The form taking shape was identical to the İrfan Kurudal already in the bed. There were now two men in the bed and one sitting opposite them: three İrfan Kurudals looking at each other without speaking.

Then the two İrfans in the bed turned their heads to the right with a slow, synchronized motion, displaying their profiles. A cold shiver went down İrfan's spine; the two faces began to crumble. Bit by bit, the cheeks, mouths, chins, and foreheads fell away. The eyes were the last to disappear. At that moment the professor had begun to scream, but a nudge from his wife had awakened him. He had been eternally grateful to her for that.

Aysel always slept so quietly that he could not even hear her breathing. He was the lucky one as he himself snored loudly. Some mornings, on waking and glancing at Aysel's face, İrfan would tell himself, "Look, this is your wife. Your wife, Aysel."

Aysel's nose had been operated on, but that was the only correction that had been made to her perfect face. She was the only woman among their acquaintances who had had so little cosmetic surgery. Aysel kept fit with calisthenics and bodybuilding exercises six times a week and never let herself sag. Exercise, as well as the latest diets and doses of fat-burning medicine, saved her from undergoing liposuction. And she had been lucky: A famous Brazilian surgeon, who had visited Istanbul to operate on a handful of well-known women, was the doctor who had worked on her nose. He was an expert, and she had suffered no serious problems after surgery, just a bit of discoloration and some swelling around her nose and eyes for a few weeks. Some of her not-so-fortunate friends had ended up with mangled noses, bulging lips, and breathing difficulties. The noses of a few of them had almost disappeared.

"Look, this is your wife. Your own darling wife! There's no reason to be afraid," İrfan told himself.

The daughter of a wealthy shipowner, Aysel had no need of his money. However, in recent years, the professor's income had been rising steadily from the various paid television appearances arranged by his brother-in-law. Every week he met his friends to talk in front of the cameras, and this brought him a substantial sum each month. With more than enough to spend, he deposited the excess in the bank, and his accounts kept on growing.

His friends who bought national treasury bonds in Turkish liras during economic crises earned a much greater amount, reaping nearly 50 percent more than by investing in dollars. Some also profited from the stock market, but İrfan steered clear of such a gamble. He was a man of learning, a teacher, not a broker, but if the bank offered high interest rates, it would be foolish to miss that opportunity.

İrfan's attitude toward money irritated his brother-in-law, Sedat, who often said that if he paid more attention at dinners when the conversation turned to business, he could multiply his earnings five or ten times over. The professor never listened.

İrfan and Aysel often ate out, preferring trendy gourmet restaurants favored by fashionable Istanbul society. Some of the restaurants were not that much different from those he visited with his wife every year in New York. Lately, they had been going to Changa, a fusion restaurant with minimalist decor. Paper Moon used to be a popular spot, but the Kurudals' circle did not frequent it much anymore, claiming it had become "too crowded and too common." They rarely went to the Bosphorus fish restaurants, either, favoring sashimi and sushi over traditional bluefish and turbot.

"I'm happy," said İrfan Kurudal, as he sat alone in his bathroom. "I'm so happy," he repeated—and began to cry.

Books that Aysel had given him extolled the benefits of positive thinking. Far Eastern wisdom, Zen Buddhism, and Tao philosophy all preached the same message: "Let life flow like a river; think positively so that everything becomes positive; the root of all the evil in the world is to think negative thoughts."

After finishing high school and graduating from the Bosphorus University, Aysel had enrolled for a course in Boston. There she met İrfan, who was then a scholarship student at Harvard, and they had married shortly after. She had never worked in her life.

İrfan and Aysel had returned home to Istanbul, capital of the bygone Byzantine and Ottoman Empires, declaring, "No city in the world is as lively as Istanbul" and proceeded to spend their time enjoying the delights of the city. The vitality of the metropolis excited them, and İrfan was fascinated by the vigor and allure of its sprawling neighborhoods. He frequently noted that it was similar to New York in this regard. Even the dismal shantytowns, home to millions of migrants from Anatolia, which had sprung up on the outskirts of Istanbul, throbbed with energy. Someone had opened a restaurant named Goodfellas in one of those poor neighborhoods, emphasizing a brutal similarity with the outlying areas of New York.

İrfan's brother-in-law, who worked in advertising, would often declare that a city had to have a certain number of murders in order to be a metropolis. "Istanbul hasn't reached that stage yet," he would say. "That's all that's missing."

Istanbul had not developed organically like other European cities. It resembled New York, since it was inhabited by people from every walk of life—rich and poor, refined and coarse. Thanks to African immigrants, Istanbul even had black residents.

İrfan thought the city must have accumulated the energy of the entire country, and he himself was one of the most learned, most esteemed, and most successful of its inhabitants. He did not squander money like the nouveaux riches but passed his time reading, attending art exhibitions, and going to the Summer Festival concerts held in the Open-Air Theater or St. Irene—all kinds of concerts by world-famous orchestras and singers.

He loved to wake up to the sound of Jean-Pierre Rampal's flute, and he would start the day with a half hour swim in the pool while listening to the same music. Aysel did not care much for classical music, though she pretended to share her husband's taste. They also followed the popular trends. An evening out at one of the city's famous nightclubs to listen to the arabesque tunes of gay and transvestite singers provided a dash of local color. İrfan relished the feeling of being a Westerner in the Orient, and an Easterner in the Occident. He was not snobbish and did not turn up his nose at lowbrow culture.

Last year, for fun, one of their friends had celebrated his birthday at an "oriental" club, and İrfan had been introduced to a new world. Fat gay singers in "third-gender" clothing strutted on top of the tables, encouraging everyone to climb up and join them in a belly dance. Before long most of the women were up on the tables, gyrating to the beat of the drum, while the men sat transfixed.

Gazing at Aysel dripping with perspiration as she danced with abandon on the tabletop, İrfan ruminated over the idea that the sexual energy of his society was being discharged in a ritual purification, a kind of catharsis. Normally, most of the men around him would fight any other male who dared to look lustfully at their wives, but here they enjoyed watching their half-naked women arouse other men with their sensual dancing. As Kazantzakis, the author of *Zorba, the Greek,* once wrote: "In Hellas, light is sacred: In Ionia it is carnal." The archaic notes of the *darbuka,* a kind of drum played with the hands, and the rhythm unique to this region put people into a state of ecstasy, arousing even the coldest and most distant to join in the mesmerizing dance.

"A common sense of rhythm has more significance for a nation than its flag," thought İrfan. Not melody but rhythm—it is rhythm that distinguishes cultures.

He had once observed his theory in action in the music department of the Virgin Megastore in New York's Times Square, where customers put on headphones to listen to the latest CDs. Divided into areas for jazz, classical, African, Middle Eastern, pop, and rock music, the place was full of people wearing headphones all moving different parts of their bodies. Jazz lovers, slightly stooped, tapped their feet to the insistent rhythm, aficionados of Latin music wiggled their hips, while those absorbed in the music of the Middle East contorted their bellies. It was amusing to watch their silent dances.

İrfan opened his medicine cabinet and picked out a bottle of Stilnox from among the countless medicines there. It would help him sleep for a while, at least. He was shaken by a storm of tears, worse even than before. Fortunately, Aysel was not awake to witness this crisis. It would have been impossible for him to have explained a fear he himself did not understand.

Was he really unable to comprehend its reason? Didn't he know the cause? "Don't lie to yourself," he advised.

Aysel would certainly have suggested a practical solution: Go to a psychiatrist. "Get professional advice, you'll feel much better. That's their job, after all." These and other clichés of the same sort were the advice she would give.

But İrfan already knew what conclusions the psychiatrist would come to.

The professor's hopelessness did not stem from being unaware of his problem, but because he knew exactly what it was. He had struggled to understand his situation, finally grasping it fully after reading a book with the title of *Sleeping Endymion.* In classical Greek mythology, a young shepherd boy, Endymion, incurs the wrath of the gods by falling in love with a goddess, and the gods sentence him by making him decide on his own destiny. Unable to bear this punishment, he chooses to remain forever young, but forever asleep till the end of time.

When he read this, İrfan realized that he, too, like Endymion, was terrified of perceiving his own fate. One's fate should always remain a secret. No mortal is strong enough to know exactly what life holds, when an accident will occur, or in what guise death will arrive.

This idea had completely upset İrfan's ideas about all the things he had regarded as secure in life, which now became ropes to strangle him. He knew he would go on living in the same house, watch television from the same chair, eat at the same restaurants, meet the same people, say the same words . . . until one day, an ambulance would rush him through the streets he walked down every day to the same hospital he always went to, and there he would die. Or maybe, without being given time to reach the hospital, he would collapse, lifeless, on the Dunlopillo bed or one of the Ligne Roset armchairs. Those pieces of furniture he and Aysel had so happily picked out together were no longer objects of comfort or joy but appeared to him like makeshift coffins. He loved Aysel. That was not his problem, yet he could not endure the image of life as inevitably the same.

During a conference in Paris, he had met a Canadian professor, a woman who had introduced him to the concept of metanoia, which had become a beacon in his mind in the same way that a lighthouse gives hope to the sea-tossed mariner. At the core of metanoia, which means "to transcend or exceed one's self and be transported into another existence," is the notion of "self."

It was the concept of self, in any case, which was the problem. What did "me," "myself," "I" really mean? To repeat one's own name over and over is enough to feel separated from self. But how could one not become a stranger to the "self" one carried with one from birth to death, nor alienated from the "id"?

The more the professor considered this question, the more deeply he recognized that most people do live with this alienation in every possible sense of the word. It is the rules of society and the material world that protect us from becoming estranged. Whenever we go astray, we sink back into the warm, relaxing waters of habit. After all, our guide is the familiar comfort of the armchair in which we always sit, the faucet we can turn on even with our eyes shut, and the imprint of our head on the pillow on waking up. In this sense, human beings are like dogs that urinate on trees, marking their territory in order to feel safe within the secure boundaries of their own smell. For human beings, familiar sensations and belongings constituted the formula for contentment.

The great Russian author Dostoevsky described his return to Russia from Europe by saying, "It's just like putting on your old *pantofles*." Sliding your feet into your old bedroom slippers—that was a good definition. That was the way people lived their lives. If they were not safe within their own familiar world, they would probably feel like a boy who was raised in a cellar, then cast out into the public square. But İrfan yearned to surmount the restrictive, tiresome security of his life, which, disguised as happiness, threatened to overwhelm him. To do this he needed to change. A personal metanoia should be experienced at least once in a lifetime.

The Stilnox had started to take effect. İrfan's eyelids had begun to droop, and his mind was becoming cloudy. In the dimly lit bedroom, Aysel slept silently as usual, like a corpse, one leg released from its coverings.

The professor returned quietly to bed and laid his head to rest on the pillow. His last vision before falling asleep was of two young men and a boundless expanse of ocean. While he stood there on the shore, on the horizon was the slowly fading silhouette of the boat carrying his friend Hidayet to Alexandria to explore the poet Cavafy's city.

"Had Hidayet reached his goal?" he wondered. Maybe he had stopped off somewhere along the way and settled down to a different way of life. Or perhaps the waves whipped up by the adverse winds of Zeus had engulfed his tiny boat.

"Good-bye, Hidayet," İrfan murmured. And he dozed off into a troubled sleep, still unable to escape the fear of advancing toward death, of being aware of his destiny.

INNOCENT BRIDE,
BEAUTIFUL BRIDE

Nine hundred miles east of Istanbul, and seventy miles beyond Meryem's village, Cemal woke up trembling with excitement in his bunk at the outpost on the snow-covered slopes of the Gabar Mountains.

He had been dreaming again of the innocent bride, whose legend had been passed down in his village for generations. In his dream, the pure young woman had glanced at the forbidden part of his body. Then Cemal exposed his private parts to her, opening his body to the delicate touch of her hands as her eyes grew wide in wonder.

Although the identity of the innocent bride was unknown, the young men of the village never ceased to talk about her—endlessly repeating to each other the same titillating story.

Once, long ago, a young girl had grown up to the age of fifteen sheltered from all evil and raised like a precious flower in the seclusion of her home, ignorant of the world outside. Her parents did not let her play with other children, shielding her from knowledge of the shameful things that could happen between girls and boys.

The year she turned fifteen, the girl was married off to Hasan the shepherd, who prized his bride's naïve innocence and was determined to preserve it. On their wedding night, he said, "I'm going to tell you a secret, my virtuous bride. I'm different from other men."

The innocent girl looked expectantly at her husband.

"I have something they don't have," he said as he revealed himself to her.

"Oh my goodness," she gasped. "Whatever is that?"

"I'll show you what it's good for," Hasan said and proceeded to demonstrate all the skills of his secret until dawn and prove to his wife that he was indeed different from any other man in the world. From that day on his wife wore an enigmatic smile. She did not share her man's secret with anyone, but, in front of others, only lowered her gaze in a knowing, half-mocking way.

Several years later, Hasan had to report for his military service. Before leaving home for this two-year separation, he hugged his wife and told her they would carry on from where they had left off when he returned. "Just wait patiently for that time to come," he said. After he was gone, the young woman's face lost its smile and her eyes were full of yearning. "What's the matter?" people would ask. "Nothing," she would answer. "It's just that I miss Hasan."

One afternoon, as she was wandering aimlessly around, she was approached by her husband's best friend, Mehmet.

"Why are you so glum?" he asked. "You're not the only woman whose man has gone to serve in the army."

"But he's not like other men." She sighed.

When Mehmet inquired what was so different about Hasan, she answered, "He has something in front of him that no other man possesses."

Realizing his friend's shrewdness, Mehmet grinned. "I have something similar," he whispered.

Hasan's wife did not believe him and thought he was telling her a lie. Mehmet took her to a deserted field, where he was able to prove the truth of his words. From that day on, he was able to prove it again and again on the many occasions he and the innocent bride met secretly at night.

Time passed quickly, and Hasan returned to the village. To his surprise, his wife greeted him with a tart look on her face instead of a smile. When he questioned her, she cried out, "You're a liar! You told me that you were the only one who had that strange part in front of him."

"My God," Hasan thought to himself. "I've lost my innocent bride!"

He then asked her who else had this strange thing, and she told him about Mehmet.

Feeling desperate and not knowing what he could do, Hasan had recourse to another lie. "I used to have two of them, so I gave one to Mehmet."

Upon hearing this, his wife burst into a storm of sobs and weeping. "What's the matter?" Hasan inquired. "Why are you crying?" The innocent bride punched Hasan in the stomach as she wailed sadly, "Why did you give him the better one?"

Just at this point in the story, Cemal, like all the other young men in the village, would laugh uproariously, so Hasan's answer to his wife's question remained a mystery. Although the story, which was repeated almost every day, always ended there, Cemal let his thoughts run free, and he imagined different endings, especially at night in his dreams. He was never able to visualize the innocent bride's face. All he could picture was a rather light complexion, but that in itself was often enough to make him resort to devilish pastimes.

In his bed at the outpost, Cemal let go of the warm vision of the innocent bride with difficulty. Feeling the sticky wetness on his sheets, he hesitated to move but lay there, wrapped in shame. The room was dimly illuminated by a single bulb, and the snores of the soldiers mixed with the crackling of the stove. The guard on duty, trying not to wake the sleeping soldiers, had opened the metal door to feed the stove by adding a few pieces of the low-grade coal he had managed to separate from the conglomerated mass.

A hollow feeling began to spread through Cemal's stomach. He enjoyed dreaming of the innocent bride and carrying the pleasurable feelings she aroused in him to their logical end, but he hated the consequences. He had to get up and cleanse himself. After plunging himself so deep in sin, he could only purify himself by ritually washing every part of his body, from top to toe.

Cemal glanced at the plastic watch on his wrist. It was nearly 2:00 A.M. Since his guard duty began in an hour, he would have no time for further rest after washing himself. If he allowed himself to snooze for five minutes, it would be more difficult to wake up again, but it was more appealing to snuggle back under the comfortable quilt and lose himself once more in thoughts of the innocent bride and her honey-colored skin. In any case, at three o'clock the sergeant would come to rouse him by pounding him on the shoulder and twisting his arm as if to break it. Perhaps he could find time to wash after his guard duty.

Just as he was beginning to relax, Cemal remembered his father. He could almost see the old man's disapproving gaze, his eyes flashing beneath his turban, his hand angrily plucking a string of prayer beads.

Cemal shuddered, chilled by the same fear, familiar since boyhood, and roused himself from sleep. He had almost yielded to temptation and let the Devil get the better of him again. Not only had he dreamed of the innocent bride, but he had also dared to think of going back to sleep without performing the ritual ablution. He had come within inches of opening the gates of Hell. Fortunately, the thought of his father had served as a warning, and he remembered the old man's words: "After being tricked by the Devil, one must perform the required ablutions and recite two prayers, asking for God's mercy. If not . . . God forbid . . ."

The long and descriptive list of the torments of Hell that would follow "God forbid" turned Cemal's blood cold. He did not have to experience those tortures to understand the deceptive and destructive ways of that creature called woman. Listening to his father's words was enough to realize how Satan used those frail creatures to ruin the world.

Something stirred in the depths of Cemal's heart, whispering that he could beat the odds—he could postpone the frigid shower until morning.

Yet there were no guarantees that he would be alive then. What if the outpost were attacked before dawn? Maybe a bullet from a Kalashnikov would smash his head to pieces while he was standing guard. Many of his friends had lost their lives in such raids. Just a week ago, Salih had been killed. No matter how strong the urge to remain in bed might be, Cemal's fear of leaving this world unclean was more powerful.

He sat up. As his bunk was the top one, Cemal could make out the motionless forms of his sleeping comrades in the dim light. Some appeared almost lifeless. Others lay on their sides, or openmouthed on their backs—dreaming, mumbling, and filling the room with the sound of snores and grinding teeth.

The coarse khaki uniforms of the soldiers, worn for many days outside in freezing weather, now hung around the stove to dry, steaming and filling the room with a sour smell. It was impossible to dry wet laundry outside. It immediately stiffened in the icy cold. Bedsheets would become rigid, stretched like sailcloth over the lonely Gabar Mountains. So the soldiers used to wrap the wet sheets around their bodies to dry them. As for their woolen socks, faded from the slush that oozed through their leaking boots, they stuck them under their undershirts when they went to sleep. In the morning, the socks were always dry.

Cemal jumped down from the bunk bed, his bare feet feeling for the familiar hardness of his half boots. It was not necessary for him to look under the bed to find them. His feet found them by instinct. Those heavy leather boots, hard as tree bark from absorbing water and drying out over and over again, were an immutable part of a soldier's life. The men had grown accustomed to the icy cold that crept in slowly through the thick leather, numbing their feet and legs. The intense pain of thawing out later by the stove was more difficult to bear. Their PKK opponents did not have combat boots but wore cheap, thin sneakers. The soldiers had noticed that all the guerrillas they killed in action wore the same light sports shoes, which offered mobility on the rough mountain terrain yet provided scant protection from the frost. As life rolled on against the odds, such details seemed more important than killing or being killed.

Although nothing could have easily awoken the twenty weary young men in the room, Cemal moved as quietly as possible. He could not help wondering which of them would live through the day and which might die. Tomorrow evening some of the beds might be empty, their present occupants lying bloody in the snow, cut down by a bullet, never to rise again, or blown to pieces by a mine.

While Cemal tied his bootlaces, the soldier on duty stared at him inquisitively from his place by the stove.

"I've got diarrhea," Cemal said. The soldiers often suffered from this ailment, caused either by fatigue or the water they drank, and it was a better excuse to go out than to say he had to shower.

Cemal threw on his army jacket and left the room in his undershirt and long underwear, his boots rough on his naked feet. He heard the wind howling outside, sweeping through the valleys and around the snowy peaks, as if playing a piece of background music belonging to a merciless world. When Cemal had first arrived here, this sound had awed him, but now it seemed natural to his ear. In two years he had become a hardened commando, familiar with these harsh mountains.

The frigid air of the corridor cut Cemal's skin like a razor blade. He hurried to the lavatory. He was still in the main building but the warmth of the stove had no effect here, and the corridor and bathroom were as cold as the air on the mountain outside. Shivering uncontrollably, he took off his underwear and upended the half-frozen water barrel over his head. He almost screamed, feeling as though his heart had suddenly become ice, but biting his lip, he managed to control himself. Steam rose from his body. With chattering teeth he washed himself scrupulously all over, especially the part that had given way to temptation. No part of his body should remain untouched by water. His teeth chattered, but his conscience was clear. He had not disobeyed the precepts of his terrible, honored, and respected father; he had eschewed sin and felt the satisfaction of doing what was right according to the laws of Islam. He had no doubt that his father was a hallowed saint: Following his instructions was a sure path to happiness in both this world and the next.

Cemal dried himself with the small towel he had brought with him and put on his clothes and boots. He returned to the sleeping quarters and was enveloped by a heavenly warmth as soon as he opened the door. The guard by the stove smiled, noticing Cemal's wet hair, but said nothing. It happened to all of them.

Cemal laid the wet towel on his pillow and climbed into bed, but he could not go back to sleep. He remembered the three guerrillas they had killed the day before, Kurdish youths in frayed shirts, baggy trousers, and sneakers, insufficient clothing for these mountains. Big holes yawned open where their faces should have been—the work of G3 bullets. Could one have come from his own rifle? In a skirmish, each side usually fired indiscriminately for as long as possible, and one could never know from whose rifle the deadly bullet had come. If you actually took aim, you might know whom you brought down, but Cemal had not experienced that yet.

He had spent two years of his life in these vast, empty mountains that had become the measure of a soldier's courage as well as his cowardice. At the end of a long climb, when they stood bathed in sweat on the peak of the mountain, they felt they were the lords of the terrain—

the silvery rivers and emerald green valleys of summer that turned white with frost in winter. Heavily armed, and in the company of bosom comrades, they felt immune to death. Patrolling the slopes, they surveyed the land below like eagles, and their gaze detected even the slightest movement. They discovered the euphoria of realizing the might of being able to destroy at will. Then they felt like gods, and their heads touched the sky.

Yet the mountains were not always so generous. Sometimes while walking over open ground, the soldiers would come under fire from a distant hill, and as the bullets whistled overhead, fear clenched their hearts—a fear like no other. Inches away from a bullet between the eyes or in the brain, they hung in the balance between life and death. A solitary PKK sharpshooter could pin down a whole unit and inflict serious damage. Armed with sniper's rifles, the guerrillas targeted officers. Sometimes a group of ten or fifteen would attack larger units with bazookas, hand grenades, and Kalashnikov rifles. On the peaks, the commandos were masters, below the summits, the prey.

The sense of superiority felt on the mountaintops did not last, especially when the soldiers had to remain in the open for many days. Rain and snow soaked them to the skin, and they forgot how it felt to be dry. Their wet clothing froze at night, adding to the torment. At such times, the soldiers thought the rain would never stop, and they imagined a life wrapped in nylon but forever soaked to the skin. Even worse was when the whiz of bullets was mixed with the sound of the rain.

Cemal, like many of his comrades, carried a plastic bag when he was out on an operation. He did not want to relive the nightmare he had been through with Abdullah.

Abdullah, a native of the city of Niğde, was a bright young man who liked to laugh and amuse his comrades with endless jokes. One late afternoon, three months before his discharge, their unit had been out on patrol. The soldiers knew that land mines lay in the snow under their feet, but they could only push forward and take their chances. It was difficult enough to recognize mines in daylight, let alone in the slowly descending darkness. Each step they took might send them to their death, and each time nothing happened, they breathed a momentary sigh of relief.

No sound except the crunch of boots on snow broke the silence until a thundering explosion shook the earth to its core. Instinctively, the soldiers threw themselves to the ground. As they did so, they saw Abdullah go flying through the air; he had trodden on a mine.

Cemal was closest to him. Oblivious to the fact that he could set off another mine, he crawled on his belly toward his wounded comrade. He did not look good. Cemal grabbed him, trying to hold his head in his lap.

"My eye!" Abdullah screamed, in a state of shock. "Something's in my eye! Oh, how it hurts!"

His face was a horrid sight, drenched in blood, but Cemal forced himself to grip his head and look at his eyes. An empty socket gaped where the left one had been. Abdullah still moaned in a voice that was faintly human, "It hurts, it hurts."

The leader of the group and the other soldiers now reached them, and Cemal heard the captain shouting furiously over the radio trying to reach the operator, "Hawk 3, Hawk 3, there's a man here seriously wounded. Send a helicopter!"

A voice crackled on the other side. Darkness was falling. It was too dangerous to fly. They would have to hold on till dawn. The voice on the wireless was so calm, as if unconscious of the life draining away there on the snow.

Blood poured from the hole in Abdullah's face. Cemal had no idea what to do. Should he plug it with a rag? All he knew was that his comrade could not last much longer. Even if the chopper came right away, he might not live.

The young captain's voice was hoarse as he continued to plead, trying to convince the other side. "I beg you, please, come! He can't last till morning. Please save our brave comrade. It's not dark yet." He continued to give the coordinates.

The radio was silent.

Cemal was looking at the bloody stump where Abdullah's foot had been. As he tried to subdue the rising fear and panic spreading through his body, he saw the severed limb a short distance away. Like some alien object, the shattered leg and ripped boot lay together in a pool of blood. Cemal's only comfort was that Abdullah was now unconscious, overcome by the pain.

Captain and soldiers gave each other measuring looks as they wondered what could be done. Suddenly, as if in answer to a prayer, the rumble of an engine and the whir of propeller blades broke the still-ness. The soldiers looked up, and a helicopter appeared over the ridge of the nearby hill. They began waving frantically, and the chopper slowly descended, stirring up a flurry of snow.

The soldiers knew the helicopter would not land, but hang a few feet above the ground, and they would have to hurl Abdullah through the open door. PKK guerrillas might see the chopper, open fire, and kill the pilot. The army could not afford the negative propaganda of losing a Black Hawk for the sake of a single wounded private. The medics on board were shouting for them to hurry up. The helicopter hovered, scattering snow, as the team on board shouted to them to hurry, though their exact words were drowned by the clatter of the en-gine.

A few soldiers picked Abdullah up from Cemal's lap and carried him through the blinding swirl of snow to the helicopter. Swinging the limp body back and forth, they threw it toward the door. The medics leaned out to grab the boy, but he slipped through their hands and plummeted back into the snow. Meanwhile, Cemal had picked up Ab-dullah's foot, still warm, and flung it into the chopper. Maybe it could be sewn on at the hospital.

The soldiers lifted Abdullah once more and pitched him toward the helicopter, but he landed on the ground again. The third attempt was successful, and the chopper rose into the air, disappearing over the ridgeline even as the body was still being pulled on board.

Cemal had thrown Abdullah's foot into the helicopter instinctively. From that day on, he began to carry a plastic bag on patrol with him. If another comrade stepped on a mine, he would use it to collect the pieces. And he knew that the other soldiers were prepared to do the same.

In the evenings, over their meals of canned food, tea, and a few carefully concealed cigarettes, they talked together, often sharing their deepest secrets. Perhaps, the following day, they would pick up the torn limb of one to whom they had revealed their intimate thoughts the night before and stuff it into such a bag.

Relaxing in his bunk after having washed himself so thoroughly, Cemal remembered a voice he had heard now and then while listening to PKK guerrillas on the wireless. It was a voice he recognized. Some-times it made a direct appeal: "Soldiers of the Turkish Republic, surrender before it's too late. Save yourselves. Tie up your commander and bring him to us. Or else you won't live through the night."

Upon hearing this, the newest of the reserve officers would grab the radio, and shout back, "You son of a bitch, come and do it yourself, if you've got the balls!"

The laugh, which would then crackle back from the other side, caused Cemal to shudder. It was a laugh he knew well. Memo . . . his childhood friend, his buddy, his brother, his confidant, Memo. Cemal recognized Memo's laughter. During the long summer days in their village, Cemal and Memo used to lie down on the meadow and watch the clouds move slowly in the blue sky. As they dreamed of their future, a future they hoped to share, the thought that they would become the worst of enemies one day had not once crossed their minds. How could they have believed it! Yet, now, one was a private, fighting in the Turkish army, and the other, a guerrilla in the Kurdish separatist movement. As two old friends, now they were fighting against one another, hoping to kill the other. This was a fratricidal fight that had been going on for more than fifteen years. A fight that had cost the lives of more than thirty thousand people, both Turks and Kurds . . . Some of the young men from Eastern Anatolia who had joined the army to do their military service had ended up on the mountains like Cemal, and others, like Memo, had joined the Kurdish separatist guerrillas, who fought against the Turkish soldiers.

As Cemal listened to Memo's husky voice on the wireless, he was not sure whether he would be able to take aim at Memo and kill him if they ever met on these mountains.

ILL-STARRED GIRLS
SUFFER

On the day on which it seemed Meryem's mother had become pregnant, she had dreamed of the Virgin Mary. Candle in hand, the Virgin approached her and said that she would give birth to a girl but would then pass away, leaving her daughter behind.

As Meryem's aunt later told the story, her sister had woken up in terror and insisted that she interpret the dream immediately. She had refused and advised her not to talk about the vision before morning since it could bring bad luck.

Meryem's mother did not return to her husband's bed that night. She was still trembling from the dream and needed her sister's comforting warmth. Hugging her twin, she fell asleep in her arms.

As soon as the first light of day began to enter the room, she woke her sister, and pleaded, "Now tell me what it meant."

Meryem's aunt, who had a talent for interpreting dreams in a positive way, replied soothingly, "I think Mother Mary wants you to name your daughter after her."

"What about passing away and leaving the child?"

"No one lives forever. Why should you be different? We'll all die one day. Even Mother Mary passed away."

When Meryem's mother died in childbirth, the family remembered the saint's wishes and named Meryem accordingly.

Whenever Meryem thought about this story—as well as countless others—she was certain that she lived in a world full of magic, full of holy people who appeared in dreams and talking animals and trees. She regretted that nothing miraculous ever happened to her and wondered if there might be something wrong with her.

In primary school, her friends used to tell stories of miracles—how they heard birds talking like humans, or how a family ancestor had alerted them to danger. Once, something similar happened at Meryem's home. Her revered grandfather had appeared to the family and warned them not to buy large amounts of soap.

"If you do," he said, "you will burn."

They did not heed his advice and bought bar after bar of soap at the market. The house did catch fire—as if lit by invisible hands. Meryem's father and uncle had great difficulty in extinguishing the flames. They ordered everyone never to disregard such a warning again.

When the grandfather made another appearance and told the women of the house to change the day of their weekly visits to the public baths, making the trip on Thursdays rather than on Wednesdays, the family obeyed the command.

Meryem loved going to the baths, which required special preparation. Food was cooked and fresh towels and clothing prepared. Then all the women, young and old, would crowd into a cart and set out, looking forward to a long day of entertainment.

At the baths, Meryem secretly studied the drooping breasts of the naked women around her and wondered whether she, too, would have such strange things one day. In this ancient building, where the sun's rays turned pale upon passing through the thick glass of the domes, the older women briskly rubbed Meryem and the other children until they glowed rose pink, and then almost scalded them with bowls of steaming water, rinsing them clean. She always noticed a pungent odor emanating from the closed partitions at the back of the room. When she asked about it, she was told, "It's the smell of depilatory . . . you'll understand when you're older."

When Meryem grew taller and sprouted two buds on her chest, the women, admiring her young, slender figure, finally introduced her to the secret part of the baths. They took her to one of the compartments, prepared a foul-smelling mixture, and removed the hair from under her arms and pubic parts.

"You must get rid of all the hair there," they told her. "If any remains, it's a sin. Use this to remove it from your body."

Soon Meryem began to carry out the procedure on her own without allowing anyone to come near her.

Depilation was the most tedious part of these days at the baths; the most pleasant was sitting in the cool room afterward, enjoying a meal of stuffed vegetables and little pasties.

Meryem tried to find a way to see the grandfather's ghost who had made these predictions, but her wishes were never fulfilled. Her prayers were of no avail; nor was it any good to rub her eyes, and murmur, "Grandpa, Grandpa!"

Her mother's father had been a wrestler, while her paternal grandfather had been a mystic who went by the name of Sheikh Kureysh. One stormy day in the dead of winter, the sheikh had walked barefoot out of the house into the snow. When asked where he was going, he replied, "To Horasan."

Some onlookers began to laugh, saying that he would not take a few steps before his feet froze solid, let alone reach Transoxiana. Despite their mockery, he kept on walking. The few villagers who followed him for a while later reported that, when a pack of ravenous wolves saw the old man approaching in the snow, they had stopped howling and turned meek as kittens. According to legend, the sheikh walked all the way to Horasan and back.

No animal, not even the most vicious or venomous, disturbed the holy man. Snakes and scorpions crawled harmlessly over his hands, up his arms, and around his neck. He was immune to evil, and he passed on this power to the newly born infants of the family by spitting in their mouths. Thus, the members of the household gained protection from all danger.

Everybody believed that the spirit of Grandfather Kureysh was forever present in the family home. That was why stairs creaked, doors slammed, and strange noises sometimes came from the kitchen.

After listening to these tales told nightly among the household, Meryem was sure that her grandfather's spirit would rescue her, but no matter how hard she tried to open herself up to these visions, he did not appear. Even during the visit to Şeker Baba's tomb, she had not experienced anything special, except shaming herself. The villagers often recounted how, long ago, when Russian troops had occupied their homes and slaughtered many of the men in the nearby streambed, Şeker Baba had rocked the sky with thunder and lightning and showered the enemy with hailstones. The Russians had scattered in fear. It was certainly Şeker Baba, too, who caused the Russian commander to put a revolver to his temple in his headquarters at the largest mansion in the town and pull the trigger. Disbelievers claimed this miracle was prompted by a telegram the officer had received from Moscow earlier on that November day in 1917, but few of the villagers agreed. Even if true, Şeker Baba must have sent the message.

Other than Meryem, almost everybody in the village had witnessed miracles: Girls flew up in the air, and chickens talked. Visits to shrines where votive rags were tied to trees, or fervent prayers during celebrations for the coming of summer and on the Night of Power, when the Holy Quran was revealed, all produced results for others, but none of what she wished for ever came true.

"I must be cursed," Meryem often thought.

And everybody secretly agreed. After all, her mother had died in agony in childbirth, as prophesied in a dream. Meryem must be ill-fated since she had caused the death and brought ill luck to the house. She was unfortunate and would probably end up an unmarried old maid. Even now, at age fifteen, she still had no suitors. No mother wished to have her as a bride in her house.

While others witnessed pleasing miracles, Meryem saw horrid nightmares. Mary the Mother, whose name she carried, had never revealed herself or given her any direct guidance through dreams. God forgive! What kind of a mother was she! She must be the one who was sending her these terrible nightmares to test her patience and the limits of her endurance.

In the cold isolation of the barn, where day and night blended imperceptibly, Meryem woke up, screaming. She had imagined herself clinging to the ground near the brink of an abyss. Far away in the mist, she could see the outline of a vast city. "Istanbul," Meryem thought. "That must be the Istanbul they are always talking of." The city was so large that she could not see its limits. Even though she wanted to stand up for a better look, she was paralyzed with fear. Suddenly the heavens rocked with thunder. Meryem looked up and saw thousands of white birds flying over her head. Their flapping wings caused a rush of wind so great that it dragged her toward the chasm. She clawed desperately at the earth. The swarm of birds flew off, then returned, repeating the same pattern of flight over and over again. Each time the flock passed overhead, Meryem edged closer to the void.

Now awake, Meryem glanced around the barn, expecting to see those fearsome birds, but the cold, dark space was empty. Her thin blanket had slipped onto the floor, and her feet and hands felt frozen.

Meryem listened for sounds of the world outside. The village had been oddly silent for the last few days, the house, too. Every now and then she heard a few agitated whispers or muted footsteps, but the chatter of the women who baked bread once a week in the earthen oven in the neighboring garden did not reach her ears.

As a child, she had loved to watch the thin sheets of bread browning on the iron trays and to breathe in the mouthwatering aroma. The women would fold the newly baked bread into big triangles, spreading fresh butter across each layer. The butter quickly melted and sizzled, filling the air with a fragrance that whetted Meryem's appetite—along with those of all the children who stood impatiently nearby—waiting for a taste of the delicacy, known as shepherd's pasty, which was one of Meryem's favorites. Once Meryem had seen a yellow chick accidentally fall into the flames at the bottom of the outdoor oven. Unable to save the tiny creature, Meryem had quite forgotten to eat her pasty and had wept all day long.

As Meryem lay locked in the barn, everything was still and hushed. Even the village, usually bustling with people and the noise of horses, donkeys, roosters, chickens, and minibuses, was shrouded in silence. The only sounds to pass through the walls were the muezzin's hoarse voice calling the faithful to prayer, the occasional grind of a distant tractor, and the infrequent rattle of a passing cart.

Meryem felt the quiet was somehow related to her—perhaps the aftermath of that terrible event in the cabin. But what did it mean? Could the whole village become silent because of what happened to one young girl?

Meryem clutched her blanket. At that moment she understood. The villagers were waiting for her to do her duty. Not only her family but the entire community was waiting silently for her to end the problem.

As soon as she hanged herself, everything would return to normal. The villagers could get on with their daily routine—shopping, cleaning, praying. The sound of children at play would again fill the streets. Like other girls ruined before her, Meryem no longer had the right to live. This is what Döne had been trying to tell her. The expression on Döne's face had conveyed the message, just as the unusual quietness of the house and the silence of the village was doing.

The realization chilled Meryem's heart. She felt responsible to everyone she knew—her father, her uncle, her aunts, and Gulizar the midwife, who had helped her come into this world.

For a while Meryem wept quietly. Then she picked up the rope she had hurled to the floor the day before, threw it over the beam, tied it with a knot, and made a noose at the other end. She stepped onto the log and passed the rope over her head. Its coarseness hurt her throat.

Meryem hesitated. She was about to fulfil her duty. "All you have to do is kick the log away," she said to herself. "The others did it. You'll swing a bit, and your throat will turn black and blue. Your tongue will stick out. It will only last a minute, no longer."

"But where will I go after that?" Meryem wondered. She could not think of an answer.

She did not know how long she had been standing there when she heard a key turning in the lock and saw Döne enter the barn with a small tray of food. Their eyes met. Döne slowly turned around and walked softly out of the room without leaving the tray.

Meryem was consumed with rage.

"Bitch!" she hissed. "You bitch!" she repeated, pulling the noose from over her head.

Döne was probably telling the rest of the family that Meryem was finally doing her duty. She could see them all, waiting there in silence, and the image made her angry. She would defy them and go to Istanbul.

"Kill yourself, you slut!" Meryem cried out, thinking of Döne, and tears began rolling down her cheeks.

She closed her eyes and prayed for help from all the holy saints. Her aunt always used to say, "It's only when problems become unbearable that one is granted a solution."

Meryem had reached that point.

"I beg you, blessed Hızır, show me your face," she pleaded. "I know that whoever sees your holy face in his dream gets rid of all his troubles. Blessed saint, please hear my call. I'm in distress. Please show me your face. O God, please let the door open and Hızır come in instead of Döne. Let him take me all the way to Istanbul."

Meryem recited every prayer she knew, but when she opened her eyes, she was still alone. No one from the family had even come to check on her. Maybe they were quietly listening on the other side of the door.

Meryem remembered her school days, when she roamed the streets freely and rolled a hoop with Cemal and Memo, who were like older brothers to her.

The yearly celebrations commemorating the village's liberation from Russian occupation were among the most enjoyable times of her youth. While the villagers marched to the accompaniment of martial airs played by the municipal band, the thunder of gunfire filled the air.

Meryem loved taking part in the parade with her schoolmates in their black uniform pinafores with the white collars. She and the other students were instructed to line up, touch shoulders, and, after shuffling into position, were given the order, "Right, turn," and off they would walk down the street, accompanied by the beat of the drums. Meryem felt that all eyes were on her, and she held her head high. As they marched under the triumphal arch, she imagined that she was passing under a rainbow. Cannons would fire, and their thunderous roar made everyone recall Şeker Baba's miraculous shower of hail on the Russian troops. Afterward, she and her schoolmates would sit in the places reserved for them in the square to watch a reenactment of the liberation.

Dressed up like Russian or Turkish soldiers, the young men of the village performed the same show every year. Village youths who were fairer-skinned and huskier than the others were chosen to act the part of the Russians and attack the darker, shorter youths who were the Turkish troops. At the decisive moment, the brave Turks would gain the upper hand and force the Russians to flee. They would hoist the Turkish flag, with numerous explosions being set off simultaneously, while the crowd cheered and dense smoke filled the square. The band would then strike up a rousing march.

Cemal and Memo took part in this performance every year. Well built and fair-skinned, Cemal played the part of a Russian, while

Memo, who was smaller and darker, acted the role of a Turk. The municipality paid the participants, but the Russians received more than the Turks since they had to take a beating. Even though Cemal earned twice as much as Memo, he felt playing the role of a Turkish soldier was more honorable. Sometimes Memo would say to Cemal, "I'm Kurdish, and you're a Turk, but I always end up being a Turkish soldier in the performance."

Everybody would laugh, but their roles remained unchanged.

Once the festival had been spoiled when the performance deviated from the established script, angering the provincial officer, mayor, and gendarmerie commander. As usual, the Russians launched the attack, then fell back in the face of the Turkish counterassault. Inflamed by a nationalistic frenzy caused by the martial music and the patriotic verses they had heard, the Turks beat and kicked the Russian soldiers, who fell passively to the ground. They were getting paid to take the blows but had not bargained for such a beating. But the roll of the drums, the call of the trumpet, and the roar of the cannons had stirred the Turks' blood. Shouting war cries, they kicked and punched their opponents with all their might, and the performance area started to resemble a real battlefield. Blood flowed from the noses of the Russians, and their faces were cut and swollen.

Meryem heard her cousin Cemal shouting at Memo, "Are you crazy? Stop!"

All the Russians were yelling, but it was useless. Finally, the Russians' patience broke, and they stood up and fought back. Battered unmercifully, their blood was up by then, and their superior physical strength forced the Turks to flee.

The Russians were victorious that year, and the local authorities, furious, immediately stopped the celebration. The crowd dispersed, and the village settled back into its accustomed torpor.

Meryem remembered the bruised and bloody faces of Cemal and Memo, and she started to giggle. Then she thought of those listening on the other side of the door. Would they not be surprised to hear a dead girl laughing?

LIFE IS A JOKE

Can a man turn into a totally different person and start a new life?"

İrfan Kurudal was asking himself this question as he sat among a boisterous group of friends in a small fish restaurant on the Bosphorus. The lights of a passing steamer were reflected in the glass of the tightly closed windows. Although spring had arrived, it was still too cool to sit outside, so the heat was on.

Sunday lunch with a few close friends, sitting by the water chatting and sipping *rakı,* used to be one of İrfan's favorite activities. He still laughed at the jokes, but had lost his enthusiasm for this pastime. The same question kept coming up in his mind—could he change his life if he so wished?

Someone was telling a joke. Jokes about the war in the southeast had recently become popular, and İrfan pretended to be amused.

"One day PKK guerrillas set an ambush for a unit of soldiers that they know always passed by the same spot at seven o'clock every evening. Half an hour goes by and nobody arrives at the ambush . . . an hour and there's still no one in sight. Then one of the guerrillas says worriedly, 'I hope nothing has happened to our boys!' "

Everybody laughed, and Metin, a banker, continued with another joke—speaking through his nose to imitate a Kurdish accent.

"PKK guerrillas raid a village and kill everyone except for an old woman and an old man. One of the guerrillas points his gun at the woman and asks, 'What's your name?'

" 'Fatima,' says the hapless woman.

"The guerrilla tells her that his mother's name is also Fatima so he won't kill her.

"He turns to the old man and asks, 'What's your name?'

"Quivering in fear, the terrified man stutters, 'My name's Omar—but everyone calls me Fatima.' "

The group erupted into laughter. İrfan had not heard this joke before, and he found it amusing.

Before joking about war had become popular, jokes about sex had been the norm. Women sometimes told bawdy jokes, but if the stories were too risqué, they might pause coyly and look at their husbands for approval. When a man told such stories, he would lower his voice and use figures of speech to cloak the meaning. Sex, İrfan believed, dominated the subconscious of all social classes in Turkey.

İrfan was not good at telling jokes. He generally failed to emphasize the right word at the right moment, and he did not have a talent for mime. Nevertheless, he decided to share a joke he remembered from his time in the States.

"Do you know which word the great Jewish thinkers used to explain the meaning of the world?

"Moses said, 'God.' Jesus said, 'Love.' Marx said, 'Money.' Freud said, 'Sex.' Finally, Einstein stated, 'Everything is relative.' "

İrfan's friends laughed politely and went back to telling their jokes about the Kurds.

Light is carnal in Ionia . . . Though Istanbul was not Ionia, it shared the same culture. The dynamic potential of this society and the basic motive that determined its behavior was suppressed sexuality. Singers whose lyrics had sexual undertones and who stressed their own sexual identity achieved popularity. Was it a coincidence that most of the leading singers were gay? Even in his day, Naima, the great seventeenth-century Ottoman chronicler, had written about young men who seduced older men by performing erotic dances in women's garb.

Recently, in a public survey, a gay singer and a man who had undergone a change of sex were chosen as singers of the year. The historical chronicles and manuscripts over which İrfan pored revealed widespread male homosexuality in the Ottoman Empire. Many a pasha and gentleman of note had visited the baths to be massaged and bathed by male attendants. Some texts even described the rules for such encounters.

İrfan's researches aimed at decoding the sexual behavior of Turkish society. He published articles that, as always, were mercilessly attacked by his professional colleagues. In the university, easily compared to a scorpion's nest, everyone was the enemy of another. Many university academicians who were İrfan's opponents were perpetually hostile. They would never get tired of accusing him of using others' ideas in his articles. They were claiming that the subjects he delved into had been discussed earlier in depth by others. As a sociologist who had not majored in history, how did he dare to repeat such stereotyped ideas and call it a scientific approach! In Turkey one had to make liberal use of the word "science" in order to defend his views. Personal ideas not explained "scientifically" were considered not of value, unless one had a certain title in front of his name such as professor, doctor, or associate professor. As a result, Turkey had an abundance of professors, since anybody who spent a number of years teaching at a university automatically received the title.

İrfan featured this glut of professors in one of his television programs. He referred to ignorant professors who could not even use their own language well. This stirred up a hornet's nest, and his detractors responded vehemently, deriding him as a faker and a freeloader, who lived off his wife's fortune.

Sometimes, sitting alone in his office at the university, İrfan wondered how he had managed to acquire so many enemies. It was hard to comprehend such hatred, but at the end of these sessions of self-pity he always reached the same conclusion—there was no need to take things personally. In this country, everyone detested each other. Soldiers despised civilians; air force officers disdained their counterparts in the army; political science graduates had no time for those who had received their diplomas in law; businessmen loathed politicians, and vice versa; pundits of the media gained kudos by bringing down idols. Where else were newspaper columns filled with profanity and invective? The intellectuals themselves were a breed apart. They fostered animosity, and their conversations were full of mockery, spite, and malice.

Until recently, İrfan had not minded all this. He felt that to live in such an atmosphere was quite natural. Success inevitably aroused jealousy, but now the local scene stifled him. He no longer enjoyed going to clubs, and he was disenchanted with the lifestyle of Istanbul's so-called elite. He began to feel helpless, like a driver in a skid, seeing himself as a useless prattler, worthless and cowardly. The ways he used to defeat his opponents he once thought so successful, those barbs accusing them of being worthless, weak, arrogant, cheap, or unprincipled, weapons that had been his armor against them, he now cast at himself. They were right. He began to see himself as no better than the people he had so heartily despised.

İrfan used to enjoy attending international conferences and seminars, but now he felt isolated at such meetings and withdrew to a secluded corner to watch the others. He would manage to carry on a conversation with Western academicians, but when the topic turned to the philosophies of the ancient Greeks or Romans, he would fall silent. He lacked a common background. It was no better with Arab intellectuals; he did not belong to the Eastern world either. The philosophical and scientific terminology of Latin, Greek, and Arabic were not internalized in his being. He was the victim of a shallow, groundless culture that mocked concepts that could not be expressed in single words or clichés.

İrfan thought he was, like most other Turkish intellectuals, a trapeze flyer, swinging between the Eastern and the Western cultures. He, like many others, suffered the vacuum that was created after an "Eastern" society of hundreds of years suddenly became "Western" in the twenties when the Arabic alphabet was abolished and replaced by the Latin alphabet. He was a trapeze artist who had let go of the fly bar of the East yet floated in the void, unable to land in the catch trap of the West.

İrfan's nights were full of fear and weeping, and he felt he was losing control over the self he knew. He had to lose his identity, find a way to alter his destiny, and overcome the fear of death, a fear that had been sown in him and grew stronger day by day. He could not accomplish these things as long as his life revolved around that house, the coffin that symbolized his destiny, and his office at the university. İrfan could no longer play the role of either husband or professor. Like Sleeping Endymion, he would be obliged to determine his own fate, yet his destiny should not be one that resulted in an eternal sleep.

İrfan remembered his surprise upon reading that Dostoevsky had once approached his worst enemy, Turgenev, saying that he wanted to confess something to him. Turgenev was taken aback by this unexpected confidence.

"I once seduced a nine-year-old girl in a bathtub," Dostoevsky declared, then turned to leave.

Astonished, Turgenev asked, "Why tell me this?"

"So you realize how much I despise you," Dostoevsky replied, without looking back.

Only a courageous man could do that, and İrfan wished he could pay similar visits to his enemies, but he had no interesting stories or even lies to tell. His "successful life" was utterly insignificant. He was shit, and his friends were, too. The places he frequented were shit, as well. Istanbul itself was a rubbish heap, with its restaurants, its streets patrolled by wild dogs, its hills of refuse, those potential explosions of methane gas picked over by beggars and seagulls alike, its nightlife where children were exploited as prostitutes, and transvestites in high-heeled shoes held knives to the throats of taxi drivers. It was full of ignorance and filth. İrfan even felt that the waters of the Bosphorus, not just those of the Golden Horn, had begun to stink. And in the restaurants of these fetid areas, his alleged friends thought they had become members of the elite just because they paid hundreds of dollars for a bill that included carpaccio, pesto, sashimi, or other dishes with foreign names. He could bear neither his surroundings nor his life of imitation anymore, yet he had no idea how to communicate this, especially to his wife, whom, in fact, he loved sincerely.

He already knew Aysel's response, "If you're depressed, let's go on holiday," she would say, or, "We can find new places to eat." A short, easy way of dealing with the problem. Nothing and no one was worth anything anymore.

Once again, İrfan remembered Hidayet, who had sailed off to see Cavafy's city. When İrfan's family had sent him to university in Istanbul, Hidayet's refusal to follow the same path, putting out to sea instead, was now a precious memory.

"Why should I go to Istanbul and study?" Hidayet had asked.

The two of them were sitting in a small waterfront café at the former Customs House in Izmir, drinking cold beer and watching the setting sun paint the waters of the gulf wine red, just as Homer had described.

"That's not the life for me," Hidayet continued. "Predetermined, limited, inactive. I expect more from life than that."

"What more do you expect?" asked İrfan.

"I've no idea; and that's the best part—not to know what life will bring you!"

A few days later, Hidayet, in his homemade boat with its makeshift sail, had become just a faint outline on the horizon. The wind might have carried him to Crete, perhaps, or to some unknown shore; or, perhaps, he had been lost at sea.

İrfan began to miss Hidayet with increasing nostalgia.

CEMAL'S SECRET

Someone unfamiliar with the terrain would probably not have noticed the village in the distance. Only by coming very close could one discern the single-story houses built on the slopes of the mountain, as drab as their barren surroundings. That day not a tree, brook, or even a fountain was visible under the blanket of snow.

When Cemal's unit entered the village, there was no sign of life. The low roofs of the houses were heaped with snow. No smoke curled from the chimneys, and the sound of neither man nor animal broke the silence.

Cemal was used to such sights. Caught between the PKK and the army, the Kurdish villagers retreated into their homes, trying to avoid both of them.

According to intelligence reports, guerrillas had been in the village the night before. They had already left, but Cemal's unit was under orders to evacuate the buildings and torch them. The village would no longer offer shelter for the PKK.

Cemal had heard that thousands of villages, as well as acres of forests that might provide refuge, had been set ablaze. He had personally taken part in burning twenty villages, and it no longer seemed out of the ordinary.

Forced out of their houses at gunpoint, the villagers were interrogated in the school, which had been transformed into a makeshift command post. As usual, they offered little information. While the women wept, the men who did not cooperate with the authorities were made to strip and stand naked or forced to walk barefoot over jagged stones. Deaf to their pleas, the captain ordered the village emptied in a half hour. The command to surrender their firearms was met by stubborn silence. The soldiers knew that no weapon would be handed over. Villagers never disclosed where their guns lay buried.

Cemal was convinced that the most important things for these people were their guns, their mules, and their testicles. They guarded their firearms closely, protected their mules, so essential for their livelihood, and whenever beaten, they always begged, "Please don't hit my balls!" Having learned Kurdish from Memo, Cemal was the only member of the unit who could understand and follow most of the conversations.

The weeping women were now piling a few sticks of furniture out in the snow, children were carrying hastily tied bundles through the doorways, and the men were still pleading helplessly. The captain told them to go wherever they wished. Many would probably end up in Diyarbakır, though some might journey to Istanbul, Izmir, Antalya, Adana, or Mersin. Their destination was of little importance to the military, whose aim was to clear the area of safe havens for the PKK.

Cemal remembered the voice on the wireless. Memo's voice. Feeling strangely close to him, Cemal wondered if perhaps his friend had spent the previous night in this village. At the same time, he was conscious of the distance between them. The war resembled the plays they had performed on the anniversary of their liberation from the Russians, but the thought of bullets whizzing overhead in battle made Cemal shudder. This was no make-believe.

At the beginning of his military service, Cemal's mind had often wandered back to the days when he and Memo picked melons in the fields, cooled them in the stream, fried fish in an old can, and opened a bottle of *rakı* with their friends. He had recalled their fantasies about the innocent bride, the sins he committed in his sleep, and the resulting shame. These were the shared secrets of youth. Ambushes, Kalashnikovs, land mines, and the bloody pieces of a friend stuffed in a plastic bag had erased them, one by one, from his memory.

Every year, on the anniversary of the liberation, Memo had always played a Turkish soldier, Cemal a Russian. Now the roles were reversed. Cemal wore a Turkish uniform, and Memo was the enemy dressed in the garb of the PKK.

Over the intercom, Cemal would overhear Memo's conversations in Kurdish with other guerrillas and listen to him calling on the Turkish soldiers to surrender. For a long time he did not utter a word about this to anyone in his unit. It was not easy to be indifferent to that voice on the radio, and finally, one day he had shared his secret with Selahattin, his bunkmate.

"Don't tell anyone," Selahattin had responded at once. "You'll get nothing but trouble."

Respecting his friend's knowledge and experience, Cemal had taken his advice.

Selahattin was from Rize on the Black Sea coast, as was obvious from his prominent nose, a hereditary feature common to most Black Sea people. Most of Cemal's comrades were from the west, Thrace, the Aegean, or the Black Sea. There were only a few easterners like himself. Selahattin often spoke about his family, who had moved to Istanbul, and Cemal enjoyed the tales of his family's shop in the wholesale fish market, his uncles' boat at Sarıyer, and their fish farms on the Aegean coast.

Selahattin was a devout Muslim, and he and Cemal prayed and fasted together. He treated Cemal, the son of a sheikh, with special esteem, and constantly asked him about his father. Although Selahattin, a member of the Ushaki sect, was deeply religious and had studied the Quran for eight years, he had never heard of the Cemaliye sect, of which Cemal's father was spiritual leader. Cemal told him as much as he understood of his father's teachings, related in a language that mixed Turkish with Arabic and Persian, which described how the Cemaliye sect was founded on the principle that the face of God made itself manifest in everything throughout the world. Selahattin did not find his explanation very convincing, and he started to wonder if Cemal's father was a false sheikh, like so many others in Anatolia.

. . .

After the village had been evacuated, the soldiers conducted a house-to-house search to make sure the dwellings were empty of all inhabitants. Then they poured gasoline over each building and set them all ablaze. As the flames rose, the grief-stricken women began to wail, and their screams soon filled the air. The fire was consuming their homes, their belongings, and their hearts. Holding fast to the halters of their mules, the men watched silently. Not tears, but hate filled their eyes.

Months ago, Cemal would have felt their anguish, and perhaps even tried to console them, but his experiences in the mountains had numbed him. A few houses collapsing in flames paled in comparison to what he had witnessed. Just two weeks ago he had gazed at the corpses of two schoolteachers executed by the PKK. A band of guerrillas had stopped their minibus, ordered the couple out, and shot them on the spot. Cemal had been struck by how quickly their bodies, especially their faces, had turned black.

During his broadcasts over the wireless, Memo declared that the guerrillas were the "rulers of the mountains and the night." They certainly knew each crag and cave better than the soldiers. The local Kurds, as well as their animals, also liked them. Whenever Cemal and his comrades approached a village, they were immediately set upon by dogs and were often forced to kill one or two. Yet, when the PKK entered the same place, the dogs did not even growl. Cemal finally solved the mystery when he heard a Kurdish villager calling out to some dogs one day in a strange, guttural voice that silenced the animals. Even though he knew Kurdish, Cemal could not imitate that sound, and like the rest of his comrades, never learned to communicate with the dogs.

The villagers also directed their mules with strange cries, like a foreign tongue. In this they were not always successful, perhaps because a mule has a mind of its own.

Several days earlier, Cemal's unit had been lying in a streambed. The terrain in front had been mined, and they saw an old man with his mule walking slowly toward the danger zone. If they warned him, they would disclose their position, but an explosion would attract even more attention.

"Stop," they shouted, "the area's mined!"

The man halted in his tracks, but despite his frantic calls, the mule did not. Desperate to save the animal, he chased after it. The mule had almost passed through the mines when the ground erupted under its feet. The explosion blew off its front legs, and Selahattin put the creature out of its misery with a shot from his rifle. The old man sat in the dirt beside the dead animal. His livelihood gone, he wept inconsolably.

Cemal imagined Memo as being one of the snipers the guerrillas positioned on the high hills. Memo had always been a good shot, even as a child.

Cemal no longer felt any warmth when he heard Memo's voice, and each time someone in his unit was killed or wounded, he blamed his former friend. His anger soon deepened to hate. If he ever came face-to-face with Memo, he vowed he would shoot him without a second thought. He would avenge all those youths, dead, or missing an arm or a leg, and kill Memo or any enemy of his country and nation.

Their faces reddened by anger as well as the heat of the flames, the villagers turned away from their burning homes. With their bundles on their backs and their mules and children in tow, they trudged slowly down the hillside.

Near the edge of the village, an old man with a long white beard and sunken eyes was lying on a mattress in front of his house, untouched because of its distance from the other dwellings. Standing beside him was a small boy of nine or ten. These two were the last survivors of a family wiped out by the war.

Tears staining his cheeks, the old man was pleading with the captain, "Please, commander, let us stay. I'm crippled . . . we have no place to go."

With little other choice, the captain relented, and Cemal saw the boy's face light up. The boy knew nothing of the world beyond these hills and the routine of taking their few animals out to pasture. Leaving these mountains for some distant place would, for him, have meant losing all that was familiar and dear.

Trying to avoid the glances of the other soldiers, Cemal quickly took a few coins from his pocket, placing them surreptitiously in the boy's hand as he patted his head. He was careful to frown as he did so in order not to spoil the child with kindness. The boy looked up, smiling his gratitude.

Back at the outpost that evening, Cemal again heard Memo conversing with his comrades on the wireless. As usual he cursed the Turkish army, then said, *"Ez dicim Nuh Nebi"* ("I'm going up to Noah").

Cemal understood from this Kurdish sentence that Memo was going toward Mount Ararat, where the remains of Noah's ark supposedly lay. Memo had once related to him how he wished to climb the mountain one day and discover the ancient ship.

Cemal at once suspected that the guerrillas, having seen the flames, were withdrawing from the peaks where they had spent days sniping at them and retreating toward Mount Ararat, a mountain where the soldiers knew the trails well. After they had eaten, he turned to the captain saying, "I have something important to tell you, sir," his face flushed hot with excitement.

WHY DON'T THE COCKS CROW?

Meryem had prayed to god and the virgin Mary for a miracle, and when, instead of Döne, she saw Gülizar, the village midwife, enter the barn, a wave of gratitude swept over her as she felt her wish had been granted. Joyfully, Meryem noted the old woman's white muslin scarf, her invariable headcovering, her tender eyes, and gentle hands. Through the open door, the sun streamed in and lightened up the darkness of the barn.

Gülizar had been a midwife for so long that she had been at the birth of everyone in the village under a certain age. It was as if they were all her children.

She had played a very special role in Meryem's life. The tiny girl, weighing just one and a half kilos, had emerged into the world unable to breathe, strangled by the umbilical cord around her throat. It was Gülizar's deft hands that had unwrapped the cord from her neck, and it was Gülizar who then breathed into her lungs, enabling the blue baby to start breathing on her own. Although she could not bring the mother back to life, she had succeeded with the child.

Whenever she thought about death, Meryem remembered this incident and would say to herself, "I've already died once." Others in the house would add, "Meryem was born dead. She can't die again!"

After so many frightening days of solitary misery, Meryem flung herself into Gülizar's arms. The scent of her headscarf was fresh and sweet, and Meryem began to weep.

"They've done awful things to me, Bibi!" she cried, using the childish name for the midwife. "They want me to kill myself."

"I know," replied Gülizar. "Make sure you don't."

Then she explained to her what a cruel fate it is to be born a woman and the difficult path each woman has to tread. She emphasized the fact that women are born accursed. "God rot womanhood," she cried. "You know, even the blessed Mother Mary had her troubles to bear."

When Meryem asked her what she meant, she exclaimed, "They killed her son. Didn't you know?"

"Oh, I know that!" Meryem replied. "They also killed our Mother Fatima's children—the grandchildren of our blessed prophet."

"Yes, at Karbala . . .

"Look here, my dear. I've been through a great deal of trouble to get here. They don't want anyone to see you. I've had to plead with them for days before they would consent. Your father seemed about to relent, but your uncle refused to hear of it. Listen to me . . . this may be your last chance; I may not be able to come again. Everyone in the village has been feeling bad about you ever since the day you were found by the graveyard, flapping around like a wounded bird."

Her face scratched with thorns and with blood running down her legs, Meryem had been a pitiful sight when she was found lying in the road near the cemetery, uttering terrible cries, scratching the dust and jerking her arms and legs in the air, her headscarf in the dirt beside her. The young men who discovered her thought she had been bewitched, but when they saw who it was they took her by the arm to take her home. She did not go quietly but kicked and struggled, at times conscious, at others falling in a faint to the ground. They had to drag her like this through the square and marketplace, where all the villagers came out to watch.

Meryem lay in bed at home for two days, fever-stricken and moaning as she drifted in and out of consciousness. Called to examine her, Gülizar quickly realized she had been mercilessly raped. The old woman used all her skills to heal her, placing pieces of cloth moistened in vinegar on her forehead, swabbing iodine in a crisscross pattern across her chest, and forcing her to sniff hydrochloric acid to bring her out of her delirium. As soon as she seemed to be herself, Meryem was condemned by the family council to be thrown into the barn.

"Many respected people in the town have spoken up on your behalf and talked with your uncle," Gülizar continued. "They've tried to convince him you're not to blame, and old traditions shouldn't be followed. Everyone wants to rescue you."

"Don't they want me to hang myself?" asked Meryem.

Gülizar was silent for a moment. "Some might, but others want you to live."

"They could send me to Istanbul, like other girls in the past."

"Child." Gülizar sighed, caressing Meryem's hair. "My poor child. Istanbul's no solution. It's best that we persuade your father and uncle to let you out. You must help me by telling me everything that happened . . . everything! Who was the monster who hurt you?"

Meryem said nothing. Her eyes clouded and her head drooped. "Tell me his name," said Gülizar gently. "You must tell me who the wretch was, or who they were," Gülizar said, "to save yourself. Don't worry. He'll be punished. The gendarmes will break his bones and lock him up. Or your family can take care of it."

Meryem remained silent without opening her mouth, as if afraid to draw breath. She began to rock back and forth as if in a trance.

In spite of all Gülizar could do, Meryem still refused to say a word, and after trying for a long while to reason with her, Gülizar gave up, convinced the girl could not identify her attackers. Perhaps they covered her head with a sack, or she had lost her memory from shock.

Even if she did remember, it would have been of little use. Gülizar had suggested to Meryem's uncle that the best solution would be to find the rapist and force him to marry Meryem. But he had snapped back, "Whether a bastard or a rapist, it's all the same. Neither of them is entering my family!"

Realizing Meryem would not give her any information, Gülizar changed the subject.

"My child, if you've become pregnant on account of this happening, so much the worse. If they realize you're carrying a bastard in your belly, God forgive us; if that's true, and I think it may be, we must try to get rid of it."

Meryem continued to rock silently, as if she heard nothing and knew nothing of what had happened to her. Her eyes were fixed on the stream of light coming in though the open door, and she seemed lost in her thoughts.

Suddenly, Gülizar began to spit out all the curses she had ever heard in her life as she bewailed the fate of this unfortunate child. Arms outstretched, as if in supplication, she railed, "God, strike down those who violated my innocent girl, let them be dragged on their backsides till they die!"

After this outburst, she looked at the girl and saw that she had returned to normal and was back in the real world again.

Staring at her with her green eyes, Meryem asked softly, "Bibi, do you think they'd let me get washed? My hair's greasy, and I stink. All I want is a bucket of water."

Meryem, however unwillingly, had to eat something, even if only a few spoonfuls of what the women put on the tray for her. Afterward, it was unbearable to have to go out into the garden, take down her panties and squat in the snow under Döne's disdainful gaze.

Gülizar must have understood her feelings, because she rose and left the room. Since it was daytime and the men were out, she settled the matter with Meryem's aunt, returning half an hour later with a small plastic tub, a metal bowl, and a bucket of hot water.

Meryem heaved a contented sigh. At least her aunt had given permission for her to wash.

"Bibi," she said, "Auntie never came to see me."

"That's no surprise," Gülizar muttered.

They both knew that her aunt blamed Meryem for her much-loved sister's death. If her sister had not told her the dream about Mother Mary, she would have tried to feel that, like other women, her sister was simply a victim of circumstances. The ill-omened dream, however, was proof of the girl's guilt.

As a child, Meryem could not comprehend her aunt's behavior. Later, when she understood the reason, she did her best to win her approval, hoping that one day her aunt would forget her grudge and give up her taunts. But Meryem was never forgiven, and, because of the way her aunt treated her, gained a reputation for being ill-starred.

Gülizar gently undressed Meryem and started to wash her in the plastic tub as though she were a little child. A long-forgotten feeling of warmth enveloped the girl as the steaming water poured over her head, and the old woman tenderly washed her hair.

Gülizar wrapped Meryem tightly to protect her from the cold in a towel she fetched from outside. One hand massaged her gently as she rubbed her dry with the other.

"Now, dearest, do what I tell you and we'll get rid of that thing in your belly. I know it's there, I can see it in your eyes."

Meryem said nothing. Obediently, she let Gülizar rub her with poisonous hemlock balm and drank without protest the foul-smelling liquid she gave her.

Gülizar was more cautious than other midwives. She never used dangerous methods to induce a miscarriage, such as thrusting a chicken quill or dried eggplant stalk inside the woman's body.

When she had finished, Gülizar laid Meryem's head in her lap and softly stroked her hair.

"Bibi," Meryem moaned, "my tummy hurts!"

"Don't worry, love. It will soon pass."

Meryem felt herself falling asleep under Gülizar's soothing caresses. Just before she dropped off, she murmured, "Why don't the cocks crow anymore, Bibi?"

"The cocks always crow, sweetheart—some can hear them, some can't."

"I don't hear them."

"Because you don't want the morning to come."

AT NIGHT DON QUIXOTE, SANCHO PANZA IN THE MORNING

İRFAN HAD NOT CLOSED HIS EYES ALL NIGHT. Without feeling the need for sleeping pills, he had stayed awake till morning, pacing through the house, tidying up the papers in his study, and sitting by the covered pool in his rattan chair, watching the refracted movements of light as they shifted here and there. Oddly enough, for the first time in years the terror chilling his heart had evaporated. Sitting by the pool, he planned the coming day—a day of emancipation from a life ruled by fear and the restrictions imposed by others. Like a man drowning, his feet caught in weeds, İrfan wanted to kick the bottom, rise to the surface, breathe the fresh air, and see the light again. Purified of fears and weaknesses, he would feel the indescribable joy of changing his life and creating a new sense of well-being.

He had not said anything to Aysel yet. She was sleeping peacefully upstairs, quite unaware that her life, too, was about to change.

When he got to the university that morning, the first thing İrfan would do would be to visit the department chair and instead of greeting him formally as he had done for years, he would punch the man right in the middle of his disgusting face. İrfan was younger and stronger, and nothing could prevent him from hitting the man, who

had secretly accused him of being shallow and commonplace and ruined his reputation, that miserable old man whose face it would be a
delight to batter.

What relief he would feel. Like Gulliver, İrfan had to rip off the invisible ties of Lilliput around him. He would make sure the door was
open so the secretary could see the fellow's ugly mouth lose a few rotten teeth. No doubt, the scandalmonger would be stunned. A few minutes later, once İrfan had left, the man would come to his senses,
shout, and threaten to make İrfan pay for what he had done. Struggling to save his ego, he would order his secretary to call the rector, a
lawyer, and, of course, the police. He would wipe the blood from his
mouth, trying to console himself by imagining how İrfan, landed in
jail, would be finished and done with once and for all.

News of the incident would spread quickly through the university.
Hundreds of telephones would ring at exactly the same minute, and
the press would soon be hot on the story. Like hungry wolves following the smell of blood, İrfan's friends would erupt into the corridors to
follow the trail of fresh gossip.

After paying his respects to the department head, İrfan would drop
by the office of that abominable woman, Şermin. After finishing his
business with the old dinosaur, he would visit her next. He wondered
how best to display his feelings for her. Peeing on her desk as she
gazed at him with astonished eyes might be appropriate. It would
probably cause her to have a heart attack. All he would have to do
would be to walk into Şermin's office and open his zipper. She was
certain to lose her presence of mind and scream hysterically. The secretary would make one frantic call after the other, and soon the department head with his bloody mouth would arrive on the scene to
find out what was going on and to join in the outcry. İrfan would have
already made a hasty exit.

As might be assumed, not only did İrfan not carry out his plan but,
in fact, he acted even more foolishly than usual. With the light of day,
the fantasies of the night vanished, and the sun appeared like a mes-
senger to bring him back to reality. His plans, so feasible in the darkness of the night, seemed nothing more than delusions in the cold light
of day. Like many people, İrfan was Don Quixote at night and Sancho
Panza in the morning. It was for this reason that he felt constrained to
go to the university, if only to prove to himself that his plans for re-

venge, which he had dreamed of so happily by the pool, were just not practical.

He knew this even before leaving the house but when, upon entering the building, he immediately came face-to-face with his department head, this unexpected encounter merely made it clearer. The door was only wide enough for one person so İrfan stepped aside, murmuring his usual halfhearted greeting as he let the man whom he had dreamed of beating up go first. The man whose face he had smashed like a melon in his dreams the night before was now treated with great courtesy. This really was proof of how little character he had. Instead of insulting the man or making him look small, he had almost licked his boots.

Needless to say, he did not even think of visiting Şermin.

When İrfan entered his office, he was so full of self-doubt that he felt an overwhelming need to compensate. He sat down to write an e-mail to his wife, feeling as if he had to burn all bridges and cross the point of no return. He typed Aysel's address, but then sat staring at the empty screen.

Feeling uneasy that he might never realize his dream, İrfan wrote "My Love" at the top of the screen but then paused. That was not honest. A farewell note should not start that way; but how else could he address a wife of twelve years standing, "My dear wife," "Dear Aysel," "Aysel," or just "Hi."

He decided to keep the two words that were the most meaningful for him. Aysel had to understand that his departure had nothing to do with her.

My Love,

You know the legal term "self-defense," or what we call "legitimate defense," meaning defense of the self. I can no longer hide the fact that for months I've been imprisoned by fear. It has nothing to do with you, or the love I feel for you. I love you more than ever, but I have to leave.

Please try to understand.

This is not the consequence of free will; it is legitimate defense. If I don't go, I cannot survive another day. I must either leave or commit suicide. Of these two options, I can only choose to live.

My foundation is shaken, and in order to breathe at all I must find another place to live where I can be on my own. I hope that you will understand that I must do this.

Don't try to find me. Pretend I'm away on a long trip. If I get over this terrible fear of mine, I'll call you.

Good-bye, my love.
İrfan

İrfan stared at the screen and imagined the impact of the message, picturing all the possible consequences. After questioning the household, the chauffeur, the secretary, relatives, and friends, Aysel would feel utterly abandoned. Realizing that his resolve was weakening, İrfan quickly clicked SEND. The message disappeared from the screen. He had crossed the point of no return.

One more thing, İrfan thought, and went to the locked closet, where he kept his research notes related to the book he had been planning to write for some time. He took out all of his notebooks, a couple of loose pages, and picked up a book about the Bogomils. After cramming them into his briefcase, he left his office. He took a taxi to the bank, leaving his car in the university parking lot. He had already given instructions for a withdrawal from his savings account. His financial adviser, Nilgün, had warned him that the interest was due the following week and he would lose a large sum on the $72,000 in his account. "Never mind," he replied. "Just have the money ready. I'll pick it up before noon."

He would lose much more if he waited for the interest to come to term.

AMBUSH AND LAUGHTER

CROUCHING BEHIND THE ROCKS, THE SOLDIERS silently cursed the change in the weather, which had turned the snow to rain. They would be out all night, and no matter how many layers of plastic they wrapped themselves in, the rain always seeped through, like a snake slipping into their clothes and slithering over their skin. The icy water seeped into their boots, soaking their socks and numbing their feet. The only advantage of this weather was that their enemies were suffering, too.

Under his blanket, Selahattin was smoking a cigarette. Despite the precaution, he was putting the whole company at risk. Any light, no matter how faint, could draw the sniper's attention and, once before, the very same action had resulted in the smoking soldier's death. If they allowed the enemy to suspect an ambush, they could all be killed, without inflicting any casualties of their own. Cemal reached over, pulled the cigarette from Selahattin's lips, and extinguished it. He looked so serious that Selahattin raised no objection.

Cemal hoped that Memo and the rest of the guerrillas would soon fall into the ambush and all die at the same instant. Memo was no longer a friend but a ruthless, bloodthirsty enemy intent only on slaughtering Cemal and his comrades. Cemal hated Memo more than any other terrorist and wanted him punished. When he had told Sela-hattin this, he had said it was Cemal's own fear of death that made him think that way. Cemal thought he had become immune to fear, yet he obviously still suffered from it. It was hard to forget the images of com-rades lying dead, with a bullet between the eyes or torn to pieces by a land mine.

Cemal remembered how he and Memo used to hunt partridges to-gether. Memo was a crack shot, and he carried his rifle differently from the others, as if it were an extension of his body. He could bring the gun effortlessly to his shoulder and hit the target without waiting to take aim.

Cemal hated Memo with a hatred he felt for no one else. He was sure that Memo's rifle was now pointing at him and his comrades. At moments like this, he always sensed the unseen barrel. Memo must be on the hilltop, ready to pick them off one by one, like partridges.

The fear of death was always present among the soldiers. The pos-sibility of a rocket attack hung over them whenever they hastily ate their two hundred grams of canned rations or tried to drink a cup of half-frozen water. When, constipated from eating dry food for days on end, they bent down to defecate bloody stools, they could feel the en-emy breathing behind them. When they occasionally lit a small fire to soften up their bowels with some hot food, the thin smoke took the form of death. Death haunted them even as they stretched out on their thin mattresses on the frigid ground. In these hostile mountains, they could not help wondering if they would survive the next minute.

Some of the soldiers broke under the strain and rushed into the fray, willing to die. Such boys would say, "Going home in a flag-draped coffin now is better than waiting for death in these mountains."

Cemal knew that Memo was ready to kill him. They had spent many nights at each other's homes, sharing meals and talking end-lessly. Yet, now, Memo wanted to send him to his grave. Cemal's only escape from his rage was to imagine killing Memo first. It would be just punishment. Memo would not even have time to reach for his rifle. "Bastard!" hissed Cemal. "Murderer, traitor, bastard!"

Hours passed, but there was no sign of the PKK. No one could sleep during an ambush; the soldiers had to be on the alert every sec-ond. They could not even whisper. Cemal knew that each of his com-rades was lost in his own daydreams.

Suddenly, Cemal saw Memo's face in front of him. His heart pounded. He realized his mind was wandering between sleep and wakefulness. Tonight no soldier could afford to make any mistakes, and he tried to get hold of himself, but soon he felt drowsy again.

Cemal recalled the games he and Memo used to play in the village, the taunts they threw at each other during soccer matches, the disputed goals, and the fights that ensued. Dripping with sweat, they would shout curses at one another, but their anger was soon dissipated.

Once they played together against a neighboring village. To guarantee victory, Cemal visited a maker of charms and potions before the match and had him prepare a talisman. He buried the charm in front of their goalpost so no ball would pass through.

In the first half of the game, the charm seemed to work like magic and even the hardest shots of the opposing team did not find the goal, going wide or rebounding from the goalpost. Cemal's teammates were so ecstatic that he told them about the talisman until someone remembered they had to change ends for the second half, which meant the charm would then work in their opponents' favor. How could they shoot against the talisman they had ordered? Their goal would be without its defense. During the second half, the talisman remained true to its promise. Every goal they attempted either went wide or rebounded from the goalpost. The team from the other village won three to one. After the match, Memo shouted at Cemal, "Idiot! If you could think of using a charm, why didn't you think about having to change ends!"

Cemal had no answer to these words of truth and kept silent.

Memo was after him now. It was Memo who was killing his friends: attacking them with rocket fire and murderous bullets; blowing them up by his side with devastating mines; and Memo wanted to kill him, too.

Icy rainwater oozed down the neck of Cemal's jacket, but he remained still. Soldiers had to endure everything: rain, cold, pain, fatigue, sickness, coughs, fever; even the lice, whose bites irritated their skin. But in the open, in the freezing rain, they had to endure all this for days at a time.

Cemal's thoughts turned to his village, his father, mother, uncle, sisters, Döne, and Meryem. He could see his father, uncle, and himself as they placed a lump of sugar between their teeth in readiness to strain the freshly brewed hot tea through it, and he tried to feel the warmth as he drank it down. He could not. It was as if he had never had a life before he became a soldier; as if he had been born on these mountains. Those hot dreams of the innocent bride, to whom he made love in spite of never having seen her face, and the image of his mortal enemy, Memo, were all that remained from the past. As the vision of his home and family blurred, Memo's features became crystal clear—his gaunt face, thin moustache, and the sarcastic smile on his crooked mouth.

And the image of his father, of course, came into his mind. Sometimes it was even as if he heard his voice, giving him advice on how to avoid danger and keep away from sin. His father was a constant teacher, always with him.

Toward the morning, Cemal could feel that the soldiers were getting restless. In the darkness no eye could penetrate, they strained their ears to hear the footsteps of those who called themselves the "rulers of the mountains and the night." Cemal knew that the captain was holding his breath though he himself could hear nothing. Then came a sound that was different from that of the drip of melting snow. Faintly, a strange indistinguishable noise came through the dark. Not even sure that it was a sound, the soldiers silently raised their guns. Cemal's heart felt as if it were no longer pounding in his chest but in his throat. In a little while the sound would come closer, the firing would start, flares would light up the sky, and the machine gun in his hand would spurt forth sudden death.

"Fire," shouted the captain, as the indistinct sounds came nearer.

Every weapon in the company erupted with a deafening retort. Flares did little to illuminate the darkness, and the soldiers fired blindly. It was difficult to know whether there was really anyone there in the darkness, but surely their efforts must show some result.

Eventually the barrage ceased. Maybe no one had been out there, or maybe several PKK terrorists were lying dead in the dark. They would not know until the first light of day. The soldiers remained in their positions, eyes fixed ahead. The rain had stopped. After the roar of the guns, the silence of the valley was frightening.

The night was finally over. Rays from the rising sun shot out from behind the mountains, causing Cemal to squint. He could make out the line of the peaks glowing red in the distance. A peculiarly bright star was still blinking in the morning sky. He shivered. It was now light all around, but there was nothing unusual to be seen. The valley was oddly tranquil. Perhaps the shooting had been futile, one or two thought, and began to yawn and stretch their arms. The captain was hesitant. If they really had opened fire on an empty valley, he would look extremely foolish. He commanded his men to stay low, and they waited another hour.

Suddenly the bright yellow sun rose above the mountaintops.

The captain stood up and surveyed the terrain through his field glasses. "There's no one here," he murmured quietly.

The next instant he was lying on the ground, blood jetting from his throat, pouring out in crimson waves onto the cold earth. Cemal had never seen anyone bleed so much before. The soldiers were sobbing, "Captain, captain!" while one of them tried to telephone the news. Behind a distant rock, Cemal saw a flash that flared and went out all in a moment. But this was enough for him to realize that this was where the sharpshooter who had hit the captain was concealed. They went on the offensive immediately.

The entire company opened fire at the rock. A storm of bullets battered against the stone; hand grenades flew through the air; the earth erupted in flame and smoke. Cemal was certain that no one could have survived that barrage.

After the dust had settled, the soldiers advanced cautiously, wriggling over the ground on their stomachs. Another grenade was thrown, and only when all danger seemed to have been averted did they stand up. They found a body behind the rock, but it would have been difficult to say if it was human. The torso was in pieces, the head ripped apart and burned, but Cemal could see it was not Memo. A strange fit of laughter rose within him, and he controlled himself with difficulty. "My nerves must be shot to pieces," he thought.

They discovered two more dead guerrillas, but Memo was not among them either. Perhaps he had fled under cover of darkness while those wounded had only been able to take refuge behind the rock. "Cunning, ruthless Memo," Cemal said to himself. "What a fox you are!" He began to laugh then, softly at first, then louder, rising to a hysterical crescendo that reverberated among the rocks. His behavior would be remembered by his friends for the rest of their lives and used as an example of a person who had been driven crazy by the events of the war. They looked at him in consternation until the sergeant stepped forward and gave him a stinging blow across the face. And another and another as Cemal continued to laugh, the tears running down his face. It took a long time for him to come to his senses and become calm again.

The team had lost its captain, and Selahattin had been wounded in the leg. Like Cemal, he was almost at the end of his tour of duty. Cemal would be demobilized forty-five days early, since he had not taken any leave. As for Selahattin, he would be hospitalized for the remainder of his service.

Even in the final days there was no relief. During Cemal's last week, an unfortunate event occurred. A new, young lieutenant had been assigned to their post. He was inexperienced and nervous. One evening at dusk he saw a figure on a nearby hill and, without hesitation, gave the order to shoot. Actually, even their former captain would have done the same. No one but the PKK came into these far hills, and there in the evening, even a shadow constituted a threat. The soldiers opened fire, and the figure fell.

When they went to inspect, they found a small boy lying lifeless on the ground. Around him grazed a small flock of sheep and goats, straying here and there without direction. Cemal looked at the bullet-riddled body and remembered a pair of grateful black eyes amidst the flames of a burning village. Cemal imagined the anguish of the crippled old man waiting for the grandson, who would never return.

"I'm getting soft," he said to himself. Perhaps it was because his military service was ending that he felt such mixed feelings.

The hearts of all of them had been coarsened in the months spent on the mountains and had become dead to human feelings. Just like breaking in a new pair of shoes, when the skin becomes inflamed for some days before becoming callused and immune to pain, they had hardened their hearts in order to survive the cruelties of war.

THE FAMILY HOME

Sitting alone in the business-class section of Airbus Flight 310 en route to Izmir, İrfan felt as if he was being swept along by the current of a raging river. When the flight attendant inquired what he would like to drink, he asked her for a glass and some ice. Opening the bottle of Royal Salute he had bought at the airport, he poured himself a shot of the tawny whisky and inhaled the rich aroma of cognac, mahogany, morocco leather, and tobacco. "I am being swept away," he thought, "and I'm dragging all the others after me."

The professor always thought in long, complete sentences, as if writing a book or dictating a letter to his secretary. He had developed this habit from writing so many articles, speeches, and television scripts. He felt responsible for organizing his thoughts. As was his custom, he started to take notes on small pieces of paper. "Everybody is being swept away," he wrote. "All reference points are lost in this society, deprived of its Eastern and Islamic roots and far from being united with Western values. No one is happy. The unwritten rules that keep a society together are nowhere to be found. We are going through a nihilistic period, in which everyone is yearning for a better life, but no one knows what form it should take. There is no prescribed form;

therefore, the people have neither a mythology nor an ideal. The torrent is forcing us along. Some try to save themselves by clinging to the branches of the trees that overhang the river. Some grasp the branch of religion, others nationalism, "Kurdism," or "nihilisim."

İrfan poured himself another drink before admonishing himself. "Stop preaching! You're full of hot air! Get to the point—confess your fears and relax!"

At that moment, the tall, attractive flight attendant approached İrfan and told him that the pilot would be honored if he would visit the cockpit. İrfan wanted to be alone, but found himself agreeing to accompany her to the cockpit. The pilot must have recognized him from his television program and seized the chance to have a conversation with him.

As he entered the cockpit, İrfan was struck by its electronic tranquillity. Listening to garbled messages from the flight control towers, comprehensible only to the pilots, they adjusted direction without interrupting their conversation. İrfan reflected on how handsome a uniform made everyone seem; even long-distance bus drivers looked smart in their tailored suits and dark glasses.

The professor felt a sudden urge to grab the flight instruments, pull down the lever, and send the plane into a nosedive. He would later recall this moment, trying to understand why the fear of dying led him to desire death. It was a fierce impulse. It was not hard to understand how people who suffered vertigo could choose to commit suicide by jumping from a high place.

Being a man of thought rather than action, İrfan did not allow his feeling to overcome him. He conversed pleasantly with the pilots, even opening the topic of "how Turkey would never solve its problems." The professor found an opportunity to cut the conversation short, returned to his seat, and gulped down another drink before landing.

As the plane lost altitude over Adnan Menderes Airport, İrfan thought about the changes Izmir had undergone during the last thirty years. Like him, it had lost its innocence. The Aegean atmosphere was slowly evaporating, causing the city to fade like an old icon from which time has worn away the gilt. The Kurdish war, or "low-intensity skirmish" as the General Staff called it, which had resulted in the deaths of tens of thousands in Eastern Anatolia, had also caused hundreds of thousands of Kurds to migrate to the west. The inhabitants of three thousand devastated villages had flocked to the Mediterranean and Aegean coasts, bringing with them their own culture to mingle with those of Ionia and Mesopotamia.

At first, İrfan doubted that these villages had really been burned down and depopulated, but later accepted this fact when he saw it mentioned in the supervisory reports of the prime ministry. Unfortunately, the struggle against terrorism was carried out in similar ways all over the world. Although it would have been better had this devastation not taken place, every state had the legitimate right to protect itself against armed rebellion.

The taxi driver, a skinny youngster with a thin moustache, who was taking him to Karşıyaka from the airport, must have come from the east. He thought he recognized İrfan from somewhere and talked to him throughout the entire trip. Had İrfan ridden in his taxi before? Where was the Turkish economy going? Since gasoline was so expensive, he had had LPG fuel installed in his vehicle. Did the professor want a cigarette? Yes, smoking was harmful, but it calmed you down. Perhaps the gentleman would like to listen to music; he had new cassettes and a Pioneer cassette player. They were cool, weren't they? Suddenly, the small car was transformed into a concert hall, where moaning violins, the percussion of drums and tambourines, as well as the melancholy wail of desert pipes accompanied a popular song of the type known as "arabesque," played at full volume.

If the professor had felt any peace previously, it disappeared immediately. This urban kitsch music had no harmony, and İrfan felt as though a screwdriver were being slowly ground into his ear. He was not a musicologist, but he was sure that arabesque symbolized the country's decadence. The music was not genuine like the blues, the fado, the tango, or the rembetiko, all of which expressed a cry of oppression. Arabesque—the music of migration to the big city—was not the outcry of a wounded man but the whimpering of one pretending to be injured. The most famous singers carried diamond-studded Rolexes, drove Mercedes, and wore silk shirts, half-unbuttoned to expose their hairy chests, yet they sang songs of pain, sorrow, and despair. Their music reflected the unreliability of the Middle East. It was a deception, a lie, and an example of how the weak were trampled on as they bowed hypocritically in front of the powerful.

İrfan was surprised by the change in himself. Just a month ago, he had viewed this music as a colorful part of Turkey's subculture, even expressing that opinion on the media. What had caused the change, shattering his comfortable life and bringing him to the brink of madness? Fear of death perhaps? İrfan could not pinpoint the answer. He only knew that the music lacked honesty, so unlike the traditional folk songs. The music was getting on his nerves, but İrfan refrained from insulting the young driver and kept quiet, allowing him to enjoy it to the fullest.

After what seemed an eternity, they finally parked on the narrow road in front of the neglected apartment building where İrfan's mother lived. He gave the driver a big tip. Maybe the young man would think his generosity was in appreciation of the music and turn up the volume again the next time he picked up a customer.

The older, lower-middle-class women of the Mediterranean region resemble each other. With her worried eyes, tired face, and weary movement, İrfan's mother was no exception. Without hiding the apprehension this surprise visit aroused in her, she hugged the man who once had been the center of her existence but now belonged to higher circles. İrfan, in turn, embraced the old woman, who occupied a space in his present life no bigger than her tiny frame, and kissed her on the cheeks.

İrfan's mother performed the *namaz* and prayed without fail, visited her neighbors frequently, always listened to the evening news, never missed her son's programs, and accepted congratulations from her acquaintances with embarrassment. She shopped at the local street market, bargained with the vendors—a longtime habit of her frugal life—and invariably complained about the high prices. Like most elderly women of the Mediterranean, who receive little medical support or advice during menopause and have no idea of bone loss or the correct calcium intake, she had ended up with bones distorted from lack of proper care. The sight of her bent body, once that of a lissome girl, shoulders bowed and hips distorted, making it difficult for her to walk, grieved the professor deeply.

Inhaling the scent of his old home, he realized that it had been a long time since his last visit. How strange to think that this modest apartment, the down payment on which had come from his father's retirement bonus, the monthly installments for which had been paid by his father for the rest of his life, had once been the center of İrfan's world. Here he used to read his books and daydream endlessly of what the future might hold. He had not truly appreciated all the precious gifts of his adolescent years: the soft-porn magazines that had aroused his first sexual awakenings, the secondhand bicycle his father had bought him, the tires of which had forever needed mending, the ferries from which he used to jump before they were fully docked, his flirtations with girls on summer evenings, the fresh mussels fried and eaten on the beach, the fairground he had sneaked into without paying, the harmless jokes played on people on the street, the buses he had pinched rides on, and the love affairs he had thought would last forever.

His father's railroad uniform was still hanging in the creaky old closet. During his early childhood, when the family had lived in lodgings for railway personnel, İrfan regarded his father as very handsome in his brown uniform and gold-braided cap. As the years went by and İrfan saw how miserable a life of poverty made his father, the impression changed to one of a lean man with hollow cheeks, sunken eyes, and trembling lips. Life was hard on some, and İrfan had experienced many of its difficulties in his childhood. He had never felt at ease around wealthy kids at school and, even as an adult, still felt shy in the company of the rich.

People who were born into wealthy families and never experienced money problems were different from those who acquired money later in life. İrfan could immediately tell whether or not someone had grown up in poverty. Perhaps it marked one for life as it had done him. Aysel was a good example of someone born rich. Without the slightest discomfort, she could say to a friend, "I don't have a dime on me; you pay the bill!" İrfan would be ashamed to say such a thing.

As a child, the brand-new shoes of the wealthy children dazzled him, and he did everything to hide his own shabby ones. Maybe that was the reason he had filled his closet with so many pairs of shoes once he started earning good money. Yet, on this trip, he was wearing an ordinary pair of trainers.

There were times in his youth when İrfan had seen his father in his wrinkled railroad uniform as a tired, distraught, and defeated man, especially when he compared him to the rich businessmen who were the fathers of his friends. Filled with anger, he would repeat to himself that he had not chosen this man as his father. He set himself a single goal—not to be like his father.

Despite his vow, İrfan realized he missed his father deeply. On that April evening, filled with the scent of an Aegean spring, and the smell of fried squash, which reminded him of summer, he felt sharp pain when he remembered his past efforts to avoid meeting the old man. After leaving Izmir, he had not seen his father again, nor given him the least opportunity to share or to take pride in his success.

He had not invited his parents to Istanbul for his magnificent wedding reception, nor even informed them about the wedding. He could not introduce his pitiable father and humble mother to Aysel's rich and successful family of shipowners. They would not fit into his circle of businesspeople, politicians, and media personalities. Aysel, herself, had encouraged İrfan to invite his parents, whom she had not met, saying that poverty was not something to be ashamed of. Besides, it would be fun to have a few "genuine" people at the event. It was all a game for Aysel; she could never understand how deep his insecurities ran.

İrfan had not visited his father when, reduced to mere skin and bones, he lay dying of stomach cancer, nor even attended his funeral five years ago. Now, he would never see him again. The reasons seemed totally incomprehensible to him now and, what made it worse, was that his mother had never uttered a word of reproach for his failure either to invite them to his wedding or to attend his father's funeral.

İrfan's mother, talking nonstop, was preparing food for him in the kitchen. She was so proud of him. Everyone in the neighborhood congratulated her on being the mother of a professor who appeared on television, and this made her feel very respected. Of course, her main concern was that İrfan, as well as his sister, Emel, were happy and healthy. She was thankful that both of them had gone to the university and were happily married. Emel had a good life in Ankara, where İrfan's mother spent a month every winter. For some time, she had taken care of Emel's second child, Ebru—such a cute little girl. İrfan would love her. İsmail, her older brother, was jealous, of course. When they were children, İrfan had been jealous of his sister, too. After Emel came home from the hospital, six-year-old İrfan had hidden under his bed for days, saying that he would not come out until his parents sent away that ugly baby. Laughing at the thought of it, she seemed to have returned to the days when her husband was still alive and all her happiness had been bound up in him and their two children.

Watching his mother's glowing face, İrfan thought, "Ah, mother! Nothing is as you think it is. Your beloved son, so admired by the grocer, is in deep trouble. He will either lose his mind or kill himself. As for your daughter, she knows that her husband has a lover, but she has chosen to shut her eyes to the affair and let her life slip away as she shoulders the responsibilities of two kids and a job. Your son-in-law, a general manager in the Ministry of Public Works, of which you are so proud, lives on bribes. He squanders money on a sixteen-year-old manicurist called Zeliha. You don't know that Emel calls me every now and then, crying that she cannot go on living like this and threatening to end her life. I tell her to be patient. After all, everyone has a lover nowadays. Before she puts the phone down on me, her elder brother whom she thinks a fool, I tell her to go along with the times and find a lover herself. Later, when I reflect that Ankara is not like Istanbul, I feel some regret."

İrfan started talking to his mother about the old days. "Let her be happy for a while," he thought, "and imagine that she is doing me a favor by cooking my favorite dishes." Soon, however, his mind drifted away to Aysel. What was she doing now?

She must have come home and taken a shower. She might have been curious about the whereabouts of her husband but had probably not dwelt on it. How long would it take her to see his e-mail message? As it grew late, would she panic and call some friends or even the police before reading it? Whatever the case, she would eventually read the message, and anguish would replace worry.

İrfan began to feel uneasy, yet he reminded himself of his promise to be thick-skinned. For some things life was too short, but it was certainly too long to worry much about a faithless husband. He had no doubt that Aysel would soon forget him and get on with her life. Now was not the time to let sentiment overcome him if he were to be true to his resolution.

Later in the evening when he was alone, İrfan took an old pair of scissors from his mother's sewing box and cut up his credit cards. Now, he had no personal documents other than his passport, with its

U.S. and other visas. He felt relieved, free of all bonds and elated by the lightness of his being.

Now he was sailing with Hidayet as the small boat glided silently across the still, mirrorlike waters of the Aegean. The white sail billowed gently in the breeze, like a cloak blown by the wind. It resembled a ghost from some mythological story of the Aegean.

THE HERO IN TOWN

One DAY WHILE LISTENING TO MUSIC ON THE static-filled radio at the military post, Selahattin told Cemal the story of a young musician named Halil, who was recognized as the best *kanun* player in Istanbul. When Halil was a child, his father used to tie iron weights to his wrists and force him to play the *kanun,* a stringed instrument placed on the knees and plucked by means of plectra on each finger. At first, the boy could barely move his small hands over the strings, but he soon learned to play faster. For years, his father made him use the weights. When Halil was a teenager, his father finally allowed him to play without them. The boy's hands flew over the *kanun,* and up to that time, no one had surpassed him in talent or art.

On the bus going home to his village, Cemal felt as if he had cast off his own iron weights, which he had carried for two long years. He did not know what to do with his hands now they were free. Accustomed to the roughness of his uniform and the weight of water-soaked boots and a cumbersome cartridge belt, he felt naked without them. His arms and hands were so light now, he no longer had a gun, hand grenades, or wireless set to carry.

Cemal felt defenseless, confused, and a little frightened. If the PKK stopped the bus, they would surely recognize that he was a soldier, even without looking at his ID. Those who had killed someone could easily recognize another like them even among a thousand people, and they would take him off the bus and execute him immediately. After surviving the dangers of the mountains, it would be ignominious to be hauled out of the vehicle and shot by the roadside. The army usually sent members of special units home by plane, but since Cemal lived so near, he had been given a bus ticket.

The best day of his military service had come. Cemal had been discharged and was free to go home, yet he had an unpleasant feeling that something was wrong or soon would be.

Plans he had made for his return to civilian life had kept him awake on many nights, but now they were buried in a thick black mist. The people in the bus looked odd to Cemal. The driver wearing sunglasses, his assistant sprinkling cologne on the passengers' hands, those who got on the bus and off it; all belonged to a strange and different world. Cemal felt lost. By chance, the adjacent seat was empty so he could stretch out his long legs, but he found it impossible to relax. He was in readiness at any minute to take shelter behind his seat if he heard a suspicious sound. After a while, he drowsed off, still feeling tense. At one point, when the driver's assistant softly touched his arm to wake him, he sprang up to stand to attention in the center of the bus, mistaking the boy for his sergeant calling him for guard duty. The other passengers began to eye him distrustfully.

When awake, Cemal fixed his eyes on the road ahead, looking for signs of danger, especially at the bends along the road and at gas stations. He was not even carrying a knife. How could he be so defenseless, so vulnerable in this unfamiliar place and among these strangers?

When the bus stopped at a rest facility, he went to the men's room and washed his hands and face. The grimness of his face shocked him when he looked in the mirror. That bony, sunburned visage framed with closely cropped hair could not be his. Suddenly, a man pushed him aside, grumbling, "Come on, leave off looking at yourself, man, the bus is about to leave."

Without looking to see whether the man was young or old, weak or strong, Cemal whirled around and threw him to the ground. There was not a sound to be heard as, stunned, the people looked at the man being helped back onto his feet. Then workers from the restaurant and gas station rushed in to break the tension. Cemal watched as in a dream while, in answer to their questions, the people there explained what had happened. "OK! OK!" one said. "It's all right. The young man's a soldier. Come, let's go."

Someone patted Cemal on the shoulder, and he flinched but restrained himself from further reaction. Afterward in the restaurant, however, everyone avoided his gaze, and he ate at a small table, alone.

When the bus finally arrived at its destination, the noise and bustle of the terminus dazed Cemal. His head ached from the sounds of the call to prayer, the wail of music, and the shouts of the street vendors selling sesame rolls, grilled sheep's intestines, and meatball sandwiches. He felt as if danger might come from any direction. Once, when a car's exhaust pipe exploded, he threw himself to the ground. Eventually, he found a minibus that was about to depart for his village. The vehicle was not crowded, and no one seemed to recognize him, so he was able to sleep for the entire journey.

When Cemal arrived home, Döne opened the door and let out a scream of surprise. All the women of the house came running. Upon seeing him, Cemal's mother wept and thanked God for sending her son back safe and sound. Many boys had returned home in a coffin, or missing a leg, an arm, or an eye.

The women immediately sent word to Cemal's father and his uncle. They came in haste. When Cemal saw his father, he grasped his hand and kissed it. The old man hugged him warmly. "May God bless you, my boy," he said. "You fought like a hero and defended your country. Thank God you were spared." Cemal was pleased to hear his father's words and to see the way he looked at him.

The next day when he went out, everyone in the village greeted him warmly. Cemal felt a rush of pride. He was their latest hero. Lean and sinewy, he bore the expression of a mature, experienced man and looked very different from the youth they had sent off to be a soldier. In spite of this, he was still their Cemal, and they sunned themselves in his reflected glory.

Turks and Kurds lived together in the village and had intermarried, so it was not easy to tell them apart. Men who completed their service in the Turkish army were welcomed back as heroes, and everyone wept at the funerals of those who died in combat. The families of boys like Memo, who joined the PKK, were insulted publicly but often supported secretly. When Cemal saw Rıza Efendi, Memo's father, in front of the coffeehouse, he lowered his eyes. "Welcome, our Cemal," the old man said. "God spared you for us." Rıza Efendi's words concealed a question, but Cemal pretended not to understand and walked hurriedly away.

The only direct question about Memo came from Gülizar, the midwife who had helped at the birth of both Cemal and Memo. Cemal told her that he had not set eyes on Memo and did not know whether he was alive or dead.

After a few days, the excitement and warmth of the homecoming vanished. It soon became clear, first to his family, then to the whole village, that Cemal had changed. He hardly touched the food prepared especially for him, not even his favorite dish cooked for him by his aunt. He had become accustomed to being in the mountains and preferred to lie wrapped in a thick blanket on the stones in the courtyard, or in a corner of the garden, rather than on the soft mattress his mother prepared for him. Every day, he woke up at the first light of day, and the slightest sound—the flip-flop of a slipper, a cough, or the creak of a door—caused him to jump up in terror. One morning, Cemal's mother went to the coop to pick out a chicken to cook that day. Suddenly, Cemal grabbed the chicken from her hands, saying, "I'll do it," and ripped off the creature's head with one twist of his hands while his mother looked on in consternation.

When Cemal noticed that Meryem was not around, his mother told him she was guilty of a grave sin and had been locked up in the barn. He shrugged his shoulders and asked no further questions.

Most days, Cemal walked up and down the garden for hours or strolled under the poplars, gazing up at the sky. His mother was worried, but there was no use trying to discuss Cemal's behavior with her husband, because the old man spent all his time chanting with his disciples.

The sheikh wanted his son to participate in the religious rites, too. Cemal went to the hut, chanted repetitively to the point of ecstasy, then lost consciousness. The rituals did not touch him, and he promised himself that he would not come again. He scolded himself for such thoughts, but the whole thing seemed nonsensical. His heart was like a dry twig with no feeling in it for such devotions.

Cemal often withdrew to his room with paper and pen bought

from the village shop to write letters to friends he had made while on military service. Most of these consisted of accustomed formulas and generalities and did not include any personal details. Only those to Selahattin were rich with information.

At night when he lay down in the courtyard, Cemal barely spared a thought for Meryem in the nearby barn. Most of his memories of that thin, weak girl who, in his childhood, had always been underfoot, had vanished. Meryem was a stranger now, and Cemal cared neither to inquire about her faults nor to ask why she had been locked up in the barn.

Then one night in the garden, half-asleep under his rough blanket, he heard the muffled sound of crying coming from the barn. For the first time, he began to wonder about the little girl in the dark barn and the reason for her misery and tears.

LAST FAREWELLS

Meryem heard the door of her prison creak and a tall figure enter the barn. It was her cousin Cemal. "Meryem?" he called out, but she was not able to reply. Her throat was too hoarse for her to speak a word, although she tried.

Cemal called her again, only to be met once more with silence. Then he stepped forward, took her hand, and gently led her outside. The courtyard was dark and deserted. Everyone in the house was asleep. Cemal opened both sides of the main gate, which was used for the sheep and cows each evening and the laden carts at harvesttime. For some reason, he did not open the smaller door in the gate, through which people generally entered or left the courtyard.

Cemal led Meryem out. After so many days in the barn, Meryem heard a cock crow. "Listen, Cemal, a rooster is crowing," she said.

Cemal laughed and started walking with big strides. He moved so fast that Meryem could hardly keep up with him. She was soon breathless. They had come to the outskirts of the village and were heading for the steep hill.

"Where are we going, Cemal?" Meryem asked.

"Over the hill . . . to Istanbul."

Meryem was elated. She would not have to kill herself. "They are sending me to Istanbul," she thought, "just like the other girls." The image of the majestic city she had seen in her dreams stretching toward infinity formed itself in front of her eyes, and she was full of joy.

They were nearing the top of the hill now. Panting, Meryem took another step forward and heard someone say, "This is the city of your dreams." She turned to see who was speaking, but no one was there.

At that minute Meryem realized that she was there in the barn, alone, and she began to weep silently. She was damned. A miracle was out of the question. The extraordinary things that happened to others were not part of her world. Neither Holy Hızır on his ash gray horse, nor Cemal would come to rescue her. Even Bibi had abandoned her.

As Meryem sat there sobbing, Cemal was discussing her fate with his father and uncle in the house a short distance away. "You've come back a hero, my son," said the sheikh. "Your return has pleased us. But that girl—may she go to hell—has ruined our honor!"

Cemal nodded, but he was not paying attention. He was thinking about Selahattin. His friend's wounds must have healed by now. Selahattin had given Cemal his address in Istanbul and told him to come to visit him. "Don't forget me when you've been discharged," he had said, "or, by God, I'll come and find you." But Istanbul was far away, and Cemal was penniless. How could he go there?

Cemal heard his father's words only in fragments. "Our family doesn't deserve this!" cried the old man. "But what can we do? It's our fate."

Cemal remained silent.

Immersed in his own thoughts, Uncle Tahsin said nothing, either.

Then something Cemal heard grabbed his attention.

"You must go to Istanbul, my son," said the sheikh. "This girl is guilty in the sight of both God and man. If the bitch doesn't wag its tail, the dog doesn't follow . . . who knows what else she's been up to on the sly? You know what the custom is, and it's up to you to put things right. I know you've just returned home, but we can't wait any longer. Everyone is talking about us and ridiculing our family! There's no other man in the family capable of carrying out this task."

Cemal at first thought it was just another of his father's moralizing speeches, but then he realized what he was being asked to do. Startled at first, he then withdrew into his usual impassive self. It was as if everything was happening somewhere else. His father's words held little importance for him. Meryem had to be done away with, and he was the one chosen to do it. That was all. It was nothing to make a great song and dance over. What was a human being anyway—just a creature that took only a second to die.

Of course, the deed could not be done in the village. "You'd be caught and put in jail immediately," said the sheikh. "Take the bitch to Istanbul and finish her off there, far away, just as it has happened to other girls. You could stay at Yakup's for a few days. Get rid of her in the big city, where no one will notice you, it's so crowded. Or, do it on the road . . . but don't get caught."

Cemal found his father's detailed plans tiresome. What was the point of talking about such a simple thing? He pitied the girl for a minute, but everyone knew that customs are customs and had to be followed. Meryem had no chance to survive. Even if her father forgave her, and the sheikh did not interfere, she still could not live. Even if everyone in the village came together to forgive her, she could not be saved. More important, by taking Meryem to Istanbul, Cemal would get the opportunity to see Selahattin.

Tahsin Agha was grimly silent. He had not uttered a word during the sheikh's speech. He did not say anything to support his older brother but just sat there in troubled silence.

The women of the house were silent, too. They remained busy with their chores, one of which was stuffing a bag with Meryem's few belongings.

Early the next day, Döne entered the barn. "Get up," she said gruffly, rousing Meryem, "you're leaving. You're going to Istanbul."

Meryem could almost have hugged the woman she hated. The miracle she had been waiting for had happened. "When am I going?" she asked.

"Right away."

"Let me kiss the hands of my father and my aunt and ask for their blessing."

"No!" Döne hissed. "You'll not see anyone. Let's go! You're leaving now."

Döne thrust a bag and a frayed green sweater into Meryem's hands.

Without heeding Döne's words, Meryem ran up the stairs and into the courtyard. The bright sunlight blinded her momentarily, but she did not stop. She ran into the house, crying out for her aunt. But all the rooms were locked. She knelt in front of one of the closed doors, sobbing desperately. "Auntie, please open the door! Let me kiss your hand! Give me your blessing."

Meryem's aunt had been like a mother to her, caring for her and teaching her about life and the right way of doing things. When Meryem had started school, her aunt had taught her to read. Although her aunt had taken pains to care for her, Meryem had always felt a certain coldness, even dislike, in her behavior. The woman performed her duties punctiliously, but when Meryem felt sleepy and wanted to put her head on her knees, she would always find an excuse to push her niece away.

Her aunt's door was locked now, and no matter how much Meryem pleaded, it did not open. She had to face the fact that both the door and the house were closed to her forever. She had been expelled from the house where she was born without anyone bidding her farewell or wishing her luck.

Meryem heard Döne's harsh voice, and she rose and walked out of the house, tightening her scarf around her head. Cemal was standing in the courtyard, casually smoking a cigarette. He was different somehow, like a stranger. He looked taller and older, no longer the boy with whom she used to roll a hoop. "Brother Cemal," she murmured softly. He gave no answer but began to walk toward the village. Meryem followed him without a word.

Spring was coming. The snow had begun to melt, making the ground spongy. At each step, Meryem's thin plastic shoes stuck in the mud. The sun seemed very bright to her eyes, grown used to half darkness for so long. It was not easy to say whether they were merely watering or she was, in fact, weeping.

As Cemal and Meryem passed through the marketplace, Mukadder, the attorney, noticed them. He was sitting outside his office, enjoying the sun and playing backgammon with his friends. When he saw Cemal followed by Meryem walking three paces behind, he stood up, along with the others, and walked toward him. "Hey, hero," he called out, "are you off to Istanbul?"

"Yes," Cemal replied brusquely, spitting the word out between his teeth.

Turning to Meryem, Mukadder smirked. "Well, well, aren't you the lucky girl. Not everyone has the chance to see that city."

His friends all laughed. There was something carnal in their grins.

Meryem wished she could disappear. Everyone in the marketplace had stopped their work. Men with big bellies and moustaches all gathered around them. They patted Cemal on the back and told Meryem how lucky she was. "You'll probably forget this small village," one said. "You won't come back—just like the others. Why should you?"

Meryem was frightened. Since leaving the barn, a slight fear had started to take hold of her. She had grown accustomed to being defiant in the barn, but now she felt weak and vulnerable. For the first time in her life, she was the object of the villagers' attention and felt ashamed of being the target of such interest. She imagined that the dogs were barking her name, the cats were meowing "Meryem," and the birds were whistling at her.

Cemal and Meryem walked on with a group of villagers in tow. They passed the cloth shop, the bakery, the police station, and the mosque. As they neared the school, Cafer ran toward them. His mouth was crooked, and his eyes had a strange expression. The crowd began to laugh. Cafer ran up to Meryem, stared into her face for a long second before beginning to cry. A few of the villagers picked up stones and hurled them at the half-wit. "Beat it!" they shouted. "You should be going to Istanbul, too!"

Cafer yelped like a beaten dog and scurried away.

Meryem saw Müveddet and her daughter Nermin among a group of women walking along the road. They must be on their way to visit someone's home, she thought. She dashed forward and grabbed Müveddet's hands, pressing them to her lips. "I'm going to Istanbul," she said. "Please give me your blessing."

Müveddet hesitated briefly, and then hugged Meryem. "I know, dear girl," she said. "Everyone knows you're going there. God be with you."

Meryem also wanted to hug Nermin, her friend from primary school. With a quick glance at her mother, Nermin kissed Meryem, and whispered, "Good-bye."

The other women wished Meryem a safe journey, telling her how lucky she was to go to Istanbul. "Life must be good there," they said. "If it weren't, the other girls wouldn't have stayed." In spite of their words, their tone made her feel she was being deceived as though she were a child. A few of them giggled, and so did the men nearby.

Meryem, eager to kiss her father's hand and say farewell, looked anxiously for him in the crowd, but he was not there. She did not have the courage to ask why.

In the distance, Cafer let out a shriek and waved his arms wildly at Meryem. "Don't go!" he screamed, but a shower of stones sent him running.

After spending so many days alone in the barn, Meryem was frightened of this attention. She wanted the comfort of one warm, reassuring face before she left the village. Turning to Cemal, she pleaded, "I want to see Bibi before I go. She will be upset if I don't say good-bye to her."

Cemal did not answer but directed his steps toward Gülizar's house. The crowd followed them.

Meryem knocked on the door, but nobody answered. She felt a dull ache in the pit of her stomach. Perhaps the old woman did not want to see her. She banged on the door, and the third time she knocked, Bibi finally opened it. Her eyes were red and swollen. Glancing at the crowd thronging the doorway, she hugged Meryem.

"I'm going to Istanbul, Bibi."

"Yes, child," the woman replied, her voice cracking. "I know."

"Maybe you could come, too . . . later, I mean."

"Maybe, my darling girl . . ."

Then a strange thing happened. Without any warning, she broke into a fit of weeping, hugging Meryem so tight the girl felt as if her ribs would crack.

Becoming calmer, she sobbed, "Forgive me."

Meryem was stunned. She kissed the old woman's wrinkled, bony hand. "Don't cry, Bibi," she said. "Please give me your blessing. You've done so much for me."

"Forgive me," Bibi answered. "Forgive this feeble old woman. I did try, but it was useless."

Then she turned and shut the door.

The crowd followed Cemal and Meryem all the way to the bus stop, where three dilapidated minibuses waiting for passengers were standing outside the cemetery where Meryem's mother was buried. "Please let me visit my mother's grave," Meryem begged Cemal.

He hesitated for a moment, but, looking at the passengers and seeing that the minibus was about to depart, he said sternly, "Get in."

The passengers on the bus greeted Cemal, without even looking at Meryem. With a loud rumble, the vehicle set off, and the crowd waved. "Have a good trip," some called out, laughing.

The minibus turned on to the main road and started toward the distant hill. Meryem felt faint. She had been in such a vehicle only once before. Then they had been on a trip to the public baths, with their bags and the bundles of food they had prepared. That time she was nauseated and this time it was the same. Clutching her ancient bag to her chest, she rolled herself up into a ball and gritted her teeth. She only had to endure the feeling of nausea until they reached the top of the hill. Once there, she would see Istanbul, and the journey would be over.

Curled up in her seat, Meryem began to think about something that had always puzzled her—the other girls who had gone to Istanbul. If it was only just over the hill, why had they not come back at least for a visit? Even on foot it should not take too long to go there and come back. Meryem decided that she would be different. She would walk back home as soon as all the trouble was forgotten. This promise consoled her as the village faded in the distance, and she became filled with the excitement of actually being in that wonderful city that so far she had only seen in her dreams.

As they came toward the top of the hill, her excitement reached a crescendo, and she shut her eyes. She wanted to see the city all at once spread out before her as it had been in her dreams. When she opened her eyes, the dreamy smile on her face quickly changed to bewilderment. They had crossed the hill, but there was no city to be seen, just a vast plain stretching out toward a line of hazy purple mountains in the distance. Farmers, tractors, and villages could be seen among the cultivated fields, and the narrow road wound among them like a snake. Every now and then, the windows of a passing minibus reflected the sun, sending a flash of light into Meryem's eyes. She was confused, but did not have the courage to ask Cemal where they were. Her childhood playmate had vanished, giving place to a strange, frightening, older man.

"Was I mistaken?" Meryem thought to herself. "Maybe Istanbul is actually beyond those far-off purple mountains."

A SAILBOAT ON THE
OPEN SEA

This Benetau sailboat had nothing in com-
mon with the craft İrfan and Hidayet had sailed as teenagers. Their boat
had started out life as a dilapidated two-and-a-half-meter-long rowboat,
and they had worked hard for many days to make it into a sailboat, fash-
ioning a makeshift mast and a cotton sail out of odds and ends. The result looked more like a toy than a boat, but it was on that boat that they
had learned everything about sailing—how to handle the helm and rudder and how to read the winds, the stars, and the movement of the sea.

They had learned everything about sailing by themselves, as if
learning to walk for the first time. Once you got used to doing it, you
never forgot.

İrfan was able to determine the direction of the prevailing wind by
the prickling of his neck, the roll of the waves, the vegetation along the
coast, the seabirds, and the smell of the air. He sailed in the comfortable security of his childhood knowledge. The Benetau was a large
three-cabined boat with all kinds of technological innovations including a sliding keel, making it easy to maneuver. The rental company in
Ayvalık had been eager to offer the best boat available to such an honored client and was overjoyed when the professor was prepared to
hire it for the entire spring and summer.

İrfan could have rented a boat in some other, nearer coastal town, but he had chosen Ayvalık. He wanted to start his journey from the spot where Hidayet had sailed out to sea so many years before.

The boat had been in need of some last-minute adjustments. Had he stayed in the town overnight, he would have had time to load provisions and make a few other arrangements. However, İrfan had been adamant in deciding to weigh anchor as soon as possible. Feeling as if his life depended on heading for the open sea that very night, he could not postpone his departure for a single day.

Early that morning, when he had woken up in his old bed in his mother's house, he had known that he would spend that night at sea. As soon as he got up, his feet instinctively searched for his slippers. One of his mother's inflexible rules was that you did not step on a stone floor with bare feet. With the passing years, his mother's authority had dwindled, but İrfan was conscious that he still adhered to certain habits she had instilled in him.

İrfan started the engine, weighed anchor, and left the harbor. Tiny whitecaps dotted the green Aegean Sea. Islands stood out in the distance. İrfan unfurled the sails and stopped the engine, letting the boat glide with the comforting tailwind. An occasional rub from a rope, the whistle of the wind, and the cries of seagulls were the only sounds he heard. He submitted himself to the will of the sea, as the noise of the town slowly faded behind him.

Although the young men working for the boat-rental company had fallen over themselves to help him, the professor had set out to sea with only two bags of supplies they had managed to get to him at the last minute. İrfan believed that at sea he could solve any problem. Hidayet had thought the same. Their small boat had capsized many times, and the sailcloth had often ripped, but they had always saved themselves, enjoying every moment of their adventures.

İrfan considered that it was the Greeks who more often had such strong feelings for the sea. They were the real seamen. Even though the Turks had lived on the Anatolian peninsula for a thousand years, they remained a steppe people, never becoming skilled seamen. But the spirit of Xenophon's soldiers, who, after fleeing from the Persians, shouted *"Thalassa, Thalassa!"* upon reaching the Black Sea, must have somehow made an impression on the Turks now living on the Aegean coast. That *"Thalassa"* represented a belief: "We have arrived at the water, with which we are familiar. Now that we have reached the safety of the sea, we will surely find our way."

İrfan had a similar belief to comfort him. Surrounded by phosphorescence, salt, fish, wind, the sun, and Homer's wine-dark sea, he would be able to solve all his problems. Those who had not seen the Aegean in all its moods could not understand why Homer had called it the "wine-dark sea." İrfan was now sailing at full speed over that same sea, which he would swear was wine-colored in the afternoon light. He could now try to escape from thoughts of the city, civilization, and all the rules that had oppressed him and follow his initial plan of finding a deserted island on which to spend the night.

The boat that was to effect the professor's escape seemed to İrfan like a boat from some mythological fantasy, its sails filled with a wind from the Cyclades sent by Zeus, the king of the gods, to save the soul of its passenger.

As night descended, the wind dropped, and the sea became calm. The purple-brown waters slowly darkened, and İrfan, filled with an indescribable content in the face of all this beauty, realized that the island where he wanted to spend the night was still quite far away. "Who cares?" he thought. He would spend the night on the boat.

The depth finder showed about nineteen yards of water under the keel. When the anchor found bottom, the boat began to turn, performing a barely discernible waltz. İrfan furled the sails and started to enjoy his first Aegean night—or rather, the first night of his new life.

It was quite dark when İrfan opened his bag of provisions and took out some cheese, bread, tomatoes, and a bottle of white wine. He set the table in the stern with the greatest of care. He even found wineglasses though he did not need them. He preferred to tip back his head and drink from the bottle: He and Hidayet had emptied many a bottle of cheap wine together in this way, paying for it by spending the next few days in bed.

İrfan was a free man now, bound by no one else's rules. He had abandoned all codes of human behavior and chosen to be alone to find his metanoia. He felt proud of having done what everyone dreams of, but few have the courage to do, and he was as free as the gulls circling above the boat. Alone in the middle of the Aegean Sea, he raised his bottle in a toast to his new life, one full of adventures as yet unknown.

The professor had finally altered his life. He would not collapse and die among the expensive armchairs and beds. No ambulance would rush him through his neighborhood streets to a hospital. He was free of a computerized life full of bank accounts, classification systems, tax records, cholesterol measurements, and calorie counts. He had time to make up for the life he had wasted in conforming to social rules, in being sober-minded, and in suppressing the storm in his soul.

He remembered a time long ago, when he had been drinking beer with Hidayet at the old Customs Pier in Izmir, and his friend had asked him what he would do after high school.

"Go to university, of course," İrfan had replied. "I've passed the exam, and I've been given a full scholarship. I'm going to Istanbul."

"And after that?"

"A job, a wife, money—a life!"

"You're trying to be just like your father."

Hidayet's words wounded İrfan. To be like his gaunt father, the chain smoker, who seemed to shrink farther into his brown uniform with each passing day, was the last thing he wanted.

"No, I'm not," he objected. "I'll have money, fame, and power."

"You know best, skipper."

Hidayet's tone indicated that their paths would part. "I'm leaving soon," he continued. "All I want is to put out to sea, without knowing beforehand what life has in store for me."

With the money he had saved by working at the shipyard, Hidayet had found an abandoned wreck, which he had converted into a seven-meter sailing boat using planks and lumber from other scrapped vessels. It was beautiful and sailed perfectly.

İrfan now raised his glass to Hidayet, the Aegean Sea, and to his own recent decision. "I'm following in your footsteps, my friend—finally, after thirty years."

Darkness enveloped the boat. It was a moonless night, the wind was still, and the sky more full of stars than he had seen for years.

İrfan guarded himself from thinking of Aysel, Istanbul, his wife's brother, the university, or his television program. Before confronting his past, he needed to feel he was a completely different person. The process of becoming a new man had to be gone through first.

The night was well advanced when İrfan finished the bottle of wine. He felt like singing a joyful song, but began shaking like a leaf instead. An unexpected wave of terror gripped him, unprepared as he was for the forceful blow of the same icy wind that had often chilled his heart.

İrfan grabbed the mast and began to weep, without realizing what he was doing. The boat seemed strange and alien, reminding him of a coffin. On that dark sea, in that darkened boat, surrounded by the darkness of night, the total blackness of death held sway all around him. He was losing his mind. What could he do on this death trap in the middle of the sea? There was no one to hear his cry for help in the middle of the impenetrable darkness, no one to save him.

"Pull yourself together, İrfan!" he screamed aloud. The sound of his cry muffled by the darkness terrified him. He turned off all the lamps, since they only accentuated the darkness. Panic-stricken, he reached for his tranquilizers and, shaking them into his hand, gulped down a couple, almost choking himself with the water he drank so hastily.

"You wanted this!" he told himself. "This is what you planned, what you intended to do! So why are you frightened?"

"I don't know," he said, in answer to his own question. "I just don't know."

The game of question and answer lasted for a few minutes and did him good, helping him forget his terror of the dark.

He took the game a step further. He imagined he and his self had separated into two personalities who were engaged in endless debate. İrfan's reference points were rooted in books rather than in life. He was more affected by fictional characters than real people.

"You're a coward!" exclaimed the first voice.

"No!" the second voice answered. "If I've risked everything by facing up to my life and have had the courage to initiate a change, I can't be called a coward. Not everyone could do what I did."

"All you did was run away. You left your problems unsolved. You should have stayed in Istanbul and confronted them."

"There was nothing to confront in Istanbul. I had a happy life. I was successful and rich. There was nothing to bother me—except the trouble inside of me."

"You're lying, İrfan Kurudal."

"No!"

"You're lying. You're a cowardly liar."

"No, no, no!"

"What will you do when I prove that you're lying? Your life in Istanbul, which you call 'happy,' was garbage. You felt worthless, and you were right. You never created anything worthwhile. You only grabbed what opportunities were available and climbed the social ladder. As a scholar, you're worth nothing. It doesn't matter if people treat you with respect. What novel idea have you come up with? What noteworthy article have you published? Didn't you always feel embarrassed, ignorant, and shallow at the congresses you attended abroad? Come on, admit it."

"Yes, yes, in a way I did."

"That's because you're not genuine. You're a man of straw. You're ignorant, cowardly, and paranoid, hiding behind your title of 'professor.' Your television talks are a great example of mediocrity."

"You've turned this debate into an academic examination."

"Okay, let's talk about other things then. You weren't a good teacher, but were you a good husband?"

"Aysel was happy—very happy."

"Maybe she looked happy, but that was because she kept all her troubles to herself. Isn't it true that you just made love to her because you felt it was your duty?"

"That's a lie!"

"You can't fool me. I'm your other self. Are you going to deny that you never enjoyed caressing her—that you never desired her flesh? You were not drawn to her, not even when you were young. Isn't that the reason for her unfaithfulness?"

"Now you are lying. Aysel was never unfaithful. Like everything else you've said, this is mere invention."

"Remember, I'm you. I know your secret doubts. Didn't you know that she regularly met Selim in an apartment in Maçka?"

"No."

"Let's suppose you suspected it. Actually, you realized the whole thing when you saw her enter that building one day, but you pretended not to notice. Why did you feign ignorance? Because you weren't jealous. You've mistreated everyone in your life. First you deserted Hidayet, then your parents, your sister, and finally your wife. You're small-minded and selfish. Your life is a fake. You've always lived according to the standards of others since you aren't brave enough to be yourself. Your colleagues at the university looked down upon you because they sensed your fear. Your enemies multiplied."

"Now you're calling me paranoid."

"The fact that you're paranoid doesn't mean that you don't have enemies."

"I'm not the man you describe."

"Listen, Professor, you don't even know who you are!"

"Are you going to treat me to a Delphic oration?"

"Indeed, I am. I'm going to ask you to know yourself. Is there something the matter with that? Or what about thinking of the great mystic Sufi poet Rumi?"

"Who said I was talking like a book? Who's doing it now?"

"I'm not Athena talking to Odysseus on this boat. Have you forgotten? I'm you. Your habits are my habits. I can't escape from your limitations, can I?"

"So why the hell are you picking on me?"

"I'm trying to show you what an unhappy, timid, worthless liar you are."

"But if you're me, then you've got these characteristics, too."

"Absolutely. But I'm the realistic part of you. I see things as they are and try not to console myself with fantasies and lies."

"What benefit does that bring you? Self-pity?"

"Don't you know that the feeling of ceasing to exist can please a man? It gives a unique kind of pleasure to know you are destroying yourself, making others despise you, that your standing has sunk to the lowest rank, and you are falling into the deep pit of being human. Don't reject all the values that every sensible person struggles to attain."

"You sound like a nihilist."

"Don't underestimate nihilism. If you listen to yourself long enough, you'll realize that nihilism is the philosophy closest to you. Remember that your temperament enjoys being detached from everything and every belief, of making fun of the ideologies that terrorize this country, and of secretly despising those around you while pretending to enjoy their company. That's why you never felt close to any group—either as a student or later in life. The groups you shunned would not have accepted you, anyway. You tried to look like an independent, disengaged intellectual, but I know that you don't take any ideology as seriously as those weird dreams of yours. I've caught you out. Admit it."

"My dreams?"

"Yes, your dreams—the biggest realities of your life. They're the only moments when you become yourself as a real human being. Your dreams are the most sincere moments of your existence."

"You're exaggerating. Dreams aren't the truest moments in life. You know very well that I don't have dreams."

"You do, even if you don't want to admit it. That suit of armor you wear, even when making love, falls to pieces in your dreams. It's only then that the truth surfaces, and you reunite with your own personality. Since your childhood, there's been a single vision in your dreams, hasn't there? It's the only thing that excites you—a shadow, an obscure being, maybe not human even. . . ."

"Stop!"

"Since you want to confront it, let's open this subject now, so that you can begin your new life as an honest man."

"Shut up! I don't want to talk about it."

"Take a realistic look at yourself for the first time."

"Enough!"

"What do you see in your dreams?"

"Nothing!"

"Whom do you see?"

"No one!"

"Are you sure?"

"Yes! Yes, I am, damn it! I don't see anything or anyone. Enough! Shut up!"

When the professor regained consciousness, he was lying on the teak planking of the deck. The night dew had dampened his clothing and caused his muscles to become stiff. In front of him, a crimson dawn was breaking. The sailboat lay becalmed on the motionless water. The offshore breeze unique to the Aegean coast would probably not arise until afternoon, after the land had heated up.

İrfan considered the nighttime "crisis" a result of wine and a mixture of various tranquilizers. His mind must have been completely confused, but now, under the gleaming blue sky, all he had gone through during the night seemed distant and ridiculous. Fortunately, no one had witnessed it. Sentimentality, overreaction, a passion for literature, alcohol, and pill-taking—all these excesses had caused the night's troubles.

İrfan's head ached. He was sure that swimming would cure the pain and clear his perception. The water would be chilly at this time of the year, but he did not care. He threw off his clothes and plunged into the salty water. It was icy, taking his breath away at first, but he quickly adjusted to the cold. The longer he swam, the more invigorated and alert he felt. The night, which had begun with thoughts of Russian novels had ended like one of them. In most Russian novels, some public servant of whatever rank would wake up in his bed one day with an awful headache. Recalling the disgust and ridicule he had aroused the previous night while under the effects of vodka, he would purse his lips and swear never to let a single drop pass his lips again.

His oath would last only until the same evening.

THE BLACK TRAIN

Meryem was disappointed when she did not see Istanbul on the other side of the hill near her village, but her hopes revived when she saw a line of purple mountains in the distance. Yet beyond that range there were only more boundless fields. She tried to console herself with the thought that Istanbul was probably behind the next line of hills. Then she wondered if she had not been mistaken and Istanbul was, indeed, a great way off.

As the minibus bumped and swayed along the dusty road, the excitement of discovering new scenery replaced the hurt of leaving her hometown. Meryem was able to adapt to new circumstances quickly.

On the other hand, Cemal's presence made her uneasy. She did not know how to approach him, or how she should behave toward him. The boy of the past—her childhood companion and playmate—had vanished to be replaced by a completely different person, this silent man who sat there sleeping, his large frame fitting awkwardly into the minibus's narrow seat. She glanced out of the corner of her eye at his sunburned face and the rough hands folded in his lap, neither of which showed any tenderness. The sight of this man dressed in jeans and an old anorak with his Adam's apple projecting from his thick neck among numerous pale wrinkles of untanned flesh, his rugged, unshaven face and short-cut hair emphasizing the grimness of his expression, made Meryem afraid.

Meryem looked at herself. What a wretched girl she was. She felt miserable in the dirty, shabby clothes she had worn all those weeks in the barn—the baggy traditional trousers known as shalvar, worn under a shapeless cotton dress of faded blue flower print, and the old green sweater Döne had given her. As usual when outside the house, her head was covered. The black plastic shoes on her feet were caked with mud.

Meryem could not comprehend why her childhood days had gone by so quickly, leaving her so dreary and so desolate. She wished she had never grown up but had gone on playing with the other children and mingling easily with the villagers. Once into puberty, when hair had started to grow in unfamiliar places and her breasts had appeared, the magic had been spoiled. What if she said, "Cemal, do you remember the day we were playing in the miller's garden and we saw his hens? I don't remember who started it, but we both started throwing them up in the air as high as we could, pretending they were airplanes. We laughed so much to see them cackling and flapping their wings as they fell to earth. We thought they were flying, like real planes do. I can still smell them and feel the feathers that fell around us, sticking to our clothes. We hadn't considered that the poor creatures would get hurt. Then someone, I don't know who, saw us and shouted, and the miller's wife burst out of her house and screamed when she saw her hens fluttering on the ground with broken legs. You remember, we ran away along the bed of the stream? My aunt punished us both, but in the end, you were forgiven—as always—and I ended up in the barn. I've been locked in that hole so many times! I was blamed for everything I did: Don't laugh loudly, Meryem; don't flirt, Meryem; you're grown up now, Meryem; don't play with boys!"

By command of her uncle, the bearded patriarch of the village, her family had stopped sending her to school after the first grade. It would be immoral for a girl to sit beside a boy, he decreed.

From the window of the minibus, Meryem watched the world pass by. The minibus went past the road signs too quickly for her to read more than the initial letters of the places along the road. Yet, as far as she could understand, there was still no mention of Istanbul—none of the words on the signs started with the letters "Is."

Her aunt often reminded Meryem how she had had to take care of her. "It was hard raising you," she used to say. "I washed your diapers so many times! Your shit's still under my fingernails." This was the same aunt who had not opened her door to Meryem. The ruthless woman had sat in her room waiting for the poor girl to leave. Meryem still could not understand why she was being sent away. Neither her aunt nor Cemal had behaved in a way that encouraged questions. Cemal was like her aunt, she thought. He hardly spoke and even refrained from looking at her.

It was getting difficult to keep her eyes open. She dozed off a couple of times, but woke up abruptly when her head fell forward. Then, without knowing it, she fell into a deep sleep.

When Meryem woke up much later, it was dark. Houses, people, and cars had replaced the fields and hills. And what a lot of houses, people, and vehicles there were.

"At last, we're in Istanbul," she thought. "It's as wonderful as they said!"

Meryem glanced at Cemal. He was awake, also, and looking out the window. The traffic slowed, and they had to stop several times. People were hurrying in and out of brightly lit shops that lined both sides of the street.

The minibus came to a place swarming with people and vehicles, and the driver turned off the engine. All the passengers grabbed their suitcases and got out. Meryem's head began to spin.

Cemal told her to follow him. They got off the bus and walked toward a row of lit buildings. He stopped in front of one. Women and men were lined up separately at opposite doors. Cemal gestured to her to wait with the women.

When she finally got inside, Meryem was overcome by the smell of urine. She saw her ghostlike face in a filthy mirror in the corner. She looked older in the dim light, but her green eyes were still the same. A woman pushed past her, going toward the basin and washing her hands. Meryem waited for the woman to finish, then asked, "Is this Istanbul?"

The woman looked at her and laughed. "No, my dear. Istanbul is two days farther on from here."

Meryem was confused. When she left the toilet, she saw Cemal waiting for her. He told her to follow him.

The street was full of vendors: Some were selling rice with chick-peas from their carts covered by a glass dome, others boiled corn on the cob or meatballs. The smell of different kinds of food reminded Meryem that she was very hungry. Cemal led her to a street vendor with a small cart illuminated by a single bulb. He bought two sand-wiches filled with meatballs, tomato slices, and fried onions and handed one to Meryem. They went to a secluded corner and devoured the sandwiches that Meryem found incredibly tasty. As if synchro-nized, the call to prayer began at the same instant from all the mosques in the city.

"This place is marvelous," Meryem thought. She could not imagine what Istanbul would be like. She had already forgotten about her aunt and her strange and humiliating departure from the village. An inde-scribable joy had enveloped her. After being locked up in the barn for so many weeks, and, indeed, after having had a rope around her neck, life had begun to seem like an enjoyable holiday. Even Cemal's rude-ness did not spoil her happiness. She followed obediently in his foot-steps when they left the bus terminus, and together they trudged along the streets for a long time. To Meryem, accustomed to everything be-ing at most only a few minutes' walk away, the road seemed endless. But at the end of this long march, a surprise awaited her. For the first time in her life, Meryem found herself in a train station. The noise, the hurry and bustle of the crowds, and even the pungent smell of smoke from the trains captivated her. For the first time, she was seeing things that she had only heard of. She wanted to laugh aloud and shout, as in the past, "Hooray, Cemal!" She felt so grateful to him for saving her from the barn and bringing her to the doors of heaven.

At one point, some military policemen stopped Cemal and ques-tioned him gruffly, in answer to which Cemal took a paper out of his pocket and showed it to them. They smiled after looking at it carefully and walked away.

Meryem noticed that the women around her were dressed in a va-riety of styles. Some, like her, were wearing the baggy pants of vil-lagers, but others wore dresses of the kind suitable for the wives of city officials. The contrast was striking. Some women had their hair cov-ered, others let it fall free on their shoulders. Looking at the various sights, seeing how people behaved toward one another, and trying to understand what it all meant was an engrossing occupation for Meryem.

Cemal led her to a crowded platform, and they boarded a train, along with hundreds of others. Even the corridors were crowded, but Cemal and Meryem managed to find two empty seats in what Meryem thought of as a "room." Meryem sat next to the window, Cemal beside her. Opposite them were an old woman wearing a scarf and a girl with her head bare. Next to the women, an old man with a gray moustache coughed continuously. A young couple, newlyweds perhaps, sat beside Cemal. The girl was bareheaded and wore a short skirt. It revealed her bare legs.

Meryem tried to engrave all the images in her mind, delighted to make the most of this unexpected adventure. She watched the young couple hold hands and saw their thick wedding rings. She looked at ·the girl across from her, sitting modestly between her parents. Meryem noticed, however, that she was secretly making signs to a young man outside on the platform. The girl's mother, with melancholy eyes fixed straight ahead, was oblivious to their silent communication. The young man walked backward and forward in front of the compartment, from time to time glancing discreetly at the girl, who sometimes tossed her head and sometimes allowed her gaze to meet his in silent farewell. Meryem was amused. Even though they had been on the train for only a few minutes, she felt comfortable, as though she had been accustomed for years to this form of travel.

Meryem had always enjoyed watching what went on between boys and girls, but she had often been reprimanded for talking about such subjects. She remembered the time she had been scolded at the village clinic for laughing at the little balloons. It was during a public health session, when the nurses were teaching the village women birth control methods and had showed them some condoms. For fun, they inflated a few, and the sight of the colorful little balloons bouncing on the floor had so amused Meryem that she started to run around chasing them until her aunt slapped her on the neck.

Later in the afternoon, when the women in the family had gathered for their afternoon nap, they joked about the balloons. The story that made them laugh the most was about a man from the village, who had gone to the clinic to ask for a condom. Not knowing what it was called, he had said to the nurse, "You know, that thing . . . the pleasure balloon!" The women immediately collapsed into a chorus of girlish giggles.

Her aunt had scolded her for having fun with the same things, thought Meryem. Well, let them share their everlasting gossip behind the doors they would not open to her. She did not care anymore. She wouldn't think about Döne with her snake eyes ever again. It was as if she had left there a month ago, not just that very morning.

Suddenly, the train lurched forward, and Meryem's heart missed a beat. A water bottle on the small table in the middle of the compartment started to fall, but Meryem reached forward and caught it. The old woman across from Meryem smiled at her warmly as the train went on puffing along, wheels rattling, whistle blowing, reminding her of a song she had sung as a child. She started to hum an old melody, "I hope the black train won't come, I hope the black train won't whistle."

If only Cemal would smile and act as he used to. But she did not despair of putting things right on the journey so they'd be like childhood friends again. Poor Cemal. The army had turned him into an old man.

"Where are you going?" asked the old woman sitting opposite Meryem. Of course, the train would stop at many stations.

"To Istanbul," Meryem replied proudly. "We're going to Istanbul."

Meryem glanced at Cemal. Had she said too much?

"Is the young man a soldier?" asked the old woman.

"He's just finished his military service," said Meryem.

"Is he your fiancé?"

"No." Meryem giggled. "He's my cousin."

She was grateful to the old woman for breaking the wall of silence that had enveloped her since leaving the village. Perhaps it would make Cemal think of speaking to her. "Where do you get off?" Meryem asked, as if she knew all the stations the train would stop at on the way to Istanbul.

"In Ankara," replied the woman. "This is my daughter Seher. We're going there to visit her brother . . . if we can get there in time. . . ."

The old woman's eyes filled with tears, and she lowered her head.

Conscious of the woman's pain, Meryem turned to look out of the window. It reflected all that went on inside the compartment. She saw herself and the other passengers in the glass. The newlywed couple were leaning close to each other as if asleep, the old man was smoking a cigarette, while the old woman wept silently and wiped her eyes. Seher was lost in thought. Cemal sat still and silent like a statue. "Yes," thought Meryem, "he is not a human but a lump of stone."

NOAH'S ARK

Tacka-tack-tacka-tack-tacka-tack!

A machine gun was blasting off, but there was something strange about the noise Cemal thought, especially as it continued without stopping. It was too regular and went on without a pause, like the rattle of a train. He sat up in his bunk and saw that all his comrades were dead, lying under white quilts covered with blood from their smashed-in faces. The machine gun continued its rhythm. I'm going to die, too, if I don't get out of here, he said to himself.

He slid down from his bunk bed and crawled to the door. Just as he was about to go through it, he realized that there was water outside the door. It was higher than the door, higher even than the building. How could it stay there like a transparent blue curtain without flowing into the room?

The machine gun continued its rattle.

Cemal realized his only escape was to plunge into the water. Surprisingly, it was not cold but warm, even warmer than the lake he used to swim in every summer. He swam upward toward the light. Reaching the surface, he stuck his head above the water and gasped for breath. There was no sign of the military post, nor of the mountains and valleys either. Everywhere was flooded, and Cemal found himself in the middle of a sea of water.

Suddenly, he heard a sound. A boy with big black eyes was rowing toward him in a small boat. "Come here, or you'll drown," he called out.

Cemal recognized the little shepherd boy. "I thought you were dead!" he exclaimed.

The boy laughed.

"I saw your head explode under the force of a G3 shell," Cemal continued.

"It's still in its proper place," the boy replied. "Climb in."

"What happened?" Cemal asked, pulling himself into the boat.

"It's the Flood," the boy answered, "and this is Noah's ark."

"Where are we going?"

"To Mount Cudi . . . to Noah."

The boy's features were slowly transforming themselves into those of Memo when Cemal woke up.

The conductor had just entered the compartment and was checking everyone's tickets. The monotonous clicking sound was the noise made by the train as it ran over the rails.

Cemal took the tickets out of his pocket, thinking how much quicker and more comfortable a bus would have been. But it would have been too expensive. His father had given him only just enough money for the long journey to Istanbul, partly from poverty, partly from his ignorance of the world outside his village. So it had not been enough for two tickets on the bus, and the train was so much cheaper.

Opposite Cemal sat a black-haired girl with what must be her parents. The man next to him was hugging a woman who was obviously his wife. Cemal turned to look at Meryem. She was sitting still, quietly staring out of the window.

"What am I going to do with this girl?" he wondered, reverting to the problem he had been trying to push from his mind since the beginning of the journey by reminiscing over his days in the army.

He could not oppose his father's will and defy his family. Killing her would be easy from what he remembered of her as a small girl, but doubts had begun to grow in his mind after he had spoken with Emine when they had met in the seclusion of the poplar grove.

"The whole village knows the duty you've been given," she said. "That poor girl's being sent to Istanbul, just like others before her. Can such a thing be happening in this day and age? Your family's crazy. At least, don't you murder her! What's the poor child done?" Then, more to the point, she added, "I've waited two years for you to come back from the army, and I'm not waiting for you to come back from jail."

Cemal had not had the courage to explain to his father that he wanted to marry Emine, with whom he was deeply in love, and these words struck him a great blow. He knew there were many previously rejected suitors waiting to step into his shoes if he should go to prison, and here she was telling him she would wait no longer.

"Let somebody else do it," she said.

"There's no one else in the family who can."

"Then spare her."

How could he possibly explain that to his father, in front of whom he had never dared to open his mouth? For years, all he had done was meet and talk with Emine in secret and suffer the frustration of not being able even to touch her hand. He was too afraid of what would happen at home. His hope was that if he did what his father wanted, an opportunity would arise to tell him about Emine. He had often thought about her during his military service, but never in the same way that he thought of the innocent bride. Emine was his wife-to-be. The innocent bride was different. Even though he never saw her face, his thoughts about her always caused him to have wet dreams.

However hard Cemal might try to forget Meryem, she was real and sitting there by his side. However much it might cost him, he had to fulfill his duty. Emine was right, but the matter was beyond his control. He had no choice.

Maybe he could take Meryem to the end of the carriage that night while everyone was asleep, strangle her, and throw the body into a deserted field. In two minutes the train would have left that place behind. Someone would probably find her the next day, but what could they prove? Maybe it would be better to push her off the train while they were crossing a bridge. Even if her body were found at the bottom of a gorge, who would care about a dead girl in baggy pants?

Cemal had become familiar with death during his time as a soldier.

In fact, life without death seemed strange. He never forgot the captain's words spoken during their training: "It is you who will punish the traitors who are trying to destroy the nation and divide this country created through the blood of countless martyrs, who died in the service of the Turkish state. It is your honorable duty to protect the unity of the Republic and the nation. Whoever dies for his country goes straight to heaven. Kill the terrorists on sight, my sons—remember, it is they who are murdering your friends."

The captain then told them that there was no such language as Kurdish, and that those who called themselves Kurds were actually mountain Turks who had come to Anatolia from Central Asia like all other Turkish peoples.

Cemal did not understand the meaning of this as he knew that Kurds spoke a different language. He himself could speak their language a little. Even the dogs in the region understood Kurdish, not Turkish, and would attack if the soldiers used Turkish to send them on their way.

Cemal got up, left the compartment, and went to the toilet on his way to inspect the door at the end of the corridor. On the floor there was a sick woman lying on a pile of newspapers. She was moaning, as a man and two children looked on.

When Cemal returned to the compartment, he found himself in the middle of a commotion. Everybody was talking at the same time. He sat down. Seher was exchanging words with the young man sitting beside him, while everyone else was either taking sides or trying to hush things up.

Curled up in her seat, Meryem sat watching in silence. The quarrel had broken out because of her. Taking advantage of Cemal's absence, she had tried to strike up a conversation with the old woman by asking her why she had cried earlier when she had said, "If we're in time."

The woman said that her son, a university student, had been put in prison where he was taking part in a hunger strike. Along with several others, he was protesting against the conditions in the jail. For the past seventy days, the protestors had not taken any nourishment. All that had passed their lips was a little sweetened water. With red bands tied around their heads, they were lying there waiting for death. Each day their condition worsened. First their eyesight failed, then they began to suffer from amnesia. A few days ago, she had seen her son on television and had hardly recognized him. Even when the microphone was held out to him, he said nothing. He just stared blankly at the camera. The leader of the protest had sworn they would starve themselves to death. The woman's older daughter, who lived in Ankara, had gone to the prison to see her brother, but had not been allowed to do so. Most of those who had begun fasting with her son had already died, or were at death's door. The old woman was going to Ankara to try to see her son and beg him to abandon the fast. As a mother, what else could she do!

When the old woman finished her story, the young man across from her said that he could understand a mother's pain, but that terrorists had been using the strike for political propaganda. All hell had then broken loose—just as Cemal entered the compartment.

"What kind of person are you?" Seher was shouting at the young man. "Hundreds of young people are dying. Besides doing nothing to help them, you tell a mother her son's a terrorist! What right have you to say such things?"

"Wasn't your brother arrested under the Prevention of Terrorism Act?" replied the young man calmly.

"My brother isn't a terrorist. He never joined in any of their activities."

"Why was he arrested then? Wasn't it for terrorism?"

The young man was an aggressive, quarrelsome type, whom his wife strove in vain to keep quiet.

"My brother worked for a student association and read books," Seher retorted. "That's all."

"But this law only punishes terrorists."

"Ten thousand people are in jail because of that law," Seher yelled, "and nine thousand of them are there because they wrote slogans on walls, read certain books, or set up student associations! You have no feelings."

Seher's mother tried to calm her down. "Don't get upset," she pleaded. "Keep calm."

Silently smoking his cigarette, Seher's father looked on without taking any part in the argument, careful not to meet anyone's eyes.

"Student associations?" the young man sneered. "I know what kind of students they are!"

"What do you know?" Seher exploded. "Have you ever met my brother?"

"No, not your brother, but I've come face-to-face with those like him. I've fought against them. I know their type."

Seher's mother suddenly reached over and covered her daughter's mouth with her hand. It was clear that the man was either a policeman, a member of the secret service, or part of a special military unit. She did not want more trouble.

But Seher could neither forgive nor forget the insult. Her brother was on the brink of death, and her parents' hearts were breaking. Turning to Cemal, she cried, "You were a soldier, brother. This girl said so. Is it right to throw such insults at a heartbroken mother? My brother's an angel. He's never even seen a gun, much less used one."

Cemal did not know what to say. He could never find words in such situations.

"Where did you do your military service?" the young man suddenly inquired. When Cemal told him, he asked, "Were you involved in much action?"

Cemal nodded.

The man held out his hand. "My name's Ekrem. I'm on duty in the State of Emergency zone. This is my wife, Süheyla."

He waited for a response, but Cemal did not extend his hand and remained silent.

The clatter of the train was the only sound to be heard.

Without warning, the old man, who had been sitting there so quietly during the altercation, suddenly spat in Ekrem's face.

Everyone was stunned.

Ekrem jumped up immediately, utterly furious. He grabbed the old man with one hand and made as if to reach for his pistol with the other. The old man took no notice of his gesture and even had a slight smile on his face.

"Don't hurt him, please, sir!" begged the wife of the old man, taking hold of Ekrem's arm. "He's sick. He doesn't know what he's doing. . . . He's out of his mind! Here, look at the doctor's report!"

Ekrem hesitated. His wife was pulling at his other arm. "Can't you see he's ill?" she appealed. "He's not worth it."

Ekrem threw the old man back in his seat, opened the compartment door, and walked out.

A happy smile lit up Seher's face. Even her mother looked pleased.

Her father, pathetic as he was, had gotten his revenge. "Rotten official!" she cursed. "Thanks to our taxes, he gets a salary!"

"You'd better shut up," warned Ekrem's wife. "You were lucky I stopped him. He can cause you trouble."

"What can he do!" said Seher in a surly tone.

"I'm telling you. You'd better keep quiet."

A few minutes later, Ekrem returned to the compartment with the conductor. "Get up," he said, looking at Seher and her parents. "There's a sick woman outside. We need your seats for her."

He pointed to the corridor where the sick woman's husband was supporting the woman's head and looking curiously into the compartment.

"This gentleman's right," agreed the conductor. "We need you to give up your seats."

"Why our seats?" Seher protested. "What about the seats over there?"

"There are two separate families on this side," Ekrem said. "There are four of us, and my wife's not feeling well. We can switch places later," he said, hiding a grin.

"Come on," said Seher's mother. "Let's go. Don't argue with these people."

Taking their luggage off the rack, they left the compartment.

The sick woman was carried into the compartment and put down carefully on the green leather seat. She was one of those Anatolian village women of indeterminate age who could have been either thirty or fifty. A piece of cloth was swathed around her head. It was obvious that she was in great pain. Her husband and two children hunched down on their heels below her.

"God bless you!" the man said to Ekrem.

But Ekrem ignored him. He was still burning with anger. "Don't let them fool you, brother," he told Cemal. "They're all red-hot communists. They don't know what 'family' is. Women like that old hag aren't mothers. . . . They're all Kurdish rebels! This land belongs to the Turks. Whoever calls himself a Kurd, Alawite, or Leftist should get the hell out of here!"

Ekrem lit a cigarette and offered another to Cemal.

The sick woman's husband opened the basket beside him and took out some bread and cheese. "Have some," he offered.

When nobody wanted any, he rolled a piece of cheese up in the bread and began to eat. He did not look at his wife, who was moaning.

"Won't you give some to your wife?" Süheyla asked him.

"No. She can't swallow. I'm taking her to Ankara for an operation. Her brother works at a hospital there."

As soon as he swallowed the last of his bread, the man fell asleep and began to snore loudly. The train rattled on into the night.

Meryem's legs were numb. She wanted to stand up and walk a little, but was afraid of waking up Cemal, who was sleeping next to her. He had done hardly anything but sleep since they started on their journey.

Plucking up all her courage, Meryem slowly got to her feet and tip-toed toward the door. She had taken no more than two steps when Cemal asked, "Where are you off to?"

"Just into the corridor."

When he did not object, Meryem slid the door open and went out.

It was empty. Seher and her parents must have gone to another carriage to find seats, not wanting to give Ekrem the satisfaction of see-ing them sit on the floor.

The train was rushing along at great speed as she had realized once she stepped out into the corridor. The swaying carriage creaked and groaned, making a tremendous noise. Holding on to the wall, Meryem walked to the end of the corridor and found the toilet. As soon as she entered, she looked in the mirror, comparing herself to Seher. With her eyes outlined with kohl and her uncovered hair falling to her shoul-ders, Seher was a pretty girl. The official's wife used makeup of various kinds on her eyes and cheeks so she looked beautiful, too. Her hair was not covered either.

Meryem untied her scarf, letting her long hair go free. But it was sticky and tangled; a long time had passed since Bibi washed it.

Abruptly, she bent over the washbasin and began to wash her hair, using the small piece of soap lying on the side of the basin. After doing her best to rinse it in the trickle of water that came from the tap, she tied her scarf around her wet hair and, just before leaving the toilet, pinched her cheeks to make them red. Yet Meryem knew that no mat-ter what she did, she would not look like the other girls as long as she was wearing her horrible clothes. She had noticed every detail of their well-kept hands, polished fingernails, shining hair, bright necklaces, and the big watches that made their wrists look so slim. She imagined herself in a tight black skirt like Süheyla's. Excited by the thought, she wondered if she would dress like that in Istanbul and become as pretty as Süheyla and Seher. Meryem remembered her grandmother's words: "eyes that outshine the sun." Yes, her eyes were different, but, alone, they were worth nothing. No one would notice the brightness of any eyes under a dingy headscarf.

Meryem opened the toilet door and stepped out. She saw Cemal standing in the corridor, silently smoking. He was frowning. Should she say nothing and just pass by him quietly? What else could she do? Wishing she were invisible, she walked forward to go past him. "Stop," he said suddenly, stepping in front of her and taking her by the arm.

Meryem was surprised and relieved. Cemal had begun to talk to her again. She did not mind what he said, even if he got angry and scolded her. She just wanted him to talk.

The train swayed suddenly, and Meryem held on to the rail in front of the window.

"Look, girl," said Cemal. "This is the door of the train."

"Yes, I know," replied Meryem before she could stop herself. "That's how we got on last night." It seemed to her that Cemal became a little angrier.

Suddenly, Cemal opened the door, and a rush of wind and deafening noise filled the corridor. Cemal bent forward and looked out. Almost immediately, he pulled his head in, gasping for breath. "Here, take a look," he ordered Meryem.

Meryem, uncertain whether it was some kind of game like the ones they had played in the old days, was afraid to lean out, but felt she had no other choice.

Clinging to the side of the door, she leaned forward, thrusting her head out. The wind whipped her face, and the train's whistle screeched, terrifying her. She could feel something in her eye and quickly drew herself back inside, fearing she would smash her head against something in the dark.

Cemal stood there wordless, looking away, as though ashamed of something.

"There's something in my eye, Cemal," Meryem whimpered, her eyes filling with tears. "It hurts. . . . Can you take a look at it?"

Cemal turned and walked away without a word.

THE ISLAND SUSPENDED
IN AIR

AFTER MANY DAYS AT SEA, İRFAN OPENED HIS eyes at dawn one morning and saw a miracle in the shape of a cone-shaped island ascending toward the sky in front of him. It did not touch the sea but floated in the air above the water, as if suspended by divine power. Only in a painting by René Magritte could something like this happen, created by the magic genius of an artist who could change the dimensions and appearance of an object by disregarding gravity.

The professor had never seen an island suspended in the air, not even in his dreams. Shrouded in mist, this gigantic, scrub-covered piece of rock hung there between sea and sky.

"I must be losing my mind," he thought, yet he did not feel afraid. He weighed anchor and started to sail toward the island. He wanted to land on that fairy-tale rock but, unfortunately, the rising sun was slowly reducing it to an ordinary island. The mist that concealed the shoreline where it met the sea gradually disappeared, and it turned into one of several thousand similar Aegean islands. The transformation did not diminish İrfan's delight in the miracle of the island floating on air that he had witnessed in the magic light of dawn.

Mythology could only have developed in this kind of environment, he thought. The Aegean Sea was full of wonders: the ever-changing color of the water, the divine rays of light that shot through the clouds in late afternoon, and the enchanting smell . . . that vitalizing scent, which could inspire one to do all sorts of wild and extraordinary things, making one feel happy just to be alive.

İrfan had lost track of the days since he had not bothered to keep count of them. His only contact with the shore was when from time to time he stopped in small coastal towns to pick up provisions. It was as if all dimensions of time and place had vanished. He went wherever the wind blew him. In his former life, he had used this saying metaphorically, but now it was literal.

The wind was mainly in his favor but, occasionally, he had to start the engine to escape some pressing danger, but he did so with great reluctance. Using the engine was shameful to a true sailor. He also had to use the sails, in a sometimes-unbecoming way, as he had realized after a couple of days that the Aegean Sea was not without its dangers. This sea was also a theater of war, where Turkish and Greek navies tested their strengths. Some of the Greek islands were so close to the Turkish coast that it was often difficult to recognize which piece of land belonged to whom. The Greeks prohibited boats from coming within three miles of their shores, and if the professor accidentally crossed the line, a Greek assault boat would immediately rush out of Mytilene or Samos and race toward him. Then, if he hurried too quickly toward the mainland, the Turkish Coast Guard would become suspicious.

In some places, not even half a mile separated the Turkish coast from the Greek islands. For instance, one could easily swim from Samos to the cape near Kuşadası. İrfan passed through the strait there easily, without being chased. Perhaps there, geography overruled the regulations.

Now and then, he saw Turkish naval ships on maneuvers. They would come sailing in line formation menacingly close to the Greek islands, their missiles primed and ready. If İrfan passed too near the ships, the officers and sailors on board would threaten him with icy stares. The soft splash of the water under his boat as it peacefully glided along in the gentle wind was sometimes broken, too, by the deafening roar of Turkish and Greek fighter jets overhead or the scream of a plane playfully diving headlong toward the sea before straightening out at the last minute. Sometimes it was a khaki-colored helicopter that noisily patrolled the sky.

İrfan was fed up with assault boats, warships, fighter aircraft, and the hostile atmosphere. He felt neither Turkish nor Greek. He was just a human being who wanted to enjoy the sea. The neighboring states playing their games of power disturbed his peace—just as they disturbed the goats grazing on the nearby shores.

İrfan knew that if other Turks perceived his thoughts, he would be burned at the stake. "How can a child of the Turkish nation think like that?" they would exclaim. "Don't you love your country? Do you have Greek blood in your veins? This nation has raised and educated you, and now you are stabbing it in the heart."

"What have I done to be born in such a country?" İrfan often wondered. He had no strong feelings about patriotism, religion, or ideologies. It was a long time since he had upheld anything he would have designated as a "value."

After the Republican revolution in the twenties and the collapse of the Ottoman Empire, the new secular government had excluded religious education from the national curriculum program at schools. Most children educated during this Kemalist era had little interest in religion, but their national consciousness had been well-developed. For some reason, İrfan had no affiliations with either.

When he was in high school, the leftist movement had been in vogue. The world was affected by the young generation during 1968. The student unions, which were set up after the students occupied the university campuses, later turned into left-wing organizations. İrfan's lack of belief in anything had prevented him from becoming a leftist, even though not being one was considered quite peculiar in those days. Demonstrations, protests, proclamations, and clashes with the police were commonplace. He forced himself to find a place within one of the movements, but his efforts never came to anything. He found the left as fanatic as the right or the advocates of religious parties.

Much later, a student in one of his university classes had risen from her chair and started to ask him a question by saying, "In 1968, did your generation . . ."

İrfan immediately cut her off, replying, "I was more interested in 69 than '68."

With the rest of the class, he had laughed, as the girl sat down blushing with embarrassment.

İrfan felt about as close to Islam as he felt to Turkish patriotism. On national holidays, when poems such as the one starting with "Your eyes were green, Lieutenant!" were recited, he used to run away to smoke a cigarette. He had never recited the ritual prayers for *namaz* or fasted during Ramadan.

Once, he and Hidayet had decided to perform *namaz* on the first morning of the Feast of Sacrifice, saying that their only aim was to have some fun. The time of prayer was set for three minutes past six in the morning, and thinking that the mosque would be very crowded later, İrfan and Hidayet went there the night before. They took off their shoes, entered, and sat at the very front of the building. A few old men, absorbed in worship, were the only others there. İrfan and Hidayet began to chat quietly. As time passed, more worshippers began to arrive, filling first the front, then the space behind until the place was filled with hundreds of people.

The imam, in his turban and black robe, rose to address the congregation, droning on about good morals, religion, the Prophet, Atatürk, and the heroic Turkish army. The boys, who had been sitting there for hours, were beginning to lose patience. They had hoped the prayers would start and end quickly so they could leave.

Finally, the imam took his place to lead the prayer, and it was then that İrfan and Hidayet realized that they were sitting right behind him. The muezzin called the faithful to prayer, and the imam started the ritual. "God is almighty," he said in a loud voice, placing both hands behind his ears. İrfan and Hidayet imitated his action.

Before coming to the mosque, they had asked their friends about the rules of the ritual. They had been told that after the imam intoned "God is almighty" for the second time, they had to bow their heads and put their palms on their knees, while at the third "God is almighty," they were supposed to prostrate themselves.

But the morning service on the first day of the Feast of Sacrifice was performed differently.

İrfan and Hidayet bowed their heads when they heard the second "God is almighty," then realized that neither the imam nor the congregation was doing the same. Among the hundreds of worshippers, they were the only two bending forward. They wanted to burst out laughing. The silence and solemnity of the situation affected their nerves, which were stretched to their full extent after a sleepless night, and they had to struggle to maintain their self-control.

When they heard "God is almighty" for the third time, they quickly prostrated themselves on the floor. Touching their foreheads to the ground, they closed their eyes. They had a strange feeling that something was wrong. When they looked up, they saw that everyone else in the mosque was standing up. They immediately got to their feet, but the urge to laugh was now stronger than ever.

When the imam once more declared, "God is almighty," İrfan and Hidayet thought they had to stay on their feet, but to their surprise, the congregation bent down. The two boys were the only ones left standing. Unable to suppress their laughter any longer, they started to run toward the exit, tripping over prostrating worshippers along the way, some of whom lost their balance and toppled over without realizing what had happened. İrfan and Hidayet finally got out the door, grabbed their shoes, and ran off down the street, laughing uproariously.

This was İrfan's first and last religious experience. To eschew religious practices was quite normal in the Kemalist Republican circles to which he belonged. In the secular Republic, where imams and muezzins were forbidden to wear religious garb outside places of worship, religion was not taught at school. Thus, İrfan never developed a sense of piety.

Perhaps this was the reason for his uneasiness at academic meetings in foreign countries. He did not classify the scholars he met there as Christian or Jewish, yet he had quickly realized that they regarded him as a Muslim, as part of a collective identity, even if this was not true. In the Turkish Republic, unless someone was Jewish, Armenian, or Greek, the word Muslim was automatically printed in the section indicating religion on the ID card, though many people were unconscious of this.

At the age of seven, he and Hidayet had experienced the terror of circumcision together. After being dressed in festival white clothes and soothed by a thousand promises of entertainment, the shock of seeing the tip of one's penis being pulled forward from the foreskin, which was then cut with a sharp razor, was nothing in comparison to the pain of dressing the wound afterward. Modern methods had simplified this procedure, but when he was a child, the circumcised organ had been wrapped in gauze. After a while, the blood on the gauze dried hard, and when it was pulled away in order to dust the scar with penicillin, the pain was intense enough to cause a scream. When İrfan saw his penis, bloody, wounded, and purple, he had thought that he would never be able to show it to anyone ever again.

Most Turks believed that circumcision was good for one and promoted cleanliness, but İrfan had a different view. He thought that the dilemma of both worshipping women and being hostile to them at the same time experienced by that species of humanity known as "the Turkish male" was a direct result of the early trauma they experienced at an early age in the ritual of being circumcised.

Many Turkish men believed that circumcision protected them against AIDS. Few took precautions when sleeping with the many Russian girls who first came to towns on the Black Sea coast. Some ridiculous beliefs developed. For example, Black Sea men sometimes squeezed lemon juice between the legs of the Russian girls to disinfect them before making love. Of course, lemon juice could kill AIDS. There was no need for other precautions as long as one had lemons. The men of these regions were not frightened of sexual diseases.

When electricity first came to Anatolian villages, many men who were warned against the danger of live electric wires had mockingly said, "What has a plucky man to fear from a few strands of wire?" Taking hold of the live wires, they had courageously held on as the current raced through them, making their teeth chatter and their bodies vibrate until they became victims of their own foolhardiness. Similarly, for Turkish men to show any fear of AIDS did not suit the image they had of themselves.

After the establishment of the Soviet Union, thousands of White Russians had come to Istanbul; likewise, after the collapse of the Soviet Union, fair-skinned Russian girls flocked to Turkey. After the revolution, gentlemen had become used to drinking yellow vodka and eating chicken kievski at the Rejans Restaurant in Pera in the company of chic ladies with fur collars. They would finish the evening listening to the piano in one of the district's stylish music halls. The more recent immigrants, slender blond Russian and Ukrainian girls with long legs and transparent skin, had made certain districts of the town their place of business, with the occasional trip to the Aegean or Mediterranean coasts as the sexual companions of Turkish businessmen. In the Black Sea region, the girls had lemon juice squeezed between their legs, but those who went to the Mediterranean were treated to the luxury of a holiday resort. They were luckier—at least those who did not have to share a bed with a short, plump man covered with thick black hair.

Some of the Russians managed to work their way into wealthier, more refined circles. One of İrfan's friends had told him an interesting story. According to this tale, some businessmen, who regularly vacationed at expensive hotels in Bodrum and Türkbükü with their families, had developed a special form of recreation. When one of them was sunbathing on the beach with his family, a few of his close friends dressed only in their swimsuits would come near the shore in a speedboat and invite him for a tour of the bay. Completely at ease, the man would leave his wife and children on the beach and go off on his own. What could be more innocent than a boat ride with a group of friends dressed in nothing more than a pair of swimming trunks?

But rather than touring the bay, the speedboat would direct its course to a big yacht anchored behind a nearby island. The lovely Russian and Ukrainian girls on board, exclusively selected and brought from Istanbul, were available for ready cash. İrfan's friend described the transparency of the girls' complexions by saying that "the redness of a cherry could be seen as it passed down their throats." The men who enjoyed the company of these girls preferred condoms to lemon juice. After a "tour" of an hour or so, the cheerful group would return to the beach, and the businessman would be reunited with his family—undoubtedly dreaming of the delights to be had on the following day.

After the polygamous Ottoman era, the change to monogamy over the next fifty or sixty years after the establishment of the Turkish Republic had not been easy. After the twenties, Turkish men were pushed to find other options, and, thanks to circumcision and lemon juice, AIDS held no terrors for them. In spite of that, they became a little worried when Western journalists wrote that circumcised men were only a little less prone to catch disease. Did that mean they were not invulnerable, after all?

İrfan caught a downwind and sailed south at full speed. He knew that the coastal conflict between the Turks and Greeks lessened in southern waters. The north was tense, but the south was viewed by both sides as a vacation spot. That was the place to head for.

One calm and peaceful afternoon, İrfan anchored his boat and watched the reflection of the sunlight on the sea. He gazed at the distant shores covered with ancient cypresses, the white buildings of Orthodox monasteries just visible on the islands, and, on the Turkish coast, miniature mosques, their tiny minarets piercing the sky. He could not help remembering the prayer of the great author Kazantzakis: "Dear God, please don't let this harmony be ruined. I don't ask you for anything else. Just don't let this harmony be spoiled."

What İrfan wished for was exactly the same.

As the days passed, he knew he had been right to change his life. He could feel himself becoming a free and different man, joy fluttering inside him. The night crises were diminishing. He kept taking his pills but was convinced he was sleeping better. In the dark of the night the boat no longer seemed like a coffin—at least not a closed one.

One day İrfan bought a big piece of cardboard and cut it in half. On one piece, he translated into free verse in English a poem by Robert Frost, whom he admired:

And I may return
If dissatisfied
With what I learn
From having died

On the second piece, he wrote in red felt tip a verse by Rumi: "Appear as you are or be as you appear!"

İrfan had not shaved for many days. His gray beard, which used to cover only his chin, had now spread across his entire face. With his shaggy hair and imposing physique, he felt like a mythological god. The more he freed himself from his bonds, the more relaxed he became. His heart beat at a slower pace.

If the day went well, and a big Mediterranean scad or bream seized his bait, İrfan would become the happiest man on earth. He would clean the fish immediately, and after pouring on some olive oil and lemon juice, eat it raw. The music that accompanied his meals was always the same. Jean-Pierre Rampal's flute blended with the cries of the gulls to create a new melody.

HAVE YOU EVER SEEN
A MIRACLE?

MIXED FEELINGS OF FEAR AND ANGER HAD OVER-come Cemal when he took off his commando uniform and handed in his cartridge belt, combat knife, and field radio kit. The confused feelings he experienced when he put on the weightless clothes of a civilian gradually became replaced by indifference. If the argument on the train had occurred in the first days after his discharge, he would probably have thrown someone out the window. Now, everything seemed a pointless game he did not care to play. He stayed on the sidelines and watched life do the running. The only thing on his mind was how to get rid of the girl by his side and return to his village and to Emine. He had been separated from Emine by his military service and now by this girl, sniffing as she sat in a hunched ball near the window.

"She looks miserable," thought Cemal. The previous evening she had seemed fine, but in the morning as the train moved through the endless Anatolian steppes, he had seen that she was ill. He should have shoved her out of the wagon in the dark. He would have been a free man already, and the journey to Istanbul would have been done with. The fervent longing Cemal felt for Emine had overtaken his desire to see Selahattin. Cemal could go to Istanbul anytime, but he was in imminent danger of losing Emine. If his task had been finished, he could have gotten off at the first station and hurried back to the village. As it was, every minute took him farther away from her.

Cemal wondered why he had not been able to grab Meryem by her skinny neck and push her off the train. Perhaps it was because he really had no desire to do it. Then he decided that he had probably been wary of the government official in the compartment. He might be in touch with the police, and he would have been suspicious if Meryem had disappeared. And if he himself had also disappeared, that would have looked even worse. So he had to wait until the man disembarked at Ankara. Between Ankara and Istanbul, Cemal would be free to act.

He was amazed that the simple killing of a girl was turning out to be such a lot of trouble. During the fighting on the mountains, no one was held accountable for the deaths that took place, but, unfortunately, civilian life was not like that; Cemal would have to heed Emine's advice and be careful not to get caught.

In the morning, Meryem had woken up with an awful headache. Her body ached, her throat was sore, and she had difficulty swallowing. She remembered that the previous night, after washing her hair, she had stuck her head into the icy wind. That was what had made her ill. Why had Cemal, who never addressed a word to her usually, been so insistent that she look out of the door?

Before she had fallen asleep, Meryem thought about all the women she had seen on the train, mulling over each and every detail she had observed: their painted fingernails, rings, tight-fitting pants, or slit skirts through which their white thighs were visible, their unrestricted behavior, and the way they tossed their hair. Seher's bold and furious response to the young man, who had insulted her parents, impressed Meryem. When, in the presence of her father and mother, Seher had shouted at the man, whom she had certainly never met before, Meryem had been astonished. Although the man, on hearing her words, had shouted back in Seher's face, he had not raised his hand to her or attempted to shove her to the floor. And even when the old man had spat in his face, no violence had followed! What a strange world it was!

In the village, women were not allowed to talk in the presence of men or eat with them. They had to hide their natural needs and conceal their pregnancies. When a new bride became pregnant, she tried to keep it a secret, though her mother-in-law would probably guess her condition from a growing appetite for pickles or pomegranate syrup. The girl had to continue working until the last day of her pregnancy without crying or complaining. When the labor pains started, the midwife would be summoned to do her job with the minimum of fuss. If a girl like Seher got pregnant, it seemed likely that she would announce it with pride and be pampered by her family.

Meryem could not say that what she had seen around her had affected her adversely in any way. At the bus terminal, for the first time in her life, she had eaten with Cemal and other men. Opening her mouth in front of them in order to eat had embarrassed her initially, but hunger had soon overcome this feeling, and she had followed her natural inclination to adapt by eating her sandwich and drinking her buttermilk without more ado. Drinking tea on the train had been easier and even enjoyable. If only she could have gotten rid of her scarf, baggy pants, and muddy plastic shoes, she would have felt quite at home. With any luck, when she got to Istanbul, she would be able to dress like Seher. Clothes like Seher's must be expensive, and Meryem had no money, but she hoped to find a way of getting to look like her.

Her headache and sore throat were getting worse. Her joints ached as if she had been given a good beating. She needed to go to the lavatory but could not find the will or the strength to stand up. Suddenly, she felt a familiar dampness between her legs, and she was overcome by fear and embarrassment. She had thought that the pain in her belly was from a chill, but this had to be her period, the first after Bibi had aborted the baby. She was stricken with panic. What could she do among all these people? If she stood up and turned around, would they see blood on her dress? She would rather throw herself from the train and avoid the shame. If it had started while she was asleep, her dress would be badly stained. There was no way of ascertaining this without standing up.

Even if Meryem made it to the toilet, she did not have anything to staunch the flow. Her aunt used to give her pieces of cotton cloth cut from old undershirts, which she would place between her legs. Immediately after use, they had to be washed with cold water; otherwise, worms would infest them. If they were cleaned with hot water or soap, the stain would never come out. If only she had a few of those rags now. Döne with her snake eyes had hastily shoved a few things into a bag for her but would surely not have put in such necessities even if she had thought of doing so.

Meryem was so frightened that she forgot her pain. Cemal was sitting next to her with his eyes shut. The government official and his wife were sleeping. The sick woman lying on the opposite seats was as motionless as a corpse, and her husband was snoring loudly on the floor.

Meryem decided that she had to stand up, take an undershirt from her bag on the rack above, and tear it into pieces in the lavatory. If people saw her, they would probably notice the stain, but she had to take the risk. "God, help me," she said to herself, and stood up. With her back to the sick woman, she reached up for her bag but did not have the courage to open it there and take out a shirt. Holding the bag behind her, though she was sure the stain could still be seen, she tiptoed out of the compartment. If Cemal were awake and looked at her, he would be sure to notice the blood. Meryem remembered Bibi's complaints about being a woman. She agreed with her. Since childhood, it had been this sinful part of her body that had always caused Meryem trouble.

After closing the compartment door, Meryem walked toward the lavatory at the end of the carriage. She tried to feel the back of her dress to see if it was wet but could not be certain.

Meryem started to cry, her head feeling as if it would split in two. As she waited outside the lavatory, she opened her bag and took out an undershirt. She had begun to tear it into pieces when she felt that someone was watching her. She had forgotten the glass doors between the carriages would make her visible to Seher, whom she saw smoking a cigarette and looking at her. Her heart began to pound. Seher opened the door of the other compartment and stepped into the junction between the carriages. The rattle of the train, which she heard as Seher opened the next door, beat in concert with the pain in her head.

"You're sick," said Seher, putting her hand on Meryem's forehead.

Meryem was obviously in pain, and Seher's heart was moved to see her in such a pitiful state. The young girl's green eyes stood out in her pale face like two extraordinary wildflowers. After seeing her struggle to tear up the undershirt, Seher understood the situation. "What's your name?" she asked.

Meryem could barely whisper her name.

"Don't be ashamed," Seher said softly. "Pretend I'm your sister. Wait here. I'll be right back."

Meryem felt terribly ashamed but sat obediently on the folding seat in the corridor.

A little later, Seher returned and handed something to Meryem. "Take this, go to the bathroom, and put it between your legs," she said. "Don't worry, the blood won't leak through."

Meryem, embarrassed, looked doubtfully at the strange little thing in her hand.

"Trust me, we all use them. We get them at the pharmacy," Seher insisted, pointing at the picture on the box.

Meryem went into the lavatory and locked the door. She washed herself clean and placed the little pad between her legs. After hesitating for a moment, as a safety measure, she also put a piece of the cloth ripped from her undershirt. She took off the baggy pants she was wearing under her dress, put them in her case, and left the restroom to return to where Seher stood waiting for her.

"Good," said Seher. "Now you can be comfortable. Let's see what else we can do for you. Come to our compartment. Some people have left, so there's room for you."

Meryem wondered whether Cemal would allow this or not, but she felt so weak and in need of attention that she could not refuse this kindly offer and followed Seher down the corridor.

After they had been thrown out of their compartment, Seher and her parents had sat in the corridor for a long time before finding seats in another carriage. As it went along, the train was slowly emptying.

Seher's mother and her father, his face still wearing a strange smile, were the only people in the compartment when Meryem and Seher entered. The two girls sat down side by side, and Seher gave Meryem an aspirin dissolved in water. Then she offered her some hot tea. After drinking three glasses, Meryem felt better and surrendered herself into their hands. Seher's mother stroked her scarfed head tenderly, murmuring softly as she did so.

Then Seher told Meryem to lie on the two empty seats next to her. Meryem bent her knees to fit into the space, rested her head on the hard green leather cushion, and felt someone cover her. Soon she was lost in the rhythm of the train, which was like a lullaby, the carriage swaying like a cradle. As she dozed, Meryem thought with gratitude of Seher and her mother, though this was accompanied by a niggling worry as to whether any blood had leaked through to her dress. Soon, she fell into a deep sleep. She looked so peaceful and innocent that she reminded Seher and her mother of a child, a pitiful child, wretched, weak, and fragile in her faded dress and green sweater, worn-out at the elbows.

Seher went out of the compartment to smoke another cigarette. She never smoked in front of her father. She wondered curiously about the relationship between Meryem and the soldier traveling with her. Meryem had said that they were cousins, but they had not exchanged a single word. The soldier was always dozing off, tossing, turning, and talking in his sleep, staring at nothing when he was awake. He never took any notice of Meryem, who was obviously scared of him. He was certainly intimidating. Even when completely still, he radiated an energy like that of a predatory bird, which, even when moving slowly, causes its prey to think that it can dart with lightning speed. "Maybe he's killed a lot of people," Seher thought. "But he's still not as underhanded as that official. He may be frightening, but he's not sly."

Seher's brother, Ali Rıza, and his friends were sacrificing themselves for men like the government official. She did not approve of the hunger strikes, because she did not want her brother to die and his enemies to be pleased. When a young man killed himself behind the silent prison walls, people like Ekrem rejoiced to think that another of them was done for. Was it ever possible to harm an enemy by hurting oneself?

On visiting days, when her brother was still strong enough to talk, Seher had tried to make him understand her point. She had pleaded with him to stop his fast. "They want you to die, and you're doing them a favor by killing yourself."

Unfortunately, Ali Rıza and his friends believed that they were engaged in a winning battle. "By sacrificing our bodies, we are struggling on behalf of democracy for our people," he replied. "As we die one by one, those outside these walls will rouse themselves to put pressure on the government. This is a political struggle. We fight by destroying our bodies. The price we pay is nothing compared to that paid by our people."

"Oh, Ali Rıza," Seher had wept, "the public doesn't care one bit about you! Outside these walls, people laugh and get on with their lives. The only things they're interested in are television shows that report who's with whom or which model has been seen at which bar with which soccer player."

Seher would have said more, but she did not want to upset her brother. She was not able to ask him, "Don't you read the newspapers and look at the television? The papers are full of photographs of models with naked breasts, of transvestite singers, and grinning prostitutes posing on water skis. 'Your people' are not individuals but an enslaved herd. Nobody has any personality, honor, or virtue."

Seher's brother and his friends believed that through the media their slow deaths were creating an impact. But it was not so; few people knew about them. It was a ridiculous, bloody game, yet Seher was not able to convey this to her brother. He was in a different world as if bewitched. His mother was now on her way to try to convince him to give up his hunger strike, but Seher was sure that Ali Rıza would not do so. If efforts at mediation did not succeed at this point, Ali Rıza would become like a living corpse, with no memory, unable to walk, see, or take care of himself. And society pretended not to recognize this as a tragedy. Some people, like the government official, were hostile, while others, like the girl sleeping in the compartment, were completely unaware of what was going on.

Seher understood why the Alawites did not trust anyone and why they married among themselves. This was not an attitude born of ignorance, but the result of hundreds of years of massacre and oppression. Nowadays, Alawite youths like Ali Rıza chose to commit suicide, with red bands wrapped around their heads.

When they were young, Seher and Ali Rıza used to perform the *semah* dance. Men and women, young and old, would whirl together in their red and green clothes to the rhythm of the *saz,* like cranes revolving around and around. The best part of the *cem* ritual was when the adults, approaching on their knees, would confess their sins to the *dede,* or sheikh, and receive their penance.

One rite was engraved into Seher's memory. Smeared with henna, about to be sacrificed and have its flesh distributed to the poor, a sheep had been brought before the *dede* and held there by one bound foot. The *dede* played his *saz* and sang three songs for the sheep. All three were apologies, asking the sheep for forgiveness and praising it for its good attributes. After the *dede* finished singing, he ordered the sheep to be untied. The animal then walked freely among people before being sacrificed. No one was allowed to disturb the sheep as it wandered about, sniffing the food set on trays on the ground and pricking up its ears to the music.

Ali Rıza was being sacrificed, but no one apologized to him. He was seen as a hated political activist. Had the feeling of being unfairly treated for centuries, which lay coiled in the Alawites like a venomous serpent, caused Ali Rıza to join an illegal organization at the university? These groups had sympathizers, like Ali Rıza, who distributed literature without being aware of its other activities. Most of the time, such young people were the real victims. Ali Rıza was so tenderhearted that he could not even watch a hen being slaughtered. How could he be a terrorist?

Since there were no mosques in Alawite villages and their women did not cover themselves, many Muslims did not accept Alawites as true believers. For such Muslims, it was unacceptable to drink alcohol or pray while music was being played, as the Alawites were accustomed to doing. Seher had cried many times when her friends criticized her for not fasting during Ramadan. She was fed up with being insulted for being an Alawite.

A woman, an Alawite, and poor—what could be worse than that? As if her problems were not enough, now she had a "terrorist" brother. She had little hope of finding a good job or marrying someone who was not from her community.

"Oh Ali, my Ali," she said to herself, "why weren't you stronger? Why did you let yourself be murdered? Even though you were the lion of God and the son-in-law of the Prophet, you endured so much cruelty and left your children forlorn. After hundreds of years, we still suffer because of you!"

She was able to reproach Ali through the courage derived from listening to ancient folk songs. In Alawite sayings, Ali was praised to the heavens, but in the old songs, both he and the Prophet, even God himself, were not beyond blame.

Once Seher had recited to her friends at school a poem by the fifteenth-century poet, Kaygusuz Abdal. When she came to the part

"God, loftier than the loftiest / God, more like the night than the day / You have a name but not a body / God, you resemble nothing," her friends had screamed "God forbid!" and had run off. Later, they complained about her to the school authorities. Seher soon learned, not by disciplinary punishment, but by the way her friends began to avoid her, that such songs and poems, which had been orally transmitted from generation to generation for centuries, had to be kept secret. Alawite children were often confused by the contrast between the religious tolerance in their homes and the Sunnite pressures outside.

The poor girl sleeping in their compartment was obviously not Alawite. She covered her head and was not comfortable in the presence of men. She must have faced a lot of trouble, Seher thought. Meryem was one of the millions of girls who became old without really enjoying life. They never had the chance to change their fate. Should Seher tell Meryem about the old sayings, in which her name was mentioned— the words of mystic poets from hundreds of years ago who considered themselves to be at one with God. Even toward the end of the twentieth century, it was still not possible to recite their verses openly. *"When Adam and Eve were not yet present in the universe / We were faithful to God in the incomprehensible secret / We were guests within Mary for a single night / And we are the true father of the Prophet Jesus."*

If the girl sleeping in the compartment heard this, she would probably never talk to Seher again.

When Seher returned to her compartment, Meryem suddenly opened her eyes, and asked, "Have you ever seen a miracle?"

Without waiting for an answer, she dozed off again. What did she mean? Why did she ask such a question in her sleep? "Strange girl," thought Seher. "Perhaps she needs a miracle."

Cemal woke up when the train stopped at a station. Since he knew that they still had a long way to travel, he paid little attention to the names of the places the train stopped at. He stretched and looked around. Meryem was gone! She must have gone to the restroom, he thought.

Cemal opened the door to the compartment and looked into the corridor. Surmising that Cemal was searching for the girl, Ekrem said, "She left while you were sleeping. She took her bag."

Cemal was shocked. Had Meryem escaped? No, that was not possible. Where could she go? She had no money and no idea where she was.

Cemal ran down the corridor, opened the carriage door, and jumped down onto the platform. Desperately, he ran among the vendors, station workers, and the passengers getting on and off the train. He looked everywhere, but Meryem had vanished. What would he tell his father? How could he look the old man in the face again? He would rather die than confess that he had lost the girl.

The conductor gave the signal for departure, and the locomotive began to move. Cemal could not stay on the platform any longer, and he jumped back onto the train. He was overcome with anger and hopelessness. As the train left the station, he scanned the platform in the desperate hope of catching a glimpse of her. Suddenly, Ekrem appeared beside him. "Don't worry!" he said. "The girl's on the train."

Cemal felt like hugging the man.

"I had a look around," Ekrem continued, "and, just as I suspected, those damned communists have her in their compartment. Maybe they're going to brainwash her into becoming one of them since she has such a hero for a relative."

"Where is she?" Cemal growled.

Ekrem took Cemal to the next wagon and pointed out Seher's compartment.

Cemal burst inside, grabbed Meryem, and shook her violently. Everyone was stunned, including Seher, and they made no move to stop him. "What the hell are you doing here?" he screamed.

Meryem was still groggy with sleep as she looked at Cemal with dawning fear, trying to utter an excuse, but before Cemal could strike her, Seher's father grabbed his arm. Cemal turned and looked at him in disbelief. How could that weak old man dare to hold him back? Would the lunatic spit on him, too? Then Cemal noticed the look in the old man's eyes, as if pleading with him to show mercy. Cemal pushed him back into his seat.

Seher stood up and grasped Meryem, protectively. "Can't you see she's sick?" she cried at Cemal. "When I found her in the corridor, she was about to faint. I gave her some medicine and brought her here to rest!"

"Yes, that's right," Seher's mother added anxiously. "The girl's been asleep since then."

Cemal looked at Meryem's reddened eyes, nose, and pallid face. She really was ill. "Follow me!" he yelled.

When they returned to their compartment, Ekrem was holding forth, saying, "The enemies of the Turks, who have destroyed our empire, are now fighting to seize our last piece of land." According to him, the communists were not important; they had been beaten, the few that remained committed suicide when they found themselves in jail. The real fight was that of the Turks against the Kurds and the supporters of the Shari'a. These enemies should be given no quarter since they were threatening the last Turkish state in history. He ended by saying, "Whoever doesn't consider himself a Turk should leave this blessed country immediately."

Cemal hardly heard a word Ekrem was saying. He was thinking desperately of how to get rid of the girl. With so many people around, there was nothing he could do on the train during the day. The landscape had changed; the mountains and the hills had given way to barren steppes. Not a single tree was visible. If he pushed the girl out of the train, his action would be seen for miles. Whether he liked it or not, he would have to wait until they got to Istanbul.

The conductor was announcing the train's arrival in Ankara. Ekrem and his wife prepared to leave. The ruddy-faced peasant nudged his sick wife, who had lain like the dead all through the journey, and the woman stirred slightly.

The train switched tracks and soon came to a halt inside the station. Meryem glanced at the platform, noticing that there were many more stylishly dressed people in Ankara. Although there were village people among the crowd, no one was wearing baggy pants or tight-fitting headscarves. Most of the women left their hair loose, and there were even a number of blondes.

At this point Seher entered the compartment and handed Meryem a small plastic bag. "Medicine," she said simply, kissing Meryem on the cheek. "We're getting off here." She then turned and walked out of the compartment, without looking at Cemal. Ekrem and his wife followed her out of the compartment, and the peasant, having picked up his wife and slung her over his shoulder, also departed. Meryem noticed that some people were waiting for them on the platform. One of them was probably the sick woman's brother. He had a wife and two children with him. Together they loaded the sick woman onto a wheelbarrow they had brought with them, treating her just as if she were a sack of cement, and walked away, chatting happily among themselves.

Two men greeted Ekrem and his wife on the platform. Ekrem said something to them and pointed toward Seher and her parents, who were heading into the distance. One of the men began to follow the family.

Meryem saw that Cemal had gotten off the train to smoke a cigarette. She was alone in the compartment. She opened the plastic bag and looked at the medicine Seher had given her: some pills that dissolved in water, a few aspirins, and a box with the name ORKID on it, like the one she had shown her in the corridor. She suddenly remembered what magic that little pad between her legs had worked, as she realized she felt no dampness there. In fact, she had forgotten about it, but she was sure that it was now time it was changed.

NEW PASSENGERS

In Ankara, the train filled up again. A young couple and their ten-year-old son took the seats opposite Meryem and Cemal, with a young woman and a blond man in a white coat next to them. Trying not to appear rude, the passengers cast furtive glances at each other, wondering what their companions for the long hours ahead would be like.

Meryem's headache had lessened, and she was not so worried about bloodstains on her dress anymore. She felt very grateful to Seher and glad that she had ventured out into the corridor. It was clear that Seher did not believe in God and, indeed, talked in a sinful way like a non-Muslim, but how helpful she had been. Meryem was confused.

Soon, her nose started running again, and her throat began to hurt. The pain got worse when she tried to eat the sesame-seed roll and drink the buttermilk Cemal had brought her from the station buffet. Even so, she felt much better than before, and, eager to learn more about this new world, she examined the woman sitting across from her.

The woman was slim and wore very tight pants and blue-and-white sports shoes. The thick belt around her waist was ornamented with the letters D and G. The thin white blouse she was wearing was so tight it emphasized her breasts. A colorful handkerchief was tied around her neck, and her light blond hair was strangely darker at the roots.

She took a glossy magazine out of her handbag and began to read. Meryem could see that on the cover there was a picture of a naked woman. Her breasts, long legs, and buttocks were completely bare, and she was looking straight at Meryem as she leaned forward to apply scarlet lipstick to her pursed lips. Meryem shuddered. How could the woman read such a magazine?

In the seat next to her, the woman's husband, short-haired with glasses, wearing a blue sweater, was casually reading a newspaper. He didn't seem at all worried about his wife's choice of reading material.

Their son was humming something between a melody and spoken words, as he played with what looked like a small black box. When he pressed a button, the box made strange noises. His shoes were similar to his mother's, but one of the laces was untied.

The blond man sitting next to Cemal was speaking to his companion in a language Meryem did not understand. Meryem knew Turkish and a little Kurdish, but she had never heard the language this couple was using.

She looked at Cemal and saw that he was staring at the magazine cover. Every now and then, he lifted his eyes toward the ceiling, but could not refrain from taking another look at the naked woman. Meryem noticed that he was disturbed, and this gave her some satisfaction. For the first time since they had set out on their journey, Cemal's hard shell of indifference was cracking. In fact, his hands were almost trembling.

Meryem gazed out the window. Houses and factories had replaced the uncultivated and uninhabited terrain. Trains traveling in the opposite direction startled her as they rushed past, making a terrifying noise, an explosion followed by a mighty wind.

She looked again at the family in the seats opposite and realized that the little boy was staring at her. He seemed to be studying her, running his eyes over her dress, woolen socks, and muddy shoes.

Showing her the box he held in his hand, he suddenly asked, "Do you know how to play this GameBoy?"

Startled, Meryem shook her head.

"Why not?"

"I don't know," Meryem said.

The boy did not give up. "We have a car, but my mom had an accident, you know. That's why we're going by train to my grandparents' house in Istanbul. My mom's afraid of airplanes."

Meryem listened to the boy and nodded.

He started to hum again and began to play with his odd-looking toy. Then he thrust his shoe with the unfastened lace toward Meryem, and said, "Tie it up!"

Meryem immediately bent forward, but the boy's mother looked up and said, "Shame on you, son! Is that the way to talk to your elders? You're a big boy now. You can tie your own shoes."

"But isn't she a maid?" asked the boy.

"No, she's not."

"But she looks just like our maid."

The woman smiled at Meryem, and said, "Please forgive him."

"It's all right," Meryem replied. "I can tie his shoelace for him."

Yet she felt reluctant to do so in front of the others since she did not know how to tie a bow. She hesitated, and the boy tied his own shoelace, huffing and puffing indignantly as he did so.

Meryem realized that, for the first time in her life, people were speaking to her politely. It seemed like a miracle to her that a woman who could so openly read a magazine with a naked woman on the cover as well as a woman who argued with men should treat her like a human being.

Meanwhile, the young woman next to Cemal said, "Have a good journey." It was not clear whom she had addressed, but the man opposite her said, "You, too." Everyone nodded.

"This is Peter Cape, an American journalist," continued the young woman, introducing the man next to her. "He's come to Turkey to interview people for an article he's writing. He wants to talk to all kinds of people. I'm his translator."

She took two business cards out of her bag and handed them to Cemal and the boy's father. "My name's Leyla. Peter would like to ask you a few questions if you don't mind."

"Not at all," the short-haired man on the opposite seat readily replied. Then he said something to the American in the foreign language that Meryem had heard earlier. He spoke it with difficulty, but he was eager to communicate with the journalist.

"We've visited many parts of Turkey," said Leyla. "We've traveled to the east, to the west, to the Black Sea region, as well as the Mediterranean. We've ridden on trucks, and climbed up to mountain villages on donkeys. Now we're taking the train. Peter wants to meet people of all backgrounds."

The American took out a small notebook and asked the man opposite him a question. Leyla translated.

"He asks what you do as a job."

"I'm a urologist. And my wife works in a bank."

"Do you live in Ankara?"

"Yes."

"Some of the people we've talked to say that the clash between the supporters of the right wing and those of the left in Turkey is over. Today, the country has three poles: Turkish nationalism, Kurdish nationalism, and political Islam. Do you agree?"

"No," he said emphatically, without taking pains to hide his surprise and discomfort. "I will never accept that the Republic of Turkey is divided in any way."

He knitted his brows and raised his chin, as if he thought that by saying anything more he would be accused of being a traitor, giving secret information about his country to foreign spies.

Without consulting Peter, Leyla continued, "Please don't misunderstand. He's not saying that Turkey is divided. He's saying that there is polarization—the country has three centers of attraction."

Somewhat bewildered, the man fell silent, trying to puzzle out her meaning. Taking advantage of her husband's silence, the woman entered the conversation.

"There is no such division," she said. "On the one hand, there is the modern and secular Kemalist Republic. On the other, there are the Kurds and the Islamists who are trying to destroy the Republic."

Leyla translated for the journalist.

"Does this situation frighten you?" Peter asked.

"Yes, a little, in fact," she answered, "because everyone knows what the Kurds have done and how many people they've killed."

She paused and continued reproachfully, "They've done it with the aid and support of Western states."

"What's frightening about it?" Peter asked.

"The Islamists want to turn this country into another Iran. They want to veil all Turkish women, like those 'cockroaches,' who cover themselves in black from head to toe. If they could, they would force us all to veil ourselves immediately."

"What do you think about the riots in the universities over the Islamic headdress?"

"Those actions are all directed from some central headquarters. What they wear is not a scarf but a political symbol. That's the way it started in Iran. They plan to plant thousands of headscarfed women first in the universities, then in government offices. Next, they'll want to use the Arabic alphabet or demand that Friday become an official holiday. Finally, they'll establish a Shari'a state—something like the Taliban."

"But don't you think that a student has the right to dress as she wants?"

"Not if her aim is to support a political agenda. Our grandmothers also covered their heads, but these women cover their heads in a different way. For them it's not a normal headscarf, but a political symbol, a uniform."

"What do you mean?"

The woman struggled to explain. Then, all of a sudden, she pointed at Meryem. "Look at her," she said. "This girl covers her head but not in the way they do. This is the way the traditional Anatolian woman covers her head, unlike how those freaks do."

Meryem was embarrassed. Everyone in the compartment was staring at her dirty headscarf. Even the non-Muslim foreigner was looking at her.

"Where are you from?" Leyla asked.

"Near Lake Van; that is, from Suluca," Meryem stammered.

Peter then started to ask more questions, and Leyla translated.

"Are you Kurdish or Turkish?"

Meryem looked at Cemal to see if he objected to her speaking. He did not seem to mind, so she whispered, "Praise be to God, I'm a Muslim."

"He didn't ask that," said Leyla. "He asked whether you're Turkish or Kurdish."

"Where we come from, Turks and Kurds are mixed," Cemal interrupted. "They've always married each other—but our family is more Turkish than Kurdish."

From Cemal's appearance, Leyla understood that he was a soldier, and she told Peter this.

The journalist then became very interested in the young man, and after a few more questions, they discovered that Cemal was a former commando who had fought in the mountains. Peter wanted to know what kinds of things he had encountered during his service. Were Kurdish villages really razed to the ground? Did the village guards tyrannize the local inhabitants? Had any of Cemal's friends been killed? How many guerrillas had he himself killed? What did he think of the actions he had taken part in? Had he crossed the border into northern Iraq? Had he ever been wounded?

Cemal soon began to feel uneasy. He was afraid that if he talked too much, he would be giving away military secrets and betraying those who had died in the service of their country. The brotherhood of soldiers followed unwritten rules. One was to stay out of such conversations.

The stranger who was questioning him had never been in the mountains. No bullets had whizzed over his head. He had never felt the all-pervading fear of stepping on a land mine. He had not lived in the open, soaked to the skin for days and nights on end. Cemal could not explain this to him, so he gave evasive answers, "I don't know much. I was in a supply unit away from the fighting."

Peter finally realized that Cemal would not give him any information.

"Tell the journalist that Kurds in this country receive equal treatment," the doctor said abruptly. "He should stop trying to stir things up. Whoever is a citizen of the Turkish Republic is Turkish. It's similar to America. There are many different people in the U.S.: black, white, Hispanic. . . . Aren't they all American? So are we all Turkish, and we won't let anyone divide our country."

Peter Cape listened politely. "But in America," he replied, "everyone speaks the language he or she wants and dresses as he or she chooses. Kurdish education and Kurdish television are forbidden here, aren't they? It's also against the law to go to school wearing a 'turban.' That's all I was asking about."

For more than a month, Peter had been traveling around this remarkable country so full of conflicts. He had never been to a land that had so many different lifestyles. Even to say that the people in the compartment were all of the same nationality would be difficult, and this was only one of the things that amazed him. The war in the southeast between the PKK and the Turkish army had lasted fifteen years. Tens of thousands had been killed, but that did not prevent Turks and Kurds from living together or marrying their children off to each other. What an extraordinary contradiction!

Although there was no current dispute between the Alawites and the Sunnites, they did not let their families mix; if that happened, blood would flow. On the other hand, it was only on the mountaintops that Turks and Kurds were killing each other. If you looked at it objectively, after so many millions had migrated to the cities, many of the larger ones had a considerable Kurdish population, yet there was no sign of a Turkish-Kurdish dispute within city boundaries.

Turkey was a Muslim country, but the Turks appeared to have a strong dislike for Arabs and Iranians. Apparently, Turks considered themselves Western and European. They admired and imitated the West, but they had a deep-seated distrust of it as well.

Peter was also surprised at the amount of nudity he found in the popular culture. On one hand, the police prevented female students wearing the Islamic headdress from entering universities, while, on the other, the television and newspapers were full of pornographic sex, even during the holy month of Ramadan. He found it very difficult to understand.

Peter had repeatedly witnessed the symptoms of a paranoia about a divided country, which turned people into fiery nationalists. Like the doctor opposite him, whenever a Turk heard the words "Armenian," "Kurdish," or "headscarf," he would become upset and go into a long rant about Atatürk, the blond, blue-eyed founder of the Turkish Republic. Portraits and statues of him were prominent all over the country. There was no town square or government office where his image was not present.

When Peter first arrived in Turkey, he had visited a very cold northeastern city and witnessed a peculiar scene in front of the courthouse there. The cold was intense—at minus eighty degrees it seemed possible that even hell might freeze—but some men dressed in colorful Ottoman costumes and carrying musical instruments were waiting outside the courthouse in the cold. Leyla told him that the group represented a symbolic Janissary or Ottoman military band. "Nowadays, each municipality seems to have one," she added.

"Why are they waiting outside in the freezing cold?"

"Someone from this city has been appointed a government minister. They're waiting for him."

"When is he going to arrive?"

"That's anyone's guess."

Snug in the warm comfort of his car, Peter Cape decided he would photograph the state minister's arrival. He waited for a long while, and he could see that the musicians were getting colder and colder. Although their moustaches were slowly freezing solid and their hands were turning blue, they did not leave.

Leyla told him that the city was famous for its cold weather, and that the great seventeenth-century Ottoman traveler, Evliya Çelebi, had mentioned in one of his books that when he was crossing a narrow road, he saw a cat jumping from one roof to another. It was so cold that the poor animal froze in the air halfway from one roof to the other.

"I can understand why it froze, but why didn't it fall down?" Peter asked.

Leyla told him that was what Evliya Çelebi's stories were like: full of exaggeration.

Now the bitter cold, which could freeze a jumping cat, was transforming the military band into statues of ice. They waited for more than an hour. Finally, a convoy of cars appeared in the distance. A cavalcade of big black Mercedes, accompanied by police cars, drove up, one after the other. The minister, a short, plump man, who looked like one of the peasants from that region, was quickly surrounded by fawning attendants. He paid no attention to the Janissary band but went directly into the building. Those unfortunate musicians made an effort to play a march, but could not produce more than a few weak notes with their frozen fingers, the joints of which had lost all feeling. The drum itself shattered when the drummer struck it. Neither the minister nor those around him saw or heard anything, but the band had done its duty and welcomed the minister in proper fashion.

Peter felt as if he had traveled back in time. He asked Leyla who the minister was, and she told him that he was a former tradesman, a minor wholesaler of foodstuffs. One day he had joined one of the more conservative parties. When the party succeeded in the elections, he had become first a deputy, then a minister.

"What a lucky guy." Peter Cape laughed.

"Most of them are people like that," Leyla added, somewhat angrily. "Many people, such as provincial merchants or those who've never been able to hold a good job, or others who need political immunity in order to avoid being prosecuted, join a party, then make people wait outside in a temperature of minus eighty degrees."

The minister, who had obtained funds from the state budget to make investments in his hometown, was visiting the city to lay the foundation of a sports center named after him and a park named after his deceased father. That was the reason why a foodstuff merchant—really not much liked—was being welcomed as if he were a Seljuk sultan.

Peter Cape had seen many strange things in this country. He had seen oppressive, dark Anatolian cities, full of coffeehouses crowded with chain-smoking men with sunken cheeks and thick moustaches, narrow roads, dreadful poverty, and heard of starving people who hanged themselves from trees, young people who committed suicide by throwing themselves off the Bosphorus Bridge, purse snatchers who almost ripped the arms off the women as well as taking their handbags. He had experienced communal taxis side by side with Cherokee and Lincoln four-by-fours, minibuses and limousines, five-star hotels, parties along the Bosphorus that were more extravagant than the tales in the Arabian Nights, firework exhibitions, people walking around in Afghan outfits, naked models, heavy-metal fans in Beyoğlu bars, Satanists, rock singers, youngsters with red or green hair and body piercings. This was a country that defied definition and was almost impossible to comprehend.

While Peter was immersed in his thoughts, Leyla stood up, and before they could be aware of it, snapped photographs of Cemal and Meryem and the family sitting opposite them.

Cemal felt he was suffocating. He rose, left the compartment, and once in the corridor, took refuge in a cigarette as the trees flashed past giving him a feeling of vertigo. The foreigner's questions had exasperated him. They had destroyed the silence that had enveloped him for so long. Moreover, he was worried that Leyla had photographed him with Meryem—the girl he planned to kill. The man was a journalist. What if the picture were to be published in some American newspapers and maybe later appeared in the Turkish press? He thought about grabbing Leyla's camera and smashing it, but such an act would certainly mean an encounter with the police.

After a while, Cemal realized that the cause of most of his strain was the photo of the naked woman on the magazine cover. His flesh, as yet untouched by a woman, was still on fire. The fear his father had planted in him had prevented him from being with a woman. He had not even—God forbid—played with himself. Some of his friends had satisfied themselves in this way until they felt faint, but Cemal had never forgotten his father's words: "Masturbation is one of the gravest sins."

Cemal had not even caressed Emine, even though he was tempted by an overwhelming desire to break down all the barriers that prevented him from touching her body. He had thought that he would achieve his desire after military service, but now this wretched girl had come between them.

In the army, the magazines his companions showed him used to make him suffer, too. It was obvious that creature called woman was an invention of the Devil, created to tempt men into sin.

"What am I going to do?" Cemal thought hopelessly. "How can I kill the girl?"

He had to accomplish his mission, so he struggled to keep his distance and expunge all past memories of her from his mind. Meryem had to become like a stranger to him.

She was corrupt . . . indecent . . . filthy. She had sinned.

NEW GODS
AND GODDESSES

THE PROFESSOR WISHED THAT JOSEPH CAMPBELL were alive and sitting opposite him. That wise man, who had observed that humanity needed new myths, would be pleased to drink a glass of wine with him, not minding the spindrift that would wet his snow-white hair as they conducted a serious discussion of mythology.

Perhaps İrfan was pursuing a myth now. He had set out to sea to reflect on the world from a distance—as from the moon perhaps—and to observe the differences between nations disappear. Yet İrfan was not on the moon but on the sea. Perhaps he was capable of producing new myths similar to the old ones.

Drifting over the warm, lazy water, he recalled his days in Boston: a white city, cold, clean, and well cared for, full of wisdom and the re-minders of an aristocratic Europe. During his first year at Harvard, he had memorized every paving stone, every corner, monument, build-ing, and garden in Cambridge. He bought mugs, T-shirts, sweatshirts, and caps decorated with the Harvard emblem from the university bookstore. As the son of a breadline family from Izmir, studying on a scholarship, these objects made him feel proud. Once he had been to the Faculty Club to meet a professor who had invited him there. The building was like a jewel set in a well-kept garden. On the ground floor, the big hall with its huge fireplace was filled with mahogany furniture and chintz-covered armchairs. It emanated a feeling of peace. The professors read their newspapers in reverential silence, broken occasionally by the crackling of the fire or the rustle of a page.

Whenever İrfan sat on one of the seats fixed to the floor of the classroom in serried rows, he felt that this happiness would play a great part in his life. Years later when he visitied the same classrooms as a guest, he had noted that the seats seemed to have very little space between them. Reflecting that it was rather that the years had made him stouter, he had to smile. When a student at the university, of course, he had been a stringy beanpole.

While at the university, İrfan had seen his life as a straight line. He would stay in Boston, finish his master's degree and get his doctorate, then spend the rest of his life as a Harvard professor, shuttling his way between the magnificent library and the Faculty Club.

Those dreams kept İrfan occupied until he met Aysel. She had dazzled him with her glamour and affluence. He had barely made ends meet, either when he lived with his family or at the university. Aysel went shopping in a chauffeur-driven Lincoln, wore the most fashionable designer clothes from Europe, and ate at Boston's most luxurious restaurants, gaining the waiters' respectful service with the enormous tips she would leave them.

At first, the regard that well-heeled Turks were given in the States had astounded İrfan, but after he married Aysel, he discovered the reason. Certain companies or individuals would give the wealthy an entrée to American high society. Through the services of an agent, a candidate would donate a large sum of money to a charitable foundation set up by a well-known person in order to be invited to charity events attended by people high in the society. İrfan later learned that Aysel had donated twenty thousand dollars to Ivana Trump's foundation, which guaranteed her a table at the best restaurants. Rich Turks ran across each other at these restaurants.

Although the esteem given to Turkey as a country was close to zero, rich Turks were highly respected abroad. Once, in London, İrfan and Aysel had been invited to a private club in Piccadilly. Entrance was by membership or invitation only, and their passport information had to be recorded at the desk. Black tie and fashionable dress were required. A hostess guided them up the red-carpeted marble stairs, illuminated by the light of crystal chandeliers. Rare and precious works of art were exhibited in niches all the way up the staircase, and magnificent paintings were hung on the walls. The spacious dining room was opulent but at the same time vulgar, with gold leaf glittering from every corner. The dishes, prepared by well-known chefs, were a mixture of Thai, Italian, and Lebanese cuisine. Waiters continuously offered them this or that food to taste, as if they were the guests of honor. The club was always crowded with rich Arabs and Turks in Armani suits and Versace ties. The women glittered in their Chanel gowns and priceless jewelry. İrfan had guessed that membership to this club cost more than the annual salary of the prime minister of England. The price of a dinner was perhaps more than three months' salary for a cashier working in a bookshop in Sloane Square.

This stylish glitter had bewitched İrfan, and he had given himself up to the pretentious lifestyle of the Istanbul rich rather than becoming a Harvard professor. At the beginning, he had been ashamed of how ostentatious the showiness of it all was. John Lobb shoes, for instance, were an absolute must for this kind of life. An employee of the company would come specially from London each year to take foot measurements to make the elegant, handmade shoes its customers desired.

He had met Aysel in his last year, and afterward, he was able to complete his degree. He had pursued his academic career later at Istanbul University.

One's lifestyle influences everything, even the way one thinks. Instead of becoming a creative thinker, content with a modest way of life, İrfan mutated into a pretentious dandy from an underdeveloped country. He had not produced anything worthwhile—since he judged himself to be devoid of noteworthy thoughts or feelings.

The professor felt in need of a new myth in order to go on living. Since setting out to sea, he had been able to understand the fears and crises he had suffered in Istanbul. It was not just the fear of dying, which had given him the desire to change his life immediately, but the fear of dying without having produced something significant and without having left even the smallest trace to show he had ever existed.

İrfan had not thought about Aysel since he set out to sea. He loved her very much and did not want to hurt her. Yet, in spite of this, he must have caused her a lot of grief.

Inwardly, he felt happier when he was away from her. He was often disturbed by things of minute importance, the daily repetition of which had become extremely annoying. For instance, Aysel would cuddle up next to him when he watched television as if there were no other place in all their spacious living room. When Aysel's blond hair, stiff and smelling of synthetic dye, touched his cheek, it would put him on edge. Unable to say, "Take your hair away from my face, it's scratching me," he would endure the discomfort in silence. Aysel would curl up next to him and stay there for hours, causing his legs to go numb and his neck to become stiff, yet he could not push her away. Eventually, he would invent a reason to go to the bathroom or to get something from the kitchen, but his excuse would not stop her from asking where he was going. If he replied that he wanted a beer, she would immediately say, "Ask the maid, honey. Don't trouble yourself."

İrfan could not easily give orders to the housemaids. He felt embarrassed to summon these servants and tell them to bring him a beer while all he was doing was sitting with his feet up. Aysel commanded and berated the maids with great ease—and they respected her far more than they did the professor.

Aysel's habit of interrupting İrfan in front of others to take over and finish a joke or a story he had started to tell disturbed İrfan a lot. Even though angry, he would maintain his self-control, and say, "Go ahead, sweetheart. You tell it better."

Aysel liked to correct her husband about insignificant details. For instance, if İrfan said, "Then we stopped at a grocery store and bought a pound of apples," Aysel would most likely immediately correct him, saying, "No, we bought two pounds, and some oranges, too."

İrfan did not have the courage to say, "What's that got to do with what I'm talking about?" Instead, he would mask his irritation with a smile.

He slept comfortably alone at night in the cabin or on the deck of the boat without Aysel's sticking her hair into his face or hooking him with her leg.

He usually began his musings by thinking how much he loved Aysel. If he thought a little longer, he would realize how much he hated her and cut his thoughts short.

Joseph Campbell's *Masks of God* and *The Power of Myth* were two of the few books İrfan had taken with him. That morning he had read these lines from *The Power of Myth*: "Myths formulate things for one. They say, for example, that one has to become an adult at a particular age. The age might be a good average age for that to happen—but actually, in the life of the individual, this differs greatly. Some people are late bloomers and come to a particular stage at a relatively late age. One has to have a feeling where he is. A human being has got only one life to live."

In another part of the book, Campbell wrote: "We are so engaged in doing things to achieve purposes of outer value that we forget the inner value, the rapture that is associated with being alive, is what it is all about."

These lines made the professor think that he had recently matured and become adult. He had always felt that his old world in Istanbul was devoid of inner values, but he had internalized this observation only after leaving that world behind. His friends and acquaintances were only interested in the supplements of weekend newspapers, which reported the love affairs between soccer players and models or singers and what went on behind closed doors. The television channels were full of such stories. Maybe this was what Campbell had defined as a lack of mythology.

İrfan believed that monotheism was a less exciting religion than that of the gods of mythology, which had lasted for thousands of years. Later, the people of the Mediterranean had suddenly been propelled into a dry and colorless system of belief in the one true God. There were no longer gods to console, attract, and to amuse them. The way the ancient gods and goddesses who lived on Mount Olympus used to fall in love, feel jealous, kidnap young maidens, make war and peace, rape and receive punishment, and undertake a multitude of adventures, each stranger than the other, was very human. The people of the Mediterranean would tell these stories repeatedly, but the new monotheistic religions were extremely boring. One could not tell whether the One God was male or female even. God had no form nor did He/She embark on any adventures. Humankind had to create new gods and goddesses to be able to maintain past habits. The members of the new pantheon were actors or actresses, soccer players, models, politicians, toreadors, and tennis pros. Countless newspapers, magazines, and many hours of television time were dedicated to the lives and affairs of these deities. The only difference was that Mount Olympus had now descended to become some Olympos Disco.

The new gods and goddesses, whose adventures were closely followed by Istanbul's elite, came from the impoverished sectors of the
city. Apparently, many poor families living in the outlying suburbs,
which had spread their octopus tentacles around the city, had tall,
slender long-legged daughters whom they "sold" to the television
channels. At first, these girls were timid, disheveled, and a little too
thin, but as time passed and they got used to their new occupations,
their appearances changed as a result of new hairdressers and the surgeon's knife, as well as silicone implants to lips and breasts. Once, a
columnist had described these girls as "long-legged with grandiose
lips," causing İrfan to chuckle. The shoulder straps of their dresses often slid from their shoulders, exposing their nipples. In an exagger-
ated tone of astonishment, they would ask the reporters around them,
"Did anything show?" Then the goddesses would burst into laughter,
showing off their new porcelain dentures, overlarge and a little too
protruding.

As for the new gods, they were invariably short, stout, and swarthy,
with hairy chests, huge moustaches, and an accent from somewhere in
the east.

In their miserable shacks, millions of the poor watched the adventures of these gods and goddesses on television as they sat hunched
around their coal-burning stoves, the noxious fumes from which
brought death to someone whenever the west wind blew the smoke
back down the chimney. They hoped for some kind of help from that
world of virtual reality. When the folk-dance music started, they would
clap their hands and prance around as if they were the happiest
people on earth. This the professor was able to understand, but he
could not comprehend why the social group that called itself "the
elite" shared these pleasures. There was a deep gulf between the social classes in Turkey; but a factory boss and his workers, a high-
ranking officer and his driver, or the founder of a holding company
and a beggar were all united in front of the television. All followed the
same gods and goddesses, gazed at their photographs, and watched
their shows. In this country, there was wealth, but nothing that could
be called elite in culture or taste.

İrfan recalled one of his columns. His claim had aroused much hos-
tility. He had written that the Turkish bourgeoisie was not a genuine
bourgeoisie because they had no aristocratic models to follow, from

which to learn culture and refinement. Nineteenth-century European novels often mentioned that the unrefined nouveaux riches, in envy of the aristocrats, emulated them by placing pianos and paintings in their houses, by organizing literary readings and inviting famous authors and poets to their homes, and by hiring private tutors to teach their children Latin, literature, and music.

The peasants who earned a lot of money in Turkey did not turn into bourgeoisie but adopted a proletarian lifestyle. There is a Russian saying: "Scrape a Russian, and you'll find a Tatar!" When the glossy layers of the rich Turk were scraped off, the peasant underneath was laid bare.

İrfan knew that during the six hundred years of the Ottoman Empire, great care had been taken to prevent the emergence of an aristocratic class since a single family lorded it over the whole state. The name of that family was Osman, which consequently became that of the state. To maintain their dynastic hegemony, the sultans had not married into Turkish families but had chosen brides of Hungarian, Russian, or Italian origin. When any other family showed signs of gaining power, the sultan would destroy it. Executing the head of the family was not enough—the whole family had to be wiped out and its property confiscated, such an action even being sanctioned by religious approval from the Sheikh-ul-Islam. As a result, the Turkish Republic had not received the legacy of an aristocratic social class from the Ottomans, but an odd group, which called themselves the "elite of Istanbul," had evolved: a group of people with wealth but no culture.

The sons of these "elite" families would go to the United States to study business administration, but in summer they came back to Istanbul to dance like Egyptian belly dancers in bars and at wedding parties. There was something feminine about the young men's dancing as they bowed low in front of each other, bumped hip to hip or, covered in sweat, embraced and even kissed.

The professor loathed Istanbul.

THE MAGICAL CITY

WHEN MERYEM AND CEMAL GOT OFF THE TRAIN in Istanbul at Haydarpaşa Station, they shared the same feeling as the Megarians, the Vikings, the Crusaders, and many others who had come there over the centuries: amazed admiration. They had all felt that this city was like no other city past or present.

During the last hour of the journey, the train had passed along the coast of the Marmara Sea and through the suburbs on the Asian side of Istanbul. Meryem's eyes opened wide in amazement as the train sped past the crowds of people lining the platforms in outlying stations. Soon, everyone on the train rushed to get their luggage together, putting on their coats in haste to line up at the doors, where everyone was waiting, impatient to get off.

Haydarpaşa station was full of trains, coming or going, and crowds of people milling here and there. Never in her life had Meryem seen such a crowded place. Over the loudspeaker, gongs were constantly clanging and announcements being made. Meryem and Cemal were hardly able to think straight. The jostling crowds pushed by them, careless of whose shoulders they banged or whose feet they stepped on. Cemal buttoned the front of his jacket all the way up to the collar. From childhood, he had heard stories about the amount of thieving that went on in Istanbul, and he was afraid that the few liras in his inside pocket might be stolen. He kept close watch, his eyes anxiously turning this way and that: Anyone in this crowd might be a pickpocket.

Meryem gazed at the people around her. Some were hugging those newly arrived, others waving their good-byes. She was astonished to see young people kissing each other on the lips. No one around them seemed to take any notice or stop to look, however long the embrace lasted.

Cemal and Meryem became even more bewildered as they made their way through the crowd and came to the floating boat landing, swaying on the choppy sea in front of the station. White passenger ferries with fenders made from huge, discarded truck tires bumped against the pier, causing it to rattle and shake, while the ships' sirens deafened their ears. The coal black funnels of the boats contrasted strikingly with their white paint.

According to the directions Cemal had been given, in order to get to Yakup's house, they had to cross to the European side of the city on one of these boats and take two different buses. Cemal showed the instructions, written on a crumpled piece of paper, to an elderly man with a gray moustache and a felt hat, who pointed out a ferry to him. Cemal, with an inbred suspicion of Istanbul folk, asked two other people and was only convinced it was the right boat when they both gave the same answer as the first man had.

After waiting in line to buy a token and pass through the turnstiles, Cemal and Meryem just managed to catch the ferry. The ropes were being cast off, and the boat was about to leave the pier with much churning of blue water into foaming white waves. On board, it was noisy and so crowded that they had difficulty staying on their feet. Several haggard-faced men in clothes that had seen better days were shouting at the tops of their lungs, trying to sell combs, colored pencils, music cassettes, razor blades, and various other items as they walked among the crowd. One elderly vendor, who looked as if he had spent his life on that boat, was explaining how the instrument in his hand had cured his back pain. "Here I am, alive and cured!" he boasted, ignoring the laughter of the few passengers listening to him.

The smell of burning oil from the engines mingled with the intoxicating fragrance from the rolling sea. Evening was falling, and Meryem marveled at the beauty of the Bosphorus. The lights of the city, the brightly shining palaces, and the majestic mosques were reflected in its blue waters like a scene from a fairy tale. She gazed at the long bridges connecting Asia and Europe; the Süleymaniye and Blue Mosques, whose graceful minarets were silhouetted against the crimson horizon; the imposing outlines of Haghia Sophia and Topkapı, and, farther down, those of Dolmabahçe and the Çırağan Palace, as well as the many other grand buildings visible on either side of the channel. "Oh God, dear God!" she whispered in awe. The beauty of the scene before her, the splendid buildings displayed, as it were, on a crimson velvet cloth, vivid against the blackness of the night sky, caused her to weep until her face was wet with tears.

Yachts, full of beautifully dressed ladies and gentlemen sitting idly, sipping their drinks, went past them, and enormous Russian cargo ships from the Black Sea with flocks of screaming seagulls following in their wake. The breeze from the land, which brought with it scents of aniseed and fish, took Meryem's breath away.

When the ferry came alongside the landing on the other side of the strait, Meryem saw that the shore was lined with rowboats, in which fishermen were frying fish. "Fish sandwiches, delicious fish sandwiches!" they shouted.

"My God, what a world this is, full of so many wonders," she whispered again.

After punishing her for so long after the visit to Şeker Baba's tomb, had God forgiven her at last? Had all her sins been erased? Did God love her now?

What a tremendous confusion of water, people, ships, seagulls, mosques, brilliance, and noise it all was. The red and yellow lights of the cars on the coastline dazzled her eyes like shining comets as they moved along in an endless stream.

The ferry docked at the pier on the European side, and the passengers streamed out like a swarm of ants to mingle with the people in the ferryboat station. Everyone moved fast in this city. They walked quickly, spoke hurriedly, jumped off the boat, and ran off to their destinations. What was more, not one of them took the slightest interest in anyone else. They all followed each other off the boat like a great flock of sheep. Cemal grabbed Meryem's wrist to avoid losing her in the crowd or to gain courage from hanging on to her. It was not clear.

After stopping a few people and asking which bus went to their destination, Cemal bundled Meryem across the street, in front of numerous cars waiting at a traffic light, and pushed her onto a crowded red bus. Clutching their bags, they inched their way to the back, grabbing hold of each dirty iron upright as they went. The driver braked frequently in the heavy traffic, and Meryem and Cemal struggled not to fall over or bump into other passengers when it jerked forward again. Meryem could not understand how these people could be from Istanbul. They were different from most of the ones she had seen at the station or on the ferry. The men looked like peasants, and the elderly women all had their heads covered. She was relieved to see that there were also a few young women who dressed more freely.

Cemal tried to stifle the feeling of being without a point of reference, which caused him as much panic as it did Meryem, before turning his thoughts to his older brother, Yakup, about whom he felt both jealousy and apprehension. So this was the beautiful city he lived in. Yakup had not visited the village once since moving to Istanbul with his family. Perhaps he had even forgotten the name of his hometown. It was as if he were living in Istanbul like one of the sultans, and those left behind were his slaves, unworthy to be noticed. While Cemal had been fighting with death, enduring the freezing rain on the mountaintops for days on end, and pissing blood, his brother had been lording it here. The letters he wrote to his father, and the news he sent to the soldier on leave were boastful in tone, belittling his hometown, as though he thought himself superior because he lived in a new environment. His attitude made the people in the village curious and also aroused both their envy and their admiration.

Meryem was overcome with fatigue and excitement. The ferry she and Cemal had taken had crossed from one continent to another, from Asia into Europe. From time to time, she remembered how she had thought that Istanbul was just behind the hill near her village. How ignorant she had been. It was true no one had taught her anything. Being a child of misfortune, she had been shunned. Her head had been filled with old wives' tales and superstitions. But in the short time since leaving the village, she had already learned many new things.

The bus passed through traffic-choked thoroughfares, changed direction at streets leading off from squares, stopped many times, and finally entered a main road leading away from the city center. Only a few passengers remained, and Meryem and Cemal were able to sit down. Already exhausted, the motion of the bus made Meryem drowsy, her head fell forward, and she slept.

When she woke up, she noticed that the bus had stopped at a bus station. This was a very different Istanbul. Gloomy houses in a dilapidated condition surrounded the terminal. Here they were to board another bus, and when they had disembarked, Cemal asked the driver for directions.

The bus they boarded this time carried them farther away from the brilliant city, through dark fields flanked by decrepit houses. At each stop, as the magical city became more distant, Meryem's hopes and dreams faded a little more. She felt as if she was returning to the east of Anatolia. It was as if they had traveled two long days for nothing and had never left their town. The bus stopped in the darkness in the middle of a dreary field. The driver turned to Cemal, and said, "The directions you showed me told me to put you down in Rahmanlı. This is the bus stop for there."

They got off the bus, which soon disappeared down the road, exhaling oily smoke, leaving them alone in the dark night. The air smelled of crops, manure, and burning wood. After the first initial disorientation, the commando in Cemal took over. "That's where we must go," he said. "Come on."

They began to walk across the field along a muddy path. Meryem's plastic shoes sank into the sticky clay, reminding her of the walk through the village marketplace. She could hear the voices of the villagers. "Well, my girl, congratulations, you're off to Istanbul," they had said. "Good luck to you. Istanbul is a big city, not like this place."

"The villagers should come to Istanbul and see for themselves what it is like, especially this place where Yakup lives," Meryem thought. Compared to where they were, her home was like a palace. She had no idea where they would end up.

After walking for a time, Cemal noticed two men standing a short distance away in the dark. A familiar sense of danger overcame him. "Hey," he called out in warning, fearing that if they were soldiers, they might fire on them. He heard the familiar sound of guns being primed.

"Halt!" they shouted. "Who goes there?"

"I'm a soldier, too!" Cemal shouted back.

"Don't move!"

Turning on a flashlight, the two figures began to approach Cemal and Meryem.

Cemal could hardly believe what was happening. He felt as if he were approaching sentries in the Gabar Mountains. They would now ask for the password and shoot if he did not answer correctly.

As the men came nearer, Cemal realized that they were gendarmes. This meant that Cemal and Meryem were out of the zone of police jurisdiction, in other words, outside of Istanbul.

Without lowering their guns or flashlight, the gendarmes demanded their identity cards. Cemal tried to soften them down by a few joking remarks in his native dialect, but they remained unsmiling. When Cemal handed them his discharge certificate and ID card, the situation was strange. "So you were a commando," they said, in the tone of respect due to a senior combatant. What was a former commando doing in the middle of a field with luggage and a little girl at this time of night?

Cemal told them that they were going to visit his brother in Rahmanlı.

"Okay," said the gendarmes, "Rahmanlı is at the top of the hill, but you've come at a bad time."

That morning, the gendarmes had conducted an operation in Rahmanlı and discovered a Hizbullah "grave house." The neighborhood was under curfew now.

Cemal did not understand what the gendarmes meant by a "grave house," but he asked no further questions. Since the quarter was surrounded by soldiers and especially dangerous in the dark, the gendarmes decided to accompany Cemal and Meryem to Yakup's home. The smell and the rustle of their khaki uniforms made Cemal uneasy. He felt naked and useless as he had on the day he was discharged. His comrades, the fighting, the canteen food, the stacking of weapons, the ambushes, the cigarettes smoked under cover, and even the rain running down their necks into their uniforms, all suddenly rushed back into his mind. He felt nostalgic for his former life, even a kind of envy.

Meryem was overcome with surprise as she followed the gendarmes over the muddy field that sucked and dragged at her feet. What kind of a place was this city? Had they by any chance mistaken their directions?

They passed a sentry post, climbed the hill, and came to a place that looked like a large village full of gendarmes standing guard. Meryem thought that it was too wretched and dilapidated. All the houses were single-storied and poorly built. Rather than being plastered, some of the walls had tin plates nailed to them, and most had a chicken coop at the side. Television antennas sprouted from windows and roofs. Masses of raveled wires and cables hung between the houses. The whole miserable area was illuminated by streetlights. Filthy stray dogs were running all around, but there was nothing resembling a village square. The open space they were walking across was a sea of mud.

"This can't be Istanbul, it can't," Meryem thought glumly. She felt deceived. Clearly, God had not forgiven her. He did not love her. Furthermore, He was punishing her again. First, He had shown her the miraculous city of Istanbul, to stir up her excited hopes, then came the painful disappointment of this dark, muddy, filthy place.

When Yakup opened the door and saw Cemal and Meryem standing there beside the gendarme, he was speechless. His face changed color as if he had received a sudden blow. His wife, Nazik, soon appeared to prevent the soldiers from wondering if Yakup did, in fact, know the two strangers.

Yakup's house could hardly be called a home. It consisted of one tiny room in which thin mattresses were heaped in a corner, and a metal bedstead hung from the ceiling, through which snaked the cable for one naked electric lightbulb. Yakup's three children were sitting on the floor, eyes fixed on the television, the only thing that made the room look like any other home. They were too engrossed to rise to greet their uncle Cemal. The announcer was talking at the top of his voice. Even the barn at home was preferable to this hole, Meryem thought to herself, as well as being far cleaner.

Yakup was overcome with embarrassment. He asked halfheartedly after the health of his brother and of his relatives in the village.

Meryem followed Nazik to the back of the room, which served as a kitchen. Nazik was making soup, and Meryem immediately began to help by cutting the bread. Colored plastic buckets and basins were lying on the earthen floor. The plastic jerry cans lining one of the walls indicated that the house lacked running water.

"My, how you've grown. . . . You're ready for marriage," exclaimed Nazik. "But why in the world have you come here?"

"Nazik, is this Istanbul?" Meryem questioned instead of making a reply.

"To hell with Istanbul," Nazik exclaimed angrily.

"But is this place really Istanbul?" Meryem repeated.

"We're on the outskirts of the city. Istanbul is so big, it's difficult to say where it begins or ends. This is what is called a shantytown. The rich people live in the center of the city, but where would we get the money to live there? We can hardly even keep a foothold in this place."

Nazik began asking about her relatives and friends in the village as well as the latest gossip. She was homesick, but her husband, who had bragged so much about living in Istanbul, was reluctant to return home with his tail between his legs.

The house reverberated with the noise of the television. Cemal's nephew İsmet and niece Zeliha, whom he had known in the village, and a third child, who had been born in Istanbul, answered their uncle's questions with their eyes fixed on the television. They told him that yes, they went to school, but it took them more than half an hour, rain, sunshine, or snow, to walk there. Whether one called this place a village, a township, or part of the city, there was no school of any kind in Rahmanlı.

As Yakup was telling his brother about his life in this area, he mentioned in passing that gendarmes had raided a nearby house that day.

"Look!" İsmet suddenly burst out. "They're showing our neighborhood on the TV!"

All the mud and squalor of Rahmanlı was passing across the screen as the television cameraman panned the area, dogs snapping at people's heels as they contorted their faces and bodies to get themselves on camera. İsmet and Zeliha scanned the images excitedly, hoping to see themselves.

The television announcer stated several times that the operation in Rahmanlı had led to the discovery of a house belonging to Hizbullah, an Islamic fundamentalist terrorist organization, which rented houses and buried the corpses of their victims in the basements. That morning, authorities from the municipality had come to Rahmanlı to demolish an illegal building. In fact, all of the houses in the district were illegally constructed. Whoever wanted to put up a house would reach an agreement with the local mafia and build wherever they wished. Every now and then, the municipality would decide to get rid of a few of these shacks, leaving the majority untouched. Cemal learned later that 75 percent of the buildings in Istanbul, which had a population of almost 14 million people, were illegal.

When the authorities came to demolish a home, the owners would resist. Shrieking women would attack the officers with pots, pans, and sticks. Often, in a last reckless attempt to save their dwelling, a desperate father would catch up one of his children and climb up onto the roof, and, after dousing himself and the child with gasoline, threaten to set fire to himself and the child with the cigarette lighter in his hand if anyone came any nearer. While the authorities tried to persuade him to desist, the television cameras kept rolling, not missing a second of the tragic drama.

That morning, the residents of the house scheduled for demolition had exhibited a strange response. When the authorities informed the owner, a bearded man in baggy pants, that his building was about to be knocked down, he replied quite calmly, "Okay, but there are still people asleep here. Just give us half an hour so that we can gather up our things."

The official in charge had been so astonished by this unusual and unexpected reply that he immediately became suspicious and informed his superiors. His report was passed on to the gendarmerie, who were always on the alert whenever houses were torn down in this way. A short while later, a sergeant with two gendarmes came to the house to check the residents' IDs. He pounded on the door and shouted to those within to open up on the count of three or he would break the door down. At first there was no response. Then all of a sudden, gunfire erupted from inside the house, wounding the sergeant at the door. Everyone scattered in panic, and after taking cover, the two gendarmes returned fire. From inside the house came strange cries and a unified chorus of *"Allahuekber!"* Among the hubbub, the voice of a woman could be distinguished.

Reinforcements quickly arrived, and at the end of an hour-long battle, during which there were several casualties among the gendarmes, three men and an injured woman were dragged out of the house. Later, when it was discovered that the people in the house were Hizbullah militants, the basement was dug up, as the Hizbullah were known to use the ground floors of houses as graveyards for their victims.

In the basement, three corpses were found, one belonging to a middle-aged woman. Like other victims of the Hizbullah, they had probably been kidnapped, locked in a closet or chest for a while, interrogated and tortured, and finally strangled with steel wire in front of cameras. The bodies were found tied up in the manner known as "hog-tied" and buried on top of each other to conserve space.

The media reported that the Hizbullah had initially been organized as an Islamic/Kurdish alternative to the PKK, and in its first years had been under state protection. Eventually, the state either lost control of the group or no longer needed its help, so Hizbullah members were often raided in this way and their militants killed.

Suddenly, Zeliha saw herself on television and began to flap her arms and chirp like a little bird. She had been visible for only a few seconds, but that was enough to arouse İsmet's jealousy, especially as his friends from the area were now seen on the screen, excitedly explaining what had happened.

"If you hadn't been a soldier, they would never have let you come," Yakup said. "The district's blocked off. We ourselves, even, have trouble going in and out." It was obvious from his body language that he wished they had been stopped.

That night, the women and children slept in one corner of the room and the two brothers in the other. The folded piles of mattresses were spread out on the floor, quilts were placed over them, and Meryem soon fell into a deep sleep.

Yakup and Cemal smoked and chatted for a while before going to bed.

"Newcomers to Istanbul live in Rahmanlı," Yakup related. "Immigrants from different Anatolian cities live here side by side."

After a pause, he blurted out, "So now you've seen what a lousy life we lead."

"Brother," Cemal replied, "why do you stay? You were better off in the village. You had your own house, land, work . . . your kids didn't suffer. Why did you ever come here?"

"I was after a better life—a dream. 'The streets of Istanbul are paved with gold,' you know the saying, but it's not like that, of course.

For one thing, the people here in the city despise us as newcomers and do their best to put us down."

"Why don't you return to the village?"

"I can't. There's no going back. I won't let anyone make fun of me for not doing what I set out to do. And don't look at the state we're in now. In a few years, things may be completely different. At least, it will be better for the kids."

Yakup took a long drag on his cigarette and began to tell Cemal his dreams of how to get on in the big city. New immigrants could not find the means to live in the city at first, so they would choose a place outside the city limits, however far, so long as it was near a bus route. Even though the land belonged to the state, a local mafia controlled it and sold lots. It had taken Yakup's entire savings to buy a piece of property and build this small house, with the help of other immigrants from the same area of eastern Turkey. In order to get electricity, he had hooked up an illegal line to a nearby power cable. This was connected to the bed frame hanging from the ceiling. When the metal glowed red-hot from the current, the house warmed up like a Turkish bath.

All he needed to become the legal owner of the property was a little patience. Before each election, the government in power generally issued an amnesty for the residents of slums like Rahmanlı and sold them the official title deeds. One or two years after receiving the title deed, the owners often sold the property to a building contractor for several apartments in the new building to be constructed. Eventually, they would live in a beautiful apartment of their own, as well as receive rent from tenants. Once their capital had grown, they might open a kebab shop or a pizza place, or buy a taxi. Once the housing problem was solved, the rest was easy.

A few years ago, the district where Yakup's children went to school had been a slum. Now it had big modern buildings and shopping centers, traffic lights, and a flood of cars. Its residents had become wealthy after receiving the title deeds to their property. Undoubtedly, the same would happen to Rahmanlı in the future, and newcomers to Istanbul would have to go farther beyond Istanbul's limits to build their shanties. If Yakup persevered, İsmet, Zeliha, and their little sister, Sevinç, would lead a good life as citizens of Istanbul. That was why they put up with the miserable life they led at present.

Yakup could not explain all this to those in the village. Their thick heads would be unable to comprehend this kind of plan. In fact, he had promised himself that he would never go back to live among those ignorant people. They had no idea of life outside of their small town.

Cemal was confused. How could Yakup speak so bitterly and demeaningly of their village? "Brother," he said, "I'm sure you don't mean that, especially as our father may get to hear of this. You should be more careful."

"That father of ours!" Yakup exclaimed, looking sternly at Cemal.

Cemal did not understand what Yakup meant, but he felt that his older brother was harboring some grief from the past. He did not question him further.

It was Yakup's turn to ask questions. What was Cemal doing there? Why had he brought Meryem on such a long journey?

Cemal told him briefly that while he was serving in the military, Meryem had been defiled. She had to be gotten rid of in order to cleanse the family honor, and Cemal had been entrusted with this duty.

"Just like the other poor girls, you might say," Yakup said. "I know that when you live in the village, it seems the right thing to do, and it is practiced even here."

He did not look sad, surprised, or angry. Apparently, all that he wanted was for this sudden calamity to disappear. He did not care about the village, Meryem, Cemal, or his father. He just wanted them to stay out of his life.

Yakup had blotted his hometown from his memory. He would not go back there and would make sure that his children forgot they were from Suluca. In any case, he intended to remove their records from their hometown and reregister them in Istanbul. The thought that Zeliha could suffer the same fate as Meryem caused his hair to stand on end.

"Look, Cemal," he said, "you are certainly acting on our father's orders, and I know you're as much in awe of him as if he were God. It's pointless to ask you to change your mind, but if you're going to do it, do it right away."

Yakup then told Cemal about some tall, deserted viaducts on the highway about thirty minutes away on foot. Immigrants to Istanbul committed these ritual murders at such spots. A number of girls had been thrown to their deaths from the viaducts. The media had even reported some of the incidents.

Later, as Cemal lay on his thin mattress in the dark, he made a plan. He had to act quickly. After traveling so far, they had unluckily ended up in a place under gendarme surveillance. The longer they stayed there, the more familiar they would become, both to the residents and the authorities. If Meryem disappeared suddenly, suspicions would be aroused. The best thing to do would be to take Meryem to the viaduct early in the morning and fulfill his duty. If two people left the house and only one came back, that might look suspicious. He would not return to Yakup's—his brother's disrespect toward their father and the village had, in any case, offended him. He would go to visit Selahattin, then immediately board a train for Van. He would be back home with Emine in no time, and with honor restored to the family.

His brother's words seemed reasonable to him, especially since such events took place quite often at the viaduct. It would seem like an accident that the girl had fallen from the height.

When he had reached this decision, Cemal felt a sense of relief, and he soon fell into a peaceful sleep.

GOD ALONE EXISTS
IN SOLITUDE

THE PROFESSOR WOKE UP ONE DAY WITH A TER-
rible headache. He took two painkillers before going on deck. The sea
looked lifeless. Under an overcast sky, the water was gray, turbid, and
devoid of any motion—a sea of concrete. Friendly and flirtatious until
two days ago, the sea now looked as hard as a turtle shell, cold and
merciless, almost hostile.

İrfan had been familiar with the sea since childhood, and usually
was unaffected by its vast expanse or capricious behavior, but he was
shaken from a close encounter with death he had experienced two
days earlier. In order to escape from the impending storm that flashed
and thundered on the horizon, he had been making for the nearest
harbor with sails strained to such tautness that the monstrous force of
the wind could have easily ripped them to shreds. When he finally entered the harbor, İrfan realized that the wind there was just as violent,
and his boat was careering toward the shore at full speed. When the
owners of the boats in the marina saw his craft advancing on them at
such a pace, they began to wave and shout out warnings. İrfan himself
knew well that entering the harbor so fast could cause a disaster.

At that moment, he noticed a huge ship behind him that had entered from the other side of the harbor and was getting ready to dock.

When the sailboat appeared, sirens and whistles blew a deafening alarm. The panic of the people in the marina and the sight of the giant ship bearing down on him petrified İrfan. He had to slacken sail and approach his intended mooring place slowly, using the engine, but he could not do what was necessary all by himself because the pulley was stuck. If he let go of the rudder and ran to the sails, he would lose control of the boat. If he kept on steering, he would not be able to lower the sails, which were propelling the boat along too quickly. This was the problem of being a one-man crew. A second person would have made things much easier. İrfan knew that he had to make an immediate decision, for in a few seconds it would be too late.

Gathering all his courage, he let go of the rudder and threw himself in a death leap toward the sails. As he freed the tangled halyard at lightning speed, he felt a stabbing pain in his knee. He must have bumped it. The sails were down, but İrfan could not breathe. He had often heard the phrase, "his tongue cleaved to the roof of his mouth," and he had always thought it just a figure of speech, but now, this was really happening to him and no matter how hard he tried, he could not open his mouth and fill his aching lungs with air. Finally, he hung over the side of the boat and drank handfuls of the harbor's dirty water. He took a deep breath. Never before had he experienced such total fear.

He spent the night tied up in the marina, talking with the other sailors. When they realized he was sailing single-handed, they acknowledged that he had overcome great danger by acting in the correct manner. He was a good sailor, they said, but one should not play games with the sea. It was not right to sail alone in such a large boat.

The yachtsmen invited İrfan for a drink. Though most of them were gray-haired, they were all fit, athletic men, who spent their time repairing their boats, exchanging memories, and planning frequent regattas. İrfan noted that they did not talk about anything other than the sea. Throughout the evening, no other subject was discussed. It was as if the land did not exist for them. Their hands were callused like those of laborers. This one talked about the new GPS he had bought, while that one explained at length exactly how he had repaired his regulator. They were not interested in strangers, and naturally, they did not realize that this huge, unkempt man was the professor whom they might have seen on television. Or perhaps not. These men were not citizens of the Turkish Republic but of the Republic of the Sea—a republic with imperceptible borders but very definite laws. They never had difficulty in finding a wind to billow their flags. They spent most of their time among their fellow sailors and had the air of men who had no wives, mothers, fathers, or children.

That night, İrfan realized that for him the sea meant solitude. He had been sailing alone for many days, and the enthusiasm of his first days at sea was slowly being replaced by a peculiar melancholy. During nights spent in desolate coves, he had wondered what would happen if he fell and broke his leg or had a heart attack or suffered a stroke. As he sat alone by the kerosene lamp, absolute silence had enveloped him like the silence of death. If he faced a serious problem, he could do nothing but try to survive until someone found him, and finding him would be very difficult.

The sea was full of serious risks like the one he had overcome that day. He remembered the saying "God alone exists in solitude" and had to agree with the Anatolian sages who had said this so many hundreds of years ago.

At first, he had stayed away from the coast as much as possible, choosing the most deserted bays in which to spend the night, but now a secret drive was directing him toward the coastal towns and the small villages with their rickety landings. In such places, he always found a reason to visit the small grocery store, where he bought bread, sausages, or beer.

Was his life changing? Was change actually the freedom of shopping at old-fashioned groceries in small Aegean resorts, empty of tourists at this season, instead of the gourmet delicatessen in Istanbul? Could metanoia be defined as lying lazily on the deck day and night, watching the flying fish leap from below the surface, startling shoals of small fish that scattered in all directions through the turquoise water, as he listened to Jean-Pierre Rampal play the flute?

That night, for the first time, İrfan thought about going home. In fact, he did not think about it—one could not call this thinking—rather, he heard a barely audible voice inside him that troubled him greatly. He did not let the voice die away, for he wanted to confront it as it whispered to him, "Can you go back? Can you return to your old life, your old home, Aysel, the university, your friends, or your clever and very successful know-it-all of a brother-in-law? Can Istanbul be your Ithaca, you foolish professor?"

"No! I can't go back," he told himself. "I don't want to, and even if I did, they would all kill me."

İrfan knew very well how Aysel treated people who angered her. If he returned to Istanbul, everyone close to him, especially Aysel and her brother, would see him as the Devil and want to tear him to pieces. And no one would build a tomb for him.

İrfan recalled an afternoon spent with Aysel in a pleasant hotel room on a comfortable bed with starched white sheets and embroidered pillowcases. They had been very happy. It was as if no other couple had ever been as madly in love as they were. That day, Aysel had pushed him away from her warm, slender body at the climax of their lovemaking, crying, "Get away! Leave me alone!" He had been stunned, unable to decide what to do. He listened to Aysel's screams, not knowing what he had done wrong.

They had been staying in Scotland at the Turnberry Golf Hotel, which resembled an enormous birthday cake placed down on top of the moist, fertile earth, where manicured putting greens swept down to the sea. In the mornings, they would walk to the lighthouse, play golf in the afternoon, and go to the Edwardian bar, where they would sit toasting themselves in front of the fireplace, with its fire of oak logs, sipping Lagavulin whisky.

Until that day, everything had gone fine. After golf, before even taking her shower, Aysel had pulled İrfan into bed and pressed her slender body onto his like a lecherous clam. Then, at the highest peak of their lovemaking, she had pushed him away. He had felt like a student, punished by being sent to stand on one foot outside the door.

Having gained enough experience to stay away from Aysel at such moments, İrfan had taken a quick shower and left the room. He had gone downstairs to the bar, where mahogany, morocco leather, and noble coats of arms reigned supreme. A few minutes after he ordered a drink, Aysel came and sat next to him on the green leather chesterfield. "I'm sorry," she said. She was calmer but still tearful, apologizing to him once again. İrfan was used to this habit of hers. If he responded, her madness would intensify, but if he kept silent, stayed away, and ignored her insults, she would calm down and come to apologize.

He could not understand her fury. Sipping his whisky, he had racked his brains to comprehend his mistake: an inappropriate joke while playing golf, an act of rudeness at the hotel, a word, a glance? He could remember nothing to cause this outburst. "You don't have to apologize, darling," İrfan said. "We must forgive each other, but I really don't understand. What happened? Everything was going so well."

Aysel glanced at him helplessly. "It's difficult to explain," she said. "Sometimes you make love to me because you feel you have to. You're a strong, clean, healthy man, but you don't enjoy making love to me. Even at that moment of extreme pleasure, I realized without a shadow of a doubt that you weren't enjoying it."

İrfan tried to raise an objection, but Aysel silenced him. "I'm not blaming you," she said. "But a woman knows. You make love as if you're playing golf." Then she gave a brittle laugh as if she wanted to lighten the atmosphere, and asked him to order a drink for her.

The subject had been sealed. They continued to make love, though less frequently. Aysel felt that she was facing a fact too serious to be changed by rebelling against it and felt scared, like a little girl lost in a great forest.

After so many weeks on the sea, the boat meant solitude for İrfan—a loneliness that would last forever. He wondered how a man would feel who, after dreaming of happiness and success all his life, suddenly realized toward the end of it that he had long ago missed his opportunity. Would his dreams collapse? Yes, of course! Maybe that was why his heart felt so heavy sometimes with the weight of such morbid feelings.

He thought often of the emptiness of his life. Although from being an indigent student in Izmir, he had gone on to study at Harvard, he had not succeeded in creating anything noteworthy. His life had been spent in vain. After he died, he would not leave anything behind about which people would say: "This is İrfan Kurudal's work." All he had achieved was the flimsy book he had written for his professorship.

İrfan had been considering an interesting subject for a book. For years, he had been researching, while waiting for the right moment to start writing it. He knew he would never find a better place finally to start his project than on this boat.

His book would be about the Bogomils. A gnostic Christian sect of the eleventh century, the Bogomils had first appeared in Samosata in eastern Anatolia, the hometown of the great, ancient writer, Lukianos.

The Bogomils' dogma had disturbed the orthodox church so much that they had been forced to leave Samosata and go to Alaşehir in the Aegean region. Unable to establish themselves there either, they emigrated to southern France via Marseille, where they built Montsegur Castle. They were known as the Cathar Knights, until the French army forced them to leave after the famous Montsegur siege. The Bogomils fled in many directions, some to Italy and others to the Balkans. According to some historians, the Bosnians in the Balkans were descended from the Bogomils. They had converted to Islam in order to escape from the tyranny of the Church.

If this theory were true, the Bogomils had met a terrible fate. As heretic Christians they had suffered for hundreds of years in eastern Anatolia, finally converting to Islam on arriving in the Balkans. Then, in Bosnia, they were persecuted and killed by Milosevic's forces for being Muslims. They believed in the wrong religion in the wrong place at the wrong time, a mistake they had persisted in for a thousand years. Theirs was a nine-hundred-year story, beginning in Samosata and extending all the way down through the ages until the war in Bosnia. Writing the story would be involving work if only İrfan could start writing it.

One day, after mooring the boat at the big tourist town of Kuşadası, he bought many books related to the subject, but something prevented him from reading them. He seemed unable to pick up his pen and begin to write.

Perhaps it was impossible for him to get inside the story as long as he was on the Aegean Sea. If he went to eastern Anatolia and talked to people there, studied their faces, habits, and traditions, then, perhaps, he could become immersed in his project.

İrfan knew that these thoughts were futile, because a bloody war was going on in the east and he doubted that it would be possible to go there for many years. In spite of having been to many foreign countries, he would probably die before seeing the eastern part of his own. Better to surrender to the sweet, offshore breeze, watch the wine-colored sea and merely daydream about his book on the Bogomils. Maybe in the coming days, the first sentence would appear, and the rest would follow.

At a town where he had stopped to buy some food, İrfan happened to see a lean-to teahouse under the cool shadow of some old plane trees. After he sat down, the owner came over and said to him in English, "Hello! Tea, coffee?"

İrfan's height and long beard had caused the man to mistake him for a foreigner. İrfan did not bat an eyelid but answered in English, "Turkish coffee—with only a little sugar, please."

The man recognized the word "coffee" but not the rest. He struggled to understand. "Sugar?"

"Just a little," İrfan replied.

The man thought that İrfan wanted his coffee without sugar, and asked again to make sure. "No sugar?" His eyebrows had risen way up.

İrfan shook his head.

Thinking that a better knowledge of English was needed, the owner called his son.

"Come here," he shouted. "This unbeliever is trying to tell me something."

İrfan was enjoying himself. Obviously, this man, like all the other shopkeepers, had learned a few words of English, like tea and coffee, but nothing else.

A slim youth appeared.

"Welcome!" he greeted İrfan, who repeated his order. The young man said to his father, "He wants Turkish coffee with a little sugar."

The man cursed. "Why don't you say so, you son of a bitch!" He was a corpulent man and beads of sweat were rolling down his face.

"He said what he wanted, Father," said the boy.

"Shut up and stop trying to show off, just because you've learned a few words of English!" the man roared.

A few minutes later, he brought İrfan's coffee.

"You tourist?" he asked İrfan.

"Yes, tourist."

"American?"

"American," the professor replied.

The shop owner's face lit up.

"Come here!" he summoned his son again. "Ask him if he'd like to buy some land around here."

The young man paused. "He came here for a cup of coffee. Why ask him that?"

"Don't interfere," the man scolded his son. "Last summer an American came here and paid cash down for Nevzat's fig orchard.

These people come here to buy land. What else would they come for?"

The lad made a tremendous effort and said, "You want . . . You want . . ."

İrfan realized that the young man's English was limited and that he did not know how to say "land," but to prevent him from being humiliated in front of the father, and also to tease him a little, he asked, "Are you lonesome tonight?"

He was sure that the young man knew Elvis's famous song.

The young man looked at İrfan suspiciously.

His father kept repeating, "What did he say?"

The young man lied. "He's not interested in land. He said he's going to drink his coffee and go."

"There's a very nice piece of land by the seaside," the owner insisted. "Ask him if he'd like to see it."

With great difficulty, the young man said, "She loves you yeah, yeah, yeah!"

İrfan could hardly contain his laughter. He was right. The young man had probably never gone to a language school but had spent his time hanging around in front of tourist bars in order to strike up an acquaintance with foreign girls. So, of course, he knew the names of all the songs.

"It's now or never," İrfan said. Then, thinking that a single sentence would sound too short, he quickly added, "Tomorrow will be too late!"

The young man turned to his father, and said, "He says that he's only here to travel. He's not interested. I'm off."

"Stop right there!" his father ordered. "I've spent a bundle of money sending you to English courses. Ask him if he has any friends who would like to buy land."

Unable to look into his eyes, the young man said, "Un, dos, tres, Maria! Chikki chikki, bum bum!"

İrfan nearly burst out laughing. After getting by in English, it was now time to shift to Spanish.

Taking the game a step further, İrfan said seriously, "Cindy Crawford, Linda Evangelista, Eva Herzigova, Letitia Casta."

The young man answered with an even more serious air, "Sharon Stone, Claudia Schiffer, Madonna."

The young man's father was following the conversation intently. It seemed like a long one. Perhaps, like Nevzat, he was in for a streak of good luck. He would be in clover if this foreigner bought the useless plot of land he had inherited from his father.

When the young man finished speaking, his father asked him, "What did he say?"

"He said that he's only here to travel around and that he's tired of our questions. He asked you to leave him alone. He also said that if you keep it up, he'll lodge a complaint."

The plump man muttered, ". . . ucking infidel. So he'll make a complaint against me in my own country. I wouldn't sell him land now even if he begged me to. Tell him to finish his coffee and get the hell out of here!"

"Okay."

Then the boy turned to İrfan and said, "Cicciolina, bye bye!" before retreating along with his father.

İrfan was amused.

After finishing his coffee, he paid the bill and stood up to leave. In Turkish he said, "Thanks. Keep the change."

The teahouse owner's eyes popped out of his head, and his son's face turned crimson. Wishing he might disappear, he kept his eyes fixed on the ground.

When İrfan returned to his boat, he was still laughing, pleased by the unexpected delight these few minutes had brought him.

IS THIS WHAT DEATH
IS LIKE?

W HEN OBSERVED FROM THE UNFINISHED, DESO-late viaduct, the view of Istanbul presented a picture of misery, a scattered, mournful city, like the ruins left behind by a defeated army. It extended into the distance like a wounded giant—and all out of proportion, deformed.

No glimpses of the glamorous temples of the Paleologues, combining the form of the basilica with that of the dome, of the Ottoman mosques with their triple-balconied minarets, of the cheerful messages spelled out by festive Ramadan lights strung between these minarets, of Catholic or Orthodox churches, of imperial galleys with forty banks of oars, or of the palaces with porphyry columns, which transformed the Bosphorus with their brilliance, could be seen in this part of Istanbul.

This was a city distorted by immigration, its tissues swollen and its joints displaced. Under a gloomy, gray sky, drizzle and yellow haze blurred the outlines of jerry-built concrete-block shantytowns, green spaces saved from the axe either because they were military zones or cemeteries, and the distant skyscrapers.

On this wet, unpleasant Istanbul day, the two thin figures standing on the half-built, high concrete bridge paid no attention to the city, or the drizzle, or the occasional lightning flash or crack of thunder that livened up the dismal scene. This was any one of many unfinished bridges and roads around Istanbul, abandoned once the rapacious construction companies in league with a few ambitious bureaucrats had made sufficient profit from illegal deals and shoddy workmanship.

When Meryem looked down, she saw an enormous empty space stretching away beneath her toward a rocky piece of ground. It reminded her of the precipice in her dream, which had made her inmost being shiver and prompted her to take shelter from the coastal wind. This time, it was not the birds flying above, but Cemal, standing silently behind her like a serpent, who made her blood freeze.

Early that morning, Meryem had been woken abruptly and bundled out of the house. The way they had left Yakup's house at dawn without bidding a proper farewell, the absence of Yakup himself, the expression of terror on Nazik's face, and Cemal's implacable attitude indicated that the fate she had tried for so long to ignore was about to overtake her.

As they walked along the road wet with rain, then through muddy fields, Meryem realized that the day of reckoning had arrived. Cemal had taken his own bag but left hers behind at Yakup's house, suggesting that Meryem would no longer need that ragged bag or the few pieces of frayed clothing. She understood now the real reason for their sudden journey to Istanbul.

Now, here she was, trembling on the edge of the precipice, waiting to be thrown down like a used tissue. She recalled the fat, oily faces of the village women, who had grinned and wished her good luck in Istanbul. She remembered the hens she and Cemal had thrown into the air, to make them fly like airplanes. It was as if she had to review every small detail of her short life. She recalled how the birds' feet and wings had been broken. "I'm so sorry," she thought. "Cemal, are you sorry, too? Did you ever think about those hens? They hadn't far to fall. It's higher here—so high. Is Istanbul always so deserted and lonely? I'm cold, Cemal. My dress is wet. My back is freezing. Actually it's not the cold that is making me shiver, but fear. Have you ever felt such fear, Cemal? I have no wings to flap like that crow flying away over there. I can't look down while flying as it can, my heart would stop. God, why don't you love me? Why have you gone on punishing me ever since the day I was born? Cemal, God doesn't love me. He loves you. Why doesn't he love me? Forgive me, Şeker Baba. I didn't sin on purpose. My aunt with the stony heart, who shut the door in my face, didn't warn me. If God had only loved me just a little . . ."

Meryem did not know whether she was thinking those words inside her head or saying them aloud. Dizzy and nauseated, she felt her stomach contract each time she looked into the void. Her belly perceived its depth, and gravity exerted its pull.

Suddenly, she heard Cemal say, "Say your prayers and show you believe in God."

He did not sound angry, and his voice was surprisingly soft. The warmth in his tone encouraged Meryem to turn around to look at him, but Cemal caught her by the shoulders and forced her to face the drop.

"Show that you believe in God," he said again. "After committing so many sins, at least say your prayers before you stand in front of Him."

After she had chanted three times in a loud voice the Islamic confession of faith: *"Eşhedü en la ilahe illallah, Muhammeden resulullah,"* the sudden, total silence made Meryem desperate. There was nothing more she could do now. God, who had never loved her, was punishing her for the last time, and here she was at the edge of this fearful drop. Cemal was merely the means, a wretched murderer fulfilling God's will that Meryem be punished.

"Cemal," said Meryem, the courage and determination in her voice startling even herself. "Cemal, I have one last wish to ask you, for the sake of the times we shared together in the past. Please blindfold me. I don't want to see the rocks when I fall. Please, I beg you, blindfold me." Her words ended with a hiccup and a sob.

Cemal did not answer, but then she heard the sound of his feet approaching over the loose gravel as he drew near, loosened her scarf, and tightly blindfolded her with it. Finally, he knotted its ends at the back of her head. She shuddered when she felt Cemal's warm breath on her bare neck. The scarf hurt her eyes, but she felt better now that she could not see the world around her. She began to sway backward and forward as though she were about to fall.

The tranquillity that had enveloped Meryem when talking to Cemal a few minutes ago was replaced by the agitated beating of her heart and a ringing in her ears. Her breath came in pants, and the blood rushed to her head. Terror was like a bird flapping its wings inside her chest. All she could hear was the ringing in her ears. The entire city of Istanbul was buried in silence.

Meryem tried to think of all the good people in her life. She tried to picture her mother's face, yet she could do no more than imagine a vague white shadow standing with a lamp in her hand at the door of her bedroom at the top of their house. She had never been able to imagine her mother any differently.

Then she tried to think of Bibi. She remembered the hurt look in the old woman's eyes and how she had begged her forgiveness.

Meryem realized that thinking of people who had never harmed her increased her fear, whereas thinking about Döne or her aunt aroused her anger. She could not help remembering the hens lying on the ground with broken legs and bloody wings.

As Meryem lost herself in her memories, Cemal was preparing to shove her over the edge. It was then that he saw a single transparent bead of perspiration, as if her mortal fear had condensed into a single drop, trickling down her delicate neck. "She's afraid to die," he thought. The smooth, lucent drop resembled rainwater. What a frail neck the girl had. He noticed a few strands of auburn hair blowing in the breeze. Then he realized that Meryem was no longer able to control her breathing. Her chest and shoulders were heaving involuntarily.

That morning, after leaving Yakup's house and walking through the fields, Cemal had felt as though he were being chased by the PKK terrorists. His shoes sank deep into the mud, and he walked quickly, as he had been trained to do in the army. He could keep this pace up for hours and walk a whole day and night without rest, but soon he realized that the girl with him was out of breath, and though she had broken into a run, the distance between them was widening. He heard her stumble and fall more than once, but she always got up again and struggled to keep up with him. Finally, he had slowed down.

Since the beginning of their journey, Cemal had felt he must remain emotionally unattached to the girl. This was not through cruelty but the attitude of a predator. His instincts told him that Meryem must remain a stranger to him, so he had tried to suppress all memories related to their childhood. Now he heard the girl's fitful breathing as she stood there with her back to him. He noticed the goose bumps on her neck, and smelled a mixture of cinnamon and dried roses when the breeze blew from her direction.

Cemal's resolve began to waver. He could not help remembering her childish giggles when they played games, her illnesses, the way they had rolled hoops together and climbed trees to look at birds' nests. Slowly, Meryem was transformed into the little girl Cemal used to know so well. He remembered how they would pull the horse cart backward into the courtyard. He could smell the bitter scent of honeydew melons piled in a corner. He remembered how he and Meryem used to break open the unripe melons by hitting them against a big stone and devour them as the juice poured down their chins. Once, during the Liberation Day celebrations, Memo, who was acting the part of a Turkish soldier, had bruised Cemal's temple with his gun. Meryem had ground up some hemp seeds, wrapped them in cloth, and rubbed them on Cemal's forehead.

When Cemal realized that his wall of resistance was starting to cave in, he immediately focused his thoughts on Meryem's sin.

In the military, they had taught him to focus on the idea that the enemy was "inhuman." Now, the girl in front of him was not the girl he knew as a child but a soiled, sinful woman, who had discredited his family. His family could not survive such shame. For centuries, this crime had been dealt with and punished in the same way. This was God's will. It was his father's will. No one could defy God's rules. Besides, this sinful girl was the only obstacle standing between him and Emine.

As he prayed *"Bismillahirrahmanirrahim!"* he suddenly remembered a previous Feast of Sacrifice. As a small boy, his father had ordered him to cut the throat of a blindfolded sheep. Then, too, he had prayed before the killing.

He collected himself and repeated, *"Bismillahirrahmanirrahim!"* Three more droplets of perspiration rolled down Meryem's white neck. They were smaller and rolled faster. He could hear the girl's troubled breathing. As a whistling sound came out of Meryem's throat, Cemal foamed with rage—vile creature, bitch, disgraceful, disgusting, filthy, sinful thing!

Then, with all the violence of the pain inside of him, he hit her.

Uttering a wild scream, Meryem reeled from the blow and tumbled down into blackness, not knowing what was happening. She felt herself hit the ground with a thud. The taste of mud filled her mouth. One side of her head felt numb.

After a few seconds, she could feel the wetness of the cold ground on which she lay. Her eyes were blindfolded, but she realized that she could still breathe. Oddly, she did not feel any pain except on the left side of her face. The oppressive silence had disappeared, to be succeeded by the sound of distant traffic and calls to prayer.

Meryem lay motionless, afraid to breathe. Then she slowly removed the scarf from in front of her eyes and saw wet concrete and ugly stones beneath her cheek. Cemal was squatting down three feet away.

Suddenly, it was as if the sun had risen inside of her. Her heart lifted, like a rainbow appearing after a day full of black clouds.

She was not dead. The way Cemal was crouching on the ground implied that she was no longer about to die. Cemal would not kill her now, and nor would anyone else.

Meryem had finally defeated her family, who had closed their doors against her and sent her out to die. Their plans to get rid of her had all been in vain.

She sat up with a triumphant expression on her face and walked toward Cemal, without even thinking about her aching cheek, now going purple from the blow.

Cemal was squatting on the ground, rocking backward and forward with his arms wrapped around his knees. It was he who was in pain now, not Meryem.

Meryem bent over Cemal with such a feeling of self-confidence and compassion that the protective energy flowing out from this young girl was almost palpable.

She touched him on the shoulder. "Come on, Cemal. Let's go. There's no need to stay here getting wet."

It did not seem strange to address him in such an authoritative way, though up to that day, she would have not thought it possible to speak to him like that.

Cemal pushed Meryem's hand away roughly, but then, like an obedient child, stood up and began to walk away slowly without looking at her. This time, Meryem could easily keep up with him. He no longer strode in front of her like a mountain commando but trudged along slowly and wearily. Overwhelmed by gratitude and compassion,

Meryem wrapped the faded headscarf around her head like a triumphal banner.

As she walked along the muddy roads of the deplorable district where hundreds of electric cables festooned the houses like dry creepers, Meryem was sure that, although Yakup and Nazik would be stunned when she and Cemal returned together, they would act as if nothing had happened.

And so they did. After the first few moments of silence, the children, the television, the Hizbullah operation, and many other irrelevant subjects were discussed until the tension in the air disappeared, and everyone felt relieved. Even the purple swelling on Meryem's left cheek apparently went unnoticed.

Yakup and Nazik were aware of everything that had happened, but the children were utterly lost in their own world ruled by the television. They sat cross-legged on the floor with their eyes glued to the screen. Even when they spoke to each other or replied to their parents' questions, their eyes remained fixed on the magic box. They knew everything about chocolate of all kinds, different brands of olive oil, credit cards, automobiles, newspapers, chewing gum, banks, washing detergent, and margarine, and had learned by heart all the advertising jingles. They participated in this ritual of watching the television with great eagerness, determined not to miss a single program, commercial, sitcom, or whatever else might be shown to them.

Watching television was not allowed in Meryem's home. Although she had seen it once or twice at a friend's, she had never watched it enough to become addicted. Now, she saw that Yakup and his family seemed to live in a world of television, as though they thought of their own lives as something temporary that had to be endured. The children knew the names of all the television personalities and their characters better than those of their own relatives. They would sing along with a bottle blonde who barked rather than sang and imitate the dancing of an excessively painted lady.

When a showman pointed his finger at the camera, and shouted, "Ay-ay, ay-ay," the children in turn would point their fingers at the screen and scream, "Ay-ay, ay-ay!"

This was a world that was totally foreign to both Cemal and Meryem.

According to the television, the weather, which had remained rainy for much of the week, was about to become colder, due to a low-pressure system coming from the Balkans. Hanging from the ceiling, the red-hot metal bedstead, through which Yakup illegally channeled electricity,warmed them like a desert sun.

"You look miserable," Nazik said to Meryem. "Let me give you something else to wear. If we wash your dress now, it'll be dry by tomorrow." At the same time, she squeezed Meryem's hand, and whispered, "I'm so glad," convincing Meryem that Nazik was a good person.

Nazik looked older than her age. She had to carry home water from the public fountain some distance away, take care of three kids, clean other people's houses four days a week, and work overtime under Yakup at night in bed.

As she lay on her pallet that evening, Meryem contemplated all that had happened that day. She tried to understand why Cemal had felt helpless enough to content himself with only hitting her, but she fell asleep without an answer.

Early the next morning, after Cemal had left with Yakup, the two children had gone to school, and the baby had been consigned to the care of a neighbor, Nazik and Meryem set off for the city center.

"I've got something to do there," said Nazik. "Come along, and you can have a look at Istanbul," and added, "I know you're wondering where we're going in the blue bus. I'm going to have an abortion. Yakup doesn't want to use condoms, so I always end up at the midwife's place. I can't remember how many times I've been there."

Meryem asked her once again why she went through all this trouble for the sake of living in Istanbul.

"Yakup doesn't listen to me," replied Nazik. "He's obsessed with this contemptible city. He keeps saying that he wants to bring his children up here."

Meryem was wearing a blue dress and a scarf with brown and yellow flowers that Nazik had given her. Her own scarf and threadbare dress, which had endured so much sweat and anguish, had been washed and hung out to dry. She felt awkward in someone else's clothes.

Meryem studied the surroundings from the window of the bus. Even though the bus passed through many neighborhoods, Meryem saw nothing that resembled her picture of Istanbul. A while later, she saw some buildings that resembled those in the small city she had seen in the East. The ground floors of the buildings were occupied by greengrocers, barbers, and electricians.

At one of the stops in a certain neighborhood, the bus driver's assistant called out, "Midwife's stop!" Many women got off the bus.

"This stop used to have a different name," Nazik explained, "but now everyone calls it the midwife's stop."

They entered an old building that smelled of gas, boiled cabbage, and mold. Many muddy pairs of shoes—men's, women's, and children's— were piled up in front of the doors outside the apartments on each floor.

Nazik rang the bell of one of the apartments on the third floor. A plump woman with a large black mole on her cheek showed them in to the waiting room. It was crowded, and Meryem felt a little afraid as she glanced at all the women waiting their turn.

The women wore strange clothes like none Meryem had ever seen before. Most of them were bundled up in black garments that concealed every part of their bodies, except for the eyes. Some had covered the top half of themselves in large shawls or even blankets, which hung all the way down below their waists. Gradually feeling more secure among other women, they relaxed and began to remove some of their wrappings.

"These women often have to have abortions," said Nazik, "because their husbands don't like to use condoms—just like Yakup. And the pill causes cancer, they say. That's why this place is always so full. The women come out of the surgery after five minutes, go back home, and cook dinner for their husbands. They constantly complain about being beaten by their men. It makes you want to vomit."

Meryem listened attentively to a conversation about being beaten. These women, who hid themselves under thick layers of clothing and kept away from strangers, were talking excitedly about the brutality they experienced at home. Sharing their stories with others seemed to relieve their feelings. Only one woman had a different twist to her story. Her young, beautiful face was blue, one of her eyes was swollen, and she had a cut on her lip. Embarrassed, she quietly shared her experience.

The day before she had had an abortion and had come back today to pay for it. Her husband had beaten her for the first time last night.

Yesterday, when all the other women had been exchanging stories about their beatings, she had told them that she was newly married and that her husband, who loved her dearly, would never mistreat her by giving her as much as a pinch. That evening, an acquaintance of the young woman, who had overheard her, had told her own husband about the boastful newlywed. He, in turn, had scolded the young woman's husband in front of everyone at the neighborhood teahouse for not beating his wife. "What kind of a man are you," he had said, "if you don't beat your wife and fancy letting her brag about it at the midwife's!"

The young woman's husband, whose pride was injured, had then gone home and punched his wife in the face. "You've ruined my reputation!" he shouted as he beat her.

"He can't really bring himself to harm me," the young woman said. "He was affected by the others. He wouldn't do it otherwise. He loves me too much. When we're alone, he calls me his little dove. It was the other men who led him astray."

After hearing her say this, Meryem thought the woman would probably have to endure another beating that night. Her swollen face and rapidly blackening eye had made these women, shrouded in black, with their white, double chins quivering in sympathy, consider that she, too, shared the secrets of their fate. Of course, in public they would seem sorry for her, but behind her back they would say, "Serves her right." This was only natural—whoever is badly treated wants everyone else to be treated badly, too. But those dull women did not know that the purple bruise on Meryem's cheek was the sign of her victory.

Soon it was Nazik's turn to go into the surgery. Before long, she came out, looking shaken and dazed. After she rested on a chair for a short while, they left the midwife's apartment and took the bus home. Nazik remained silent throughout the trip, and Meryem, afraid of upsetting her, did not ask any questions. Though the ways of God could not be questioned, Meryem realized that He did not love Nazik either.

Suddenly, Meryem shook with a sob that welled up from deep inside her, and she began to weep hysterically. Tears poured down her cheeks, and the people in the seats in front turned around to look at her. Nazik shook her by the shoulders and said something, but Meryem did not hear her. Pulling herself together enough to dry her eyes on the edge of her scarf, she bent forward, forcing herself to stop, but her frail shoulders continued to heave. Every now and then, a muffled sound like the cry of a kitten could be heard. She had no idea why she was crying, but no matter how hard she tried, she could neither stop nor suppress the feelings surging up in her heart, not even when they got off the bus and began to walk home over the field.

When they came near their neighborhood, Meryem noticed that Nazik was in pain and having difficulty walking. Feeling thoroughly ashamed of herself, she stopped weeping and tried to help her.

As they entered the house, Nazik hugged Meryem and said, "It had to be like this, Meryem. It's a good thing you cried. You've been like a stone ever since you came here."

QUESTIONS AND ANSWERS

After Cemal had smashed his fist into Mery-em's face, a paralyzing feeling of helplessness had overwhelmed him as the rain spat down on them.

Where was he to hide the girl he had been ordered to kill? Now that he had spared her, her desire to live would become even stronger. What could he do with her?

All night long, he pondered over this problem, as the raindrops beating on the roof dripped into the plastic buckets placed here and there. The only solution he could think of was to get on a train and go back to his village and Emine.

At dawn, Cemal leapt out of bed with the thrill of having discovered an answer to his problems. He woke up Yakup and said, "I'm leaving. If I'm lucky, I'll catch the morning train. Good-bye."

He was lying. First he would find Selahattin, and after spending a few days with him, he would leave for his village. He would remain tight-lipped about Meryem. Everyone in the village had observed his silence. The villagers would respect his unwillingness to discuss the subject. Besides, it would not be in anyone's favor to probe.

All of a sudden, he heard Yakup say gruffly, "Wake Meryem up, too."

"Brother," Cemal said, "you know I can't take her back. Let her stay here for a while. She gets along well with Nazik. She can help with the housework."

Yakup looked at him grimly. "That's not possible," he said. "I can't feed another mouth. Besides, I left the village to stay away from trouble, but you searched me out and brought it with you. Get off my back! Leave us alone, for heaven's sake."

His tone was resolute, and Cemal was surprised to realize how much his brother hated his family and his hometown. He also understood that his plan would not work.

That morning, when Yakup left home, he went with him. Yakup worked as a waiter in a kebab restaurant downtown. He could have found a better-paying job, but he had plans. The kebab business was profitable. Every day, a new restaurant owned by a person who had formerly been a waiter opened its doors. After working in a kebab restaurant, people learned such crucial details as where to buy meat, how to cook the meat by stacking it on a large, vertical spit, and how much to pay a good kebab cook. Once they had mastered this lore, they were in a good position to set up on their own.

Yakup was eager to have his own kebab place. When the first one was up and running, he could open another restaurant of the same type. After five years or so, he might end up owning three restaurants. The place where he worked now was always filled with customers. There were tables inside, as well as a booth opening on the street to sell sandwiches to passersby. All day long, customers were served from trays of all sorts of kebabs, or ate fried meatballs coated with cracked wheat and served with pita and glasses of buttermilk or beet juice. Yakup was determined to succeed in his ambition and provide a good future for İsmet, Zeliha, and Sevinç. They would not share the dismal fate of those condemned to live in his hometown but would go to good schools in Istanbul, far away from the outdated traditions and the harsh and unhappy life of the east. Every day he vowed that he would realize this dream.

As they parted, Yakup gave Cemal directions to the wholesale fish market. It was not hard for Cemal to find the market, which had the same crazy, crowded, nauseating atmosphere that Cemal had noticed the first day he arrived in Istanbul. Fishing boats were constantly coming and going. Nets spread out on the breakwater gave off strange smells, and thousands of fish poured like silver rain out of the returning boats while screaming seagulls flew madly above. Vendors in blue aprons constantly kept the fish, arranged on red wooden trays, fresh by sprinkling water over them, and called out in loud voices to attract customers. Fat cats crouched in corners, working out ways to steal the fish they had their eyes on. Doubtful customers handled the fish to see if the gills were still red and looked into their dead eyes to catch a last glimpse of life in order to reassure themselves that the fish were freshly caught. The ground everywhere was sodden, constantly washed down with a hose, no one showing the least concern as to who got wet.

Cemal stopped a few people to show them Selahattin's card and ask for directions, but since he, in ignorance, chose customers first, they could not tell him. Finally, the first fisherman he asked pointed him toward a distant fish stall.

As Cemal walked through the crowd, he wondered why people in Istanbul behaved so oddly. When they spoke, they never looked you in the eye. They answered your questions reluctantly and only after you asked them several times.

The young fishermen at the fishmonger's stall were sprinkling water from plastic buckets over their trays of fish and yelling at the top of their lungs, "Bluefish, turbot! Fresh fish! Come and get it!"

After confusing Cemal with a customer and praising their wares, they told him that Selahattin was in the office at the back.

The reunion of the two friends, who had shared a bunk for many months, was warmer than Cemal had expected. When Selahattin stood up to embrace him, Cemal realized that the bullet must have hit the joint since Selahattin limped and could not straighten his knee. Selahattin had gained weight. His face was round, and with his thin moustache, he seemed quite different from when he was in the army.

Selahattin seated Cemal in an armchair and ordered him a glass of tea, while many people came in and out of the office accompanied by the constant ringing of the phone on the table. At the same time, he answered the phone and took care of customers. He smiled and gestured to Cemal, apologizing for the disturbance. "This must be an important place," thought Cemal, and realized that his friend, who had been his equal in the army, had a higher status now. He felt embarrassed.

Selahattin took Cemal for lunch to a small tradesmen's restaurant, where he introduced him to many people as his "comrade from the military." One of the boys working at the fish stand was Selahattin's brother. He accompanied them to the restaurant, and they all ate together, chatting and joking about their life in the army.

When they returned to the office in the afternoon, Cemal several times tried to take his leave, but Selahattin would not let him go. "No," he said, "we're going home together."

At the end of the day, they got into Selahattin's Honda and drove to a district of narrow roads and high apartment buildings. Selahattin's apartment was on the second floor of one of these buildings.

A young woman, very tidy and clean in appearance, her head covered with a headscarf, opened the door. "Your sister-in-law," said Selahattin, introducing his wife.

"Welcome," she said, though she did not take Cemal's outstretched hand, indicating her strict religious convictions.

Cemal thought Selahattin's apartment was the most magnificent home he had ever seen. He had never seen so much furniture in one house. There were so many white-painted, gilded armchairs and carved, inlaid coffee tables that there was hardly any space to move around. When Selahattin saw Cemal's obvious admiration, he said with pride, "Oh, these, they're Lukens." Cemal had never heard of Lukens so had no idea what he meant, though the "Louis Quinze" style was the most popular in Turkey at that time.

The television in a walnut-paneled cabinet was tuned to a religious channel, where a woman in a headscarf was holding forth. Besides the carpets on the floor, there were more carpets on the wall, one depicting "Holy Mecca" and another an exciting deer hunt. All of the furniture, including the television, was covered with handmade lacework, probably part of the trousseau prepared for Selahattin's wife. A crystal chandelier hanging from the ceiling illuminated all this splendor.

Cemal feared that the difference in status between Selahattin and himself was turning into a huge gulf. How could he be friends with someone who lived in such a dazzling place as this?

After Selahattin had performed the evening *namaz,* they ate some fish from the stall, hurriedly prepared by Selahattin's wife, who then served tea before disappearing out of sight. As soon as the two friends were alone, Selahattin asked him, "You have a problem, don't you?

You've been acting like a broody turtledove all day long. What is it? Money? Work? Love?"

Although Cemal did not know how to explain his dilemma to Selahattin, he wanted his friend to insist on being answered, because he was the only person in whom Cemal could confide.

In spite of being intimidated by the crystal chandelier, the highly carved armchairs, and the floors covered with all those expensive carpets, Cemal told Selahattin the whole story, clearly and concisely.

As he listened, Selahattin nodded frequently. "Yesterday you avoided committing a great sin," he interrupted, finally. "Thankfully, you are not sitting here as a murderer. God softened your heart and saved you from that, I'm glad to say."

Cemal was confused. Selahattin, with whom he had many times fired at the enemy, considered the killing of a mere girl important.

"That was war," Selahattin said. "The Holy Quran judges war differently. But killing an innocent girl . . . it's not the same as fighting an enemy in battle."

The more Cemal spoke with Selahattin, the more relieved he felt and the longer he wished the conversation to continue.

"But doesn't Islam order men to kill women who've sinned?"

"No."

"But what about stoning? Shouldn't adulteresses be buried up to the waist in the ground and stoned to death?"

"No. There's no such punishment in the Quran. Such things are just made-up stories."

"How can that be?" asked Cemal. "My father says that stoning was carried out until Atatürk came to power."

"It's an incorrect punishment, which is applied in some Arab states, but it has no place in Islam. Besides, it is very difficult to prove adultery. Islamic law requires that the sword be seen in its sheath by three witnesses. What's the girl's name?"

"Meryem."

"Have you seen the sword in Meryem's sheath?"

Cemal blushed. "No."

"How do you know she's guilty?"

"My father told me so."

"How can you kill a human being just on hearsay?"

Cemal began to wonder if Selahattin was from a different religion. He had never heard of such tolerance in Muslim belief before.

"In Islam, killing a human is considered sinful," Selahattin continued.

"I think you're wrong," said Cemal. "Many religious organizations, Hizbullah for instance, kill people all the time."

"They're perverts," said Selahattin. "They use Islam in order to fulfill their political goals. Killers and terrorists can be members of any religion. One should turn to the main source of Islam—the Holy Quran, and the *hadiths* of the Prophet. Have you read Sahih-i Buhari?"

"No," said Cemal.

"You probably haven't even read the Quran. I thought your father was a sheikh. How did he educate you?"

Then Selahattin told Cemal that he wanted to take him to a ceremony that was to be held the next evening by a religious sect in the district of Eyüp Sultan, in order to correct his misconceptions about Islam.

After Cemal promised to come, they continued discussing his problem. They examined it from various angles, yet could not find a solution. Meryem could neither go back to the village nor stay with Yakup's family. She could not be left alone in this city. Even if Cemal found a job, he and Meryem could not stay in the same house as an unmarried couple. Nobody would rent them an apartment. Besides, Cemal did not want to stay in Istanbul. He wanted to return home and marry his beloved.

They spoke for hours but could not resolve the dilemma. Then Selahattin decided that they must sleep on it, and he showed Cemal to the guest room.

The heavy curtains in the bedroom and the embroidered towels laid out for him in the bathroom by his "sister-in-law" made Cemal feel awkward and uncomfortable.

Early the next morning, the two friends went to see Selahattin's father, who lived upstairs. In fact the whole apartment building was full of Selahattin's family, who did not want any strangers among them. The old man, who had presumably been captain of a fishing boat for many years, had a habit of shielding his eyes with his hand whenever he looked at the television, as if he had been through a violent storm and was preparing to shout "Land ho!" and give his companions the good news.

After breakfast, Cemal and Selahattin left the apartment for the office behind the fishmonger's stall and ate again at the same restaurant near the fish market.

At six in the evening, Selahattin parked his Honda in front of a big single-story house on a hill near Eyüp, with a wonderful view of the Golden Horn—no longer golden, perhaps, but still the shape of a horn—as well as the domes of Eyüp Sultan Mosque and the Pierre Loti Café. Many cars were parked in front of the house, and the entrance was full of abandoned footwear.

Cemal followed Selahattin inside, shy at finding himself a newcomer among so many people who all knew each other. The interior of the house resembled that of a home in his village. The large living room was full of men sitting cross-legged on the floor. From their clothing, Cemal surmised that they must be tradesmen. Some wore ties.

One of the men began to chant in a high-pitched voice a poem by the mystic poet Yunus Emre with which Cemal was familiar. Meanwhile, the men on the carpet arranged themselves side by side as if to take part in ritual prayers, but no one stood up. They wore white skullcaps on their heads. Cemal noticed one of them sitting alone at the front with his back turned to the others. "Just like my father," Cemal thought. It seemed as though a religious *zikr* ritual, like those in his father's vineyard hut, was to take place. Soon, some of the men began to chant *"Hu."* Then the sheikh's followers began to sway from side to side and moan, "God! Oh God!" as they swayed increasingly faster and faster. The faster they swayed, the more excited they became. Every now and then, one of them screamed out, "God! Oh God!" in a frenzied crescendo. Eventually, some of the men became unconscious, like those Cemal had seen in the vineyard hut as a child. Others rolled on the floor, foaming at the mouth. Cemal's father had told him that this was a state of ecstasy caused by submission to God through reciting his Holy Name. In fact, it was the result of the effect of the rhythmic chant at a tempo of 124 beats per minute. In Middle Eastern rituals, the name *"Allah"* recited at this tempo soon sends a person into a trance, this being the same tempo at which the heart beats. The same thing applies in discotheques all over the world, when the drum beats 124 times a minute.

Cemal, unexcited by this religious fervor to which he was accustomed, waited for the ritual to end and the men to calm down. The sheikh counseled his congregation on how to live a good life and recited a few of the *hadiths* of the Prophet. After some of the men left, Selahattin introduced Cemal to the sheikh. Cemal bowed and kissed his hand. Then Selahattin told the sheikh that his good friend from the military was a devout Muslim but was confused about the use of force and violence.

The sheikh stroked his white beard. Although very old, he was still full of energy, and his blue eyes reflected intelligence and wisdom.

"My son," he said to Cemal, "in our times, since right and wrong and good and bad have become inextricably mixed, most Muslims are going through a crisis, searching for something they cannot find. I don't blame them, but you must watch out for those who have transformed Islam into a religion of revenge. Don't believe them. The word 'Islam' means 'to submit, to surrender.' Islam is a religion of peace. If you want to understand Islam, do not respect anything other than the Holy Quran, the *hadiths,* and the Sunna of the Prophet, because Islam is a manifested religion. In other words, it is an open, transparent way of belief. Politics spoils religion and sows discord among the believers. Listen to what the thirty-second verse of the *al-Mai'dah* Sura of the Quran has to say. . . ."

He first read the verse in Arabic and then explained its meaning in Turkish. "Whoever kills a person guiltless of killing others or of setting people against each other will be seen as the killer of all humanity. Whoever lets that person live or saves him from death will be seen as the savior of humanity."

The sheikh's soft voice, and the smile that illuminated his face, surprised Cemal. For the first time in his life, he felt that religion was not an intimidating force. He felt as though his heart were being purified with cool, clean water.

The sheikh continued, "Son, the fortieth verse of the *ash-Shura* Sura says, 'The response to evil is an equal amount of evil. However, whosoever forgives and brings about peace will be rewarded by God.' There is no doubt that God hates tyrants."

The sheikh talked for a long time. He recited passages from the Quran about kindness and peace, the *al-Baqarah, al-Mai'dah, al-An'am, al-A'raf, bani I'srail, al-Hajj, al-Mumtahanah, al-Mu'min,* and *an-Nisa'* Suras. His final words from this beautiful Quranic verse stirred Cemal's heart, " 'Do good unto your mother, unto your father, unto orphans and the poor, unto close neighbors and distant neighbors, unto the friend near you, unto the traveler, and unto those who depend upon you.'

"This is the thirty-sixth verse of the *an-Nisa'* Sura." The sheikh then asked, "Are your doubts cleared? Are you convinced that those who act in line with the word of God and the command of our Holy Prophet are peaceful and tolerant people, who eschew tyranny and violence? Do you now understand that murderous organizations have nothing to do with God?"

Cemal felt embarrassed in the presence of this wise sheikh but was finally able to mumble, "I am convinced, teacher. May God pour his blessings on you."

He kissed the old man's hand again.

On the way back to Selahattin's house, Cemal wondered how the sheikh had instinctively understood his feelings and spoken as though he knew that he had only just avoided killing Meryem. He grew suspicious of Selahattin. Had his friend told the sheikh about Cemal's dilemma? The sheikh had even talked about orphans, as if he knew that Meryem was one, but Cemal quickly realized the absurdity of his doubts.

When they entered the house, there was a young girl with Selahattin's wife. Selahattin introduced her to Cemal as his sister. The girl did not shake hands with Cemal but greeted him distantly. Her head and neck were tightly covered in a close-fitting scarf, which she had tied at the back of her neck. In spite of all this, Cemal could see that she was pretty, observing, however, that she had a cut on her cheek. Saliha— as Cemal heard Selahattin call his sister—began to tell them about what had happened to her that day.

As always, in the morning, she and her friends had gone to the university, only to be confronted by a police barricade to prevent female students who had their heads covered from entering the campus. The students had unfurled banners and yelled that it was the right of all human beings to cover their heads or not as they wished. They had shouted slogans such as "Islam will come and tyranny will end!" and blown whistles, while the tradesmen in the area clapped their hands in approval. The male students supported the demonstration by booing the police.

This was a familiar scene that took place every day. The police were carrying out government directives that forbade students from wearing Islamic headscarves to enter the university. Those who were not allowed on campus demonstrated in front of the gate.

That day, things had gotten out of control. Perhaps the police, who were trying to impress the secular chief of police, newly appointed to Istanbul, had been overly zealous. They had attacked the protesting girls and turned water cannons on them. They took out their truncheons and began to beat them. The girls screamed. Some fell to the ground, and others fainted in terror. When Saliha shouted at the police, "Aren't your mothers and sisters covered, too? Aren't you all Muslims?" a policeman hit her on the cheek. She blushed as she told her story. One could tell that she was excited and even a little pleased. They had another protest planned for the next day and would teach "those sons of Satan" a lesson. The Kemalist satanic regime in Ankara, they said, would shatter in front of this army of girls.

"Come on, Saliha," Selahattin said, "the other day Father talked to you for hours, but it seems that everything goes in one ear and out the other. You can't play games with the government. You have to obey your country's laws. Besides, will you be less virtuous if someone sees your hair?"

Saliha looked at her brother angrily. "Those miserable nonbelievers have brainwashed you," she said. "If you want, you go ahead and kiss the hand you can't bite. We're not doing it."

"Until last year, you never covered your head. Were you not virtuous then?"

"I didn't know what God's law was then. I learned it after I started at the university, thanks to my friends. You all pretend to be religious, but you don't practice the rules of your religion. In any case, why don't you make your wife uncover her head?"

Fed up, Selahattin said, "May God give you some brains. Those people are manipulating you for their own agendas."

Saliha looked at him angrily. "Brother, why don't you become a general in the army? You're just like them—trying to turn us into nonbelievers. It's my right to decide whether or not to cover my head. It's nobody else's business."

Saliha then left the room and went upstairs to her father's apartment.

Over dinner, Selahattin talked about the danger of movements that were using religion as a weapon and fooling naïve young people like Saliha. "These people plan to use the headscarf protests to start an Islamic revolution in Turkey, just like they did in Iran."

Late that night, after everyone had gone to bed, Selahattin said, "I've been thinking about your situation, Cemal. It's impossible for you to stay in Istanbul. You can't go home, either. I've got no idea what will happen in the long run, but we must find you and the girl a place to stay. Somewhere far away."

"Thank you," said Cemal, with wholehearted gratitude.

ONLY PEOPLE AND FISH
GET DEPRESSED

THE HEAVILY BUILT MAN WITH A BEARD AND UN-
kempt hair suddenly woke up, not because of the wind caressing his
face, or the creaking of the keel or hawsers, the screeching seagulls,
the soft splash of the waves, or the roar of a speedboat passing in the
distance. A feeling of acute and burning desire, which pained him
deeply, had woken him, though he did not fully grasp what he was
longing for. It was, perhaps, a yearning for emptiness or for desire itself.

The professor opened his eyes. Dawn was breaking. At this hour,
the sea was a pale, whitish blue. The color of the horizon gradually
changed from indigo to blue, from blue to rose pink, and then a vast
cerulean hue took over the whole sky. In this overall blue floated a
single navy cloud, shaped like a curved scimitar.

After drinking so much the previous night, the professor had
passed out on the deck, and the dampness of the morning dew had
penetrated his clothing so that all his limbs ached.

He tried to stand up but found he had to limp as his right knee hurt
so much. He had hit it badly during the race against the storm to reach
the harbor. The cuts on his hands made by the ropes were painful, too.
Now it would be even more difficult to handle the boat. Since his

childhood, he had known very well that sailing was a violent struggle—the wind could throw you about; the waves could surge above your head; the mast could break; the boat could spring a leak; the clews could suddenly get loose. If you did not pay attention, any of these could kill you.

The professor had been too self-confident and made things harder for himself by renting a boat more than forty feet long. In fact, the boat was not complicated to sail, having only a single main sail and a genoa, but you never knew how the sea might act. Sudden counterwinds might blow, the halyards could get stuck, or some other unexpected problem could occur. This was not the type of boat he was accustomed to, and if he had another person with him, things would be much easier.

There were so many coves and dangerous rocky or shallow places on the jagged coasts of the Aegean Sea that he could not have sailed anywhere without thoroughly studying the charts and maps beforehand. Thankfully, at the bookstore in Kuşadası where he had bought a few new books about the history of the Bogomils, he had purchased Rod Heikell's *Turkish Waters and Cyprus Pilot*. According to the owner of the store, this was the most detailed book written about the Aegean. The charts could save him from the many dangers to be encountered at sea.

The Aegean winds, which had pleased him like a child on his first days at sea, had soon become his worst enemy. He had become tired, but the winds remained as vigorous as ever, like strong young men hiding behind each and every cape. The williwaw—a very dangerous gust of wind that descends precipitously from the mountains to the sea—was especially formidable. You could recognize it by the whirlpools it created in the water and the way the boat heeled to one side. If you were not careful, this wind could hurl your sail into the sea. One day, in front of Çıfıt Castle, the wind squall had struck, and the professor had barely saved the boat from capsizing.

After ten days at sea, İrfan was tired of sailing from one bay to the next. He felt he was wandering aimlessly around the Aegean Sea like a drunken sailor as if nothing had changed in his life, but he realized this was not true.

As he was leaving a small grocery store one day, he saw some daily newspapers and bought them without giving it a second thought. He had not read a newspaper since setting out to sea. He had not even thought about the news. In Istanbul, he used to start the day by reading the paper. First he would check if there were any articles about him or if anyone had criticized his television program.

The writers of the daily columns pursued a running battle with each other through their articles in the papers. It was entertaining to follow their quarrels, which sometimes lasted for days. Some writers got so furious with their colleagues that if they had had swords, axes, or spears instead of pens, they would have brutally hacked each other to pieces. Their jobs were like the punishment of Sisyphus—to work and write from morning till evening just to have their articles thrown into the garbage every night.

When İrfan returned to the boat, he opened the newspapers and was immediately horror-struck by what he read. The newspapers could not be talking about his country. What he read there had nothing to do with Turkey. This approach to the world, the language used, the news emphasized, and the photographs printed there were completely foreign to him. It was then the professor realized how deeply the past weeks on the sea had changed him.

Drinking his cool beer, he ran his eye over the events that were taking place in the country: quarrels between politicians or boasts about their achievements, efforts to paint Turkey as a heaven on earth; news of a Turkish fashion designer who had taken New York by storm, of a Turkish singer whose album had sold out in Europe, of an American politician who said that Turkey was the most important country in the world, or about a Hollywood star who wanted to shoot a film in Turkey and eat "shish kebab"; morale-boosting lies, and the headscarf protests that had been a part of the political agenda for the last few years.

On the front page of one of the newspapers, there was a photograph of a policeman hitting a girl on the head with a truncheon. İrfan had become used to seeing such scenes at the university. He had passed by such protests many times. He tried to understand why the girl had acted in such a militant way. He could easily understand why women in an Islamic country, forced to cover their heads, might fight to remove their headscarves. But why did these girls torture themselves by covering their heads in the summer heat and risk getting beaten up for it? Natural and biological laws should have caused them to revolt against such coverings, not protest in favor of them. What possible reason could there be for such behavior?

The professor noticed a phrase in the article: "the attempt to break the police barricade." These words hinted at an answer to his question. Suddenly, he understood what was really going on! The police barricade was not an obstacle to surmount but the goal itself. The police represented the regime, and they also protected it. They were the symbol of that vulgar, rotten system that all young people hated. And in each period of time, young people, full of honest, if rebellious, feelings, revolt against the system. In the seventies and eighties, students had tried to surmount the police barricade in front of the same university and had been harshly treated. But then, the students had been shouting leftist slogans: "Revolution is the only way! Down with oligarchy!" At that time, the way to revolt against the system had been through such leftist movements.

In the nineties, again there were police barricades and rebellious students in front of the same gate. Truncheons were raised once more, and tanks aimed water cannons at the students, who were screaming in Kurdish, *"Kurdare Azadi!"* and *"Biji serok Apo!"* They wore red, green, and yellow scarves and carried posters of Abdullah Öcalan, the leader of the PKK.

In the twenty-first century, the same square was, this time, full of girls in headscarves clashing with the police. Once again water cannons were used. In short, the police and the students played the same game time and again. The only things that changed were the slogans and the outward appearance of the students.

Youth needs to rebel and revolt in this way or that. In reality, these girls fighting to keep their heads covered were doing it just for the sake of fighting against the established regime; to demonstrate to their parents, to their school, and to the political system that they had their own unique personalities. And if these girls who were struggling to be allowed to cover their heads had been living in Iran, they would be fighting to uncover them.

Long live the spirit of rebellion! Long live revolution! Long live Kropotkin! Long live Bakunin! And long live Khomeini!

Lost in these thoughts, İrfan said to himself, "It's none of your business, idiot! Just because you were born in this part of the world at this particular time, why should you make everything your problem? If you had lived in the fourteenth century in China, other problems would have meant the end of the world to you, and you would still have been wrong. In many years from now, that hill in the distance will still be there, but you will be gone. This sea will still be here, but you will be gone. Even that ruined house over there will remain, but you won't. Stop it, for God's sake! Stop this nonsense!"

İrfan threw away every one of the newspapers and opened another bottle of cold beer.

He had been on the Aegean for a long time, but he had only been to a single Greek island, Kos. He had docked his boat in the harbor, presented his passport and visa, and had officially entered Greece. Then, for the first time in weeks, he had spent a whole evening on land.

First, he had a dinner of octopus, red mullet, *horta,* and *fava,* at a famous restaurant, and then he went to a small music hall where some local musicians were playing the *rembetiko.* The music was intoxicating, and the women and men were indefatigable, dancing to the *zeybekiko* and the *kasapiko* till long after midnight. The professor realized how intoxicated he was only after he went out into the fresh air. He did not know whether it was the ouzo or the tipsy atmosphere of the music hall that had made him drunk. As he staggered along the deserted streets, he felt as if he were a penniless *rembetiko* musician, living in the time of the ascetic saints of music, Markos Vamvakaris and Tsitsanis.

Hundreds of thousands of Anatolian Greeks, who had had to immigrate to Greece from Izmir, the professor's hometown, had created this mysterious music. This drunken music burned like acid, was as uncontrollable as the sea breeze, and as grief-stricken as the deepest part of the Aegean. Perhaps he found himself in tune with it because it came from a neighboring land.

In the marina, the professor had found his boat with difficulty. He had thrown himself on the bed in his clothes and slept until afternoon. He had woken up with a stabbing headache though he still felt drowned in the sound of the bouzouki and the brittle *rembetiko* music.

The professor felt he must go to those desolate coves again to regain his equilibrium. He longed for the solitude he had earlier complained of. In the deserted coves, a resinous scent wafting toward the sea in the serenity of the night would remind him of the pines' existence. Then he would light the kerosene lamp and sit silently in the deathlike darkness that surrounded him while cold shivers ran up and down his spine. Afraid to make the slightest sound, he abandoned himself to the will of nature.

During the day, the professor would amuse himself by casting a line and enjoying fishing. He usually caught at least one of whatever fish were to be found in the channels between the islands but, no matter how hard he tried, he was not able to catch the colorful *lambuka* which were always swimming around the boat. In some places, they called the *lambuka* "dolphin." The people of the Far East called this fish "mahi-mahi," and the Aegean people called it "the naked fish." As if intending to drive him crazy, the *lambuka* would appear every afternoon at the same time, taunting him. One day, another fisherman noticed his lack of success and told him to use a trotline. "Throw out the trotline and let one of them get hooked on it, but don't pull the line in. Soon you'll see that all the others will come."

It happened just as the fisherman had said. When a fish seized the bait, the others enthusiastically tried to get themselves hooked as well. "Exactly like humans," thought the professor.

One morning, he forced himself to write the first sentence of the book he had been struggling to begin. He had done all that research over the years, and now that he had his notes with him, he could begin. The first sentence went: "That day in the marketplace of Srebrenitza, Ibrahim, a ten-year-old Bosnian boy, was killed by a bullet from the rifle of a Serbian sharpshooter. He died without knowing that he shared the same fate as his Christian ancestors, who, centuries earlier, had lived thousands of kilometers away in Samosata."

Then he added: "This was the fate of the Bogomil."

After that he could not think of another word or idea to write down. He read the first sentence over and over again, enjoying it more each time. A book that started with that sentence would surely attract attention, but how would he write the rest of it? Thousands of words had to flow to be able to write a book, but it seemed that he did not have the talent to be a writer.

Until evening, the professor contemplated the first sentence of his book, but then a sudden, strong wind began to rock the boat. Then he gave up. He had to cope with the much more vital problem of finding a tranquil cove to take refuge in. With an injured leg, he could not risk the danger of being caught in a storm on the open sea.

He took out Heikell's book, established his location, and discovered that there was, in fact, a nearby cove where he could spend the night. Perhaps it could not be called a cove, exactly, because, according to the map, the sea went inland like a twisting river. It would have been easier to enter it in daylight, but he had been absorbed by his book.

When İrfan found the entrance to the cove, darkness had already descended. It was a moonless night, and visibility was nil. He moved very slowly, taking extra care, as the chart indicated some perilously shallow water. İrfan looked at the depth sounder and changed his direction when the numbers began to decrease. He did not want to run aground.

As he went deeper inland, he felt as if he were moving up a real river, one that twisted and turned. He had turned on the spotlight, which allowed him to see a little of the coast and water in front of the boat.

At least there was no wind here. After moving very slowly for a while, İrfan discerned a pyramidlike hill in the darkness, and he realized that he was approaching the end of the cove. This was a magical place, which did not look like any of the coves he had been to before. He was excited, yet he did not know why. He began to move toward the hill. Perhaps he would be able to cast anchor soon. Maybe he would not even need to tie the boat to a tree in such a serene cove. Nothing stirred; the air seemed solid and tangible.

The professor scanned the shore, using the spotlight, and suddenly started with fright. In this deserted, lonely place, a man was shouting at him, "Turn off the light! Turn off the light!"

The man's tone was threatening, almost as if he was about to grab a gun and shoot if he was not obeyed. İrfan switched off the light and was left in complete darkness.

Who was that man? Were there others with him? Why did he shout, telling him to turn off the light? Where was he?

The professor cast anchor. The sound of the chain frightened him. "I wish I hadn't come to this ill-omened cove," he thought. What a sinister river! He felt as if he were on a spellbound shore, like the one that had caused Ulysses so much trouble.

After he cast anchor, he sat silently in the dark. Would they be angry if he lit the kerosene lamp? With the help of a flashlight, the professor poured himself a glass of whisky and began to sip it as he looked at the dark hill that resembled the pyramid of Cheops. Not even the smallest light could be seen, and no sound broke the silence.

A few minutes later, İrfan heard a splash as if someone was rowing toward him. "Peace be with you!" said a man's voice.

The professor was not sure which of that evening's events was more surprising. Now, in the middle of the night, a stranger in a rowboat was hailing him with a religious greeting. The man was obviously not a sailor.

İrfan aimed his flashlight at the stranger. He saw a tall young man, with a fine-boned, slender face, a striking contrast to his sturdy figure. İrfan invited him aboard, and the young man jumped onto the deck.

"Sorry," he said. "There's a fish farm here for sea bass and gilt-head breams. If a strong light shines on them, they get scared and might kill themselves by swimming into each other. We've been warned to protect them from lights."

İrfan relaxed a little and asked where exactly the fish farm was.

The young man pointed to the left bank. "We live there, too—in a hut on the shore. You can't see it now, because the light is behind a tree."

"Doesn't the light frighten the fish?" asked İrfan.

"No. Nothing happens when you turn on an ordinary light. They only get disturbed when a spotlight is turned on them. Noise bothers them, too. When you catch some with a net, that also affects them. The rest get white spots on their skin, then they die."

"What sensitive fish."

"Yes. We're new here, and we've learned all this just recently. If you're here tomorrow morning, I can show the fish to you."

İrfan introduced himself, and they shook hands. The young man's name was Cemal. İrfan felt an extraordinary power in Cemal's coarse hand. He offered him a drink, but Cemal said he did not drink alcohol. Then he said, "I should go back now. The girl is alone in the hut, and she's afraid of snakes and centipedes."

That night, İrfan was too busy thinking about his strange encounter and the frightened fish to add a new sentence to his book. He drank half a bottle of Jack Daniel's and passed out.

Next morning, the razorlike sharpness of the sunbeams woke him up. He looked around and saw that the spell of the previous night had worn away. Together with the night, the ghosts of Homer had stolen away from the cove.

İrfan looked at the breathtaking aquamarine water and the green hills covered with thick pine forests that descended to the sea. Near the shore he could see the buoys of the fish farm. The sensitive fish, protected from the light, must have fallen asleep. The cove was so peaceful and so lovely that he decided to stay for a few days to work on his book.

He took out some sheets of paper, bit the end of his pencil, and thought for hours. Over and over again, he read what he had written the day before and added a few new sentences: "Ibrahim's fate had been determined centuries before; after his people in eastern Anatolia had been converted to Christianity and become members of a heretical sect, they were oppressed for centuries by the Orthodox Church. Fleeing their home, they adopted a Muslim identity, only to be persecuted by Christians at the end of the twentieth century. This is a story of the dangers of remaining unreconciled with the dominant power."

The new lines were not as striking as the first sentences he had written the day before, but the most important thing was that he was writing. He felt that he deserved a drink of cool white wine in the midday sun before he took his nap.

İrfan's nap lasted until late afternoon. When he woke up, he perceived though a groggy haze Cemal rowing toward the boat. Cemal looked like an interesting young man. He seemed friendly, but also gave the impression that he could be dangerous. He had come to pick up the "teacher" if he still wished to visit the fish farm. İrfan realized that with his unkempt black hair and gray beard, he had acquired the image of a revered elder in the young man's eyes. Cemal said he could show him around the place and would be happy to share a modest dinner with the professor in his hut. Pleased to be welcomed with such warmth, İrfan accepted the invitation.

As they rowed toward the shore, Cemal showed him the buoys, the underwater cages, and the fish. "There must be millions in there," İrfan thought, observing that the fish did not have enough space to swim without touching each other. İrfan looked away from this fish prison and glanced at the shore. A tiny hut stood there under age-old olive trees. Beside it, sacks of fish feed were stacked on top of each other. Later, Cemal told him that the feed was made from the bones of anchovies. When they landed, the fishy smell pervading the air was immediately noticeable.

A young girl with big green eyes, a childlike face, and a cotton scarf wrapped around her head came out of the hut. She greeted the professor shyly with a slight inclination of her head. She seemed to be fifteen at most. In America, even caressing a girl this age would land you in jail labeled as a pervert. But in Anatolian villages, older men would climb on top of little girls without anyone opposing it. "So this guy is with this little girl," thought the professor scornfully, but he smiled and merely remarked, "Good evening!"

As darkness fell, Cemal jumped into the rowboat and went to cull some fish from the cages. The young man rowed the boat, as tense and balanced as a tiger. He plunged the net into the water carefully, but the professor wondered if he would still frighten the fish no matter how careful he was.

Meanwhile, the girl prepared dinner without looking at İrfan. Taking a few tomatoes, onions, and cucumbers from a fisherman's basket hanging from a beam under the ceiling, the girl began to slice them.

Cemal returned to the hut and cleaned the fish he had caught, scraping off the scales, slitting them open, and ripping out the innards while they were still alive. Two wild cats suddenly appeared from nowhere and grabbed the remains at lightning speed. There were probably many animals in the forest. Cemal had said yesterday that the girl was afraid of snakes and centipedes. İrfan glanced around him apprehensively.

When it was completely dark, Cemal lit a small lamp, provoking a riot of flies, mosquitoes, sand flies, and moths that flew in and began to flutter around the brilliant light. İrfan was caught in a mist of flying bugs. Mosquitoes attacked his neck, arms, and legs. He scratched himself until his skin bled.

He began to slap himself everywhere, and asked Cemal, "How can you survive here, for God's sake? These damned things are going to kill me!"

Watching the professor jump up from his seat, slap himself, and curse, the girl could not help giggling. "They usually come to me," she said, "but tonight they seem to like you more."

When İrfan realized that the mosquitoes would not stop coming, he and Cemal got into Cemal's boat and rowed out to the sailboat. İrfan took all the insect repellents he could find and they returned to the hut. He rubbed the medicine on himself and gave some to the girl.

Only then did the girl fry the fish and serve it with the salad. İrfan regretted that he had not brought some wine along, but he did not plan to spend too much time in this wretched hut. He wanted to return to his boat as soon as he finished his meal. He planned to listen to Erik Satie's *Gnossienne*, which he now preferred to Jean-Pierre Rampal's flute. The sad tune of the piano in the first melody enchanted him. He wanted to listen to those tunes and feel as if it was only to hear them that he had been born. While he listened, the velvety Jack Daniel's would slip down his throat in the sterile atmosphere of his Plexiglas-and-chromium vessel.

He followed his plan, but he could not get the girl's big, shining, green eyes out of his mind. "Such strange eyes," he thought, "childish and innocent, yet desirous and devious."

The elusive glance of those eyes embraced everything.

A CALL OF YOUNG BODIES

Tᴇɴ ᴅᴀʏs ᴏʀ sᴏ ʙᴇꜰᴏʀᴇ ᴛʜᴇ ᴇɴᴄᴏᴜɴᴛᴇʀ ɪɴ ᴛʜᴇ secluded cove on the Aegean, Cemal had left the house with Selahattin, whom he believed to be the most truly good person he had ever met. As if his friend had not done enough by showing him hospitality and doing him favors, he had also found a place for him and Meryem to stay. He had even put some money in Cemal's pocket without making him feel ashamed. "Don't think I'm helping you," Selahattin had said. "I'm just paying you your two weeks' wages in advance."

Then the two friends had driven to Rahmanlı to pick up Meryem. Selahattin returned Cemal's thanks by saying, "We're buddies. You saved my life so many times."

Yakup was not home when they picked up Meryem, so Cemal could not say good-bye to his brother, but he knew that there was an unspoken agreement between them to remain silent. Yakup would never tell anyone that Cemal had not fulfilled his father's command. In return, Cemal would not tell the villagers back home about the reality of "Yakup's Istanbul."

As they rode on the intercity bus, Cemal felt his gratitude to his friend. Without him, he and Meryem would have been left without shelter. Now Selahattin was sending them far away to a cove near

Çeşme on the Aegean coast, where his family had a fish farm. The caretaker had asked for two weeks' leave to look after a sick relative. During that time, Cemal and the girl could stay there safely. All he had to do was mount guard over the fish and feed them twice a day. The rest was in God's hands. His duties were easy.

As the bus traveled along the well-cared-for roads of the verdant Aegean coast, Cemal realized that in the last week he had traveled more than he had ever done in his entire life. He had set out from the Iraq border and was now on his way to Grecian shores. He had traveled so far from Emine that he could no longer recall to mind her soft skin. He had Meryem to thank for all of this, but Cemal hated her even more than he had hated the terrorists on the mountains. No matter what Selahattin said, she was a sinner who deserved to die, and yet, he, Cemal, a veteran commando, was incapable of killing her. He simply could not bring himself to murder this little girl. Who was this girl sitting next to him—a prostitute, a sinner, a lousy creature, a girl under sentence of death? Or just a kid who did not know anything about the world?

In the state between sleep and wakefulness where he took refuge when he did not know what to do, Cemal became aware of the pungent smell of lemon cologne. The bus driver's assistant, more child than man, was walking down the aisle, offering lemon cologne to the passengers. The husky voice of a folk singer was blasting out of the radio.

Cemal was starting to doze as the bus trundled along, when it occurred to him that he had not dreamed of the innocent bride recently. The fair-skinned young bride, who used to appear in his dreams every other night during those harsh days in the army and cause him to sin in his sleep, was gone. She had not appeared since the start of his journey. Cemal longed for her scent, her skin, her warmth, but it was no use. He could not summon at will a girl whom he had seen only in his dreams. She came only when she wanted to.

Cemal tried hard to keep his father out of his thoughts. Since he had not fulfilled his father's commands, he could neither write him a letter nor telephone home to ask news of him. Only after he had solved the problem of what to do with the girl would he be able to contact him, yet he had no idea of how to go about finding a solution.

Meryem leaned against the window absentmindedly. She was exhausted from having so many emotions. She was drained of strength and fearful that she would become ill as she had on the train. Her monthly bleeding had stopped and, thanks to the sanitary napkins Seher had given her, the arrival of her next period was not a frightening thought anymore. She only wondered how she would find new pads. Seher had said they were sold in pharmacies, but how could Meryem buy them? She did not have any money. She wondered what Seher was doing now. Had her brother died, or was he still alive?

Only the rather elderly women on the bus had their heads covered; in fact, not only did the young girls have their hair loose, they also wore hip-hugging blue jeans. Their sleeveless pink, blue, or orange blouses were tight across their breasts, of which glimpses were revealed when they bent forward, yet they did not seem to mind. They wore earrings in their ears, bracelets on their wrists, and thin gold necklaces around their necks. Some of the pendants on the necklaces were shaped like hearts. Perhaps there were photos of their sweethearts inside. They talked, giggled, and laughed loudly, and a few of them even smoked when the bus stopped at a rest area.

Meryem felt miserable in the presence of these girls. Nazik had washed her blue cotton dress, but the blue flower print had faded even more. Although she had washed her black plastic shoes in the fountain in Rahmanlı, they were muddy, as was the long skirt wrapping itself around her legs.

Each time she looked at those black shoes, she remembered that cursed day she had been sent away from the village. Maybe because she always looked at the ground, she had not been able to take her eyes off her shoes. Her thick socks also looked awful, but none of these things disturbed her more than the scarf covering her head. Her headscarf had not bothered her in the village, but the village was in the middle of nowhere. Wearing a scarf here made Meryem feel foolish. The weather was getting warmer, and her feet were sweating in her woollen socks. She could not breathe in these clothes.

Cemal still did not talk to her even though he dragged her behind him like a puppy from one place to another. In the morning, he and another man had come to Rahmanlı to pick her up. Then they had gone to the bus terminal. After living in the village and walking only between her home and the poplar grove all her life, she had, in a single week, seen so many buses, garages, stations, boats, cars, and people that nothing astonished her anymore. All she wanted was to know where she was going.

When they first boarded the bus, she had thought that they were returning to the village, but after listening to the bus driver's announcements and conversations between passengers, she realized that they were heading for a completely different place.

She did not know the geography of Turkey. She had no idea where the southeast was or the Black Sea region, or the Aegean. She was the girl who thought Istanbul was behind the hill outside the village. If she had considered the matter carefully, she would have realized that the big city could not be that close. But nobody had talked to her. She had always been pushed into her own solitary world of dreams. Her head had been full of fantasies: Şeker Baba's miracles, Armenians flying in the air, and weeping nightingales perching on the strings whenever the Armenian musician Bogod played the zither.

Meryem was an unlucky girl. She had caused her mother to die and brought many misfortunes upon her family. Her friends had stopped playing with her after they had grown up. She had been ostracized. No one had wanted to make her a part of his family. She had waved good-bye to her dreams of marriage and a family of her own. Whenever she had some spare time after finishing the housework, she used to go to the poplar grove and daydream. "I'm so ignorant," she lamented to herself. "How ignorant I am beside these girls who know so much!"

Still, she did not allow self-pity to overcome her. She relied on her ability, since childhood, to chase away bad memories. She did not ponder on all the evil done to her in the village; nor did she recall the fear she had felt on the viaduct. Her mind did not return to the past, and an inner strength blanked out her fears and sorrows.

The only bad memory she could not erase was that of her aunt making her cry in front of the locked door, as well as the shame she had felt returning to say good-bye as she walked down the muddy road in the village. Her black plastic shoes reminded her of those incidents.

Meryem was ready to forget the memories and begin a new life, but as she knew nothing about her future, she was unable to daydream about it.

Cemal did not say a word, not even about where they were going. Was he taking her somewhere to finish her off for good? Would he fulfill his task at the seaside? Deep inside, Meryem felt that this would not happen. She was sure that Cemal would not try to kill her again. When she had seen him on the bridge, bowed down with shame, beaten and dejected in the drizzling rain, she had known that she would go on living. But what if this were no longer true? She could not prevent doubt from poisoning her mind now and then.

Meryem marveled at how fast she had gotten used to the good things in life. She had been eating and drinking in the company of men for an entire week without feeling embarrassed. Since the day of her puberty, she had been told that women must not eat, drink, go to the toilet, or even talk when men were present. Yet now, she sat across from Cemal and devoured her soup among strangers. When Cemal went to the men's room next to the gasoline stations, she went to the ladies' room. She almost believed that she had lived like this all her life. She would feel much better if she could get rid of the scarf around her head, but she did not dare take it off. Cemal would probably hit her with his hammer of a hand and cause her other cheek to swell, too.

As the bus drove along the coast, they passed many cities, towns, and summer resorts, and finally they arrived at their destination, a small coastal town. There, girls were running around half-naked, some in bathing suits and others in shorts. Meryem was stunned. Proud of their womanhood, these women walked freely, their shorts revealing their sunburned legs, letting their long, beautiful hair fall around their shoulders. Meryem looked at them in amazement.

For the first time, she regarded the young men with interest—their slender bodies and charming smiles; the way they hugged the girls and drank Coke from the same bottle; she found their bare, tanned, muscular arms and their lithe movements attractive. In her village, she would not even think of raising her eyes to meet a man's, let alone gaze at them as she was doing now. Besides, the men in the village did not look like these young men. Meryem had discovered a new and completely different world.

The scent of spring mixed with those of perfume and suntan lotion wafting from the passersby. On one corner, a group of giggling girls and boys were eating ice cream. At that moment, Meryem felt like a real woman, even though she was wearing shabby clothes and muddy plastic shoes. She wanted to be near those boys. Oddly, she did not feel ashamed of her desire. This young girl, who had till now been called ill-starred, stupid, and sinful just because she was female, had changed in this climate. She let the desires of spring possess her body. Even the "sinful place" between her legs did not seem so dreadful, because she realized that the girls here were not ashamed of their "sinful places."

Unfortunately, Meryem's hopes of staying in the town were dashed as, after asking many times for directions, they found a man in a shop who took them to his white rowboat. Climbing into this, they left the land and rowed for nearly an hour under the hot sun, watching the glittering shore.

Having played in the lake during her childhood, Meryem was not afraid of water. The sea did look very different, but it was just water, too. And after all the experiences she had been through, little could disturb her now.

The hut Meryem saw on the distant beach had no meaning for her, but as they drew nearer to the land, she could not help thinking that they had come to an awful place. In fact, they had arrived at a heavenly cove, where emerald green trees swept down to the enchanting sea. But the hut was a ruin.

When they went ashore, Meryem studied her surroundings in gloomy silence. The hut was filthy and smelled foul. The walls were patched with rusted tinplate or sheets of plastic here and there. Dirty baskets and bags made of reeds hung from the low ceiling. The whole place was oppressive. The bed in the corner was covered with a dirty piece of cloth. Meryem was used to having clothes washed in boiling water in a cauldron. The sheets at home were washed by scrubbing them with bleach and rinsing them in several changes of water. The floorboards were scrubbed with a wire brush and soft soap until they shone. Meryem felt like vomiting. The people in her village not only cleaned their houses thoroughly but also cleansed their bodies with hot water, soap, and sponge until their skins turned red. For the last few weeks, Meryem had been covered with dust and dirt, and the thought of her body made her feel sick. She had not been able to get rid of her body hair, either. If the women in the village knew about that, it would have certainly been considered a great sin.

The man who brought them there explained to Cemal how to feed and care for the fish and how to guard them from every danger. Then he left. Meryem did not understand what they were doing in this place, or how they would be able to live in that hut. Behind the hut, toward the forest, a small hole had been dug and covered with reeds. The stench emanating from that direction and flies buzzing over the hole indicated that it was the toilet.

It was almost evening when they arrived. Meryem sat by the water and lost herself in the beauty of the cove, of the pine trees on the opposite shore, and the intoxicating scents of spring. The air smelled of rose geranium, jasmine, cherry laurel, and pine needles. The pine trees themselves were reflected in the water. Seashells and shiny, colorful pebbles glittered like jewels beneath the surface. Meryem could not take her eyes off their varied and speckled hues of green, red, brown, purple, dark blue, and yellow. Perhaps the following day, she would walk into the sea and feel the coolness and soft, slipperiness of the ground beneath her bare feet as she had done when a child on the shores of Lake Van.

Cemal was busy inside the hut pulling and pushing things around. Meryem suspected that he would make her sleep in the hut while he himself spent the night outside in the coolness under the stars.

Silently, she removed her plastic shoes and thick socks. The cool water was delightful and refreshing. Then she washed her shoes and put them on again without the woollen socks, which she quickly stuffed into her pockets. She suddenly felt much lighter.

When darkness fell, Cemal lit the small lamp in the hut. Suddenly, hundreds, thousands even, of flying insects attacked Meryem's arms and legs, and began to suck her blood. Her skin began to itch and swell. Although she continuously slapped her arms and legs, Meryem could not win the battle against such an army of mosquitoes. She wondered how Cemal could endure this torture with such calmness.

Cemal had also been dismayed when he saw the hut and was wondering how they would survive imprisoned in these few square meters of space. The dark forest and aggressive mosquitoes did not disturb him as they did Meryem. He was even slightly pleased, for these small creatures reminded him of his survival training as a commando.

When he returned to shore, he caught a glimpse of a spotted snake slithering through the grass. "This place must be full of snakes and scorpions," he thought. Recalling all he had learned during his military training, he began to think of ways to keep Meryem safe from these kinds of creatures. Then he realized with a start that he was trying to protect the girl whom he had been ordered to kill.

If a snake bit the girl in this wild, remote place, his problems would be over. He could not have thought of a better solution.

"Let's wait and see," he thought, even as he sprinkled the floor with some sulfur powder he had found in a jar. No insect would get inside now.

In a few days, Cemal and Meryem got used to the hut and its foul smell, but they had a new problem—boredom. Since Cemal did not say a word to her, Meryem did not speak either. She spent the days sitting on the narrow strip of sand with her feet in the cool sea. Cemal lay on the ground in the open air most of the time, but Meryem was not sure if he was asleep or awake. Sometimes he took the boat and rowed to the opposite shore.

Once, he disappeared for many hours. Taking advantage of his absence, Meryem undressed and got into the water. She washed herself all over with a piece of soap she had found in the hut. She tried to cure the open sores on her arms and legs she had made from scratching the mosquito bites by rubbing them with salt water. Then she loosened her long, shoulder-length hair to let it dry in the sun. At the same time, she kept a close lookout for Cemal so she could cover her head with her newly washed scarf as soon as she saw him coming.

IT TAKES ONE HUMAN TO
HEAL ANOTHER

As THE ROWBOAT GLIDED OVER THE STILL WATER in the evening mist, Meryem thought that the big sailboat they were approaching resembled a tower rising from the sea, imposingly white in the still air. Cemal rowed and drew up alongside it.

Meryem had difficulty climbing the aluminum ladder, so İrfan caught her by the arm and pulled her up. She shuddered when his fluffy beard rubbed her face, and she smelled the alcohol on his breath.

Unaccustomed to the alien and sterile atmosphere in which they found themselves, both she and Cemal sat down meekly in the seats the professor indicated to them. Their host had already prepared dinner and the table was set. Candles were burning, and wine was cooling on ice.

Meryem had become accustomed to eating in front of men, but now she was faced with the realization that she was about to be served by a man, with food he had cooked himself. Not only was he a man, he was an older man, from the city, an educated man—a professor, in fact. She stirred restlessly in her seat and did not know what to do as the man leaned forward to put food on her plate. This was the first time in her life such a thing had happened to her, and she was too covered with confusion even to look at what was being served.

Cemal was also confused though less so than Meryem. He did not understand the reason for the professor's invitation. Why would such an important man want their company? He was even more awe-inspiring than his commanders in the army had been. This man was a university professor as well as being as old as Cemal's father.

Cemal refused with a shudder the wine İrfan offered him and looked askance as the elderly man filled his own glass. He had never sat at a table where alcohol was served. Was he betraying his father again? He burned inside, yet he had to remain respectful and silent as long as he was with the old professor. "Each to his own sin," he thought.

On the sailboat, motionless on the still, dark waters of that enchanted cove, the three diners sat buried in ambiguous silence. Each was aware that there was something peculiar about their situation without comprehending exactly what it was.

An intense scent of jasmine suddenly filled the darkness. The incredible sweetness of it seemed to pervade even their bodies. Dizzy, they silently ate their food in the warm light of the kerosene lamp.

After overcoming her initial embarrassment, Meryem realized how delicious the food was. It was somewhat like spiced sausage and tasted even more delicious after days of eating fish at every meal.

Apart from the day of the professor's visit, they had eaten only the small fish Cemal caught. They were not supposed to eat those from the farm. Every day Cemal rowed out into the cove and, after waiting patiently for hours, would catch a few small fish. Meryem could not bear to clean and gut them, so Cemal did that job. Feeling squeamish, Meryem would fry them and set the table under the hungry gaze of wild cats waiting for the innards. She and Cemal would finish their silent meal in a few short minutes.

Dinner on the big boat, however, was quite different. Compared to the filthy hut, this place was like heaven. Everything was immaculate, well kept, and well cared for.

After dinner, İrfan offered them some chocolate out of a fancy box. He himself continued to drink steadily until his speech became slurred, and his movements slowed down. When he stood up to clear the table, he staggered and had to grab hold of it for support.

Cemal immediately reached out to help him, saying, "The girl will clear the table and do the dishes. It's her job."

Meryem carried the dirty plates toward the ladder which the professor had climbed up with the food. Downstairs, she found a small kitchen, and though she had a hard time finding a garbage can and the faucet, she quickly washed and dried the dishes. Her sharp eyes saw where everything should go, and she even worked out how to use the detergent and rinse the foaming bubbles from the dishes.

Meanwhile, İrfan was talking to Cemal, trying hard to extract information from the reticent young man. What were the two young people doing on this fish farm? Where had they come from? Why were they there? What kind of a relationship did he have with the girl?

Slowly, in dribs and drabs, the young man began to answer his questions. İrfan felt he was slowly disentangling the mystery of this young couple, yet some things were still unclear. He had worked out that they were cousins, and Cemal did not talk about the girl as though they were lovers, but what were they doing in this cove? Perhaps they were fugitives.

Suddenly, İrfan had an intriguing thought. When someone changed his own life, could it affect the lives of others, too? Or, could he change his own life by transforming other people's lives?

The idea of participating in the fate of these two young people excited İrfan as though he were playing an entirely new role. Moreover, with his commando training, Cemal would be a great help on the boat. The girl was already doing the dishes. Meryem had had an amazing effect on İrfan, who found the little girl oddly attractive. He liked her large, round, moist eyes that always seemed wide open in amazement. These youngsters could do many tasks on the boat that he could not do himself because of his injured leg, and he would no longer be alone, traveling from one bay to another. He remembered something his mother had said: "It takes one human to heal another."

Here on his boat were these two people from eastern Anatolia. İrfan had not been able to go there, but the atmosphere of the east, which was a necessary part of his book, had come to him.

Cemal, like İrfan, was immersed in thought. The caretaker of the fish farm was to return the next day, and he and Meryem would not be needed anymore. Where would they sleep the following night? Would the guard allow the girl to stay in the hut? He recognized that Selahattin could only help him for two weeks. Then it was up to him to take care of his own affairs. Cemal had to find an immediate solution, but, without help, he and Meryem could not go anywhere. They needed someone with a boat to take them to a village on the coast.

Should I ask this old man for a job? he wondered. He was willing to work on the boat in return for food and a place to sleep.

At the same time, İrfan was considering how they would react if he offered them a job and gave them some money.

Meryem, having finished the dishes, came out and sat down silently in a corner, breathing in the intoxicating scent of jasmine and wishing that their visit to this boat would never end. The boat was so beautiful, so clean, so different. It did not resemble the hut in any way, nor the shanty in Rahmanlı. The man himself was very different from any other man she had met. He treated her respectfully and, maybe, he even liked her. Yes, Meryem felt quite sure that he liked her.

On those spring evenings, when the sap began to rise and the air was filled with intoxicating scents, Meryem was filled with an indescribable longing for life. She wanted to live. Her body burned with the desire to live. With all the yearning of her fifteen years, she felt the need to touch and embrace another body. Those scents, the young men on the seashore, the half-naked girls licking their ice cream, the boys' slender bronze bodies, their laughter, their smooth white teeth, their earrings, and the bangs falling free over the girls' pretty faces— she could not stop thinking about what she had seen. On this boat, there was something that belonged to "that world," something different from her own, a freedom in the atmosphere, full of life and joy. The humidity rose with the rising mist, and the enchanting scent of jasmine seem to enter into the very pores of their skin.

The professor tried to remember Constantin Cavafy's line: "The jasmine was like a second skin," or something like that. His mind was too bemused to remember it clearly, and in any case, the quotation in itself was a reminder of another time when he had not been quite sober.

As they sat in silence letting the smell of jasmine waft over them, each of the three realized that they had come to a decision which did not need to be put into words, it was so obvious.

As Cemal and Meryem left, İrfan said, without getting up, "Don't come too early tomorrow, but don't wait till evening either. We've got to leave the cove while there's still light."

The next day toward lunchtime, the fish farm caretaker arrived in a rowboat towed by another that had an outboard motor. He was a coarse, unfriendly man with yellow teeth and a three-day-old beard. He did not pay much attention to Cemal and Meryem. He immediately went into the hut, sat down on the bed, and lit a cigarette.

Cemal and Meryem no longer had any business there. Cemal asked the man if he could row them to the big sailboat. For the first time, the surly man smiled, or rather grinned. Perhaps he was happy that these two uninvited visitors were not about to become a burden to him. He was quick to get up and row them to the boat.

When they climbed aboard, İrfan woke up. As if she were already familiar with the place, Meryem made him a cup of Turkish coffee. This unexpected kindness pleased him. She was a strange little girl—quick, efficient, and friendly.

Before weighing anchor, İrfan gave his crew their first crucial lesson. He taught them how to use the life jackets and the fire extinguishers. He also told them a few things about the engine and explained how the boat moved forward and backward. Then it was time to teach them about the sails and the fenders. He showed Cemal how to throw the fenders over the side when they docked.

İrfan's explanations were too garbled for the inexperienced crew to grasp, but their captain was patient. He did not expect them to learn everything at once.

İrfan sent Cemal to shore in the dinghy to tie the painter to a tree. Then he limped toward the front deck and weighed anchor. Using the engine, they began to move slowly out into the current.

The cove was so winding and treacherous that İrfan was amazed he had passed through it safely in the dark without any accident. He steered the boat and gave orders to his crew at the same time. The way they kept bumping into things, getting tangled in ropes, or slipping and falling made him roar with laughter.

Soon they were out on the open sea. The misty, humid air of the cove was replaced by bright, open sunlight. A gentle wind was blowing from the northwest. İrfan let out the sails and turned off the engine. The boat listed to the right and began to speed over the glassy water as it hissed beneath the keel.

Meryem closed her eyes and let the wind caress her face. She reveled in this environment full of new and charming things. The loathsome feeling of dirtiness that had dominated her in the hut was washed away by the open sea, the wind, and the crystalline sky.

After passing the headland, they were caught by a strong cross-wind. The captain was at the rudder, trying to adjust the sails to the new breeze, while Cemal stood behind him. Meryem was sitting in the prow.

Involuntarily, she had an idea. She would take the first step in testing her desire to belong to this new way of life. She was frightened at the thought, but a burning desire to live impelled her to take that crazy step. Turning slightly, she stole a glance at the two men and waited for the right moment. While neither of them was looking, she loosened the knots that held the scarf around her head. The cloth slowly freed itself in the wind, and Meryem could feel it move. She waited impatiently. It was time to rid herself of that ugly piece of cloth. Later, one by one, she would shed the rest of her clothes—the faded cotton dress, the black plastic shoes that now seemed so out of place.

Suddenly, the wind swept her scarf away into the air behind her, filling Meryem with joy and fear. With an expression of disbelief, she turned and cried out. The wind had plastered her scarf to the rudder.

Meryem was devastated; she had failed. Now she had to go and pick up the scarf and cover her head again. No one would fall for the same trick twice. Frowning, Cemal watched her in silence.

At that minute, İrfan picked up the scarf fluttering on the rudder in front of him and shouted so she could hear, "Why do you cover your head?" he asked. "You have beautiful hair. Let it breathe."

Under Meryem's startled gaze, he released the scarf into the wind and let it go. The cloth fell into the water, floated for a while, then disappeared under a wave.

Meryem shut her eyes tightly. "Oh, my God!" she thought. "Dear God!"

With every passing second, the boat gliding over the turquoise sea carried her farther away from that hateful scarf.

Meryem did not have the courage to look at Cemal—even though it was too late for him to do anything. She guessed that he would not be able to go against the wishes of the long-bearded professor who was as old as his father.

Finally, Meryem was a girl without a headscarf; she could have grown wings and flown for joy. With her hair blowing freely in the wind, she stretched her bare feet toward the foam and lost herself in the swift movement of the boat cutting the water like a knife.

She did, in fact, feel a twinge of guilt. Since she was little, she had been taught that covering her head was one of the most important of God's commands. Now she had defied that divine order, but her joy was so intense that she did not really mind. "God doesn't love me anyway," she thought. "He's never shown me any miracles as he has others."

As they flew over the water, it reminded her of the way she had flown through the air when pushed on the swing they had rigged up in the garden in her childhood. It was the first time since then that she had felt so carefree. Foam from the prow splashed against her legs and cooled her down.

After a while, she heard someone call her name. When she turned, she saw İrfan offering her a bright red can of Coke. It was ice-cold in her hand.

Then he did something strange: He smiled and winked at her. Meryem glanced at Cemal, whose eyes were glued to the rudder. Flushed with excitement, he was too preoccupied with steering the boat to notice her. Meryem winked at the professor. They were accomplices now and had exchanged their first secret message.

"Thank you, grandpa!" Meryem said exuberantly.

İrfan's face fell, and he recalled a line from a poem: "A girl called me uncle, what shall I do!"

For the first time in his life, a young girl had called him "grandfather." He was not old enough to play that part yet—at most he could be her father. Perhaps it was the long, gray beard that created an impression of age.

These young people who had come aboard made him feel old and worn-out, but at the same time, they instilled in him the jasmine-scented enthusiasm of youth.

"It takes one human to heal another," he thought.

That evening, they anchored in another lovely cove. There were three cabins on the boat, so there was no problem with sleeping arrangements.

The next morning, Cemal and Meryem woke up very early and went on deck. When İrfan appeared around midday, they were shocked. At first, they thought there was a stranger aboard.

After waking up around 11:00 A.M., İrfan had first taken the scissors and cut off his beard, before giving himself a smooth shave. Seeing his hairless face in the mirror had surprised him, too. His face looked thinner, more elegant. "I'm still young!" he thought to himself.

As he left his cabin, İrfan was sure that the youngsters would be surprised. He felt as if he were in a scene from John Dos Passos's novel *Manhattan Transfer*, set at a time when everyone wore beards. There the bearded hero sees a Gillette advertisement in a pharmacy window and, wishing to look like the clean-faced man in the ad, he goes in and buys himself some shaving gear. Then he goes home and shuts himself up in the bathroom to shave off his beard. When he comes out, his children all scream and point at him as if he is a stranger.

İrfan's prediction was right. Cemal and Meryem were bewildered at first by the difference in his appearance, but they were also astonished to realize how young he really was.

Meryem would never call him grandpa again.

AN INCOMPETENT
CHAMELEON

ONE MONTH AFTER THAT BRIGHT, JOYFUL DAY on which Meryem's headscarf had blown into the sea, İrfan was once more alone on the sailboat, driven by the wind and lost in a despair that gave him more pain than his broken teeth and bloodshot eye.

The adventure was over. He cared nothing for his aching bones or about which direction the boat went, but let it be blown hither and thither by the wind. Slumped on the deck with a bottle of gin, warm from the sun in his hand, İrfan recalled the events of the past few days.

His life had taken a crazy turn. His quest for metanoia had failed. He felt dizzy when he looked into the dark depths of the void he had discovered inside himself.

Now he understood why most people did not want to leave the safe waters of their lives or to throw themselves headlong into adventures. Security was the reason they remained in their prisons. Their homes and possessions did not prevent them from being free; rather, they protected them against a greater danger—themselves. The established system prevented man from meeting himself face-to-face. Did those who tried to escape end up as he had?

İrfan wondered about Meryem's effect on events. He did not know where she had gone, but he knew that he was sailing farther away from her with every passing minute. This gave him pain as well as pleasure.

He had no idea where the wind was taking him. Would the voyage end on the sharp rock of a Greek island or somewhere along the Turkish coast? He did not want to know. At least, another boat was unlikely to hit him. It was almost impossible, because anyone who noticed the aimless direction of his boat would take pains to keep away from it.

Among his confused thoughts, the name Martin Eden frequently surfaced. İrfan tried to remember what Jack London's tragic hero had been thinking of as he was drowning. İrfan had abandoned many things, but he had not lost his habit of perceiving life through fictional characters.

He no longer recalled how he had spat out his teeth after being punched in the mouth. He only remembered Meryem's extraordinary character. After that happy day when she rid herself of the headscarf, she had made herself noticed like gradually rising water, eventually becoming indispensable.

Meryem had surprised the professor by quickly learning everything he taught her about seamanship. She grasped new information much faster than Cemal, and her reasoning was more developed. She could make connections between things she knew and could reach intelligent conclusions. When İrfan issued a command, Meryem would already have leapt forward and raised the sail or thrown the boom as swiftly as a sparrow by the time Cemal figured out what to do. Cemal would then frown and cast hostile glances at Meryem and the professor. He did not know how he should behave, and his anger toward the girl increased.

One day, Meryem had seen a log in the water coming their way and shouted a warning. Now and then, logs would roll off freighters into the sea. They could damage or even sink the boat. Meryem had warned them in time. İrfan shivered as the enormous log rolled by harmlessly. Although Meryem had never encountered this kind of danger before, her intuitive warning had saved them from a catastrophic collision.

Soon Meryem was able to determine the position in which to moor the boat when they entered the bay where they would spend the night. Sometimes when İrfan directed her where to cast anchor and where to tie the painter, she would object, and say, "The last time the wind blew at two o'clock in the morning, it shook us badly. The same thing could happen again, so I think it would be better to tie the rope to that tree." İrfan was left openmouthed in astonishment. What Meryem said was true, but he was surprised at her saying it. He had to laugh at her audacity. Was this the ignorant village girl he had first seen with her head tightly covered with a scarf?

The professor discovered that Meryem had difficulty reading, so he began to tutor her. He enjoyed listening to her pronounce sentences from the newspaper syllable by syllable. Once he asked her to read the words "God willing," together with him, but before they had finished the first two syllables, she quickly said, "God willing! That's something I know very well."

Another day, while cleaning the boat, Meryem had seen the Magritte reproduction in İrfan's cabin and stunned him by asking, "Are those people flying in the air Armenians?" Even if he had contemplated it for a hundred years, he would not have imagined that those people wearing felt hats and suspended in the air in the picture *Golconde* were Armenians. What strange thoughts this girl had. When he asked her to explain, she blushed, and said, "One day a great wind blew in my village, and all the Armenians flew away. I thought those people in the air were them."

How could this ignorant girl, whose head was full of fantasies and superstitions, learn so rapidly and, more importantly, reason things out so well? Two weeks after coming aboard the boat, she had changed so thoroughly, it was as if she bore no relation to the girl she had been.

Her appearance had changed, too. İrfan had freed both Meryem and Cemal from their odd-looking clothes. He had taken the girl to the market in Bodrum to buy her some new things.

At first, Meryem had been too shy to walk along the marina in her cotton dress and black plastic shoes when others were dressed in bathing suits. At İrfan's insistence, she allowed herself to be taken to the fashionable shops there.

Under the puzzled glances of the clerks, İrfan picked out cotton T-shirts, white pants, jeans shorts, bathing suits, and Nike trainers for Meryem. Then, ignoring her protests, he told her to go and try them on in the dressing room. Though she was too shy to put on the shorts,

Meryem tried on a pair of white pants, a pink T-shirt, and the phosphorescent sneakers. İrfan almost fainted when Meryem came out. How elegant she looked. Her breasts, which had been invisible under the loose dress, sprouted like two small peaches under the T-shirt.

Meryem was so self-conscious she could not look anyone in the face, but kept her eyes fixed on the ground and held her arms awkwardly at her side. It was obvious she had undergone a great shock.

İrfan bought a pair of sunglasses for her as soon as they left the store, so that she could lift her head and look around. As she walked along the marina, Meryem sometimes caught a glimpse of herself in the shop windows. She had become one of those girls she had so longed to resemble. She felt indebted to the professor for everything, especially for releasing her from her headscarf.

A miracle was taking place in her life. This man had now become one of those miracles that had always been reserved for others, never for her. Maybe he was that very holy man, Hızır, who, dismounting from his gray horse, had boarded a boat and disguised himself as a sailor. Bibi and her aunt always used to say: "It's only when a man's problems become serious that he is granted a solution to them." That was when the holy man would come to your aid. She would tell the professor her thoughts later and explain it all to him. Meanwhile, before returning to the boat, they went into a men's outfitters and bought clothes for Cemal, too.

At first, when Cemal saw Meryem in her new outfit, he did not recognize her. Then his eyes opened wide in astonishment and fury. But when he saw his new clothes, he forgot his anger. The professor was able to encourage him to replace the thick, creased trousers and dirty yellow shirt for knee-length, white sailor's shorts and a navy T-shirt. Now he was involved in thinking about his own appearance.

The sight of Cemal wearing shorts reminded Meryem of a chicken with feathered legs and made her want to laugh. The sudden appearance of his hairy legs, which had never seen the sun and were somewhat bandy as well, made his self-image of the strong man a little ludicrous.

Thanks to the rapidly changing circumstances, the clothing revolution went smoothly. In the village, Meryem would never have been allowed to wear such an outfit, but, on the sailboat and in coastal towns full of tourists, her other clothes would have made her stand out and attract attention.

Once again, İrfan admired the human ability to adapt to new conditions and accept a new order of things so quickly. He regarded the experiences of the past weeks as a sociological experiment. It seemed he had been right when, in an article written years before, he had compared people to passengers on a transatlantic liner. When things went well, the passengers had a good time in the formal ballroom; people stood aside for each other, men rose to their feet when ladies entered, and they toasted each other in champagne, clinking their fine crystal flutes, while listening to lively tunes played on the piano. When the ship began to sink, these same people, struggling in the sea to catch hold of a piece of driftwood that would enable them to survive, would mercilessly push others away from it.

Human beings were chameleons, with the ability to survive by adapting to their surroundings. Yet some were incompetent, like himself. İrfan was a chameleon who was ready to try everything to adapt to his environment but who struggled in vain to change color—an incompetent chameleon.

That would be a good name for a book, but it was already too late for İrfan to dream about the future. Sooner or later, the boat would hit a rock and sink. The incompetent chameleon would be buried at the bottom of the sea, and his lifetime of incompetence would disappear forever.

From where he lay, İrfan could see the blazing red sky. A little later, darkness would descend like irresistible, absolute death. The boat had to be in a strait somewhere, because the wind was rocking the boat. İrfan was determined not to get up and look. Whatever would be, would be.

In two weeks, Meryem had learned to read fluently, then he began teaching her how to use the charts. He would lay a yellow chart on the table, and, as they bent over it to study the headlands and bays, he could inhale the girl's fresh scent. Sometimes, he would ask her which headland they would encounter next. Even when she answered incorrectly, he would applaud and say, *"Brava!"* He knew it was impossible for her to learn to read a map in just a few weeks, and the headland she had pointed out bore no resemblance to the one he had asked for, but he felt he was helping her develop her self-esteem.

Besides his usual attitude of bad-tempered silence, Cemal had begun to cast angry glances at them both. There were two conflicting poles on the boat: İrfan and Meryem at one pole, and Cemal at the other. The closeness between the professor and the girl and the way he praised her infuriated Cemal.

The fact that she was obviously streets ahead of him in intelligence and understanding was something he could not accept. How could this snot-nosed girl, this feeble creature whose life he had spared, have changed so much? In the village, it would have been her duty to serve him, and there she would not even have been allowed to eat or talk in the presence of men. On this boat on the Aegean shore, it seemed as if she were the superior being. That professor was spoiling her completely. Could it be that he was making advances to her? If Cemal discovered such a thing, he was ready to defend the family honor by immediately throwing him off the boat. With every passing day, his grudge against them grew, and he began to spend more time alone. Sometimes when they were at anchor he jumped into the water and swam long distances. At least he could swim better than Meryem.

İrfan insisted that Meryem should learn to swim. He said that if they ever had an accident or she fell into the water, she might drown if she could not swim. But Meryem was not brave enough. To learn to swim, she would have to wear a bathing suit, and she was not ready to expose her body.

Actually, she longed to wear her pretty new bathing suit. In fact, every day when she woke up, she put it on and wore her pants and T-shirt over it.

At first, she had felt naked in these clothes, but gradually she got used to them. But going around in a bathing suit in front of two men was out of the question.

İrfan continued his efforts to encourage her. "You'll get used to it," he said. "Human beings quickly get used to good things. And you've really scared me with the speed at which you adapt to new things!"

One evening, after they had cast anchor, İrfan had the opportunity he had been waiting for. "There's an incredible little bay nearby," he told Meryem and Cemal. "Let's get in the dinghy and go see it."

Cemal shook his head as usual. He did not want to join in anything they did. So Meryem and İrfan left together.

There were many interconnecting bays in this area of the coast. Idling along the virgin, green, pine-scented coast, they sailed over the blue water, so transparently crystalline that one could see clear through to its aquariumlike depths.

Meryem trailed her hand in the cool water and watched small silver fish swimming below the surface. İrfan was telling her about their destination, a narrow piece of land between two bays. In the age of Cleopatra, the local inhabitants had unsuccessfully tried to dig a channel across the narrow peninsula to connect the two. Since then, everyone who had tried to do the same thing had died in mysterious circumstances. In just a little while, he would point out to her the ancient ruins.

The sun was setting when they entered the bay, but Meryem was still able to see the ruins. On one side, they faced the setting sun, and on the other, the rising full moon. As darkness deepened, the moon shone brighter.

After a while, they took the rubber dinghy and made for the shore that was beginning to gleam silver in the light of the moon. They sat down on the pebbles. İrfan opened the two cans of beer he had brought along and handed one to Meryem.

Meryem was lost in a dream. The beauty around her, the silvery moonlight shimmering over the bay, the intoxicating scents, the gentleness and care of the man sitting next to her made her head swim. She felt as if she were being drawn along by a stream that was carrying her where it wished.

She accepted the beer without showing too much reluctance. Her lips touched the cold can first, and then she felt a momentary tickle of foam before a somewhat bitter taste. She was content and stretched out her feet toward the waves rippling along the shore. Cemal's absence—the lack of a controlling presence—was enjoyable. Maybe for once she could spend a few hours without being told what to do.

The respectful attention of this wealthy, learned man with his sensitive ways made her tremble inside and opened the door to a mixture of feelings. For the first time in her life, she felt valued, intelligent, and beautiful. Lost in these thoughts, she did not realize how quickly she had drunk the whole can of beer.

İrfan felt intense compassion for the girl sitting beside him. He wanted to grasp her thin shoulders and hug her. This was not from sexual desire, but rather from a feeling of sympathy. All he wanted was to clasp the girl to his breast and hold her like that for a while. He could not hug her. The girl would misunderstand.

The moon was rising fast. İrfan asked Meryem if she could see a shape in it that resembled a woman's profile. She could not. One night long ago in Izmir, when the air was heavy with the scent of rose geraniums, İrfan's father had taught him to look carefully at the moon until he could distinguish that figure. The full moon was like a medallion on the face of which was the profile of a beautiful woman, her face turned slightly upward. İrfan described the face of Meryem in great detail, but the girl could not discern it. What she could see was something completely different.

He decided to teach Meryem how to swim. He made the proposal with such eager enthusiasm that Meryem, already tipsy from the beer and the magic of that strange night, was not able to resist. After İrfan got into the water, she took off her clothes, hoping that the darkness would conceal her body. With only her bathing suit on, she stepped into the sea. Her bare feet, unprotected from the sharpness of the stones, made it difficult for her to walk. The sea, however, felt warm and protective. She was afraid that the professor would see her half-naked body in the light of the moon, but she did not resist when İrfan took her hand and pulled her into the sea. Soon, the water rose to the height of her chest. Terrified, she clutched İrfan's hand.

When he laid her abruptly on top of the water, she screamed. "Don't be afraid," he said. "I won't let you go. Just keep your back straight. The water will hold you. Lie on the water as if you are lying in bed." At first in her panic, Meryem could not relax and lie flat. Afraid of drowning, she allowed her waist to drop and began to sink, but İrfan's protective hands were ready to catch her. He would not allow her to go under. Soon, she learned to trust him and began to float on the water unafraid.

Meryem shone in his hands like a white fish in the waters of that moonlit bay. He was holding a miracle. With light touches, he corrected the girl when she started to sink as she tried to float by herself. Each time, he admired her slender body more. The two resembled animals playing in a splendid bay by moonlight. The bays, which

Cleopatra had tried to unite, were filled with laughter and little screams of pretended fear.

Gently, İrfan turned the girl over and began to help her to swim, holding her by the waist and the shoulders. A pearly radiance gleamed from the white fish sliding through his hands.

He had not felt this happy since he had begun his voyage. This was perhaps one of the most joyful moments of his life, and, strangely enough, sexual desire was not a part of it. Carnal desire would spoil their childish, innocent fun.

He remembered that night as two children at play. He had become a young child like her. She, in truth, was a beautiful, innocent girl—a pure, intelligent, excitable, rosy-cheeked child, a child who had not forgotten how to blush—a baby dolphin, a silvery fish jumping up and down in the water.

The cynical, sharp-tongued professor, who had spent his adulthood lost in nihilism, realized that he had changed after meeting this girl. Meryem had softened his heart and taken him back to his childhood and youth. He was doing what he had formerly criticized and sneered at.

İrfan realized the girl was getting cold. She had stayed in the water too long for one not accustomed to it. He started with her toward the beach, carrying her over the sharp pebbles. Then she stood up, water dripping from her as she walked ashore; reaching the beach, she threw herself down on the pebbles.

The wind had got up. The professor could sense that Meryem was shivering with cold in her swimsuit and her teeth were chattering. She was not only unaccustomed to being in the water, but the beer and the excitement had also affected her. In spite of the cold, she had fallen asleep on the stones. Like a cat protecting its young, İrfan wanted to put his arms around her and keep her warm. He tried to quell this feeling, but could not. He bent over her and took her in his arms. For the rest of his life, he would recall this moment as one of the biggest mistakes he had ever made.

As soon as the girl had sensed the man bending over her, she leapt up and kicked him away with all her might, screaming at the top of her lungs, "No! Don't! No, Uncle! Don't do it!" Her bloodcurdling cries in the dark of the night were so unnerving that İrfan froze. He did not know what to do. He realized he had to calm her down and stop her cries, but he did not have the courage to approach her.

Covering her face with her hands, the girl ran back and forth over the pebbles, screaming like a madwoman. Then she fell to her knees and began to speak deliriously. İrfan got even more frightened. He could not understand what she was saying. A couple of times, he heard the words "uncle" and "hate you." Then she would scream and pound the stones with clenched fists.

İrfan had never witnessed such a scene before. Afraid to breathe, he waited, not knowing what to say or do. If he slapped the girl, would it bring her back to her senses? What if it made things worse? He had already behaved like an animal and frightened the girl into this. Maybe it was best to wait for her to calm down.

Finally, drained of energy, Meryem collapsed in a heap. İrfan saw that she was only half-conscious, but he still hesitated to approach. He knew something that triggered this incident must have happened to the girl. It was more than likely that she had been raped. Again more than likely by an elderly man. Could it be that the girl's uncle, Cemal's father, had raped her? But wasn't the man a sheikh of some religious order? But what difference did that make!

If his suspicions were right, Meryem had just revealed the deepest secret of her life. His heart wrenched with the knowledge that she had been hiding such a painful, horrifying secret. And it was he who had caused her the shock of remembering it. Yet this same shock she had experienced could also help drain the poison from inside of her.

İrfan gathered all his courage together and approached the girl. He lifted her head, placed it gently in his lap, and began to stroke her hair. Cautiously, he whispered, "Don't be scared, Meryem. There's nothing to be afraid of."

In a few minutes, she regained consciousness. She did not speak but İrfan felt warm teardrops fall and wet his leg. It was good that she was able to cry, and it also meant the crisis was over.

"I'm sorry I frightened you," he said. "I didn't mean any harm. I only wanted to protect you, I swear. Like a father . . ."

The girl continued to cry.

İrfan realized that he had entered dangerous waters again. "Did a man hurt you?"

Meryem wept silently.

"You thought I was your uncle, didn't you?" he asked. "Did he rape you?"

Meryem sobbed, and İrfan concluded that he was right. She did not deny it. Respecting Meryem's distress, he remained silent.

He recalled his past conversations with Kürşat Bey, a retired judge who was Aysel's uncle. Kürşat Bey had worked for many years in various Anatolian towns and cities. Once, when İrfan had asked him what kind of crime was most common in Anatolia, the judge had startled him. İrfan had expected the answer to be homicide or larceny, but the old man told him that it was incest. "Since the girls in the case are ashamed and embarrassed, these incidents are usually not brought before the law. For instance, after a young man gets married and leaves for his military service, his father begins to harass the young bride. Uncles and in-laws rape their nieces. Unfortunately, such incidents are common, and in the end, it's always the women who pay, either by committing suicide or being murdered."

The sobbing girl fell asleep on İrfan's knee. So Meryem was one of those who had somehow been spared from suicide or death. Her figure looked so vulnerable in the moonlight. Trying hard not to disturb her, İrfan stretched over to get her T-shirt and pants in order to cover her. Afraid to breathe, he then waited for her to wake up.

On the way back to the sailboat, Meryem held her head between her hands, bent over as if in great pain. İrfan apologized again as the dinghy moved silently forward. He had not intended to hurt her; his only intention had been to do good. Perhaps, after all, what had happened might help her overcome her feelings of shame.

He told her that, according to the psychologists, a secret once disclosed would cause the pain to be obliterated. "My mother says that only a human can heal another human. Tell me your secret so that you can let the poison out."

The girl did not move or speak.

"Was it your uncle?"

She did not answer.

"Was it Cemal's father?"

She had remained silent, looking as if she had surrendered to a power greater than herself.

Suddenly, as he was lost in his thoughts, there was a tremendous crash, and İrfan was flung across the deck. The sailboat had hit something. Was it a Greek island or the Turkish shore? Or was a rock in the sea breaking the boat into pieces?

İrfan heard the sheet iron tear like paper, making horrific noises, yet he was determined not to get up from the deck. He was not afraid. His fear—the bird fluttering its wings inside his chest—had been replaced by calm submission. Soon, the cool water touched his face and İrfan felt the vast, cold, magnificent darkness of the Aegean Sea. He smiled.

EVERYONE HAS A SECRET

That night, Meryem had dreamed again about the phoenix tormenting her with its black beard and pincerlike beak. It was the first time she had seen the creature since leaving the barn. On the narrow bed in her cabin, she writhed and moaned, begging the bird to let her go. The creature did not listen but went on ferociously stabbing at the sinful place between her legs.

Meryem had almost forgotten that place of sin. In fact, she had no longer considered that part of her body sinful. When she woke up in her cabin with a terrible headache, she felt as hopeless and miserable as she had in the barn. All the bad memories she had blocked out came rushing back to her once again. No matter what she did, she was unable to release herself from the fear and guilt that flooded her heart. Her bloody flesh felt immersed in sin. Maybe it would have been better if she had tied the greasy rope around her neck. By now, her name and her face would have been forgotten, and no one would remember her. As it was, she felt that her sin would haunt her forever.

She hated the new clothes she had put on with such excitement just a few days before. She was different from those others and had no right to wear them. Those pants, T-shirt, and belt were part of her sin. She wanted to wrap herself up in her threadbare dress, put on her black plastic shoes, and cover her head tightly with a scarf. The courage she had found on the sea had completely disappeared, and she had become a timid little girl again. She felt she had gone out of her depth.

Meryem oscillated between extremes. One moment she felt at the height of her courage, and the next she plunged into the depths of cowardice. She did not believe her fear would ever go away.

For some time, she lay curled up in bed moaning. Then she sat up and took off her bathing suit. Once more she put on her long underpants, cotton dress, and woolen socks. She also covered her head with a thin muslin cloth she found in the cabin. Then she felt better.

She considered she had been led astray by the professor, a man from the big city. If that evil man had not suggested it, she would never have worn a bathing suit or entered the water in the presence of a man. She hated the professor and never wanted to see him again.

She was comfortable in her old clothes. What scenarios she had pictured in her mind when lying in that bed: She had seen herself returning to her village and walking through the marketplace in her new clothes. People would be stunned by the sight of her new pants, pink T-shirt, sunglasses, and sports shoes and would scarcely believe their eyes. They would mistake her for a wealthy lady from the big city or even a tourist—whether German, French, or American—they could not tell.

The small stores on both sides of the muddy road would empty, and everyone—the grocer, the cloth-seller, the greengrocer, the attorney—would come up to her, even the government officials. "Who is she?" they would ask each other in awe. "Who is this rich lady?" Meryem would not say a word, but secretly, she would be laughing at them. All the women in the village would come to stare at her in envious amazement. Her aunt would be among them, with her pinched face, receding chin and tightly wrapped headscarf. She would look at her, but Meryem would pretend not to see her and walk away. The curious crowd would follow as she headed for Bibi's house. When Bibi opened the door, Meryem would say, "It's me—Meryem. Don't you recognize me?"

She would take off her black sunglasses, then.

Amazed, the crowd would exclaim, "It's Meryem! Our unfortunate Meryem!"

Her aunt would open her arms, and say, "Meryem, my dear girl!" But Meryem would turn her back on the woman who had left her crying outside her door.

Then, making sure that the whole crowd heard, she would declare, "Everyone in this village is a liar, Bibi. They smile at you, but behind your back, they lay traps for you. Everything they said when they sent me to Istanbul was a lie. There is not a single honest person here. And the worst is my aunt. Besides, Istanbul is very different from what they think. If you had seen Yakup's house, you would have cried. Not even a dog would live there."

She and Bibi would hug each other. Leaving the others outside, they would enter the house hand in hand.

Each time Meryem recalled this daydream, she added new details. Sometimes she would wonder at how quickly she had forgotten about Döne and add her into the fantasy. Another time, her father would take part in the story.

Now, bundled inside her old clothes, Meryem felt frightened and ill. She trembled as she thought about all the things she had dared to imagine. She felt her legs burn with fire as they had the day she visited Şeker Baba's tomb, when her aunt had placed a burning match between her legs and Meryem had felt the heat of the flame. The boat began to smell of depilatory wax. "You have not waxed your hair in such a long time! You sinner! You'll burn in hell!" The spiteful hags were touching her all over.

In the cabin next door, Cemal heard Meryem moan and sob a few times before falling silent. His ears were sharp. He lay motionless on his bed as if he were on the mountains, listening for every sound.

He should not have let the girl go alone with the professor; he should have taken steps to prevent it. A strange man and a girl from his family should not have been permitted to go anywhere alone together. In their village, this could have been a reason for murder. Circumstances had changed so much in the last few weeks that when something unfamiliar or unexpected happened, he did not know what to do. He could no longer tell right from wrong. In the village, Meryem would not have been allowed to dress like this, but on the boat, she looked very outlandish in her village clothing. He even wore shorts himself.

Cemal was amazed how clothes could change a person. In his

commando uniform, with his equipment and weapons, he had felt like the ruler of the world. In these funny shorts, he was an incompetent boy. Besides, he had no money, no job, no home, nor anywhere to go. He was like a refugee on the professor's boat.

After Meryem and İrfan had left, he had gone to the professor's cabin. The old man had the biggest cabin, of course. There was a strange painting on the wall, depicting flying men wearing peaked felt hats. Next to it, the professor had placed a poem which spoke of coming back to life if you did not like being dead. It did not appeal to him. Cemal's favorite poem was one he had learned during his army days and had never forgotten: "A flag is a flag only when there is blood on it / A country is a country only if you die for it!" When they shouted this in unison, his heart had swelled with pride. The poem this man had pasted up was utter rubbish. "In your dreams!" said Cemal. "I'd like to see you come back if a Kalashnikov bullet smashed your head. Death is no child's game."

He had rummaged through the drawers in the cabin. In the first two, there were underwear, a notebook, and a lot of pens. In the third drawer, he found money—American dollars. He did not count the notes, but there were obviously a great number.

Holding the money in his hands, Cemal had sat down on the bed and begun to think.

When the girl and the professor returned in the dinghy, why shouldn't he strangle them both and throw the bodies into the sea? Nobody knew that they had anchored in this isolated bay. It would take only a few minutes to get rid of them. Then he would take the money and leave in the dinghy. No one would find him or be able to accuse him.

Cemal got carried away with his planning. He could just as easily get rid of them before they boarded the sailboat. As the dinghy approached, he could hit them over the head with something or give them a lethal blow to the throat with the side of his hand, as he had learned to do in his commando days.

He put the money in his pocket and went on deck. The green dollars warmed his pocket. He felt happy and secure. With this money he would be able to start a business and become respectable like Selahattin. Or maybe he would go back to Istanbul and open a kebab restaurant with Yakup. He could bring Emine to the big city, where they would get married. Going back to the village did not appeal to him, because he would have to give the money to his father.

As soon as he had remembered his father, his blood went cold. The thought of his father's black-bearded face, which had always stood between Cemal and sin, made him shiver. He had nearly committed a sin. He had forgotten that God, who saw everything, even a black ant on a black stone, was watching him. Hurriedly, he had returned to the professor's cabin and put the dollars back in the drawer.

Now as he lay in bed listening to Meryem's sobs, he was annoyed. Since leaving the army, he had become a nobody. In the village, they had patted his shoulder, praising him as a hero, but he had broken his bonds with the past after leaving there. In Istanbul and here, by the Aegean, nobody paid attention to him or respected him as a veteran soldier.

However, in the mountains, he and his comrades had been told that they were fighting to prevent the breakup of their country and were making the greatest sacrifice in doing so. Soldiers who died or were wounded in the service of their country would live eternally in the nation's memory. They were fighting for the honor of the red flag with its star and crescent. Here, no one seemed to care about such things.

Who did the professor, that poor excuse for a man, think he was? It was obvious that, old as he was, he felt no shame in lusting after Meryem. No wonder he flattered her by saying how smart she was and how she grasped things faster than Cemal. None of it was true. How could an ignorant little girl be better than a trained and seasoned commando? He would love to take both of them to the mountains and see how long they survived. Neither the girl nor that old sinner of a drunkard would last long there. Cemal did everything better than Meryem, but since the old man had eyes for no one but her, it was she he went on praising.

Without nodding off, Cemal had waited for them to come back. If anything seemed strange, he would have come forward and broken İrfan's neck, but everything had appeared normal. The professor and the girl had boarded the boat in silence and retreated to their cabins.

Cemal felt they had united in a conspiracy to make fun of him and put him down. They had both laughed when he first put on his shorts.

Had Cemal, the great commando, the ruler of the mountains and of the night, become their clown?

He felt that his anger intensified. He would finally be able to fulfill his duty and kill the girl. First, the witnesses on the train and the commotion in Istanbul had confused and prevented him from doing anything, and later, the sick, forlorn look on the girl's face had softened his heart. But he was a soldier; he should not have been affected by such things. Now the girl had joined the old man and was carrying on some funny business behind his back and, so, was coming closer to her death; she and that drunken old man, both.

The wind had changed direction during the night. The boat was rocking and the ropes were creaking. The professor lay in bed, covered with shame and sorrow, unable to assuage his guilt at having caused the girl such extreme shock. "It's none of your business," he tried to convince himself. "Her uncle raped her, then threw her out. None of it is your fault." He tried to return to his old cynical, sarcastic self. "What a pervert the fellow is! Who knows how much pain he must have caused the poor thing."

No matter how hard he tried, he could not forget the girl's trembling shoulders and unspeakable torment. Why did he feel such pity for her? Was she the means to bring about the change he had been looking for, which was to make him into a new man? Was he becoming like one of those people whom he had always mocked for their credulity and sentimentality?

The man she called "uncle" was probably Cemal's father, but İrfan did not think that Cemal was aware of the incident. He reflected on the girl's fear of Cemal, the lack of communication between the two, and the icy tension between them.

Why were they traveling together? Had Cemal run off with the girl? If he had, why did he treat her so harshly? As if struck by lightning, the penny dropped and İrfan understood.

His heart began beating like a drum. It seemed a murder was about to take place on his boat! He could not believe it. He remembered all he had heard about crimes of honor and girls who were condemned to death by consensus of the family. He had read such stories in the newspapers, but he never would have imagined he would have a role in such an event. In the past, these killings used to take place only in remote parts of eastern Anatolia, where a girl might be murdered or forced to commit suicide simply because she had been seen talking to a young man alone in a poplar grove. In the last few years, traditions had also transported along with the people who migrated from the poor areas in the east to the big cities. Young girls were pushed off viaducts, shot, or strangled by the men of the family.

When he read such accounts, he wondered chiefly about the mothers of such girls. How could a woman consent to the death of her daughter, whom she had nursed and raised? Or did they have no choice?

Articles criticizing such crimes of honor were often published in the newspapers. If those who had committed them got caught, they were accused of homicide, and according to the Turkish Criminal Code, the sentence for this was capital punishment. Although judges frequently exercised their judicial discretion and modified the sentence, the general amnesties that were issued periodically allowed the murderers to go free. In short, the justice system tolerated and protected those who committed such "crimes of honor."

İrfan's friend Altan, a professor of anthropology in Paris, had told him about a case he had experienced in France. One day he had been invited to the Colmar court by a judge who wanted to ask his advice concerning the murder of a young girl. The daughter of a Turkish guest worker who lived in Colmar had become friends with a French youth. The family had wanted them to separate and had forbidden the girl to see him. When the young man protested, the family had come together and ordered the girl's older brother and her nephew to kill her. The two young men strangled her near a highway. According to the coroner's report, it had taken fifteen minutes for the girl to die. Now the whole family was on trial.

The judge, a woman, had believed that they should not be tried as if they were French, since they had different cultural traditions. According to Turkish tradition, honor crimes were not considered serious. It was for that reason that she had consulted with Altan, as a Turkish professor, to give her his opinion.

Altan told her that murder was the same in every culture and that the family's origins should not influence her decisions. In the end, he realized that the judge wanted to send the family back to Turkey instead of having to have them taken care of in a French prison for twenty years. She might have thought that the family did not belong to the civilized world anyway, and it was better to let their own country deal with the matter. As a result of Altan's insistence, the family had been found guilty. Yet Altan thought that the judge was not totally wrong, since he himself declared, "All over the Mediterranean, the concept of honor is still considered to lie between a woman's thighs, and such murders are still seen as pardonable crimes."

İrfan was furious with Cemal, Meryem's designated executioner, and he vowed to keep an eye on the girl at all times. She would be under his protection from now on, and he would not let anyone destroy her young body and fresh spirit. He might even adopt her.

Yes, maybe he would do that.

The boat yawed in the wind. The ropes and the mast creaked, and the cabin rocked like a cradle, this way and that.

He wished he had his Colt revolver with him. He had been a fool not to bring it along.

He began to feel suffocated and stood up to go on deck.

The moon had set, and the sea was dark. The wind was wuthering, but the anchor had not dragged. The boat remained steady at its moorings. He would not have to get up at midnight to see to the boat.

Meryem heard a door open and someone go on deck, but she did not know which of the men it was. Was it the professor? Or was it Cemal?

A few minutes later, she heard a soft knock at her door. When she opened it, she was face-to-face with the professor. "I heard sounds and thought perhaps you weren't asleep," he whispered. Perhaps he was afraid of waking Cemal. "I can't sleep either," he said. "Let's go on deck."

Meryem followed him.

The cool wind outside gave Meryem goose bumps. İrfan found an anorak and covered her shoulders with it, pretending not to notice that she was wearing her old clothes.

"I'd never do you any harm, Meryem," he said. "You know that, don't you?"

The girl nodded.

"Can you trust me . . . like a father?"

Meryem nodded again, and İrfan breathed deeply.

"I was afraid that you'd misunderstood me. I couldn't sleep," he continued. "I want to tell you something. You're away from that village now. No one can harm you here. They can't touch you in any way."

"What about Cemal?" Meryem whispered.

"He can't touch you either."

They remained in silence for a while. They could find nothing to say.

Meryem was unable to raise her head and look at him. She would always feel everlasting shame in front of him, now he knew her impossible secret.

İrfan picked the girl up gently and carried her to her cabin.

Before he closed the door, he did a strange thing: He pressed a light kiss on Meryem's hand, in response to which Meryem kissed his.

Then shutting the door quietly, he returned to his cabin.

Cemal had heard them whispering without understanding a word of what they said. Wondering what had happened, he fixed his eyes on the ceiling and waited for dawn to break.

THE HOUSE THAT SMELLED
OF ORANGE BLOSSOMS

After that night in the cove, Meryem lost her cheerfulness, and her health deteriorated. When they set sail in the morning, she felt cold and had found an anorak to wrap herself up in. She constantly felt nauseated and had to rush down to the toilet to throw up. Cemal did not understand why Meryem had fallen ill or why she was wearing her old clothes again. Observing her carefully, he saw that the girl, who for some days had been as cheerful as a sparrow, had now become upset by the motion of the sea. To relieve her nausea, the professor had given her some pills and a special bracelet to wear.

The atmosphere on the boat was extremely uncomfortable. No one spoke, and each person did what was to be done with a gloomy face. The hatred between İrfan and Cemal was palpable.

After thinking things over carefully, the professor decided that no good would come of sailing any farther. On the open sea, both he and Meryem were easy targets for Cemal, who was young and strong. He did not really think the boy wanted to get rid of them but, if he did, he could easily do so. The best thing to do was return to land, moor the boat somewhere, and find a place to live.

The more İrfan thought about it, the more he realized this was not a reasonable solution. Though he knew he should leave Cemal and Meryem at the nearest point on the coast and sail away alone, he could not abandon the lovely girl to die.

He studied his book of charts and saw that there was a fishing village nearby. By now what looked like a small village in the book must surely have become a tourist paradise, but that would be even better. İrfan changed course.

The wind blew from behind, and they sailed at maximum speed toward the land.

The bay and the houses on the shore, which appeared as soon as they turned the headland, surprised the professor, who had expected to see many big hotels. Instead, there were small, white two-story houses with gardens covered in pink, white, and purple bougainvillea, and a village full of ancient cypress and olive trees.

As they drew near the shore, he saw a couple of fish restaurants and a rickety pier. İrfan tied up at the pier as barefoot children screaming, "Welcome!" ran forward to help him fasten the ropes. The water was emerald green, the village serene and beautiful.

From the pier, the village appeared larger than it had at first. There were quite a number of foreign tourists around, predominantly English. Some were reading, some were drinking Turkish coffee, and others were snoozing on divans under the giant eucalyptus tree in the garden of the teahouse. On the green hills behind the town beyond the last of the houses, ancient ruins, including the remains of a half-ruined theater, were visible. How delightful it all seemed.

Having decided that this was exactly the kind of place he had in mind, İrfan went ashore alone. Meryem was lying on the deck. She raised her head to look at the village, but then went back to sleep. Cemal was studying his surroundings.

İrfan thanked the deeply tanned boys who had helped him tie up the boat, promising to visit their fish restaurant. He then headed for the teahouse in the garden with the eucalyptus, which was so enormous that not even three people holding hands could encircle the huge trunk.

The professor ordered a Turkish coffee. He loved to sit in the open air outside a café or a teahouse in the early morning, looking at the bright green sea. He remembered the previous comic scene when the boy had tried to speak English with him. Since he had cut off his beard, no one would take him for a tourist any longer. He could see the boat from where he sat and keep an eye on Meryem.

Apparently, the local tourists had not yet discovered this place. Once, he had made the mistake of spending a holiday at a fashionable resort in the south. It seemed like hell: Giant sailboats crowded the small bay; seaplanes carried customers from the airport to the luxurious five-star hotels; the helicopters of the yacht owners buzzed overhead; and speedboats madly turned circles in the sea. Every hotel and restaurant by the seaside played different music, and the beat from various discos deafened the ears. At the time he had thought he was enjoying himself, but he had realized during those nights on the sailboat how much the voyage had changed him. Now many things disturbed him that he had then taken for granted.

The peace of this hidden village on the shores of the Aegean was something different. It was a refuge. Stray dogs drowsed idly by the roadside, opening an eye every now and then to glance at passersby. Nobody meddled with them. Here, life flowed slowly on its tranquil way.

The professor shared some of his first impressions with the owner of the teahouse. The middle-aged man said, accenting his words in the Aegean way, "You're right, but more and more people keep coming. In one or two years, this place should be full."

The owner had misunderstood him. The man considered the village's isolation a defect. If more tourists came, the village would get asphalt roads, traffic lights, and big hotels. The man wanted to earn more money; what could be more natural?

İrfan then told him that he liked the village very much and asked if he knew of a house for rent.

The owner did not know of any empty ones but said a man from Istanbul, a retired ambassador, had bought an old house at the other end of the village. And he sometimes rented rooms. They would not find anywhere as comfortable as that house. The old man was a bit strange, but they would have to put up with that.

İrfan was curious about the ambassador. The son of the teahouse proprietor accompanied him to the house, the last building at the end of the bay. It was a simple stone structure in the midst of a grove of orange trees with their fragrant blossoms. At least five hundred trees were giving off the provocative scent that embraced İrfan. This orange grove beside the sea was surrounded by tall cypress trees to block the wind. The garden ran right down to the sea, near to which a giant olive tree attracted the professor's attention. Just beyond it, he noticed a landing stage, ramshackle and rickety, but nevertheless a place to moor the boat if the water was deep enough.

He walked around the side of the house and came to the front garden, where a thin, white-haired, well-dressed man was crouching next to a splendid cypress tree. He gestured to them to keep silent before signaling them to come quietly.

İrfan walked softly toward him. The old man was holding a baby sparrow in his hand. The poor thing could not even open its eyes, let alone flutter its wings. The man carefully placed the tiny bird on the garden wall and took a step backward. When he was far enough away not to disturb it, he said, "There are sparrows' nests in the cypress tree. That little one had fallen out, and the mother was chirping anxiously. I've put it where its mother and father can see it. Let's see what happens. Soon we'll find out if it fell out of the nest accidentally, or if the parents pushed it."

"What will you do if it's been pushed out?" İrfan whispered.

"Then I'll take it home and look after it."

"So you'll change its fate, you mean."

"Yes," replied the ambassador, and for the first time, looked closely at İrfan. "Who are you?"

The professor introduced himself. He said that he was looking for a place to rent for himself and the two people with him.

"You may stay here, but there are certain rules," the ambassador said.

"What are they?"

"There's no television here, and you can't bring one in. Radios and newspapers aren't allowed, and neither is any discussion of politics. Singing popular songs and talking about celebrities is not permitted. Nor is support of any football team whatsoever. In short, any behavior that would cause the nation of folly to enter this house is banned."

İrfan was stunned.

" 'The nation of folly'?"

"Yes. Foolishness is so widespread in this country that it could enter a house through the air if one did not shut the windows and doors. Foolishness is the most contagious disease in the world."

"All right," İrfan said. He had never met such an ambassador. "How much is the rent?"

"As much as you offer."

"What?"

"As much as you want to pay. I don't hide the fact that I need money—the oranges don't make enough to cover their cost. People no longer want oranges that have seeds, when they can buy navel and Jaffa oranges, even though ours are tastier and more aromatic. Anyway, that's why I take a tenant every now and then. They pay whatever they can. You look wealthy, so you should pay more."

"How much more?"

"One or two million dollars."

Upon hearing this, İrfan realized that the old man really was an oddity, but he liked him for all that. The old man had tremendous energy and subtle irony—a good combination.

"You're as odd as they say."

The ambassador laughed.

İrfan checked the jetty and determined that the water was deep enough. After walking along the fine sandy beach for about ten minutes, he arrived back at the boat.

Meryem was still asleep. He asked Cemal to take in the fenders and untie the moorings. They turned on the engine and went to their new anchorage. The garden looked magnificent from the sea, and even from the boat they could smell the intoxicating scent of orange blossom. Meryem sat up and looked at the garden. Then she lay down again.

When they arrived, the ambassador was inside. He looked sad. He was sitting in an old armchair on the verge of tears. İrfan asked him what the matter was.

"Guess what happened to the little sparrow," he said.

"What happened?"

"Guess."

"Its mother came and took it back."

"No."

"You brought it home."

"No."

"What happened then?"

"A cat ate it."

"What did you do?"

"I shot the cat. So now, both the sparrow and the cat are dead."

"Don't be sad," İrfan said. "You've lost a bird and a cat, but you've made three new friends."

As soon as the words left his mouth, he realized what an idiotic thing he had said, but it was too late to change it.

The ambassador looked at the three of them. There was a mischievous twinkle in his eyes. He looked at Cemal in his shorts and Meryem in her village clothes and headscarf. "Who are they?" he asked.

"My friends."

"Are they professors, too?"

"No."

"Then they must be associate professors. Oh, who cares . . . your rooms are on the upper floor. Did you inform your associates of the house rules?"

"Yes. Don't worry."

As they carried their belongings to the second floor, the ambassador said, "You told me I was a strange man, but you, Professor, are no less odd."

"You're right." İrfan smiled.

The old man smiled, too. İrfan decided that the ambassador was not so strange after all but a very intelligent man who was simply teasing him.

Maybe everything he had said about the bird and the cat was a merciless joke.

"That was a fine game you played," he told the ambassador.

"What game? The game of becoming a child?"

In the evening, after İrfan had drunk a glass of half-frozen whisky, he asked the old man what he had meant by "the game of becoming a child."

The ambassador laughed.

"Human beings go through a 'camel phase' during which they carry all the foolish prejudices society burdens them with. Then comes the 'lion phase,' when they fight against all such prejudices. But there's another phase only a few achieve: the childhood phase. It's the highest phase, which requires one to consider life with the naïveté of a child, to play games, to be open to all kinds of influences, and to find one's lost innocence again. That's why I play games."

"I would never have thought that you would be an admirer of Nietzsche," said İrfan, as he toasted the old man.

"Well, I only accept his theory up to a point," the ambassador replied. "All that superhuman stuff is crap."

The healing scent of the orange blossom mixed with the salty smell of the sea. Surrounded by the delicately sweet fragrance of the breezy garden, İrfan enjoyed his ice-cold whisky. He considered living here till the end of his life. Meryem could stay with him, but he had to find a way to get rid of Cemal, who made him feel nervous.

"What's the girl's problem?" asked the ambassador.

"She's ill."

"What's her illness?"

"A nervous breakdown, I guess. That's why she can't get out of bed."

"The will to return to the womb," said the ambassador.

"Wilhelm Reich," replied İrfan.

The ambassador laughed. They had made up a reference game. Whenever one of them said something, the other had to refer it to its source.

"Why did she have a nervous breakdown?"

"I suspect she's been raped."

"What should we do?"

"Let's leave her alone for a few days. She may pull herself together."

Then the ambassador asked about Cemal.

"He's her uncle's son," said İrfan. "He's just finished his military service. As far as I can tell, he was ordered to kill the girl but couldn't do it."

"Maybe he fell in love with her."

İrfan laughed.

"That would be a perfect Hollywood script," he said. "Even the most mediocre writer would think twice before writing such a story."

"Sometimes real life is more melodramatic than Hollywood clichés," replied the ambassador. "Actually, it's often like that."

"You're right," İrfan agreed.

The ambassador remarked that in Anatolia there was a belief that women were evil, sinful, and full of guilt. This belief was at the root of the country's underdevelopment, since in this way half of the nation became ostracized.

"Yes," agreed İrfan. "But women are seen as guilty and sinful in the Western culture, too!"

"What do you mean?"

"Think about the word 'evil.'"

"Yes?"

"Don't you think this word comes from the word 'Eve'?"

The ambassador frowned, and said, "Perhaps you're right . . . Eve, evil, the first sin . . . You're right. At least, there's no such word for evil derived from 'Havva,' the name for Eve in our language."

According to the bits and pieces of information İrfan gathered from the ambassador as they drank through the night, the old man had worked as a Turkish ambassador in several European capitals. After he had retired, his wife had died, then he had bought this lonely house in this secluded bay. It was not the house he had bought as much as the orange grove, because his first idea had been to pick the oranges, pack and sell them. Later, the idea of living in the house had attracted him as much as selling the oranges.

"For years, I thought I represented the state," said the ambassador. "Then I began to wonder if the state was eligible to represent me. The honesty and intelligence of the people in charge did not measure up to my expectations. In the end, I decided to withdraw from the world I had always lived in and come here to write my memoirs."

"Did you write them?"

"No. Because I realized that the problem in this country is not a lack of knowledge or comprehension. We cannot teach them anything. They know everything better than you or I, but they lack good intentions. They insist on having their own way. You can't influence those who have the power of decision-making in this country, because the public is foolish and naïve. Democracy in a country where the public is uneducated is no different from having a dictatorship or an elected king. Therefore, I cut my ties with this country. I don't know who the prime minister is, even. The sparrow chick of today is more important for me than the prime minister."

"What really happened to that bird?"

"Come with me." The ambassador grinned.

He took the professor to his room. He had placed the sparrow on a bed of cotton in a birdcage.

"I wasn't wrong," he said. "It was the parents that threw the poor thing out of the nest, but I won't let it die."

Meryem was lying in bed in a small dim room with only a tiny window. She could not get used to her bed and was tossing and turning. This house reminded her of the vineyard cabin near her village. Whenever she closed her eyes and began to doze, she thought she was in that cabin and kicked wildly in the air to repulse the black-bearded shadow bearing down on her, but the sinister shadow did what it wanted and made the place between her legs bleed. Then she began to moan. The sound of her own voice woke her, and she found herself soaked in sweat.

The part of her brain that was working soundly whispered to her that even in the barn she had not suffered so much. Much time had elapsed since then, and she was far away from the village. Just when she thought she had forgotten everything, how could the horrifying memories return to haunt her?

Meryem tried to make her mind numb and expel these images from her mind to become as pure as a child once more. Yet, she could not manage it.

As Cemal squatted in a corner of the garden and watched the two drunken men, his hatred swelled to the point of bursting. Those two were laughing together—maybe even making fun of him—and talking in a language he did not understand. It was clear that they despised him, as though he were lower than a farmhand or a servant in the east.

Yet it was the heroism of Cemal and his comrades that allowed such men to live comfortably in this country. If Abdullah could see these two repulsive alcoholics, he would question whether they were worth sacrificing an eye or a leg for.

In Cemal's opinion they were not. The professor, in particular, was a traitor. He flew a foreign flag—larger than the Turkish one—on his boat. Every night, Cemal changed their places and put the glorious Turkish flag above the other, which, to him, resembled pajamas with its red and blue stripes. The next day, İrfan would say that it was against maritime rules and put the Turkish flag back in its former place. Cemal would not say anything, but at night, he would change the flags over again. The most important thing was the nation's flag. After so many of his brave comrades had become martyrs for their country, what maritime rule could prevent the Turkish flag from blowing in the wind above the foreign flag?

The next morning, Cemal found an opportunity to show the professor and the ambassador some of his photos from the mountains. In one of the pictures, Cemal was seen on the crest of a hill in his commando uniform, with his bandolier and cartridge belt, and his G3 gun pointing in the air. The photo had been taken from below. There were clouds in the background, and Cemal had raised his head with pride.

The two men did not pay much attention to Cemal's photographs; they gave them a cursory glance and handed them back. No matter what he did, they were not interested in him. If they had only asked, he could have talked about the war for hours.

WHAT DID THE
DONKEY SAY?

For three days, the scent of orange blossom, which had become almost sticky in the heavy air, enveloped all of them. Not only were the ambassador and İrfan, indefatigable in their consumption of whisky, intoxicated by the odor, but so was Cemal, who spent his time dozing lazily on the boat or in the garden.

The scent came in through the open window of Meryem's dim room, suffused her body like a balm, and healed her wounds. Compassion had turned into the scent of orange blossom pervading her room. The intense fragrance caressed her hair like Bibi's hand. In the rare moments when she half opened her eyes, she had visions of butterflies. Butterflies with dark blue wings and yellow spots flew above her head, landed on her face and hair, and covered her blanket.

Within a few days, the scent of the orange blossom and the vision of the butterflies brought Meryem back to health. She woke up with a tremendous feeling of boundless energy and well-being and sat up. Her bones ached, but she devoured the food the professor had left for her while she was sleeping.

Tearing off her clothes as if they were hospital garments soiled with sweat and blood, she jumped out of bed. Her head did not ache anymore, and her body felt weightless. As she opened the shutters and let the sunshine fill the room, her arms and legs responded as though she were floating through water.

She saw the sun rise in a crimson cloud behind a nearby hill. From their nests in the cypress trees, the sparrows chirped nonstop. Her happiness overflowed. On the chair in front of the bed, she saw a white dress. It must be a surprise gift from the professor. After admiring herself in the mirror in her new white dress, she went downstairs.

There was no one to be seen. It was too early for anyone to be awake. She went out into the garden and walked to the jetty. She watched the boat, which had become like home to her, sway gently in the morning breeze. She looked around at the orange trees as if witnessing a miracle. How could this fragrance be so pervasive? It was even more enticing than the smell of jasmine.

As Meryem walked around the garden, she discovered a chicken coop. Like a child, she joyfully collected the warm eggs. Back in the kitchen, she made tea, boiled the eggs, and set the table for breakfast in the garden.

The first to wake up was the ambassador. Still groggy from sleep, he did not recognize Meryem at first. In her white dress, so fresh and lively, she seemed a completely different girl. Then he noticed the breakfast table. "You did all that!" he said in surprise.

"Yes!" said Meryem proudly, as she poured the tea.

As they were eating, the ambassador asked Meryem, "Were you seasick?"

"Possibly," she replied.

"Had you ever sailed on a boat before?"

"No. I was in a rowboat on Lake Van once, but that was different."

"I get seasick, too," said the ambassador. "That's why I don't go sailing."

"It's so beautiful here," said Meryem, looking around. "It's like heaven."

Cemal came down a little later. Glancing surreptitiously at the girl, he took his seat at the table. In a little while, the professor also arrived. He was glad to see Meryem, but refrained from giving her a hug.

Looking down at her dress, the girl said, "Thank you."

"It suits you," replied İrfan. The dress of fine cotton he had bought in the local market fluttered in the morning breeze like a wedding gown.

Two days passed happily by. No one disturbed anyone else. The ambassador read books in his room, the professor went to the village and sat in the teahouse by the sea, Meryem hoed and watered the sweet basil, mint, tomatoes, and parsley the ambassador had planted, and Cemal either fished from the jetty or went to the village.

The ambassador did not allow fish to be fried in the house since the odor would linger for as long as three days. Cemal could not bring home the fish he caught. Instead, he removed the hooks from their mouths and threw them back into the sea. However, this was not enough to prevent him from fishing; to count how many he had caught was satisfaction enough.

During the long hours on the pier, he brooded about his future. He had no money, no job, and no home. He could not live in this house forever. He was unable to decide if he should go back to his village or go to Istanbul to try to find work there, perhaps as a security guard. Selahattin had told Cemal that if the girl were not with him, it would be easy for him to find a job. Ex-commandos were hired as guards by all the big banks and companies, and they got paid well. Would it be such a bad idea to leave the girl here and go to Istanbul? But would these men accept her as their responsibility?

One day when he was immersed in his thoughts, Cemal realized that he no longer thought about Emine or yearned to be with her, a discovery that did not disturb him much. He had left his village far behind, together with everyone and everything that belonged to his past, except for Meryem.

In the evening, they all ate together. Then İrfan and the ambassador would drink whisky and talk for hours, using words neither Meryem nor Cemal understood.

Sometimes, Meryem or the professor prepared the food, but mostly it was the ambassador who cooked. They often had spaghetti. The ambassador would pour olive oil and sprinkle sweet basil over the noodles.

One evening, when the ambassador had a pot full of water on the stove, the gas ran out. "Oof!" said the old man. "We can't buy a canister of gas at this time of day. The shops in the village are closed. We'd have to find someone to open up for us."

Meryem immediately came up with a solution: "There's bottled gas on the boat."

The ambassador looked at the girl in amazement.

"I'll go and get it," said Cemal.

"There's no need to bring it here," Meryem responded. "We can take the pot to the boat, cook the noodles, and bring them here."

Cemal was irritated. "It's easier to bring the gas," he said. "We might need it later for making tea or something."

The girl and the boy faced each other angrily. Then they both turned to the ambassador, as if waiting for him to decide who was right. The atmosphere was tense. Any answer he gave would upset either Meryem or Cemal.

The ambassador hesitated briefly, then said, "Let's eat out tonight. Forget about the gas. There's a family from the southeast living nearby who make special pancakes and serve them in their garden."

Everyone relaxed, and they set out along the sandy road to the village.

It was not far to a place where naked bulbs could be seen hanging underneath an awning. The family from the southeast had repaired the house, placed a few simple wooden tables and chairs in the garden, and begun to make and sell the traditional pancakes of their hometown. Foreign tourists, in particular, loved the food prepared by the mother of the family, her head swathed in a clean white muslin scarf. She made the dough, rolled it thin, then baked it on an iron sheet; the two sons served the customers, and the father with his bushy moustache sat at the cash register. Recently, many such places had sprung up in towns along the Aegean and Mediterranean coasts.

Meryem became nostalgic when she smelled the fresh odor of pancakes baking on the hot metal tray. She recalled how, as a child, she used to watch the bread baking in the backyard and later enjoy the triangular flaky pastries spread with butter. As soon as she arrived there, she had sensed that this was a place that would arouse her feelings.

As they ate their food, they could hear the sound of the waves. Otherwise, there was only silence since the father had told his sons to turn off the radio as soon as he saw the ambassador. He did not want to make the old man angry.

Meryem listened to the unending conversation between İrfan and the ambassador.

"What about wars and massacres?" asked İrfan. "Do you think they're games, too?"

"Yes. They're all games."

"Mass murders, world wars, atom bombs?"

"Games . . . childish games—if you look at it from the point of view of the cosmos. Think about the recent Kardak crisis between Turkey and Greece. If you consider the matter from the military point of view of both countries, war might seem reasonable. But try to consider it from the point of view of the goats on Kardak island: a lot of men roaring in on assault boats, dirtying the sea with diesel fuel, and destroying the peace of centuries. They erect a pole with a blue cloth on the rocks and leave. Then some other men come on boats just as noisy and replace the blue cloth with a red one. What is it, if it isn't a game? Human beings belong to the category of mammals, yet they try to turn themselves into something else. But no animal can survive outside its biological rules. A donkey has to live like a donkey, a snake like a snake, and a human being like a human being. However, the latter falls into error through his own strength by trying to become something else, forcing himself to change his nature. This is the real reason for unhappiness and war. In short, my friend, a human has to live like a human and a donkey like a donkey."

The ambassador paused and turned to Meryem and Cemal. "Do you understand what I'm talking about?" he asked.

"A donkey has to live like a donkey," Cemal repeated.

"Meryem understands everything," İrfan said. "She understands whatever you say."

"*She* understands everything," Cemal muttered. "Who do they think they're fooling?"

Then the ambassador said, "Let's play a game. If you're all so smart, then solve this riddle by tomorrow."

The professor looked at the ambassador as if he wanted to say that it was not the right time or place for a game. "Don't look at me like that," said the ambassador. "You, too, are bound to find me the answer."

Meryem and Cemal listened attentively as the old man spoke.

"A great sultan summons his two sons to his deathbed. He tells them that he will die soon and does not want his realm to be divided. 'However,' he continues, 'you shall not fight between yourselves about who is to be the new ruler. Tomorrow, both of you will go to the hunting lodge an hour's distance from here, and you will return the following day. Whoever's horse enters the city last will become sultan.' At once, each of the two princes begin to consider the problem. A race to come first would have been easy, but in what way would it be possible to enter the city last? They go to the hunting lodge and eventually find a solution. Now, you have until tomorrow morning for the most intelligent of you to come up with the answer."

Everyone was silent, trying to puzzle it out.

As she was finishing her pancakes and buttermilk, Meryem heard a donkey bray. The sound came from behind the house. Meryem stood up and walked in the direction of the sound. Behind the tumbledown house was a garden planted with vegetables. Two dogs lay there lazing in the sun, and a donkey stood tied to a tree, braying from some unknown discomfort. Meryem went over to it, stroked its head, and whispered something in its ear. She could feel the hardness of the skin under its harsh coat. This backyard smelled like the poplar garden at home. A strange feeling welled up inside her as she heard someone coming. It was the dark-eyed boy with a lock of hair falling over his forehead, the boy who had served them.

"What are you doing?" he asked.

"Talking to the donkey," Meryem replied.

The boy laughed. "It's our donkey, but I've never heard it speak," he said.

"It talks only when it wants to," responded Meryem.

The boy introduced himself as Mehmet Ali. "Where are you from?" he asked.

Meryem told him about her hometown, and Mehmet Ali was surprised that she was from the east. "I would never have thought so," he said. "You have a slight accent, but since you're with the ambassador, I thought you were his relative."

Mehmet Ali was very talkative, and Meryem soon learned all about his life and family. They had left their hometown because of the war but had not gone to a big city like millions of others fleeing the fighting. Instead, they had come to this little coastal village where a relative of theirs had given them the idea of selling pancakes. They were just making ends meet but believed they would earn more in the future as the number of tourists coming to the village increased.

Meryem stroked the donkey's face as she listened to Mehmet Ali. A little later, they heard the professor calling her name. They felt awkward when they returned to the front garden, as if they were mutually guilty of committing some sin. Everyone was looking at them.

Later, as they walked home, the ambassador asked Meryem where she had been.

"I was talking to a donkey," she said.

"What did it tell you?"

"It told me that you were right."

The ambassador and İrfan burst into laughter. This girl was certainly as odd as the professor had said.

The next morning, the ambassador asked if they had the answer for him. İrfan spoke first. "In a horse race, one of them could enter the city first," he said, "but it would be out of the question to enter last. Since their father was aware of this, he actually wanted the princes to become reconciled and agree between themselves as to who would ascend the throne."

"You have failed, *mon cher!*" The ambassador laughed.

İrfan shrugged; he had already forgotten the question. Besides, he had made up his answer on the spur of the moment.

"Come, commander, what's your answer?" asked the ambassador, turning to Cemal.

"Please don't let him know it, please, dear God!" Meryem prayed.

"Neither of the brothers move," said Cemal. "They wait in the hunting lodge for days. Whoever gives in, loses, and the one with the strongest willpower waits till the end and becomes the new sultan."

"No, commander." The ambassador laughed. "That's not the right answer either. What if neither of them moves, and they wait there for years? Now, pretty girl you tell me."

"They exchange horses!" Meryem blurted out.

The ambassador began to applaud, and the professor laughed.

Cemal jumped out of his chair. "What do you mean by 'exchange horses'?" he shouted.

Meryem turned to him and explained slowly, as though talking to a child, "They get on each other's horses and ride them like mad in order to enter the city first. The son whose horse comes in last becomes the sultan."

"But the last, not the first, becomes the sultan!" Cemal objected.

"Not the first son," said İrfan, "but the son whose horse enters the city last. The answer is in the question!"

Cemal left the table.

"Thank you, Bibi," Meryem said to herself. If Bibi had not told her this story when she was a child, Meryem would never have come up with the right answer, but she had no intention of sharing her secret with the others.

Both the ambassador and the professor had admired Meryem's wit while Cemal had left the room abruptly, his face purple with rage.

Was she going to lessen her enjoyment by telling them the truth?

"How did you find the answer?" İrfan asked.

"I thought about it all night," Meryem replied, "and the answer suddenly popped into my head!"

Later that day, Mehmet Ali brought some pita bread to the stone house. He stayed in the vicinity that afternoon, twisting his forelock and secretly watching the house.

The following day, he came again toward midday and said that his mother had asked for Meryem. A large group of tourists had come, and the old woman needed help. Since Meryem had told her that she knew how to make pancakes, his mother wondered if she could give them a hand. Meryem was sure that this was Mehmet Ali's idea but made no comment.

She went to the pancake restaurant that day, the next day, and the following one, too. So it happened that she began to spend most of her day there. Mehmet Ali's mother hugged Meryem, kissed her cheeks, and said, "My little partridge. Don't you have a mother or a father?"

"No," Meryem answered.

"My poor girl," the woman said, and hugged her again.

Although the professor and the ambassador were good to her, Meryem felt nervous and uncomfortable near them. When she was with the family from the east, she felt at home, as if she were in her own part of the world. She felt the family were sympathetic toward her and would not cause her harm.

One day she asked the old woman, "Shall I bake some flaky butter pasties?"

"Of course, my dear," said the woman, "but let me bring you something else to wear so that your nice dress doesn't get dirty."

Together they entered the small house. The woman opened a wooden trunk and took out a blouse and a beautiful pair of baggy pants decorated with purple flowers.

Meryem was amazed at how comfortable she felt in these clothes. As soon as the trunk was opened, she had caught a whiff of her hometown, bringing her to the verge of tears.

How strange it was. The clothes she had struggled so hard to get rid of now seemed to embrace her like old friends. She would never give up wearing her new clothes, which would always give her a sense of freedom, but it would be pleasant to wear her old ones from time to time.

Putting on an apron, she covered her hair with a muslin cloth and sat down in front of the kneading trough. Soon, her arms were covered in flour up to her elbows. She sat down beside the hot metal tray, baking the thin sheets of pastry and spreading them with butter before folding them into shape. From that day on, many customers asked for her special pastries.

In the afternoon, Meryem washed her arms and face at the faucet in the backyard before she changed her clothes and went home. The next day, when she returned, she immediately put on the baggy pants.

Wearing those pants was not the only change in Meryem. As soon as she stepped into the family's garden, she felt secure. She spoke without embarrassment, and even her accent smacked of the east again.

Meryem talked nonstop with Mehmet Ali, laughing, telling stories, and teasing him. She behaved flirtatiously toward him and felt proud when the boy looked at her admiringly.

Everything flowed along like milk and honey, and Meryem smiled knowingly to herself when the old woman said, "You've brought us such good fortune. Since you came here, the customers have been flocking in."

When she caught Mehmet Ali secretly looking at her breasts, she smiled to herself again. He followed at her heels as though mesmerized and never left her side. Meryem enjoyed feeling his excitement, which she had inspired.

One day, when she was alone mixing the dough inside the house, Mehmet Ali tiptoed up behind her. He gathered up all his courage, kissed her on the neck, and rushed out of the house. Meryem smiled to herself, and strangely, was not in the least upset.

A WILD NIGHT

Life was going smoothly, and everything was harmonious and peaceful in the house that smelled of orange blossom. It seemed as though they could go on living that way forever. Even Cemal, in spite of huffing and puffing and making constant complaints, had to put up with living among people he was sure were traitors, for he had nowhere else to go.

The retired ambassador enjoyed having a like-minded friend. At first, he had said that no one was allowed to bring up political matters, but this ban only applied to others. He took pleasure in stating his ideas, and if anyone interrupted, he got angry, and said, "This is what I think. How can you have an opinion on this? For half a century, I've been racking my brains over these subjects."

The others listened to the old man without much comment. It was especially difficult for Meryem and Cemal to grasp what he was talking about.

Whenever Meryem sat in the garden during the day, she would suddenly stand up, take a few steps forward, then go back to her seat. This act might have surprised some, but there was a reason. She had discovered that the crickets were afraid of her white dress. Each time she walked toward the trees, all the noise in the garden abruptly stopped, and this made the others laugh. The ambassador would say, "Come on, Meryem, make them shut up. Show yourself."

The moment İrfan and the ambassador waited for with expectation was when they sat down at the table among the trees and sipped their whisky.

None of them knew that the day on which the professor invited them out to dinner would change their lives forever.

The professor had become tired of eating pasta. He wanted to take them to the fish restaurant in the village. Besides, he had promised the boys working there that he would come there for a meal. The others were also looking forward to a change of diet. İrfan insisted on using the dinghy instead of walking, so at sundown, they crowded into the small craft and slowly glided toward the village over the crimson waters of a sea smooth as glass. İrfan thought that the ambassador would speak of "the wine-dark sea" and refer to himself as Homer, but the old man said nothing.

When they arrived at the fish restaurant, they found it full of British tourists, a merry group of young men and women, already slightly tipsy, singing, shouting, and showing off.

The owner of the restaurant showed them to a table in the garden by the sea. The table sat awkwardly on the uneven ground and rocked like a camel journeying across the desert, but the seafood was very fresh.

The owner showed them his trays of fish, carrying them out into the garden for the inspection of such honored guests and promising them that the sea bass were not from a fish farm. Three of the people at the table remembered the fish farm where they had first met. Recalling the mosquitoes and sand fleas that had attacked her so viciously, Meryem began to scratch herself. What a hellhole that place had been!

The restaurant owner also brought the local crayfish, squirming around on the tray for their inspection. With the air of an expert, the ambassador ordered some of these, explaining just how they should be prepared and served. "Of course, just as you say," bowed the owner.

In a short while, he brought wineglasses and a well-cooled bottle of the locally produced white wine. The ambassador picked up his glass, swirled the wine around, and looked at it for some time before announcing, as if it were something very important, *"Il a de la cuisse."*

He pointed to the oily trickles running down the glass. Then he took a sip, turned the wine on his tongue, swallowed it, paused, and said, "Very nice."

The owner was surprised to receive praise for such a cheap wine, but he filled glasses for the ambassador and the professor. Cemal and Meryem declined, placing their hands on top of their glasses.

The ambassador and İrfan drank the wine down as if it were water, finishing the bottle before the salad was served. As the two men were used to whisky and hard liquor, wine was like sweet-smelling water for them. The owner's son brought new bottles one after another.

From the moment they stepped into the garden, they realized that it was another of those paradises along the Aegean. They caught the sharp scent of honeysuckle, which in this area grew like a small tree, leaning down over them and spreading its fragrance all around. At this hour, the night-scented stock released its perfume to mingle with that of the honeysuckle.

Slowly, the crimson color of the sea disappeared. As darkness descended, the intoxicating scents in the garden grew stronger, and the young British tourists at the other tables continued their boisterous laugh.

"Since the waters of Lake Van are brackish, there are no fish there," Cemal commented, "but in Erciş, where the river meets the lake, we have delicious mullet."

"Really," said the ambassador, "how interesting."

The professor said nothing, and the two men then returned to their conversation.

Suddenly the lights went off. Some of the British tourists exclaimed in surprise, but the locals, who were used to such problems, were not disturbed. The waiters immediately brought kerosene lamps to each table and hung lanterns in the trees.

That evening, the ambassador did not stop talking. It was as if he wanted to compensate for all his years of being alone. Both he and the professor began to slur their words after consuming so much wine, and each became unreasonably happy. Perhaps the merriment of the youths at the other table was contagious.

Meryem watched the girls and the boys embracing each other, but she did not yearn to be close to those slender, tanned boys anymore. When she looked at them, she thought of Mehmet Ali's dark hair falling over his forehead and the sincerity in his brown eyes.

First the smaller fish, the crayfish, then the sea bass were served; bottles of wine came and went. The ambassador talked and laughed without a pause.

"Professor," he said, "look at those candles. Aren't they romantic? Marital romance. Yet there's an invariable tragedy about marriage: Love is ephemeral, but quarreling is eternal."

Both of them laughed uproariously.

"Romance is a European invention," the ambassador continued, "which is imitated in this country. Married women are very interested in romance. As a married couple, you argue about money, then talk about your upset stomach, and discuss which medicine helps to relieve wind. Then, all of a sudden, you are sitting by candlelight, gazing into each other's eyes, unconscious of anything else. And that's the hour of romance!"

İrfan laughed heartily. "In this world," he said, "every woman has a single goal: to have a man on his knees beside her till the end of her life."

The old man waved his finger, and said, "I've got you this time . . . that's from Dostoevsky!"

Toward midnight, the young tourists became even more exuberant. First they roared, *"What shall we do with a drunken sailor."* Then three girls grabbed a boy by his arms and legs and threw him into the sea. Turning their backs to the boy, who was trying to clamber out of the sea in his soaking-wet clothes, they pulled down their shorts and displayed their naked bottoms as the rest of the group shouted with wild applause.

"When human beings became *Homo erectus,*" said the ambassador, "women's vaginas got tighter. That's why the human female gives birth with such difficulty. Her pregnancy is hard labor, and contrary to the babies of other species, a human baby cannot walk as soon as it is born. It needs care. So who is to feed the female in the cave during the long months of pregnancy and nursing; who will hunt for her? The male, of course. He has sacrificed himself for his family. Since the days of the cavemen, women have asked men the same three questions: Where are you going? When will you be back? Do you love me? It was so then and still holds true today in New York, Paris, or Istanbul."

After the ambassador finished speaking, he and İrfan howled with laughter. Even the drunken tourists turned to look at them.

"Three questions eh, ambassador!" shouted the professor, as he rocked with laughter. Supporting himself on the table as he tried to stand up without falling over, he repeated the ambassador's words before recalling in the back of his mind that this was from something by a famous journalist, but he had already forgotten what it was he would say by the time he managed to stand up. Meryem was afraid that he would fall, but the professor maintained his balance as he lurched toward the restaurant.

He was dizzy and had no idea where he was putting his feet, yet he felt exquisitely happy. He enjoyed the oblivion in his mind. He had not felt so carefree for a long time. Entering the restaurant, he paid the bill without checking it and asked where he could find the men's room.

A lantern glowed in the small dilapidated hut behind the restaurant that served as the toilet. İrfan looked at his puffy face and bleary eyes in the mirror and snapped a salute. His jaws ached from laughing.

"Where are you going? When will you come back? Do you love me?" he repeated. "Bless you, my friend! It's true, absolutely true!"

On his way back to the table, when he was passing under the lantern that hung from a honeysuckle branch, he almost ran into someone. A face appeared in the lamplight, and the professor stopped in his tracks. He could not believe his eyes. "Hidayet?" he mumbled.

It was Hidayet, his face illuminated in the yellow light, who stood there looking at him. That wavy auburn hair, those thin, rosebud lips . . . The professor remembered the words Oscar Wilde had said to André Gide: "Your lips are too straight, my dear friend. Because you cannot lie. However, your lips should be undulating like the lips of a Greek god."

This face belonged to the Hidayet of his youth, no more than twenty years of age. The passing years had turned İrfan into an old man but had not touched Hidayet.

The professor swayed from side to side and almost fell down. The young man's face came and went in the lamplight.

The young Englishman was as drunk as İrfan, and they nearly knocked heads. He gazed with unfocused eyes at this middle-aged man who was regarding him with awe and admiration.

Maybe because they both needed support to keep themselves from falling or out of drunken sentimentality, or perhaps for some other reason, they put their arms around each other. The professor laid his head on the young man's bare shoulder. "Hidayet!" he murmured, and began to weep. A taste of salt came into his mouth.

"Hidayet," he whispered.

He had never experienced such pleasure in embracing a woman or felt such overpowering desire.

"Hidayet . . . Hidayet," he said again.

The drunken youth was not in a position to understand what the professor was saying. He freed himself from the old man's embrace, pursed up his lips to kiss him extravagantly on the cheek, and lurched off to the men's room.

The professor collapsed on the ground where he sat, looking at the sea, trying to understand what had happened. He did not know if he was looking at the dark sea or at the abyss inside himself.

"Hidayet," he whispered again. "Where are you?"

If the ambassador had not come to pick him up, he would have passed out there and then. With the help of the restaurant owner, the ambassador dragged him down to the dinghy.

On the way back, Cemal rowed. No one spoke.

When they arrived at the small jetty by the orange grove, Cemal jumped out first and fastened the rope. Then he helped the ambassador and Meryem ashore. Finally, the professor stood up, accidentally grabbing Cemal's arm while he was reaching for the jetty.

"Don't touch me, you homosexual bastard!" shouted Cemal, pushing him away. The professor fell back into the dinghy and hit his face on the seat. Meryem and the ambassador stood by, watching helplessly.

Then he sat up. His nose was bleeding, and his whole body ached. He reached for the side and tried to pull himself up. After struggling for a while, he managed to get out of the boat. Holding his bleeding nose, he managed to stand up and take a step forward. Cemal loomed there above him on the jetty, looking more formidable than he really was, as if waiting for another attack. "Don't you touch me again, you pervert!" he yelled. "Everyone saw what you did at the restaurant. Fag!"

Looking at him, an intense fury swelled up in the professor. As he tried to stop the blood streaming from his nose, he screamed, "It's your father who's the pervert! He raped his own niece!"

Cemal said nothing but only gritted his teeth in answer.

"You idiot. Don't you realize that your father not only raped her but gave you the job of killing her?"

When he heard these words, Cemal went mad. He leapt at the professor and grabbed him by the throat. "Liar!" he screamed. "Liar! You'll die for what you said!"

"Ask Meryem," İrfan gasped. "She'll tell you!"

Cemal turned to the girl. "Tell this man he's a liar!" he shouted. "Tell him!"

Meryem said nothing.

"Speak!"

She remained silent.

"Don't you understand?" İrfan said. "Her silence explains everything. Your father's a pervert."

Cemal began to beat the professor, venting his accumulated rage, hitting him again and again with his hammer-hard fists. Meryem and the ambassador watched in horror, as screaming like an animal, Cemal punched the old man in the face, cutting it badly.

The professor fell to his knees, crawling along the ground as blood poured from his mouth onto the boards of the jetty. When the ambassador saw him spit out a few teeth he began to tremble uncontrollably. Cemal let go of the professor and ran to the house, howling as though in pain.

İrfan turned around and lay down on his back on the jetty. Breathing heavily, he tried to recover himself.

The ambassador was quite overcome by what he had witnessed. "You see!" he cried hysterically to Meryem. "I was right not to want anyone around. My house has been filled with the barbarity of this country!"

Meryem knelt beside the professor, and not finding anything else more suitable, wiped his face with the hem of her dress.

From where he lay, the professor looked up at the stars in the sky. The brightest was right above his head. "That must be Jupiter," he thought. Forty times bigger than the Earth. Was the Earth visible from Jupiter? At that moment he would have liked to see a shooting star, but none was visible.

The professor knew that something unpleasant had happened, an incident had occurred, but he could not remember what it was. He kept on thinking about Jupiter and the stars.

The impulse came over him to laugh. Unable to suppress this urge, he burst into a fit of laughter where he lay helplessly. Meryem and the ambassador stared at him dumbfounded. İrfan took Meryem's hand and sat up with his legs wide apart, still laughing.

The ambassador asked him apprehensively why he was laughing.

"I've been defeated," İrfan replied. "I swear to God I've been defeated. As General Trikopis once said, 'I'll retreat gracefully and go home.' I, too, have reached the decision to go back where I belong."

His speech sounded strange since two of his front teeth were broken and his mouth was full of blood.

"That's the best thing to do, my friend," said the ambassador, turning and walking toward the house. As he stepped into the garden, he shouted, without looking at them, "Have a good trip!"

The professor stood up, and, holding on to Meryem, slowly walked toward the boat. Meryem went aboard with him, continuing to hold his hand as they entered his cabin. Meryem wondered why they were going there. It was the cabin where the picture of the flying Armenians was hung.

"I'm leaving now," İrfan said. "We won't see each other again."

Meryem was silent.

"Go and fetch me a drink."

Meryem went upstairs, opened the liquor cabinet, chose at random one of the unfamiliar bottles there, and took it down to the cabin below. When she entered, the professor was closing a drawer. He took the bottle and put it to his lips. "Maybe I shouldn't have told your secret, but I think it's better that I did," he said. "It's time for you to get away from Cemal."

The girl said nothing.

They went up on deck together, out into the open air.

"Are you mad at me?" asked İrfan.

Meryem shook her head.

"Can you throw me the rope when I turn on the engine?"

"Yes," said the girl.

"Then, good-bye."

The professor kissed Meryem's hand, and she made a pretense of kissing his.

As she left the boat, the professor said, "Just a second. Take this."

He thrust something into her hand. An envelope.

When she heard the engine start, Meryem threw the rope toward the professor. He swayed and had difficulty remaining on his feet, but he managed to pull up the anchor, and as the boat faded into the distance, he waved to her for the last time. "What really happened at the restaurant?" he shouted.

"Nothing," Meryem shouted back.

The sailboat vanished in the darkness. Soon the noise of the engine could no longer be heard.

Meryem gazed into the darkness for some time, then walked to the house. The garden was empty, and the house was quiet.

When she entered her room, she realized that her dress was covered in blood. She would have to wash it immediately in cold water. She remembered the bloody pieces of cloth she used to wash every month back in the village. Blood should not be heated, she knew.

She placed the envelope on the bed and went downstairs to fill a washtub with water. She carried it back to her bedroom and dipped the dress in it. The water quickly turned red. "I'll have to rinse it many times," she thought. "Otherwise, it won't come out."

While she was wondering what to do, she sat down on the bed and opened the envelope. It was full of money—more money than she could count, and foreign money, at that!

GOD LOVES MERYEM NOW

AFTER CEMAL RAN INTO THE HOUSE AND CLIMBED the stairs, he felt a great fatigue come over him. He could hardly drag his body up the stairs; it was as if he had suddenly turned into a cloth puppet. Reaching his room, he threw himself on the bed without undressing and immediately fell into a deep sleep, like a stone falling to the bottom of an abandoned well. His sleep was dreamless, unbroken, undisturbed: a state of nonexistence.

The next morning, the ambassador told Meryem, "I want you to leave my house. Please leave today and take your relative with you."

Purple rings had appeared under his eyes, and the broken veins under his skin were more obvious. He must have cut himself while shaving that morning, as the blood was oozing slightly from a piece of cotton wool stuck to a bright red wound on his neck. His hands were trembling anyway.

"Please get out of my house. Immediately! I want my peace back. I knew it would be like this. This country's full of lunatics, and their madness has entered my house. Please go."

Meryem said they would leave and never come back just as soon as Cemal woke up.

Then she sat in the garden with the ambassador, waiting for Cemal to come down. Hoping he would soon appear, the old man kept his eyes fixed on the house.

They waited until noon, but Cemal did not come. The ambassador kept asking, "Why doesn't he get up?" until at last, quite fed up, Meryem rose and went to see what Cemal was doing. She knocked gently on his door, but there was no answer, then a little louder but still got no reply. Finally, she began to pound on the door, simultaneously calling out his name at the top of her voice. No one could sleep through that noise, but not a sound could be heard from Cemal's room.

The ambassador joined her outside the room. He looked terribly worried. Perhaps he was in a panic, afraid of facing a worse situation, a suicide or a death in his house. In great fear, he and Meryem opened the door and entered the room.

Cemal was lying on the bed in his shirt and shorts. The ambassador whispered, "Cemal. Mr. Cemal." Then he repeated in a louder voice, "Mr. Cemal!"

Cemal neither moved nor uttered a sound. The ambassador timidly shook his shoulder. Nothing happened. Then he put his ear to the boy's chest. "He's breathing," he said with relief.

That day they were unable to wake Cemal. When night descended, the boy was still in a deep sleep, as though he were in another world.

The ambassador could not understand the situation. "I've only experienced such a thing once before," he said. "Actually, I've always had sleeping problems. But once, when my mother died, I came home and slept for twenty-four hours without dreaming or knowing that I was still alive. Maybe it's a type of death. Perhaps Cemal is suffering from something similar."

Meryem went upstairs several times to look at Cemal, but he lay sleeping in exactly the same position. She touched his forehead; it was burning. In spite of having a high fever, he did not make the slightest move. Whether they liked it or not, they would have to spend another night in the ambassador's house. The old man would be upset, but there was nothing she could do about it.

Meryem went to her own room early, got into bed, and tried to sleep. Rather than being upset by all that had happened, she was calm. She felt relieved that everything was out in the open and felt that life was about to take a new turn. She had almost no fears or doubts about the future. Her resoluteness and serenity astonished her, yet she enjoyed the power that was building up inside her.

The sweet caress of a gentle hand woke Cemal toward dawn. Without opening his eyes, he felt the clean, sweet-smelling hair and silky softness of a fiery body touching his own. He began to quiver at the touch of a woman. The innocent bride had really come and mounted him this time. His heart was pounding with excitement. He embraced her, holding his arms around her slim waist and tightened hips. A little later, he felt the girl's forbidden area fluttering over his private parts like the wings of a butterfly, and he lost himself in a rush of pleasure. He did not want to open his eyes, but he knew he must. He did not want to lose the delightful sense of this lovely body ever again. He would open his eyes suddenly and see the face of the innocent bride for the first time.

Trembling with fear, he slowly opened his eyes and then closed them again, dragged into the dark corridors of a deeper sleep.

The day following that terrible night, the professor had been awakened by the piercing rays of the early-morning sun. His first thought was of death, to which he had peacefully surrendered in the darkness of the previous night. The smell of the teak deck, the breeze caressing his face, the sunlight burning his eyes, and the awful pain of the familiar headache were all so real that he sat up to look around him. The sailboat was turning on its own axis in the middle of the sea. He remembered that during the night he had pushed the button to release the anchor. When he thought that he had collided with a rock and the boat was being torn to pieces, he had actually been anchored in the offshore swell.

Realizing this made him neither happy nor sad.

He hurled the empty gin bottle into the water. His mouth tasted rusty, and his head ached as if it were in a vise. The only way to save himself was to throw himself into the sea along with the gin bottle. Jumping up, he threw himself overboard, falling into the sea just as the bottle had. He swallowed a little water. Grateful for the blueness washing over him, he stayed motionless for a while before twisting and turning himself in the water like an old dolphin left behind by its school.

When he returned to the boat, he felt so good that he believed he could endure the questions that filled his head and forget the previous night's unpleasantness, but then he changed his mind. "You've been defeated," he told himself.

Oddly enough, this thought pleased him. The feeling of submission and defeat made him indescribably content. The period of ambitious struggle, with all its fear and venomous questions, was over. He became resigned, like a commander who surrenders his castle to a stronger foe after years of resistance.

The questions running through his mind were many and varied: Was he Turkish? Aegean? Mediterranean? American? European? Middle Eastern? Muslim or atheist? Rich or poor? Man or not? Real or fake? Merciful or tyrannical? Ironic or sincere? Traditional or modern? Ostentatious or philosophical? Scientist or charlatan? Afraid of death, or not?

The calmness of surrender and the acceptance of defeat were better than bothering his head with hundreds of such questions, all of which could be united in one, unanswerable query: Who am I?

He knew exactly what he had to do. He would go to his mother, the person who loved him the most of all and who was always there for him; he would eat her wonderful food and let her introduce him to her inquisitive neighbors. He would visit his father's grave with a bouquet of fresh flowers, find a modest job at an Aegean university, and live the same life as his father, even if different in status, in the same house for the rest of his life. That was the safest thing to do.

At the back of his head, he heard a mocking voice reminding him of an article he had read in *Newsweek*. The article had mentioned a new term, "Mammismo," devised in Italy for elderly men who lived with their mothers. This term could be translated as "mama's boy" or "mother's pet." Yet neither of these nicknames disturbed him. He had already accepted defeat, so life could trample on him or tear him to pieces as much as it wanted. It could be fun to start life from the bottom rung again. He laughed.

"Come on, mammone!" he cried. "First take the boat back—and be glad that you paid for it in advance!"

When Cemal woke up in the morning, the first thing he saw was Meryem's pale face staring down at him. He sat up slowly, his body aching all over.

"Meryem," he asked, "did you come in here during the night?"

"No," she replied.

"How long have I been asleep?"

"Two days. I've been waiting for you to wake up. The ambassador wants us to leave."

"All right," said Cemal. "We'll find someplace to go."

"Find a place for yourself," said Meryem.

"What? You're coming along, too."

"No."

"Where will you go?"

"None of your business."

Cemal looked at Meryem in disbelief. Her expression was determined, even hard. Her mouth was pursed defiantly, and she looked him straight in the eye, absolutely serious. Cemal was startled. "You can't manage alone, Meryem," he said. "Come with me."

"No," Meryem repeated. "Go back to the village."

When Cemal heard the word "village" his face darkened, and his eyes flashed fire.

"I can't," he hissed through clenched teeth. "I'll never go back to that sordid place!"

"Then go to Istanbul—to your brother or your friend. They'll find you a job."

Meryem took a fistful of banknotes from her pocket and gave them to him. "Here," she said, "these will be of use. Don't worry; I have more."

"Where did you get them from?" asked Cemal, looking at the money in disbelief.

"The professor gave them to me."

Then, without saying good-bye, she turned and walked out of the room.

Cemal was suddenly overcome by a fear he had never felt before. Meryem was leaving him. He would never see her again. The thought pierced him like a piece of shrapnel. Tears welled up in his eyes. He ran after her and grabbed her arm. "You're not going anywhere," he shouted. "Do you hear? You are going to that boy at the pancake restaurant, aren't you? Well, you're not. I won't let you."

"Let go of my arm," Meryem replied quietly. "You can't stop me, whatever you do."

Cemal shook her menacingly. "Come to your senses!" he shouted. "I'm going to teach you a lesson!"

He raised his arm as though to strike her. She shrugged.

"I'll kill you!" he screamed.

Meryem stared into his eyes fearlessly.

Then Cemal felt like doing something he had never thought he could do. He wanted to kneel, put his arms around her knees, and beg her not to go. He was in a total panic, as if his life would end if the girl went out the door.

He wanted to beg Meryem's forgiveness, even bury his head in her white dress and sob, but he just stood there, frozen.

Meryem looked at him in silence.

"Look after yourself," she said, and left.

Carrying the scent of orange blossom with her, alone, fearless, and free, she walked along the sandy road beside the shore lapped by the waves and awakened by the breeze.

Her dress fluttered in the wind, and spray from the waves cooled her bare legs.

She heard the donkey bray three times.

"I'm coming. Don't worry," Meryem said.

In her mind, the pancake hut, now coming into view, was transformed into a bright, shining restaurant with pretty tables decorated with flowers. She touched the wad of money in her pocket.

If Mehmet Ali did not object, she would like to have FLAKY BUTTER PASTIES written in small colored lights over the restaurant, after it had been renovated.

The donkey brayed mournfully once again. As the sound echoed from the hill behind her, Meryem responded. "I'm coming!" she cried. "What's your hurry!"

At last she could be sure that God loved her!

Reading Group Gold

BLISS:
A NOVEL
by O. Z. Livaneli

In His Own Words

- A Conversation with O. Z. Livaneli
- About the Author

Historical Perspective

- "Peace Building and Early Childhood Education: A Critical Alliance" Highlights from the author's Harvard University address

Keep on Reading

- Recommended Reading
- Reading Group Questions

For more reading group suggestions
visit www.readinggroupgold.com

 ST. MARTIN'S GRIFFIN

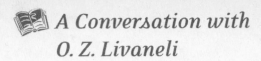 *A Conversation with O. Z. Livaneli*

Could you tell us a little bit about your writing background, and how you came to be in publishing?

I began my career as a publisher; I had a publishing house in Ankara. So I was somehow always related with the world of books. When my publishing house was shut down by the military junta and I was imprisoned, I chose to continue my relationship with books through the act of writing. I've been writing ever since.

"At night, I slept in the boat with the novel under my pillow."

The desire to write was always there in me from my youth onwards and I began by writing stories. One of my stories, "A Child in Purgatory," was filmed by the Swedish and German televisions. This year *Bliss* will be the basis for a movie. I think I have a special liking for novels that can be adapted for cinema. For me it indicates that the book has a decent story and characters.

What was the book that most influenced your life or your career as a writer—and why?

Ernest Hemingway's entire work and especially *The Old Man and the Sea* influenced my life and career to a great extent. I first read Hemingway when I was a kid and he immediately became my idol. I not only admired him as an author but also because of the feeling of adventure that he aroused in so many young people all around the world. After having read *The Old Man and the Sea* many times—I had even memorized some parts of it—I had decided to be a writer myself and lead a life of adventure just like he had done.

At my parents' home in Ankara, the walls of my room were full not with photographs of famous

people from the world of music and cinema but with portraits of Hemingway. I had read all his biographies. On Saturdays, I used to go to the American library in Ankara to check whether there was anything new about him in the journals. In time his influence over me grew to such an extent that when I was sixteen years old, during my summer holiday, I went to a fishing village, without letting my parents know, to live like him. I started to work in a fishing boat. At night, I slept in the boat with the novel under my pillow. At the end of two months, I had to return to my parents' house, but at that point I knew for sure that I was going to be a writer.

Do you have any special writing rituals? For example, what do you have on your desk when you're writing?

No rituals really. I have on my desk my notes, my reference books, and a cup of coffee...

If you had a book club, what would it be reading, and why?

If I had a book club I would start by reading *Don Quixote,* as everyone well knows today it represents the true beginning of the art of the novel.

What tips or advice do you have for writers still looking to be discovered?

I believe that one just has to write and write until one finds his true voice.

Is there anything else you can tell readers about the reality of honor killings in Turkey?

In Turkey, honor killings are most frequently seen in regions where tribal/feudal ties and relations continue to exist. In certain parts of Eastern Anatolia, patriarchal norms and hierarchies can still be found in their harshest and most anachronistic forms and women are denied all of their rights.

In recent decades, as a result of migration, honor killings have started to become more common in Ankara, Istanbul, Izmir, and other major cities in Turkey. In fact, the arrival of this ruthless tradition to the metropolis is how many people living in western Turkey have come to be aware of the seriousness of the problem. According to a report prepared by a commission appointed by the Turkish National Assembly, the majority of the officially registered honor killings between 2000-2005 have taken place in Western Turkey, whereas the majority of the suspects and victims come from Eastern Turkey.

"The problem of honor crimes cannot be solved by legal measures alone ... what is needed is a change in consciousness."

For many years, Turkish laws have reinforced the unequal treatment of men and women. However, in the last decade, important steps have been taken to improve the situation. Changes and amendments have been made to the Constitution, the criminal code, the civil code, and the laws regarding the family. Obviously, the problem of honor crimes cannot be solved by legal measures alone. Much more importantly, what is needed is a change in consciousness, which can only be achieved through education and economic development.

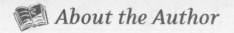

About the Author

O. Z. LIVANELI is one of Turkey's most prominent and popular authors as well as an accomplished composer whose works have been recorded by the London Symphony Orchestra. He was held in military prison during the coup of March 12, 1971, and lived in exile for eight years. He studied music in Stockholm, then lived in Paris and Athens, returning to Turkey in 1984.

Livaneli has been nationally and internationally active in promoting human rights, the culture of peace, and mutual understanding between people. Being one of the foremost defenders of Turkish-Greek friendship, in 1986 he founded the Greek-Turkish Friendship Committee together with the Greek composer Mikis Theodorakis. In 1995, he was appointed as a Goodwill Ambassador of UNESCO in recognition of his contributions to world peace. From 2002-2007 he served as an elected Member of Parliament.

His books are published in twenty-two languages, becoming bestsellers in his own country and abroad. His other works of fiction are *Leyla's House* (2006), *One Cat, One Man, One Death* (2001), *The Eunuch of Constantinople* (1996), and *A Child in Purgatory* (1978). He lives in Istanbul.

*In His
Own Words*

Photo Credit: Adil Gültekin

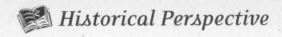
Historical Perspective

The following is an excerpt from a speech the author gave at Harvard University, May 2007

"Peace Building and Early Childhood Education: A Critical Alliance"

In the span of a century, humanity has achieved enormous technological developments. It's impossible not to acknowledge the progress and the level of civilization that's been reached. However, we also can't help being alarmed!

Violence and wars are threatening the future of humanity and the world. We see that violence is increasing in the private and public spheres. How should we deal with the dilemma of a supposedly increased level of civilization on the one hand and increasing violence on the other? These concerns are not new, of course. We have had them for quite some time now.

In the first decade of the twenty-first century… the situation seems to be getting worse. One of the main characteristics of the age we live in is violence. Be it religious, political, ethnic, or sexual; a culture promoting violence is tightening its grip on our lives.

Unfortunately, popular culture and the entertainment industries around the world act as accomplices in this process by continuously providing all sorts of images of violence. The Constitution of UNESCO begins with the following sentence: "Since wars begin in the minds of men, it is in the minds of men that the defenses of peace must be constructed."

"There [is] a connection… between [an] individual's inner peace and peace in the external world."

And the best defense for peace is culture. Culture in itself is an action for peace. What do we understand when we say culture? Culture is not an instrument of leisure as the entertainment industry promotes it to be but it's a foundation upon which all kinds of human relations are built. In this general sense, culture does not refer only to artistic creation but to an accumulation of human values and experiences. If we want to guarantee peace on earth, it's for the improvement and enrichment of this foundation that we should be striving towards. Peace, children's rights, women's rights, and democracy are all closely related.

As I was writing my novel *Bliss*, I had all these concerns on my mind. The three characters of my novel are the victims of different kinds of violence in Turkey.

The professor, İrfan, assaulted by vulgarity, insincerity, and ignorance, escapes his life in Istanbul. Meryem, a fifteen-year-old young girl from Eastern Anatolia, is the victim of rape and she's trying to escape the fate facing many other young women who have been so-called "stained." Cemal [is] a commando who's back from fighting with the Kurdish guerillas. Toward the end of the novel, fate brings them together and this becomes an opportunity for each to purge themselves of the long-lasting effects of their experiences of violence. Finally they all opt for peace.

There's a much bigger connection than we think between the individual's inner peace and peace in the external world. A culture of peace includes both.

It might sound utopian, but what we should aim for is an all-inclusive civilization of peace. And peace education has to start with children.

In a period of growing international tensions, terrorism, and wars, in order to combat the prevailing culture of violence, we need to educate our children on peace and nonviolence.

It means that we have to teach our children about democracy and human rights; tolerance; social and economic justice; gender equality; respect for different religions and cultures; environmental sustainability; disarmament; traditional peace practices; reconciliation; and nonviolent conflict resolution.

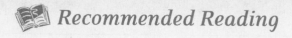 *Recommended Reading*

William Faulkner
Light in August

I read William Faulkner's *Light in August* when I was young, and I felt that it would change my life. The novel elevates a local crime to the level of a universal human tragedy, and hence creates a sense of identification with the events that may have taken place anytime, anywhere in the world. Although its style has an archaic air reminding one of the Old Testament, it at the same time has a very modern quality. Faulkner creates a shadowy atmosphere even in those parts of the novel where the events take place in daylight and in this way represents the dark and shadowy nature of our consciousness. I must say I tried hard to get rid of Faulkner's influence.

I always think that certain characteristics of the nineteenth-century Russian novelistic tradition have somehow been transferred to twentieth-century American literature. I find similarities between Dostoevsky, Tolstoy, and Turgenev and Faulkner, Caldwell, and Steinbeck.

Fyodor Dostoevsky
Crime and Punishment

One of the things I most like about this novel is the way in which Dostoevsky describes St. Petersburg; the city reflects the inner worlds of the heroes. Also, Raskolnikov's pangs of conscience due to his crime and his confession move me deeply. Today those who commit a crime go on with their lives comfortably as long as their crime remains unknown. It may be said that Dostoevsky is idealizing the human heart. Only this can explain the fact that at the end of all the novels of this great author, whose main concern is analyzing the depths of human psychology, there appears the light of hope.

Reading Group Gold

Keep On Reading

Ernest Hemingway
The Old Man and the Sea
    See Conversation with the Author.

The Book of One Thousand and One Nights
    I think that this unique masterpiece of Eastern liter-
    ature with its multitude of stories that intertwine
    and form a labyrinth have influenced many writers
    in the world, such as Jorge Luis Borges and others.
    Told by a woman, these stories on the unfaithful-
    ness of women stand somewhere between life and
    death. This book is an infinite source of inspiration
    for any writer.

Rumi
Masnavi

    Another masterpiece of Eastern literature, this is
    written by Jalal ad-Din Rumi, the great Sufi poet and
    thinker of the thirteenth century. Composed of
    intertwining tales and stories, *Masnavi* surprises
    the reader with its depth and it's full of modern
    thoughts. As early as the thirteenth century, Rumi
    opposes all kinds of religious, ethnic, and sexual
    discrimination. In my own books, I frequently quote
    stories from the *Masnavi*.

Leo Tolstoy
Anna Karenina

    I have always admired the way Tolstoy identifies
    with women in love and studies carefully the depth
    of their feelings. It's interesting that in nineteenth-
    century Orthodox Russia, this old count with a white
    beard is telling the story of a woman who would in
    the end commit suicide because of a desperate love.
    How could this be explained by anything other than
    the ability of great writers to identify with different
    people and situations around the world?

"It's not a coincidence that…Bliss has a chapter called 'At Night Don Quixote, Sancho Panza in the Morning.'"

Gustave Flaubert
Madame Bovary

I like this book for similar reasons as *Anna Karenina*. I have always admired Flaubert's strict loyalty to details and his ability to bring to life visually each scene, place, and person that he describes.

Gabriel García Márquez
Chronicle of a Death Foretold

This short but intense novel tells about the people of a village who are very well aware of a murder being committed in the name of tradition yet remain quiet. Although the suspects brag about the crime, people seem to ignore it. I like this book very much because it has so much to say on the conflict of tradition and modernity, an issue which I am dealing with all the time in my own country.

Yashar Kemal
Memed My Hawk

The most cherished classic of Turkish literature has instilled in all of us, during our youth, a feeling for the necessity of struggle against injustice.

Miguel de Cervantes
Don Quixote

In this masterpiece which I've read over and over again, I find a very sad side to the desperate struggle of Don Quixote, who tries to defend values that are being worn out by a changing world. It's not a coincidence that my novel *Bliss* has a chapter called "At Night Don Quixote, Sancho Panza in the Morning." I believe that every one of us is like this a little bit. At night, we're full of idealism and sublime feelings, but in the morning, reality makes us Sancho Panza.

Excerpted from O. Z. Livaneli's "Meet the Writers" interview
Courtesy of B&N.com
Reprinted with permission
© 2006 Barnesandnoble.com

Reading Group Questions

1. Discuss the reasons why the author may have chosen the title *Bliss* for his novel. What is its significance?

2. Did you have any ideas or opinions on Turkey before reading the novel? Take a moment to talk about your collective knowledge of Turkish history and culture before and after reading *Bliss*.

3. Who is your favorite character in *Bliss* and why? Are there those you like who are, in fact, "unlikable?" Take a moment to talk about the cast of characters—and range of personality types—in the novel.

4. Discuss the two distinct settings of the novel—the small rural village and the larger-than-life city. What does each locale mean to each of the main characters?

5. In what ways do Meryem and Cemal's encounters with different people on the train shed light on the problems of identity that characterize contemporary Turkey? Also, in what ways is sailing the Aegean Sea symbolic for them both?

6. What are the themes of tradition and modernity, religion vs. secularity, and male domination and female empowerment that resonate throughout *Bliss*?

7. Each of the main protagonists in *Bliss* experiences tragedy on a profound, indeed existential level. How would you describe each character's personal transformation? What unites them in their struggle to overcome their demons?

8. How do you interpret İrfan's final resolution at the end of the novel about what kind of a life he's to lead? And what about Meryems?

9. How would you describe İrfan's relation to Hidayet, a character who never appears in the novel but who's always in İrfan's thoughts?

10. One of the chapters in the novel is titled "At Night Don Quixote, Sancho Panza in the Morning." Were there times in your life when you felt the same? Please discuss.

11. At one point in the novel İrfan likens himself and all Turkish intellectuals to "trapeze flyers." Why?

12. Why is İrfan's relationship with his parents marked with deep feelings of guilt?

13. What are the differences between İrfan's and Cemal's attitudes about national identity and belonging?

14. Discuss the ambassador's comment that there are three phases in the life of an individual: camel phase, lion phase, and childhood phase.

15. There are numerous references to mythical figures and stories in the novel. Why do you think the idea of myth has such an important place in *Bliss*?